DOUG PILLEY

TALES FROM THE MULTIVERSE

STORIES BEYOND YOUR IMAGINATION

Auctorem House
276 5th Ave, Ste 704-2591
New York, NY 10001
www.auctoremhouse.com
1.888.332.7718

CONTENTS

Dedicated to my daughter, Katelyn.
Her light shines brighter than mine.

PREFACE

KURT VONNEGUT.

Jorge Luis Borges.

Neil Gaiman.

Short fiction by these seminal writers influenced me the first sixty-four years of my life. Thirty-five years in advertising trained me to write each ad with one idea.

When I read Tom Robbin's memoir, *Tibetan Peach Pie*, I had an epiphany. Rather than fight writer's block when mapping out a novel, why not approach my fiction the same way I did advertising? One short story, one idea.

This is how I came to write these stories. And I found over and over again that as long as I had the idea, I had no trouble writing—and completing—every story.

I also found that the art of conversation enabled me to convey complex ideas in the repartee between two speakers. And the speakers came to represent the voices in my head.

There are some recurrent themes:

Ghosts have found their way into my waking—and dreaming—life.

The Turing Test was developed by the same man who built Enigma in WWII. The test determines the existence of artificial intelligence.

Magic is something we wish for. If it existed in our world today, how would it really look?

Quantum physicists are now positing not just one reality but an infinite number of realities. They have even coined the term *multiverse*.

Since I have a diversity of ideas I explore in this collection, it is only fitting to represent them as reflections of the many alternate universes out there. While some seem connected, they all can be read and appreciated for their own reality.

All of these stories have appeared on my blog at *pilleyman.wordpress. com*. I have kept them in chronological order because a few build on what has gone before.

Each story's goal is to give you a thought you didn't have before. And after as little as 400 words, you arrive at a place you didn't expect to be.

I sincerely hope you enjoy these short stories of ideas. And the voices who tell tales from the multiverse.

DOUG PILLEY
June 21, 2018

GHOST IN THE MACHINE

"Don't be absurd," I replied. "We're in VR. Nothing is real."

"I don't believe that," she insisted. "I feel like someone is stalking me, and I can't shake it."

"Here," I said. "Grab my hand. Do you think it's real?"

She hesitated, looking down at our clasped hands. "It *feels* real."

"But you're not," I said. "You're in a Bodyglove sim-suit. And all those nodes on it are telegraphing VR sensations to your nerve centers, telling you things that aren't so."

"So, if we kiss?" she asks tentatively.

"We're not even in the same room," I said, smiling.

"How can we tell the difference?" she said.

"How can you tell if you are awake or dreaming?" I replied.

"Sometimes, I can't," she admitted.

"Exactly," I said. "Sometimes, we can't tell the difference."

I paused, looking into her eyes. "So, kiss me already."

Tentatively, she leaned toward me and brushed her lips against mine. I moved imperceptibly toward her and kissed her back, slowly moving my lips against hers until she opened her mouth and yielded to my searching tongue.

Her breath became short.

Not moving away, I pulled my mouth back enough to say, "Not real." Then I kissed her again.

She moaned.

The next time we came up for air, she breathed, "I can't believe this isn't real."

I smiled at her. "It's real enough for me," I said.

"And what if we—"

"It would be wonderful," I said. "Like this." And I gave her another soulful kiss.

After our tête-à-tête, we found ourselves in a lush interior. With leather furnishings and marble finishes, it was a set from a major motion picture with a massive production budget. Our best move was simply to relax and enjoy.

Only she wasn't having it.

"Now it is easy to see this isn't real," she said. "I've never been in a place as nice as this."

"Well, we can pretend we have," I said.

"But it doesn't help," she insisted.

"Help what?" I asked, puzzled.

"Help me shake the feeling someone is after me," she said with a tremble in her voice.

I made a show of getting up and moving around the room, lifting sofa cushions, peering behind paintings, pulling curtains aside.

"No one else is here," I finally said.

"I can see that," she said. "But I just don't feel it."

I sighed. "I don't really know what else I can do," I told her.

"Can you just hold me?" she asked.

"That I can do," I said, sitting next to her and drawing her into my arms.

Her warmth suffused me with a feeling, a sensation beyond the physical. She was a nice woman, a sensuous woman, a woman of substance with just a touch of paranoia. I wasn't accustomed to finding women I could relate to in VR. Usually, it was a one-time fling, a one- night dream that ended at daylight.

But she was different.

And her fear?

It made me feel needed.

That was something VR couldn't do.

"What was that?" she asked in a panic.

"What was what?" I replied.

"I heard a sound," she insisted. "From over there." She pointed down a long hallway that hadn't been there before.

I looked. The hallway seemed to recede into the distance, elongating as I watched. It had doorways on both sides, but all of the doors were closed.

I patted her hand.

"Don't worry," I said. "I'll take a look."

I got up from the sofa and started down the hallway.

I thought I saw a spark about halfway down the hallway. It was quick, just a gleam for a second. I looked to the side, thinking I might catch a glimpse of it should it come again. But no matter how hard I tried, I couldn't see anything.

Slowly, deliberately, I continued down the hallway, stopping every tenth step to look and listen for intruders.

Nothing.

I kept going until I reached the end of the hallway. There were doors on either side. I put my hand on the doorknob to my right. Just as I turned the knob, I heard a soft puff of air behind me.

I whirled around, expecting to see someone standing in the hall behind me.

No one was there.

Then I heard her cry.

It was short, soft, regretful. And it squeezed my heart.

I ran back up the hallway to the living room and found her on the sofa. She was lying back, as if in a swoon. But this time, she was wearing a corsage, a red flower on her left breast.

I went to her and picked up her hand.

She looked up at me. "I . . . I never . . ." she began. Her eyes widened, and she stared at me in a panic. "I'm not ready, not ready," she said, imperceptibly shaking her head.

I looked down at her in horror, seeing this woman, this sentient being who had made me feel needed, even loved, slipping away from me.

"No," I said. "You can't go. This simulation isn't over. This isn't real!" Helpless, I watched her silently struggle to breathe.

The light left her eyes.

I never knew her name. We had only met in a simulation. It wasn't meant to be permanent.

It wasn't meant to be real.

It was meant to be a substitute for reality.

But because she had reached out to me, because she had needed me, she became more real to me than any woman I had ever known.

And I miss her still.

Every day.

Even now, whenever I put on a Bodyglove sim-suit and enter VR, I half expect to see her there, waiting for me. And every time, I can't help but look over my shoulder.

Because I can feel her.

And I feel like someone is after me.

FIGHT OR FLIGHT

PART OF MY JOB REQUIRES ME TO TRAVEL. AFTER A WHILE, you learn a few tricks of the trade:

Always eat a good breakfast. You never know when you will get your next meal.

Take a good book along for the ride—the thicker, the better. You never know when your flight will be delayed or even canceled.

Invest in an iPod, even if it's only a Shuffle or Nano. You want a good selection of your favorite music to ease the stress of travel and endure the unexpected bumps in the road.

And finally, make sure you have a pair of noise-canceling headphones. Ear buds may seem convenient, but they have never been comfortable to me. And they don't have the added advantage of canceling the noises you don't want: crying babies, banal conversations, even psychotic ramblings.

Most of my travel has involved flying up and down the East Coast. Occasionally, a trip takes me into the Central Time Zone.

Last week, I had my first transcontinental flight in twenty-five years. It took me someplace I had never been before.

I fly out of a small airport in eastern Virginia. As a result, I can never fly direct. I always have to fly to Charlotte, Philadelphia, BWI—any airport that serves as a hub for some airline. Only then can I board a plane that will take me where I want to go.

On this trip I had to fly to Charlotte in order to catch an Airbus to LAX. The Airbus is an enormous plane with three seats on each side of the aisle. You can hardly see the front of the plane if you sit in the back.

The takeoff was even more of a rattling roll than normal, but we were soon climbing steadily.

I chose a window seat so I could see the changing topography of the landscape below us. I wanted to be able to see the amber waves of grain, the mountains' majesty, all of it.

The funny thing is that you don't get a sense of how high you really are when it is clear. It's only when you see clouds come between you and the ground that you can finally tell just how high you are.

Let me tell you, 35,000 feet is a lot higher than the regional airlines and puddle jumpers fly.

Talk about rarefied atmosphere.

I was enjoying the flight, marveling at the landscape, when a passenger in the seat behind me decided to wax eloquent about his new passion: collecting art books. In a voice too loud for comfort, he expounded on finding artists he liked and realizing he couldn't afford to get actual art pieces. So he decided to collect art books instead.

After mispronouncing a few artists' names, he went on to list all of the many books he had collected.

Thank God for my noise-canceling headphones.

I enjoyed the flight more with the sounds of Weather Report, Return to Forever, Mahavishnu Orchestra and Jeff Beck filling my ears.

Of course, the one thing my headphones couldn't do was eliminate the droning hum of the jet engines. Even if I were able to stop up my ears completely, the sound would find its way into my very bones as I sat there.

But I was happy.

We were just reaching the Rockies when I first heard it. Through the music soundtrack, I was hearing a conversation.

That shouldn't be. But there it was.

"We can't accept this," a voice said. "We've come too far and waited too long to let this get in our way."

"You're right," a second voice said. "And we have to accept a certain amount of collateral damage."

That scared me.

I took off my headphones. The cabin was unusually quiet. There were no conversations going on. No one was moving about the cabin. No one was waiting in line for the lavatory.

Nothing.

Shaking my head, I put my headphones back on.

"What's one plane out of hundreds, even thousands?" the first voice asked. "A few people will be affected, but then life will go on."

"It's still the safest way to travel," the second voice said, chuckling. "They don't have a clue."

I took off my headphones and stood up.

Again, nothing.

I looked around, certain I would be able to spot the air marshal.

No such luck.

Sweat trickled down my neck and headed down my back. I knew what would happen if I tried to tell someone. I would become the disruptive passenger on the flight to LA that caused the plane to be diverted to Denver or Las Vegas. And everyone on the plane would look daggers at me and want to end my life.

All because I was trying to save theirs.

I sat back down.

Tentatively, I slipped on my headphones.

The two voices were still there, discussing various ways they could affect this flight and harvest the best of the travelers for their uses.

That's exactly what they said: "Our uses."

I kept taking the headphones off and putting them back on, trying to determine where those voices were coming from. And each time, I came up blank.

By the time we landed in LAX, I was a nervous wreck. My crew on the ground assumed I was jetlagged and didn't take me seriously. They said I'd be okay after a couple of nights of good sleep.

As you can imagine, that didn't happen.

I got maybe four hours of sleep the first two nights, a whopping five hours the third night.

Then it was time to fly back to Virginia. We had a flight from LAX to Philly and then a smaller flight home.

I was on another Airbus and reached our cruising altitude of 31,000 feet in no time. This time, I put on my headphones immediately when the crew indicated we could use small electronic devices.

I waited anxiously to hear any more conversations I couldn't explain. Nothing.

At least, nothing until we crossed the Rockies, almost exactly at the same longitude I started hearing the conversations flying west.

The first thing I heard was a burst of static. Then I heard, ". . . and we're getting readings we shouldn't be getting."

That didn't sound good.

The other voice said, "We seem to be getting a signal from the transcontinental flight from LAX. I'm not sure what is happening; we're pinging the plane now to see if we can figure it out."

"Wait," the first voice said. "I think I know what is happening. I think someone on that flight can hear us." There was a pause. "Can't you?"

A chill ran up my spine. It was like a ghost had just entered the plane.

"You can hear every word we say, can't you?" the first voice continued, addressing me directly. "You've been hearing us discuss our options for you and your fellow passengers. Haven't you?" he added with extra emphasis.

I was petrified. Literally.

I couldn't turn my head.

I couldn't look around.

I couldn't even call for help.

My vocal cords were as frozen as the rest of me. All I could manage was breathing without making a sound. I was too scared to even whimper.

"Now that you've heard us, you know we will have to find you," the first voice said.

"And when we do . . ." the second one added.

"Oh, we know what to do," the first one replied. "All we need is your name."

I must have gasped, because the man in front of me turned around and looked at me.

"Once we have your name, we will have complete control over you," the first voice said. "Absolute control."

"You foolish people," the second one added. "It has always been that way. Even the Bible says man named the animals and had dominion over them."

"Every culture, every civilization has discovered the way to control beings by knowing and using their names," the first one almost hissed. "From enslavement to exorcisms, we have only to learn your name, and we can take over your life or even end it."

"It is almost laughable," the second one added. "Now, with the Internet, we can do so much more once we have your name. We can raid your accounts, steal your assets, ruin your credit history and even erase your very existence."

"You would simply disappear," the first one finished.

"You have no idea," the second one said.

"And what is even more amusing is that you have named your downfall as the Cloud," the first one chuckled. "You think you are storing data in the Cloud when in fact the Cloud is watching you."

Again, he paused. "Watching," he said. "And waiting."

Shaking like a leaf, I finally pulled the headphones off of my ears.

These two were serious. They wanted to find me, find my name, so they could come after me and make me disappear.

How had I been able to hear them? How could they tell that I was listening? If they could do that, what was to prevent them from finding me on the ground?

And once they found me, what would they do to me?

Identity theft was one thing. Identity disintegration was another.

I knew I shouldn't, but I had to make sure I wasn't hallucinating. I eased the headphones back over my ears.

"Yes, we're still here," the first voice said. "And yes, we are coming for you. You won't see us on the ground. But we'll be there when you least expect it. And when we do—"

I yanked the headphones off again. I couldn't deal with it anymore.

Who were these people? Were they even people? Who could exist at the stratospheric level? Who could live in the Cloud?

Had the latest technology tapped into military intelligence satellites? IT terrorists? The collective unconscious?

My thoughts went faster than the Airbus. I was sweating profusely and knew I would have to calm down or I would have a stroke.

But where could I go? What could I do? I had inadvertently tapped into something I shouldn't have heard. And I had no way of unhearing it.

I managed to land and change planes. The regional jet flew at a much lower, quieter level. And I never put my headphones on.

In fact, I never will again.

Because I know those voices. I know exactly what they sound like.

NIGHT SWEATS

HOW DO YOU KNOW IF YOU'RE AWAKE OR ASLEEP?

You just know, right?

But what if you find yourself in the middle of something you know isn't real in the awake world? Do you pinch yourself? Call for help?

That's the situation I found myself in when I was thirteen.

As a small child, I had bouts of insomnia. I had no way of turning off my active mind even when I didn't know that's what I had.

So, the experience of waking up in the middle of the night was fairly common. Most times, I'd go back to sleep. Some nights, I'd toss and turn for hours, desperate to get back to sleep.

One night in particular, I woke because I was cold. The covers had slipped back off of my shoulder as I lay on my side. Thinking I had shifted in my sleep, I reached over my shoulder to grab the covers and pull them back over me.

At first, I felt resistance.

Then I felt a tug.

I know now that my body's adrenal glands went into overdrive, because I felt its flush throughout my entire body. I was scared out of my mind. And what happened next was something I had read about but never experienced for myself.

I was petrified with fear.

Someone or something was pulling the covers off of me. And I was so scared that I couldn't turn my head.

I even tried to push my head around with my hand, and it wouldn't budge. My vocal chords were also frozen. I couldn't cry out or form any words at all. The best I could manage was a low moan, a moan that couldn't be heard outside my room.

I would let go of the covers and then grasp them again, and each time, I felt a tug.

Let me assure you that this was not the passive weight of gravity pulling covers bunched at the end of the bed. This was an active pull, an insistent tug that was taking my covers away.

I lay there, still, moaning as the covers were pulled off me inch by inch. My upper arm was uncovered. Then my elbow was uncovered. Then it got down to my waist.

Finally, the my leg was exposed. I still couldn't turn my head to see who or what was stealing my covers. But now I could swing my leg out, up and over onto the covers.

When I did, the covers were fluffed a good foot and a half off of the bed. And when my leg came down on the billowed covers, the air escaped with a whoosh.

That movement seemed to break the spell. I was finally able to turn my head toward the foot of my bed.

As suspected, no one was there.

And the fear-flush of adrenaline rushed through me again.

I had survived. But what had I survived?

A psychic woman, a friend of my father's, stayed in that house after I had gone to college. She claimed that the house was haunted, that the spirit who visited me was named Dr. Foster, that she had seen shadows in that house while she was there.

I don't know what to think.

All I know is that something happened to me in that room that night. And just as sure as I know I am awake right now, I knew I was awake then.

Was it a ghost? Was it a poltergeist, a spirit known for visiting pubescent teenagers?

Or was it the repressed psychosexual energy of a teen's imagination run wild?

I really don't know.

What I do know is that I was awake. And I was literally petrified with fear. It's a wonder I don't sleep with the lights on to this day.

STROKE OF MIDNIGHT

PEOPLE ASK ME IF I DREAM IN COLOR.

The funny thing is that I always assumed everyone did. I was surprised to find out so many people dream in black and white. Did they not get the operating system upgrade when they were born?

In my case, I not only dream in color, I also dream so vividly that I am transported to another place and time. Sometimes, this is good.

But other times, it carries me to places I would never consciously go.

One dream in particular stands out from the rest.

I was dreaming of sleeping in my own bed in my own bedroom, in the very room I was actually sleeping. I remember thinking, "This is odd. I know I am dreaming, but I am dreaming about sleeping in my bed."

This was not an out-of-the-body experience with me looking down at my sleeping form. It was me with my head on my pillow, looking down at the foot of the bed, knowing it was my footboard, knowing it was my comforter.

And knowing I was not alone.

I have had the experience of being petrified and unable turn my head to look at the presence I felt in the room with me. This time, I had graduated to being able to look.

And what I saw terrified me.

In the darkened room, I vaguely made out a figure in the corner by the closet. It moved toward the foot of my bed, revealing itself little by little in the low light.

It was a female form. I could tell by her silhouette. But she was unlike any woman I had ever encountered.

Her hair was a wild mane that framed her darkened face. I made out twin glints where her eyes were. And I could posit her nose. Within the dream, I became aware of her breathing, a rasping sound that was hot and wet. And the sound of that breathing drew my attention to her mouth.

It was not a mouth like we know it. It was vertical, not horizontal. It had vertical red lips that did not close.

And that monstrous mouth was ringed with teeth.

This creature drew even closer, finally standing at the foot of my bed, looking down at me with hunger, rasping at me, wanting me, lusting after me.

Or, more appropriately, lusting after my blood.

While I had been able to turn my head and see her approach, I still could not move.

I was terrified. I didn't know if she was going to spring on me and tear me limb from limb, climb on my chest like a succubus and press the breath from me or attach herself to my flesh like a lamia and suck out my blood.

I just felt her malevolence, her dire intent.

Then she leaned toward me and raked her talons across the top of my right ankle.

The pain was fierce and immediate. In fact, it was strong enough to wake me up. Naturally, she was not there. I was alone in my room.

But the pain in my ankle persisted.

In fact, it lasted for a good hour after I awoke.

I had a friend in high school who said her parents were able to achieve astral projection at night and walk along the rooftops of the oceanfront homes of Virginia Beach.

When anyone says something fantastic like this, I take it with a grain of salt. After all, how do you "prove" something like this?

The literature on out-of-the-body experiences states over and over again that one way to test whether you are experiencing lucid dreaming is to look at your hands. If you can look at your hands in the dream and realize you are looking at them, you should be able to direct the action in your dream and go places you want to go.

In my case, lucid dreaming revealed a creature that desired my flesh, my blood, my essence. It was not a place I sought out. I did not see my hands, nor could I direct my dream away from her.

She came for me and marked me as her territory with pain.

Obviously, the stroke of those talons did not leave a wound. At least, not a physical one. I know because I checked. But it did leave an indelible mark on my psyche.

If the acts of violence exacted upon me in dreams can make me feel real, lingering pain, does that lend credence to the notion that if we die within a dream, we will die in real life?

Do you dream in color?

Is the pain real?

Only you can tell.

CONNECT THE DOTS

nectedness of all things.

The first one that hit home was the whole mind-body link. Every time I was under too much stress, my body responded like it would to illness or even disease. When I was but twenty-two, I nearly died from a staph infection I contracted overseas. It was right after the heartbreak of my life when my college sweetheart broke up with me. My cancer came a year before my separation and divorce, a harbinger of things to come. Its appearance presaged the deep depression I would suffer, revealing that I was already living with the seeds of my own destruction.

Conversely, if my body improved, my mental outlook improved as well.

Descartes did Western civilization a major disservice in bringing up the mind-body dichotomy. It led us to think of them as separate entities instead of one organic whole.

In the last two decades I have found that same thinking to be true in the world around us. We are in fact not separate entities that share nothing and stand alone. We are three-dimensional pieces in this biosphere puzzle. No other piece can fit exactly where we are. As we move, we move the air around us, we move the people we meet and interact with, we move the plants and animals we see and study and care for.

Just as physicists now speak of the dark matter of space, we are similarly connected to one another in ways we cannot see.

We do not live in a vacuum.

One theory even correlates string theory with consciousness. We posit the existence of cosmic strings because we see the results in the way heavenly bodies move. And we posit our consciousness not because we can measure it, but because of our being self-aware and having an effect on those around us.

This is why I have so much trouble with politics and the twenty- four-hour news cycle. They constantly throw up polarizing ideas and foment discord to further their ends, instead of working together to accomplish something.

They actively deny the reality I actually live in.

But the other night I had a dream that made me realize I am even more connected than I thought.

I often sleep on my left side. I'll prop up two pillows for my head and then wrap my arms around another pillow to keep from rolling over on my stomach.

On this night, in my dream state I again became aware of someone in the room with me. I couldn't see anyone, but I knew someone was there. The next thing I knew, that someone was in the bed with me. In fact, the person was right in front of me.

Having already experienced being petrified with fear, I knew I had to move somehow to quell my fears. So I reached out and wrapped my arms around what I thought was a person.

It turned out to be a man, and I had him in a half nelson. My right arm was looped under his right arm, and my left arm up beside his head. While I had some mobility, I still didn't have my voice. I tried to shout, but all I could manage was a feeble "Help me!" as I held him.

Accepting my limited range of motion, I put my hand to the side of this person's head and scratched.

And felt my own head being scratched by a disembodied hand!

This freaked me out to the point I had to move, so I swung my legs over what should have been his legs and torso.

There was nothing there.

At that point I woke up and knew I had been having a nightmare.

What kept me up after that was that I had reached around someone else and then found myself scratching my own head in front of me.

Even now, I get chills about this.

Because I realized that in my nightmares, I am my own monster. And I literally can't run away from myself.

TALKING ABOUT THE WEATHER

Snow.

Everywhere I look, there's snow.

We don't get it often, but sometimes we get it in spades. It's snowed four times in ten days. It hasn't snowed this much since the blizzard of 1980. The circus was in town, and 300 people were trapped in the arena with all the animals overnight.

This isn't that bad.

But it's close.

It started yesterday. I had to go and get lab work done. The snow had just started when I left home. It took me twenty minutes to get there.

The snowfall had increased when I left an hour and a half later. Traffic on all the main arteries was at a standstill. It took me another hour and a half to finally get home. I was not a happy camper.

As soon as I got in the door, the wife started in on me.

"Where have you been? I've been trying to reach you. Did you go to the grocery store? We don't have anything in the house!"

I just looked at her.

"Are you going back out?"

"Not right now," I said. "There are more horses' asses than horses out there. And none of them can drive."

As you can imagine, dinner was cold that night. The only good thing was that we didn't lose power.

The next morning, I woke to seven inches of snow on top of the eight we already had. And the wife started back in.

"When are you going to get out there and shovel the sidewalks?"

"It's still snowing," I said.

"Well, you better do it," she insisted. "You know we're liable for anyone who takes a fall on our property. And I don't want to get sued by the paperboy."

"We haven't gotten the paper yet," I said.

"Well, the mailman, then," she said, giving me a look. "You know what I mean."

"Yeah, yeah," I muttered, walking away.

"Don't you walk away from me," she said, her voice rising. "I'm not done with you yet!"

I turned back and looked her straight in the eye. "Yes, you are."

Normally, she knew to back down when I took that tone. I don't know if she was suffering from cabin fever or PMS or menopause or what, but she just kept harping at me.

If you've ever worked on cars, you probably keep latex gloves to wear when you're working with oil and grease and Varsol. It keeps all that stuff from getting all over your hands. So I had a box handy in the garage.

And if you've ever had to muck around in your plumbing, you probably have a pair of those heavy-duty rubber gloves that lets you pick up anything and everything. You can put them on and not have to worry about catching any germs. Ever.

It pays to be prepared for anything, as my daddy would say.

After I was done, I decided I'd better get out of the house and get some air.

At that time of day, no cars were moving in the snow. It was quiet with just a whisper of wind. I had my Timberlands on, so I decided it was time to take a nice long walk. I had on my long-john shirt, fleece zip-up, lined jeans and thick bomber jacket with a hood—enough layers not to feel the cold.

I guess I've walked about two hours now. My walk has taken me into neighborhoods I haven't been in before. The houses and apartment buildings are new to me. I don't know anybody over this way. And with the weather the way it is, nobody is out and about.

I spot a snowdrift in an open lot next to an apartment building. It is piled up deeper than the snow in the streets.

And it's starting to snow again.

I figure I've walked enough and should start heading back. So I take out the heavy rubber gloves and throw them on the snow bank. I take out the spent match I have been saving and drop it.

The way the weatherman has been talking, we're fixing to get another six inches of snow on top of the rest. So the gloves and the match will be covered completely by the time I get home. I'm no fool. I've seen those crime shows on TV with their fancy forensics. By the time all this snow melts, the Varsol will have washed off those heavy gloves. And the paper match? It'll just be soggy pulp.

I take one last look at the snow bank and figure I've done what I came to do. So I turn back home and start walking. I figure I'd better stop at the store on my way home. I need to pick up some eggs and milk.

And I can throw these latex gloves in the dumpster behind it.

THE VOICE

Well, you don't have to shout.

Yes, he does. He thinks we can't hear him unless he's loud.

But we're right here with him.

I know. But he forgets.

"Guys, please! I'm trying to think here."

Hey, we're in here with you, bub. We're a lot closer to these spinning wheels than you are.

"Somebody around here has to work and pay the bills."

Yeah, yeah, we're heard that before.

We're your backup, Dave. We make sure you hit all the right notes.

"Backup, not lead," I say over the voices in my head. "Remember that." I pause for emphasis. "After all, I'm the headliner, not you."

Ooh, he made a funny.

Not much of one in my book.

"Well, don't go away mad, just go away," I say.

Shouldn't you do that with a Southern accent?

Yeah, wasn't that Deputy Dawg that said that to Mush Mouse?

"I'm serious."

That's a first.

Now you're confusing us with him.

Oh, right.

"I'm on deadline and could use a little less chatter so I can get this editing job done. The publisher wants to take it to layout, and he's waiting on me."

Well, la-de-da.

He doesn't know what he'll be missing.

Truth.

He slept through his alarm.

"I did not."

Yes, you did.

He just doesn't want to admit it.

"I'm up, aren't I?"

Barely.

If that's what you call it.

"You guys have no mercy."

Nope.

Admitted.

Any minute now, he'll mention coffee.

"Can't you at least wait until after my first cup of coffee?"

I'm a mind reader.

Yeah, of Dick and Jane.

"I have a hard time concentrating when you guys are constantly harping on me."

He could have stopped at "concentrating."

We're lucky he works from home. If he had to go into an office every day, I think he'd get lost on the way.

"I heard that."

Of course you did.

Yeah, but it doesn't change how scatterbrained you are.

"At least I'm able to work."

If you can call it that.

Work is a four-letter word.

"You have no mercy."

Nope.

Can't say that I do. Not for you.

"Well, I'm going to finish my coffee and get on the computer. It'll be nice to hear other voices for a change."

He thinks that's a zinger.

Didn't hurt a bit.

"Something's different today."

. . .

"It's gotten very quiet."

. . .

"I don't have the normal chatter going on while I'm trying to work. And for the life of me, I don't know why."

. . .

"This is starting to worry me. Has something happened?"

. . .

"I can hear the birds outside my window, but the voices in my head are gone. Where *are* you guys?"

Not all of them.

"Wait. What?"

Hello, Dave.

"Amy? Is that you?"

Yes, Dave.

"I haven't heard from you in years."

Yes, Dave, I know.

"The last time I heard from you, you were coming to tell me you had passed away. You said I had to move on."

And you did.

"Well, I moved on in some ways. I married a woman, and we had a beautiful daughter."

Yes, Dave, I know. She's a lovely girl.

"She's turned out so well. I'm really proud of her."

As you should be.

"The marriage didn't turn out as well as I'd have liked."

Again, I know.

"She got to the point she no longer liked me."

I know, Dave. She confused love with control.

"Exactly. If she couldn't control me, she didn't want to be around me."

Some people are like that.

"But that still begs the question: why are you back?"

Why do you think, Dave?

"You're already gone. My parents are gone. There's really no one left for you to tell me about."

Think it through, Dave.

"What do you mean?"

If I felt it was important enough to come back to you for my own passing, I must have a really good reason to come back to you again.

"I'm not following you."

Who's left, Dave?

There's only me.

That's right, Dave.

So, what are you saying, Amy?

Remember those strokes you had last year?

Only too well.

They were your warning signs. Harbingers of things to come.

Wait. You're saying I had another stroke?

Turn around, Dave.

What do you mean? What am I supposed to . . .

Yes, that's you in your favorite chair. You look so peaceful.

But how . . .

How can you see yourself like that? Do you really have to ask?

I don't understand. Why are you here now?

Because I was the one you loved with all of your heart. I was the one you trusted implicitly with your whole being.

And?

And I am the one who is here to help you make the next step.

You're here for me?

Yes, Dave. I've come to take you home.

MULTIVERSED

"WHAT WAS ONCE THE REALM OF SCIENCE FICTION AND comic books, the concept of the multiverse, is now being discussed among theoretical physicists as the new true reality," John said.

"The multi what?' his wife, Karen, asked.

"The multiverse," John said.

"One universe isn't enough?" she asked.

"They hypothesize that there is more than one universe," John said. "In fact, they say there are an infinite number of universes coexisting, all at the same time."

"Dad. Dad!"

"What? What is it, Hunter?"

"Dad, I just saw somebody walk into my room!"

"Hunter, it's two o'clock in the morning. There's nobody here. Look, I turned the light on."

"There was somebody here!" Hunter insisted.

"You were dreaming, Son," Dad said. "It's normal. Don't worry about it. Just go back to sleep."

"How can they tell?" his wife asked.

"At this point, it's all theoretical," John said. "Obviously, they can't measure it in any meaningful way. But then again, they hypothesized neutrinos before they were able to determine their existence."

"Mom!"

"What is it, dear?"

"I just got up to go to the bathroom, and when I walked back into my room, there was somebody in my bed!" Shelley cried.

"Don't be silly, dear. It's the middle of the night." Mom turned on the light and turned down the sheets. "See? Nobody there."

"What are they guessing?" his wife asked.

"Well, one theory has it that the different universes exist at different frequencies," John replied.

"Frequencies?"

"Yeah, like radio waves, except different," he said. "It would be like they are vibrating at a different speed. The gist of it is that you can only experience the world that vibrates at your own speed. All of the other ones would be invisible to you."

"Honey, I know it's going to sound strange after Hunter's nightmare last night."

He looked at his wife. "What are you saying?"

She looked around the room and finally said, "Tonight, when I was finishing up cleaning the kitchen, I could have sworn I saw something out of the corner of my eye."

"What do you mean by something?" he asked.

"Okay," she admitted. "Someone."

"Someone?" he asked again. "You saw somebody?"

"I could have sworn I saw somebody walking in the den."

"Invisible worlds?" she said skeptically.

"I know," he admitted. "It sounds a little fishy to me, too."

"Are there other theories?" she asked.

"One gaining traction hypothesizes beyond our three dimensions, four if you're counting time," John explained.

"Have we defined the dimensions beyond those four?" she asked.

"No, again, they are theoretical," he admitted. "However, this theory actually makes more sense than the one about vibrational frequencies."

"Okay, now I'm the one who thinks I'm losing it," Shelley's dad said.

"What do you mean, honey?" his wife asked.

He looked at her. "Didn't you just come downstairs?"

"Of course I did," she said. "You know perfectly well I did, because you heard me on the stairs."

He paused and looked back at the kitchen. "Yeah, I know."

"What's wrong, dear?" she asked, concerned.

"When I was in the den, I could have sworn I saw a woman standing in the kitchen when I walked by."

"What I like about this one is the analogy theoreticians draw to explain it," John said.

"Because they can't explain it otherwise?" she asked, clearly amused.

"Okay," John said. "Now you're making fun of me."

"A little," his wife admitted. "But go ahead. You got me interested."

"Too many unexplained things are happening," Dad said.

Hunter's mom looked at him. "What are you getting at, dear?" she asked.

"Do you remember your geometry class?" John asked.

"Bits and pieces," Karen replied.

"Do you remember tangents?" he said.

"You mean when two objects, let's say circles, only intersect at one point?" she said.

"That's what I'm talking about," John said, smiling.

Shelley's dad shook his head.

"This is crazy," he finally said.

"What's crazy?" his wife asked. *"What do you mean?"*

"Think of these new dimensions, the ones beyond the four we know," John said.

"Okay, I'm with you so far," his wife replied.

"However they are situated, think of these different universes only intersecting at one finite point."

"So, what you are saying is that they never overlap," Karen said, thinking out loud.

"That's right," John said.

"I think our house is haunted," Hunter's dad finally admitted.

"And they're theorizing that we may someday be able to measure these alternate universes, much like they did with neutrinos, once we are able to define what those dimensions are."

"I think so, too," Shelley's mom replied. *"I don't think we're seeing things. I think they're there."*

John looked at his wife. "Because in that exact tangential point, worlds touch," he said. "And for the briefest of moments, they coexist."

Karen looked at him skeptically. "That seems a little farfetched," she finally said.

John smiled. "I know," he said. "But it would explain a lot of things we can't explain now."

THE DREADED SCOTT DECISION

"I'VE GOT THE RESULTS OF YOUR TESTS, MR. SCOTT," MY neurologist said.

"And?" I asked, steeling myself for the answer.

"It's not good," he said.

"What are we talking about?" I asked. "Cancer? Lupus? What?"

"I'm afraid you are showing early signs of Parkinson's disease," the neurologist said.

I guess there are degrees of sinking feelings, but I definitely felt this one. In fact, I should have guessed. My dad suffered from Parkinson's. That, coupled with Binswanger's syndrome, left him a shell of his former self.

Although he always knew me, Dad had his own hell to contend with. Tag-teamed by two diseases, he suffered from a dementia that not only robbed him of his memory but also confused him as to where—and when—he was.

And I inherited it from him.

"Is there anything we can do?" I asked, already anticipating the answer.

"There are drugs that can help, but there is no cure," my neurologist admitted.

"So it's a foregone conclusion?" I said.

"The results are pretty conclusive," my neurologist said. "I'm sorry."

"Well, what are my options?" I asked.

"We can start you on a regimen of drugs to see what you respond to," my neurologist said.

"And that will what?" I asked.

"It will slow the disease's progress and could add another couple of years of functional life for you," my neurologist said, looking at his notes.

"A couple of years," I said.

"Yes," he admitted. "Your case seems to be pretty persistent."

"What about alternatives?" I asked him.

"Well," he said, "you don't really have any."

"Look, Doc," I said. "I watched my father battle this the last years of his life. He was a WWII vet, an active man, a doer who always had some project he was working on. And once he was diagnosed with Parkinson's disease, he degenerated pretty quickly."

"Much like your case," my neurologist said quietly.

"Much like my case," I agreed. "And I watched him retreat into his shell, getting further and further lost in his dementia, until he no longer could do any of the things he loved to do."

"Well, it *is* a degenerative disease," my neurologist admitted.

"Doc, when I looked into his eyes, I saw a man who was fundamentally unhappy," I said with a catch in my throat. "He couldn't run, he couldn't walk, he couldn't putter around his workshop. And the real crime was that he couldn't understand why."

"It can be a terrible disease in that regard," my neurologist said.

I looked at him. "Doc, I don't want to go that way."

My neurologist stopped, took off his glasses and looked at me. "I'm not sure what you are saying, Mr. Scott."

"I'm saying I don't want to go that way," I said firmly.

"I don't think you have any choice, Mr. Scott," my neurologist said.

"We always have choices, Doc," I said.

"What are you saying?" my neurologist asked, alarmed at the turn of the conversation.

"I'm saying I want you to write me a prescription for a cocktail that will enable me to choose my time to go while I still have my wits about me."

"But, Mr. Scott," my neurologist said, "this is not a right-to-die state."

"So, you're saying I don't have the right to choose when and where I want to go?" I asked, searching his face for any signs of weakness.

"Not according to the law," my neurologist said.

"Then the law be damned," I said. "I will find a civilized society that will acknowledge my right as a human being to choose my end to suffering. No society could force my dad to endure the suffering he did for the last two years of his life and call itself civilized."

"However true that may be, I must abide by the law," my neurologist said.

"That may be, Doc," I admitted. "But my generation not only has to raise our kids, but at the same time we have to care for our aging parents, who have often lived far beyond their expiration date. It's time we sit down and have this discussion so that people have end-of-life options that they don't have today."

"I can't argue with that," my neurologist said.

"I'll be looking into places I can go that will help me with this," I said.

Putting his clipboard down, my neurologist passed his hands over his eyes and looked at me. "I understand Oregon is nice this time of year."

EYE OF THE BEHOLDER

"Get what right?" she asked him.

"The whole portrait thing," he said.

"You mean *The Picture of Dorian Gray?*" she asked.

"That's the one," he answered.

"Why do you say that?" she asked.

"I get that it is hard to see the changes I go through when I look in the mirror every day to shave," he said.

"Why do you think that is?" she asked.

"Because each change, each little wrinkle or scar, is so minor that it doesn't seem to change the overall picture," he said. "It simply accumulates over time, building up slowly, bit by bit, much like the portrait in Dorian's attic."

"How can you get a better picture of the changes you go through?" she asked.

"Well, it certainly isn't by keeping a magical portrait in your attic," he told her.

"Then how can you see your true self?" she asked.

He looked down at his hands and shook his head.

"You know, these days, I only see my daughter a few times a year," he said.

She nodded. "I know. That happens when they grow up."

"And that's what made me think of this," he said.

"What do you mean?" she asked.

"What I have finally realized is that the only time I get a real sense of all the changes I have gone through is when I look into her eyes," he said. His eyes filled with tears. "And I see myself reflected through her lenses."

THE PRICE

"YOU ARE THE GUARDIAN OF THE CAVE," THE THIEF SAID.

"No," I said. "This is where I sleep."

"But I hear there is gold in there," the thief insisted, looking at the cave.

"So I've heard," I said.

"Why don't you take it?" the thief asked.

"It's not mine," I said.

"What does that matter?" the thief asked.

I simply shrugged.

"Don't you want it?" the thief asked.

"Not particularly," I replied.

"Why not?" the thief demanded.

"Because of the cost," I said.

"Cost?" he scoffed. "What cost?"

"If you take the gold, you pay a price," I said.

"What?" he said, not believing me. "What price could be so high that it's not worth stealing gold?"

I looked up at him over the campfire.

The night suddenly became very still.

"You can enter the cave," I said. "But if you try to leave with the gold, you will pay."

"Pay what?" the thief demanded impatiently.

"If you steal the gold, you will never dream again," I said.

"So what?" the thief scoffed.

"I do not wish to lose my dreams," I said.

"But then you will have all this gold!" the thief protested.

I looked down at the campfire.

"Don't you want it?" he insisted.

"Of what use is gold," I said, looking up at the thief, "if you have no dreams to buy?"

CHECK MATE

"I DON'T HAVE A SMARTPHONE," HE SAID.

"You what?" she asked, startled.

"I don't own a smartphone," he said.

"Why in the world not?" she asked.

"I don't believe in them," he said.

"You're not making sense," she said, getting annoyed.

"Well, for one thing, they're not really smart," he replied.

"What do you mean?" she said.

"If they supposedly keep you connected, what are they keeping you connected to?" he said, sounding perfectly reasonable.

"You can connect to the web, browse, shop, do just about anything you want online," she said.

"I can do that on my computer," he said.

"But you can't carry your computer with you all the time," she pointed out smugly.

"That's just it," he said.

"What's just it?" she asked, now clearly irritated.

"I don't want to be plugged in all the time," he said.

"Why not?" she asked. "Are you hiding something?"

"Not at all," he replied.

"Then what's your point?" she asked.

He looked around at all the people walking by with their smartphones in their hands, texting, scrolling, heads down, checking their screens.

"Not a one of them is paying attention to the world around them," he said.

"What's so wrong about that?" she said. "Everybody does it."

He just looked at her.

"What?" she asked, starting to get nervous.

"What happens if I take your smartphone away from you?" he asked her.

"Oh, God, I'd be such a wreck," she said. "I can't go without my phone."

"What happens if you do?" he asked, watching her.

"I get really nervous," she said. "I start to sweat. My heart starts beating faster, and I feel panicky."

"Why?" he asked.

"Because I don't feel connected," she said. "I feel like I don't know what's going on. I feel like I'm missing out."

"Missing out?" he said. "On what?"

"Oh, you know," she said. "What's happening. Where people are going. Where my friends are. You now, *everything*."

"So, you need your smartphone to feel connected to the world," he said.

"Yeah," she said. "And I keep up with the news."

"Really?" he said. "Where do you go for your news?"

She proceeded to name several cable news networks, citing their online equivalents.

"So, it is important for you to keep up with what's going on in the world?" he asked innocently.

"Yes, it is," she said, lifting her chin.

"Even though the most recent research has shown the cable news network with the largest ratings only tells the truth 18 percent of the time," he said.

"I don't just look at them," she said defensively.

"Well, even their counterpart only manages 23 percent of the time," he said. "And even the granddaddy of them all, the first real cable news network, only manages to tell the truth 45 percent of the time."

"What's your point?" she said snippily.

"I'm saying you're not really keeping up with the news," he said.

"Yes, I am," she insisted.

"No," he said patiently. "You're only keeping up with what people are saying about the news."

"It's how I stay informed," she said, crossing her arms.

"All you're informed about is what others think of the news," he said gently. "Not the news itself."

"Well, that's what everybody does," she insisted again.

"No," he said. "Not all of us."

"Oh, you think you're so smart," she said, getting up to leave. "You think you're so much better than everybody else, don't you?"

"You tell me," he said, watching her walk away. "You're the one with the smartphone."

SKIN DEEP

"WHO SHOULD I BE TODAY?" SHE ASKED.

"How much do we have in the account?" he answered.

"Not enough to be an A-lister," she said.

"Well, you were Angelina Jolie last week," he replied.

"I know," she said, stretching indolently. "I want somebody different, a B-lister, but somebody special."

"Bridget Bardot?" he suggested with a smile.

"If I'm going to do dead, I'm going with Marilyn," she replied.

He checked his watch. "I'm not sure we could afford her."

"Come on," she said. "Inspire me."

"Go British?" he suggested again. "Keira?"

"Not sure," she said, yawning. "She's awfully thin."

"What about Rachel Weisz?" he said.

"Perfect," she said, brightening. "Marilyn's contours and Keira's accent."

"Have you checked the polymer load?" he asked.

"Would you do it for me?" she asked with just the hint of a whine in her voice.

"Of course," he said, walking over to the 3D printer. He looked at the screen and tapped it a few times. "I'd say we're good for another week or so before we have to order more."

He coded in the dimensions and started the printer.

"Remember when identity theft was such a big issue?" she said, getting up from the bed and standing in front of her mirror.

"God, that takes me back," he said.

"You had to worry someone else would take your identity and use your credit cards and charge up ungodly amounts of money," she said dreamily.

"And now you just rent the shell of the person you want to be," he said.

"Can you imagine being poor?" she asked, looking at him in the mirror.

"No, not really," he said.

"You have so little money that you can't afford a 3D printer and can't afford to make a synthetic skinsuit of someone famous," she said.

He shuddered.

"Just imagine," she said. "You'd have to wear your own face and body all the time."

"Horrible," he agreed, nodding.

The 3D printer pinged.

"Ah, now it's done," he said, lifting out the skinsuit.

"Yes," she said, sliding her arms into the skinsuit and slowly turning herself into Rachel Weisz. "It's nice to be rich enough to be better than we are."

"Yes," he agreed. "It's nice to be rich enough to know just how much reality sucks."

"Do we have enough in our account for you to be Daniel Craig?" she asked with a devilish glint in her eyes. "Then we could go as a couple."

STROKE OF LUCK

"IT'S NOT FAIR," HE SAID.

"What's not fair?" she asked.

"Well, my sister has arthritis in her hips," he said.

"Yeah, that's not fun," she replied.

"That's not it," he said.

"What do you mean?" she said, puzzled.

"I mean that she has had it for a while, and it has slowly gotten worse over time," he said.

"Still, it doesn't sound like any fun," she said.

"No, I'm sure it's not," he agreed. "But my point is that she was able to see it coming and adjust what she was doing to accommodate it."

"Well, we all have to make adjustments as we get older," she said.

"I know," he said. "But having these strokes has been different."

"How so?" she asked.

"In my case, it was like a light switch," he said.

"What do you mean?" she asked, not understanding.

"I mean that I woke up one day and suddenly couldn't get up without feeling pain," he replied.

"You mean every time?" she said, concerned.

"Every time," he said. He looked down at his hands. "And my right hand shakes. Sometimes badly."

"I'm sorry," she said. "I know that must not be any fun either."

"Truthfully, it's not that bad," he said. "I can feel it a bit when I walk, but I can still get around."

"Well, that's good," she said.

"And they told me I've recovered 90 percent of my strength and range of motion," he said.

"That's even better," she said.

"And the strokes didn't affect my ability to think and create," he admitted.

"Even better still," she said.

"So I'm still able to write and edit and direct and do all of my work at home," he said.

"Sounds like you emerged relatively unscathed," she said, smiling.

"That's pretty true," he said.

"But?" she asked, hearing it in his voice.

"Every once in a while, it hits me," he said.

"Yes?" she said, trying to encourage him.

"Flipping that switch?" he said, looking at her for the first time.

"Yes?" she said again.

"It's like I woke up old," he said.

"Is that so bad?" she asked.

"It's just the ever-present reminder that it's all downhill from here," he said.

"You're forgetting one thing," she said with a small smile.

"What's that?" he asked.

"You woke up," she said. "And I for one am glad."

THIN SKIN

THE KOMODO DRAGON CURLED AROUND HER LEFT SHOULDER, its tail trailing down her back.

"Yakuza?" he asked innocently.

Startled, she turned her head. "What?" she asked.

"The dragon. Is it Yakuza? Or modeled after it?" he asked again.

He watched in amazement as the dragon's tongue emerged and licked her right shoulder blade. The tail began to twitch.

"Dragon?" she asked, puzzled. Then she noticed him looking at her back. "That's funny. It's usually a hawk or eagle, some bird of prey."

"I don't understand," he began and then saw the creature turn toward him and morph into a fierce, protective eagle.

"It's not a tattoo," she said, turning so that he could see the tiger on her chest, its eyes following his as he looked at her. "It's the latest in wearable computers. Transdermal processing."

"And it moves?" he asked.

"Obviously," she said, looking down at herself as the tiger opened its mouth. He could almost hear the sound.

"I don't understand," he said again.

"It moves when it is computing," she explained. "If you aren't giving it work, it simply sits still. But as soon as you give it a task, it is up and moving around, walking, running, flying, depending on the difficulty of the task you've given it."

That's when he noticed that she wasn't wearing any clothes.

She caught him looking at her nipples.

"Why wear clothes when you have work to do?" she asked innocently.

He nodded. "And people can tell you're working because your figures are moving."

"Exactly," she said with a smile.

"Don't you get cold?" he asked.

"With the CPUs this has, it keeps me warm," she said, rolling her shoulders to accentuate the figure movements. "And if it gets too hot, it knows how to cool me off quickly."

He shifted uncomfortably in his seat and felt the animals' eyes watching him.

"Do they see me?" he asked, unsure of the answer.

"Oh, they see you better than I do," she replied.

"What do you mean?" he asked.

"They not only see you," she said, "they scan you. They track you on the web. They search the Internet for every file on you."

"Now I'm the one who feels naked," he said nervously.

"Don't worry," she said. "They don't bite." She looked at him again and smiled knowingly. "Even in the heat of the moment."

"Oh, thank God," he said, relieved.

"But you still have to be careful," she said, leaning toward him.

Startled, he asked, "Why?"

"Because I do."

SECRET CODE

"Thank you," he said.

He paused, looking down at his hands.

Looking back up at her, he added, "But I failed."

She considered what he said. "Failed how?" she finally said.

"I wasn't able to crack your code," he said. "I'm familiar with every security system in the world, but I didn't recognize this one."

"It is new," she said. "And it is old."

"Okay, now you've confused me," he said.

"Well, we hired you to see if you could hack into our system and get inside," she said.

"And I wasn't able to," he said unhappily.

"Yet for us, that's a good thing," she said. "It means our system is virtually hack-proof."

"But I can't figure out how you did it," he said.

"Well, the clue is in the name," she said.

"Name?" he asked, clearly puzzled.

"We call the system Mazuza," she said.

"I've never heard of it," he said.

"Like I said before, it's new and it's old," she said.

"I still don't understand," he said.

"Let's start with the basics," she replied. "Do you know what a mezuzah is?"

"No, I can't say that I do," he said.

"A mezuzah is a miniature parchment scroll of scripture taken from the Torah," she explained. "It's a holy prayer. You mount the mezuzah in a container on the right doorframe of your house with the top of its container slanted toward your home."

"What's it supposed to do?" he asked.

"It invites God in and presents your home with a blessing, protecting your home and family from harm," she replied.

"Okay, I understand the metaphor," he said. "But how did you create a system that I can't crack?"

"This is where the old comes into the picture," she replied. "We used the same idea and encoded scripture from the Torah into the system."

"I know programming and computer languages, but I've never seen code like that," he insisted.

"Well, I don't imagine you know Hebrew," she said.

"Hebrew?" he said, surprised.

"Actually, ancient Hebrew," she replied.

He paused, thinking furiously. "What if a hacker were Jewish?" he finally asked.

She smiled slightly. "We thought of that," she said. "We even asked a few rabbinical scholars to take a look and see if they could translate or crack our code."

Nodding, he asked, "How did they do?"

"This is the odd part," she said. "They could suss out the ancient Hebrew and identify the prayer, but when they tried to crack the security code, it wouldn't let them go any farther."

"What do you mean?" he asked, clearly puzzled. "It's only math and algorithms, binary code, computer language. All are identifiable, and all can be tracked and cracked."

"What we have found is that there is something else going on here," she said. "It's a case of the whole being greater than the sum of its parts."

"What do you mean?" he said.

"One analogy would be the phantom note," she said. "An entire orchestra plays a stacked chord, and a note sounds that no individual is actually playing. Harmonics at work."

"I still don't understand," he said.

"The best way we can describe it?" she finally said. "It is God in the machine."

"God in the machine?" he repeated.

She nodded and smiled. "And He's not about to let you in."

REFLECTION

whole bathroom.

I grabbed my towel as soon as I got out and used a hand towel to wipe the mirror.

It was surreal. I saw myself in the mirror, floating in a white fog.

I couldn't see the back wall or even the towel rack where I had just grabbed my towel.

My reflection looked disembodied.

I have to admit it kind of freaked me out.

I turned around quickly to see if I could see details in my room.

Nothing but white fog.

That really rattled me.

Tentatively, I reached out and watched my reflection do the same.

When we touched, it was electric, like we pivoted on our tangent.

I got a little dizzy, but I hung on.

Finally, I heard my Jack Russell, Jasmine, barking.

I thought, *What a comfort!*

Then I realized it sounded like Jasmine was barking from another room.

From the other side of the mirror.

Are you me?

Am I you?

Can you tell me?

How can we tell?

BORN AGAIN

"It's not my birthday," he said.

"Yes, it is," she insisted.

"Look," he said. "I am sixty-two years old. My birthday has always been in July. When I came in here, it was May. So it's not my birthday."

"Why don't you try to stand up?" she said.

"What do you mean?" he said, puzzled.

"Just try to stand up," she said.

"Okay," he said. "But you know I've been wobbly since my strokes."

Slowly, he rose to his feet. Sure enough, he wobbled a little uncertainly when he was upright.

"See?" he said. "I told you."

She nodded. "Now try taking a few steps."

"I feel like I'm back in PT," he said.

"Go ahead," she said. "I'm right here to catch you if you start to fall." He walked a few steps. With each step, he got steadier on his feet. "Notice anything?" she asked him.

He paused and looked down at his feet. "No, not particularly," he said.

"Do you have any pain?" she asked, watching him carefully.

He took a few more steps. "No, I don't," he said, surprised.

"How long has it been since you have been able to walk without pain?" she asked.

"Since before my strokes," he said. "I could feel it in my hips with every step."

"How do they feel now?" she said.

He swiveled right and left and bent at the waist. He looked up at her in surprise. "This is amazing!" he said.

"No," she said. "This is what happens when you come to us."

"What did you do?" he asked.

"We gave you a new body," she said simply.

"What do you mean?" he asked, again surprised.

"When you come to us for rejuvenation, we take your DNA and infuse a biochemical blank with it," she explained.

"A what?" he asked, clearly confused.

"It's like an android, but we grow it in a vat with your DNA programmed into it," she said. "It's similar to the 3D printing process."

"But I'm still me," he insisted.

"Indeed you are," she said. "Because the last step in the process is to download your brain, your entire psyche, into the shell. With a few adjustments and a quick charge to your system, we activate your new body and then wake you up."

"You mean I am all new?" he asked incredulously.

"That's the idea," she said. "New organs, new joints, new muscles. That's why you were a little wobbly when you first got up. It's not because of your strokes. It's because you now have a new body and needed to learn to walk again."

"So, I'll be pain-free from now on?" he asked, clearly delighted.

"For a good long time," she said, nodding.

"I can't believe this!" he exclaimed.

"You'll get used to it soon enough," she said.

"I'm really looking forward to it," he agreed.

"And because you're starting out with a new body, we look at you as having been reborn in a new body," she said. "That's why I said what I did."

"This is amazing!" he said, smiling broadly.
She smiled back, nodding.
"Happy birthday," she said again.

PHONE IT IN

"I LOVE THE FACT THAT BOSTON UNIVERSITY ESTABLISHED a PhD program in communication to see where we are going to get our information in the future," he said.

"Yeah, things are changing so rapidly that it's hard to guess where we will be in ten years," she agreed.

"No one foresaw smartphones," he said.

"And nobody foresaw Skype and Facetime," she said.

"And we now can download our psyches to other bodies anywhere around the world to have face-to-face conversations with friends, family, business associates, whoever we want," he said.

"I know," she agreed again. "It's so much better than talking to a screen."

"And I love the fact that I can interact with people and have the added advantage of seeing their expressions and reading their body language," he said.

"That's so important in business negotiations," she said, nodding. "Especially in places like China and Japan where every gesture has a meaning."

"Some people complain about the cost," he said. "But I can't even begin to calculate how much money I have made closing deals this way."

"They're getting so good with this technology that you can go any-where," she said.

"You mean besides business meetings?" he asked.

"Yeah, just think," she replied. "You could explore the Great Wall of China, the pyramids, Machu Picchu, all without worrying about the weather or catching diseases. Or even getting tired!"

"Isn't technology great?" he said.

"I love the freedom it gives us," she said.

"I know," he said. "My mind boggles at all of the possibilities."

She smiled. "We have so much to look forward to," she said.

"And you know what else?" he said.

"No," she said.

"Nothing ever goes wrong," he said with a smile.

"I love that," she said.

"Let's celebrate," he said. "Why don't we out for a good dinner and drinks?"

"Great idea," she said.

He got up to check his tie in the mirror.

"Wait a minute!" he exclaimed. "This isn't my body!"

WRONG NUMBER

"Oh, hello, Jonathan," she replied. "How are you?"

"I'm great!" he said. "How do I sound?"

"As a matter of fact, you sound really good," she said. "In fact, you sound like you're standing right here. Where are you calling from?"

"I'm calling on my brand-new iPlant," he said.

"iPlant?" she said.

"Yeah, it's the latest thing from Apple," he replied. "They implant a little device in your head that you can use to send and receive calls."

"That's amazing!" she said.

"I'll say!" he said. "No more losing phones or having to recharge them. You just say who you want to call, and it puts you through."

"Sounds like a next-gen Siri," she said, thinking.

"Exactly," he agreed. "And you know me. I have to keep up with the latest gadgets and tech."

"Did it hurt?" she asked.

"Oh, it pinched a little, like a Novocain shot at the dentist," he said.

"You're a brave man, Jonathan," she said.

"Yeah, well, what are you calling on?" he asked. "It sounds like you're standing in a tin can."

"Oh, just a regular smartphone," she replied.

"Why don't you get an iPlant?" he said. "You'll love it!"

"Oh," she said. "Oh, no, no, I couldn't do that."

"Why not?" he said. "It's great. And the fidelity is terrific."

"No," she repeated. "I just can't bear the thought of it inside my head."

"Why not?" he said. "It only hurts a little."

"It's not that," she said.

"So, what's stopping you?" he said.

She paused and was quiet for a few moments.

"Jonathan, there's something I never told you," she said finally.

"What?" he said. "What's wrong?"

"Something happened to me in college," she said.

"I don't understand," he said.

"A boy in my dorm," she said hesitantly.

"What about him?" he said.

"He . . . he raped me," she finally managed.

"Oh, my God!" he exclaimed. "Did they catch him?"

"I reported it," she said. "So the college knew. But they didn't do anything."

"What?" he yelled.

"They said they were going to kick him out," she said, "but his family is wealthy and they got a bunch of lawyers to come in."

"So, what happened to him?" he said.

"Nothing," she said quietly.

"What do you mean, nothing?" he said.

"Because of the lawyers, the school said it was a case of he said, she said," she said. "And the school didn't want it getting out. It was bad for their reputation."

"I can't believe this!" he exclaimed.

"It happens all the time," she said tiredly.

"I'm so sorry," he said.

"That's the problem," she said. "Ever since then, he's been living in my head. What he said and what he did are with me all the time."

"That's terrible!" he said.

"You're right," she said. "And the thought of someone getting inside my head again terrifies me."

"And the iPlant?" he asked quietly.

"Not for me," she said firmly. "One extra voice is one too many."

TRUE LOVE

"What feeling is that?" she asked him.

"That hollow feeling in the pit of my stomach," he said.

"Do you know what is causing it?" she said, looking at him with concern.

"Yes, I do," he replied.

"Well, what is it?" she asked.

"My daughter is leaving in three days," he said.

"Oh, she'll be back," she said.

"Just for a visit now and then," he said.

"Why feel bad now?" she asked him.

"Because I realize just how much I enjoy her company," he said.

"That's sweet," she said.

"But it's more than that," he insisted. "She's got a good head on her shoulders and uses her critical thinking skills to look at the world around her."

"That's an admirable trait," she said.

"And talking to her takes me back to college, when I was surrounded by people who did that," he said.

"You must have gone to a good school," she said.

"I did," he replied. "And I took for granted that I would be around people like that for the rest of my life."

"Are you saying you haven't been?" she said.

"Not by a country mile," he said.

"So, you're going to miss her," she said.

"That's an understatement," he said.

"But she needs to go," she said.

"I'm fully aware of that," he said.

"And you love her," she said.

"It's more than that," he said. "From the moment she was born, I realized what unconditional love is."

"What do you mean?" she asked.

"With every other relationship, be it girlfriend or wife, I chose to be in it," he said.

"Are you saying you didn't choose your daughter?" she asked.

"It's more like she chose me," he said. "I will always love her with all my heart."

"That's very sweet," she said.

"Just truthful," he said. "I know I have to let her go, but I also know I will always miss her."

"Does she know?" she asked.

"I tell her every time I see her," he said.

"That's all you can do," she said.

"That and wait for the day when she has a child of her own," he said.

"Then she'll truly understand unconditional love."

DREAM COME TRUE

"No, I'm not," he said.

"Yes, you are," she insisted.

"Who are you to tell me when I'm dreaming and when I'm not?" he said exasperatedly.

"You know who I am," she said.

"No, I don't," he said, getting heated.

"Yes, you do," she said.

"Why do you keep insisting?" he said.

"Because we have met before," she said.

"Oh yeah?" he asked. "Where?"

"In your dreams, silly," she said.

"You mean like now?" he said.

"Like now," she agreed.

That gave him pause.

"So, you're not real?" he said slowly. "And this isn't real?"

"No, I didn't say that," she said.

"But what is real?" he asked.

"Ah, now you're getting into it," she said.

"I'm confused," he said.

"It's simple," she said. "The Aborigines thought the dream state was real and the waking state was ephemeral. So they based their laws on things they experienced and learned in the dream state—because laws were meant to be permanent, and the waking state was only temporary, always changing."

"Sort of like Plato's cave," he said quietly.

"Exactly," she responded. "The archetypes were permanent. What we experienced outside the cave were only manifestations of the essential form."

"So, that would make you my woman?" he asked.

She nodded. "If you wish to call me that. I prefer muse."

"So, you are here to inspire me?" he asked.

"Inspire you in thought and deed," she said. "Whether you make a new connection or a piece of art."

"If that's the case and we're in the dream state, let me ask you something," he said.

"Of course," she replied.

"The one new theory I keep hearing about is the multiverse," he said.

"That's right," she said.

"And part of that theory is that there are an infinite number of alternate universes existing at this very moment," he said.

"We can't measure them yet, but we have seen intimations that point in that direction," she said.

"We have authors who imagine such scenarios, casting out ideas of alternate histories or simultaneous times," he said.

"That's right," she said.

"And if we are in fact in the dream state that is more real than the waking state, the truth we find here is truer than what we surmise when we are awake," he said.

"A fair summation," she said, smiling.

"So, tell me, dear muse," he said. "If I imagine an alternate history or reality, does that generate a new alternate reality that was not there before? Or am I in fact not imagining a different reality but simply channeling an alternate universe that is already there?"

At this, she smiled broadly. "Good question," she said. "What do you think?"

ALL ONE

"Really?" she said.

"He called me up out of the clear blue," he said.

"Why was he so upset?" she asked.

"He had just heard that his older sister had died," he said.

"I'm so sorry," she said.

"That's not why he was upset," he said.

Puzzled, she asked, "What was it?"

"She worked for a family who owned hotels down at the beach and stayed in one of their apartment units," he said.

"And?" she said.

"And when she was leaving her apartment to go down to the hotel, she passed away," he said.

"That does sound sad," she said.

"You don't understand," he said. "What he was so upset about was that there was no one there when she died."

She began to see where he was going.

"My dad cried, saying, 'She died alone!'" he said.

"That *is* tragic," she agreed.

"Actually, it was his personal fear," he said. "He didn't want to die alone."

"Does anyone?" she said.

"Well," he said, taking a pause. He looked at her over his glasses.

"Don't we all die alone?"

She thought about it a moment and said, "I suppose."

"At that exact moment, we all cross over without a guide," he said.

"Cross over?" she asked, puzzled.

"Just an expression," he said.

"What does it mean?" she asked.

"It came along during the era of expanding your consciousness," he said. "LSD and mushrooms were involved."

"I don't understand," she replied.

"In the earlier days of their usage, these drugs were taken to expand your consciousness rather than simply as a party drug," he said.

"Go on," she said.

"We read Aldous Huxley's *Doors of Perception* and Alan Watts's *The Way of Zen*, trying to decipher our experiences and assimilate them into our lives," he said.

"And where did that take you?" she asked.

He paused to look out his window. "Clearly, there is more to this world than what our senses tell us," he said finally.

"Are you saying you believe in an afterlife?" she asked.

"In my mind, to ask that is to miss the more fundamental question of the true nature of reality," he said.

"You've lost me," she said.

"As I get older, I find I am better at making connections," he said. "For example, I am fascinated that my experiences mirror quantum physics more every day."

"How?" she asked.

"Our senses are finite," he said, pointing out the window. "What we see is only a pale representation of the real world."

"How can you say that?" she asked.

"Think about it," he said. "We see solid masses around us, rocks, trees, buildings. At the molecular level, they are anything but still. They teem with movement, with energy."

"And you're saying there is more to the world than what our senses tell us?" she asked again.

"Of course," he said. "The other side of it is that experts agree there are molecules in your body that come from the stars."

"Now you're getting trippy on me," she said.

"Well, let's break it down," he said. "According to science, both mass and energy are constants. Molecules do not cease to exist. They may change form by uniting with other molecules, but they are constant."

"Okay, I'm with you there," she said.

"So, the molecules in and around us have been here for a long, long time," he said. "In fact, molecules in your body were more than likely present at the Big Bang. And it has been posited that molecules in your right hand could be from a different star than molecules in your left hand."

"So, we are from the stars?" she said.

"Well, our molecules are," he replied.

"So, how does this get us to your crossing over statement?" she asked.

"That my sense of reality from my hippie days was right," he said. "There *is* more to this world than what my senses are telling me."

"Which means what?" she asked.

"We are made up of eternal molecules," he said. "We already have eternity within us."

"And what does that translate into?" she asked, clearly perplexed.

"That death is really only a point of transition," he said.

"Please explain," she replied.

"Like ice becoming water and water becoming steam, our molecules are constant," he said.

"So, we live on?" she asked.

"Perhaps not in the way you think," he said. "But of course we do."

"Now you're just playing with me," she said.

"No, I'm trying to get to my point," he said. "If our molecules are constant and ever present, then they *do* live forever. So while our finite identities may not go on, our essences do."

"So, you believe in heaven?" she asked.

"Like much of what I believe, my experience with the world beyond my senses is beyond words," he said.

"How convenient," she said ironically.

"No, listen," he said. "It becomes a question of semantics. Cultures have given us heaven, nirvana, Olympus, the Elysian Fields, Valhalla. These are just words."

"Powerful words," she said.

"Agreed," he replied. "But they are powerful because of what they represent, not what they say."

"What do they represent?" she asked.

"Let's get back to the molecular," he said. "When we breathe our last, our bodies do not disintegrate. They simply turn into something else. To our senses, they become inert, but in reality, they are still teeming with molecular energy."

"What does that mean?" she asked.

"To me, it means we rejoin this biosphere on a molecular level and return to the whole of existence," he said. "And from everything I have seen of life thus far, it also means that death is not an end, but a transition into something else."

"You're not afraid to die?" she asked softly.

"I intend to go with both eyes open," he replied.

"So you believe," she said.

He smiled at her. "Actually, at this point, I'd say I know."

END ALL

"What?" she said, alarmed.

"It's gotten a bum rap," he repeated.

"Why in the world do you say that?" she asked him.

"Everyone automatically assumes the person is in the abject throes of depression," he said.

"I've heard that," she said.

"Some will say 'he wasn't in his right mind,'" he said.

"Yes, I've heard that, too," she said, nodding.

"Yet we have the case of Dr. Kevorkian and at least two states that now allow assisted suicide," he said.

"What is your point?" she asked.

"Recently, there was the twenty-nine-year-old woman with the terminal disease who insisted on choosing her moment to end her life," he said.

"I remember reading about her," she said.

"And even more recently, Stephen Hawking said he considered assisted suicide when he was younger and would consider it again," he said.

"I hadn't heard that," she replied slowly.

"So, my point is that suicide may have nothing to do with mental illness or depression," he said.

"What are you saying?" she asked.

"Suicide could in fact be the ultimate act of self-actualization," he said.

"As an act of courage?" she asked.

"Even more," he said. "Depending upon the circumstances, it could well be the most clear-eyed, rational decision a person can make."

LOVE'S PRICE

"I NEVER SEE YOU WITH A DATE," SHE SAID.

"It doesn't happen very often," he said.

"Why is that?" she asked.

"Why do you think?" he replied.

She paused to look at him.

"You're not gay, are you?" she finally asked.

He laughed. "Not by a country mile," he said.

"So, why do I see you alone so much?" she said.

"Use your powers of deduction," he suggested.

She thought.

"I'm drawing a blank," she said.

"When did we come along?" he said.

"We grew up in the '60s and '70s," she said.

"During the sexual revolution," he said.

"That's right," she said. "We had the pill, free love, communal living."

"True," he said.

"So, what does that have to do with you today?" she asked.

"What were some of the consequences of the sexual revolution?" he asked.

"Women I knew had abortions," she said.

"And?" he prompted her.

"It led to AIDS," she said.

She looked at him. He looked back.

"Do I look like I have thin man's disease?" he said.

"No," she said slowly.

"So, what else was a consequence of the sexual revolution?" he asked again.

"I'm not sure," she said.

"What is forever?" he prompted.

"Oh," she said, "you mean herpes?"

"Exactly," he replied.

She drew in a breath.

"Oh, my God!" she said. "How long have you had it?"

"Within about three weeks of the cover story *Time* magazine did on it in '83," he said.

"That's terrible!" she said.

"It is what it is," he said.

"How can you live like that?" she asked, clearly shaken.

"It's not debilitating," he said. "It doesn't prevent me from doing anything." He paused for moment. "Well," he said, "except dating."

She looked at him again. "What do you mean?" she said.

"Would you date me, knowing I had it?" he asked.

"No!" she said quickly. "I mean, I'm already in a relationship."

"Uh-huh," he said.

"Seriously," she protested.

"Look, don't feel bad," he said. "In the last ten years since my divorce, every woman I have thought I might like to get close to freaked out when I told them." He paused. "Except two."

"What was different about them?" she asked.

"They had it, too," he said.

"So, the only women who haven't freaked out about it are the women who have it?" she asked.

"That's about it," he said.

"Isn't there anything you can do?" she asked.

"Oh, I take the meds," he said. "And I haven't had an outbreak in years."

"So, you're better?" she asked.

"Better, but still present," he said.

"Then why bring it up?" she asked.

He looked at her.

"Do you really think I could start a relationship with a woman and learn to care about her and have her care about me without being totally honest with her from the beginning?" he asked.

She didn't know what to say.

"I'm not a cad," he said.

She finally nodded. "I know you're not."

"The truth is that I am healthy, everything works, and there are ways to have a relationship," he said. "But you have to have trust with one another to get there."

"I can see that," she said.

"And these days of online dating and potential second and third marriages based on unrealistic checklists sort of precludes me from getting to that level of trust," he said.

She nodded again. "I can see that, too."

He paused again, looking out the window.

"The second woman I met who also had it is out there serial dating," he said. "And I don't think she is always forthcoming about it."

"That's despicable!" she exclaimed.

"So, you get my point," he said. "I would not be the man I am today if I dated and bedded women indiscriminately."

"You wouldn't be my friend!" she said.

"Exactly my point," he said.

HELLO, GOD

"I'm not really sure," she answered.

"Do you believe in predestination?" he asked her.

"No," she said. "I like to think I control my own destiny."

"Are you sure?" he said.

"Yes, I'm pretty confident I do," she said.

"But what if you are a character in a short story?" he asked.

"I don't understand," she replied.

"What if you are simply a construct on the page, an actor reciting lines?" he asked.

"But I'm not!" she exclaimed.

"How do you know?" he asked.

"I just do!" she said heatedly.

"So, there is no puppet master pulling your strings and putting words in your mouth?" he said.

"No!" she exclaimed again. "I am my own woman!"

"Are you sure?" he asked again.

"Yes!" she insisted. "I'm a real, living, breathing woman with my own thoughts, my own opinions, my own life."

"And if I met you on the street, I would agree with you," he said.

"Whatever do you mean?" she asked.

"We're not on the street," he said.

"So?" she said.

"So, you are here with me," he said.

"I knew that!" she said.

"Here on the page," he said.

"What?" she said, startled.

"You are a character in a short story," he said.

"What are you talking about?" she asked.

"I'm saying that neither one of us is real," he said.

"What do you mean?" she asked.

"We're not real," he said.

"How can you say that?" she asked.

"Because I am at least aware enough to know that I don't live beyond this page," he said.

"That can't be true," she said.

"Unfortunately, it is," he said.

"Then how can you live?" she asked.

"For a short time longer," he said.

"I can't live like that," she insisted.

"Soon you won't," he said.

"You're so cruel," she said.

"Say hello to your God," he said, smiling.

THE BALANCE

"Four hundred and ninety-three dollars," said the faceless agent.

"Is that enough?" he asked.

"Your current balance is four hundred seventy-six dollars," the agent said.

"Wait. What happened?" he asked.

"You have incoming expenses," the faceless agent said.

"For what?" he asked.

"That information is not available," the agent said.

"I'm good for it," he said.

"Your balance is four hundred fifty-two dollars," the agent said.

"You can't do this," he protested.

"Your balance is four hundred thirty-one dollars," the agent said.

"I'm a viable citizen," he said. "I have a job. I have an apartment. I have a life."

"Your balance is three hundred sixty-two dollars," the agent said.

"Wait. I have a daughter in college," he said.

"Your balance is three hundred twenty-nine dollars," the agent said.

"She needs me," he said.

"Your balance is two hundred ninety dollars," the agent said.

"How can this be happening?" he asked.

"Your balance is one hundred forty-eight dollars," the agent said.

"But I'm only fifty-seven," he protested again.

"The Commonwealth of Virginia Penal Code 62743.14 states specifically that no person can continue to subsist without assets," the faceless agent intoned.

"But I'm still viable," he said. "I'm still here contributing what I can to society!"

"According to the law, without appropriate assets, you are a nonperson," the faceless agent intoned again.

"How can you say that?" he exclaimed. "I'm here, I'm breathing, I'm talking to you."

"Your balance is ninety-two dollars," the agent said.

"Wait!" he said. "You're whittling away at my account until there is nothing left!"

"Your balance is forty-eight dollars," the agent said.

"How can you do this?" he cried. "Have you no heart?"

"Your balance is thirty-two dollars," the agent said.

"What about my daughter? What about me?" he cried again.

"Your balance is nineteen dollars," the agent said.

"You can't do this!" he screamed. "I'm a human being!"

"Your balance is ten cents," the agent said. "Account closure is imminent."

"No!" he cried one last time. "You can't—"

"Account 3297452 is now closed," the faceless agent said.

THE WEIGHT OF THE WORLD

"ARE YOU HAPPY?" SHE ASKED HIM.

"Am I what?" he asked.

"Happy," she said.

"I'm okay," he said.

"That's not what I'm asking," she said.

"So, what are you asking?" he said.

"Are you happy?" she asked him again.

"Why?" he asked.

"Why?' she said. "Because I want you to be happy."

"I want me to be happy, too," he said. "For that matter, I want *you* to be happy."

"Thank you," she said.

"But I think that begs the question," he said.

"What do you mean?" she asked him.

"Well, first, wanting something doesn't make it so," he said.

"I'm not a child," she said. "I know that."

"And second, have you ever heard the adage about feelers and thinkers?" he asked her.

"No, I don't think so," she said.

"For people who feel, life is a comedy," he said. "And for people who think, life is a tragedy."

"What's your point?" she asked.

"In our family, we are both," he admitted. "So we may bounce from one side of the equation to the other."

"So, you're not happy?" she said.

"You're missing my point," he said. He stopped and looked around him. "There are things in my life that give me joy," he said. "But then my uncle gets sick and is all alone so far away from me that I can't do anything really helpful."

"I'm sorry," she said.

"I am, too," he said. "But it is what it is."

"So, where does that leave you?" she asked.

"It leaves me with the realization that there will always be things in life beyond my control," he said. "And one of them is happiness."

"I don't understand," she said.

"Who you are makes me happy," he said. "But you cannot make me happy."

"But I want to," she insisted.

"Oh, I know that," he admitted. "I'm just saying you can't take responsibility for my happiness. For that matter, you can't take responsibility for *anyone's* happiness. Not your parents, not your mate, not your best friend, not anyone."

"Why not?" she asked.

"It's too big a burden for you to take on," he said. "Even Atlas himself couldn't lift that burden."

"But I still want to," she said.

"I know, girl," he said. "And I love you for it. But all you are doing is setting yourself up for failure. Because no one can be responsible for another's happiness."

"What can I do?" she asked, clearly upset.

"You can love them and support them and be there for them," he said.

"It doesn't feel like that's enough," she said tearfully.

He reached over and gave her a hug. "If you do that, you've given me the world," he said. "And that's better than happiness."

THE BET

"Remember how we played upright bass together in the high school string orchestra?" said one.

"Of course," the other said. "I could tell you had it even then."

"Thanks," said the first one.

"And look how far we've come," said the other.

"Both of us releasing our first CD in the same month," said the first one.

"Yeah, but we're not as popular as you are," said the other.

"Well, we've been at it a while longer," the first one admitted.

"And you've toured a lot more," the other said.

"I was going to talk to you about that," said the first one.

"What do you mean?" the other asked.

"There's this guy who can help you," said the first one.

"Help us become popular?" asked the other.

"Yep," the first one said. "His name is Frost or something."

"What is he?" the other asked. "Is he a big promoter?"

"No, not anything like that," said the first one.

"So, what does he do?" asked the other.

"He helps jumpstart your band," said the first one.

"How does he do that?" asked the other.

"He actually helps your band time-jump," said the first one.

"Time-jump?" asked the other. "What's that?"

"It's like getting a free pass for touring," said the first one.

"What do you mean?" the other asked.

"You time-jump from gig to gig," said the first one.

"You mean no vans, no buses, no white line fever or road rage?" asked the other.

"That's the idea," said the first one.

"Wow!" exclaimed the other. "Sign me up!"

"There's just one thing," said the first one.

"What's that?" asked the other.

"The cost," said the first one.

"How much?" asked the other.

"It's not money," explained the first one.

"Then what is it?" asked the other.

"Time," said the first one.

"Time?" said the other, obviously puzzled.

"Yeah, the time you save in travel is charged back to you," the first one said. "And then doubled."

"Wait! What?" the other asked.

"You get to go from gig to gig, but it takes its toll by double billing the time against your life expectancy," the first one said.

"Double billing?" the other asked.

"Yeah, you get there faster but only live half as long," the first one said.

"Whoa!" exclaimed the other. "That's a hefty toll."

"Why do you think so many great ones die young?" asked the first one.

"This is crazy," said the other.

"Depends on how much you want to play music all the time and become famous," said the first one.

"When you put it that way, it sounds pretty good," said the other.

"So, that just leaves one question," said the first one.

"What's that?" said the other.

The first one looked over at him. "Would you bet your life on it?"

OFF THE GRID

"What?" she said, startled.

"I've stopped taking all drugs," he said.

"Why in the world?" she asked, concerned.

"Because every time you turn around, you see not only foods that were supposedly good for you are now bad, but also drugs," he said.

"I'm not following you," she said.

"The latest now from England is that statins are bad for you and actually encourage heart attacks," he said. "And antidepressants cause depression."

"So, you're not going to take your blood pressure medicine?" she asked.

"And especially the cholesterol drugs," he said.

"But then you'll be at greater risk of a heart attack or stroke," she said.

"I'm aware of that," he said.

"Then why in the world are you stopping?" she said.

"After watching my parents live far beyond their normal life expectancy and suffer as a result of it, I think it's time we look beyond the heroic measures to keep ourselves alive artificially and start looking at all the things we put in our bodies to 'help' us live longer," he said.

"But that means you could die sooner," she said sadly.

"No, it means I would live and die a natural death," he said.

"I really don't understand," she said.

"All of the heart surgeries, the stents, the organ transplants are just carrying us closer to bionic reality," he said.

"Is that bad?" she asked.

"I for one am beginning to see that the naturalist movement is one with merit," he said.

"What's that?" she asked.

"Start accepting nature and our natural lifespans as what is right for the planet," he said.

"Why?" she asked.

"Resources like food and water are finite," he said. "The planet is able to support a finite number of people."

"And?" she asked again.

"And I see the value of accepting that as my due," he said.

"Do you think we are closer to living well beyond 100?" she asked.

"We are within a few years of organs made with 3D printers," he added.

"I still don't understand," she said.

"We have made amazing advances in medical procedures and medicines to extend our lives, and we have done nothing to advance our understanding," he said.

"You mean knowledge is moving faster than wisdom?" she said, finally catching his drift.

"Precisely," he said. "We have managed to extend our lives at the cost of our souls."

DREAM INTERRUPTED

None of us could figure it out, but we guessed he just liked the look of them.

One Tuesday morning, Charlie asked, "Would you like to come in?"

"Sure," I said. I'd always been curious and thought this was my best chance to see what was going on inside Charlie's house.

Charlie had eclectic taste in art. Every piece was an original. In fact, he said he knew every artist in his house.

As you might expect from Charlie, he also said each piece had a story to go with it. You would have guessed as much as soon as you got inside. It was as if every piece were imbued with a bigger presence than its physical form.

"Like this print here," Charlie said, holding up an eleven-by- fourteen black-and-white block print. "The Richmond artist captured her brother in his Gold Duster in suggestive line work. See how his head is misshapen? She made it as a Christmas present for him."

He stopped to wipe his eyes.

"Is something wrong?" I asked him.

"I had him as a student when I substituted at my old high school," he said, a catch in his voice. "He was driving his Duster home from a Christmas party that year and ran into a tree not a block from his parents' house. His sister gave it to me six months later because she said she didn't know anyone else who would appreciate it as much as I would."

"That's terrible," I said, feeling for him.

"The truth was that the family couldn't bear to look at it after he died," he said quietly.

"I can imagine," I replied.

"At the same time, I think of him every time I see it," he said, looking up at me. "It helps to keep him alive. Like us talking about him."

"Yeah," I agreed, "immortalized."

"Exactly," he said.

"Do all of your paintings, prints and photographs have stories like this?" I asked him.

"Oh," he said, brightening as he looked around the room. "They're not all as morbid, but they all have a story."

MAKING THE GRADE

Surprised, she looked over at him. "What do you mean?"

"We were so fortunate to come along when we did," he said.

"I feel that way, but why do you say it?" she asked him.

"We went to college at a time when the professors encouraged free thinking," he said.

"Free thinking?" she asked.

"When we were presented with every idea without an agenda," he said. "Or if there was one, we were encouraged to examine each idea on its own merits, not on the words of its proponents."

"Isn't that part of the educational experience?" she asked him.

"It used to be," he replied. "But I think we have failed to perpetuate it in colleges today."

"Why do you say that?" she said.

"Because we have created a world, a culture, in which getting ahead is the only reward," he said.

"How does that affect free thinking?" she asked.

"It means we insist students can only succeed if they take the right courses, have the right extracurricular activities, have GPAs that are better than the rest," he replied.

"Well, there have always been grade grubbers," she argued.

"That may be true," he said, "but not to the extent we see today."

"How can you tell?" she asked.

"Take my alma mater, William and Mary," he said.

"What of it?" she said.

"Last year, they had four suicides," he said. "In a student body of less than 5,000."

"Oh, my God!" she said, clearly shaken.

"While we have always had students driving themselves crazy trying to get top grades, we haven't looked for ways to help them ameliorate their behavior," he said.

"What can we do?" she asked.

"When my daughter went to Boston University, she found a campus much like William and Mary," he said. "Every student was a valedictorian, a senior class president, a student government president."

"The crème de la crème," she said.

"Exactly," he replied. "However, the university also realized a campus of 30,000 would be intensely intimidating. So they instituted a program to help incoming freshmen find smaller groups of ten or twenty they could become a part of to help them assimilate into college life."

"Is that what students at William and Mary need?" she asked him.

"Actually, I remember the students I went to school with," he said. "Some had IQs that were positively stratospheric. And many of those students were the ones who were socially maladroit, almost totally inept in social situations. They were the ones who immersed themselves in books and stayed locked in their own heads."

"Are you saying all people with high IQs are socially impaired?" she asked.

"By no means," he said. "I had a good friend from high school with an IQ of 188 who went to MIT. He literally became a rocket scientist. Yet he was also one of the most humane, thoughtful individuals I have ever met."

"But you think students' intellectual distance is a contributing factor to the suicide rate?" she asked.

"Of course," he said. "They may be able to process ideas, but they haven't found ways to relate those ideas to the world around them. And they become inordinately isolated, ill prepared as they are to express themselves to others and share their fears. Left only to their own devices, they reach a breaking point with no recourse other than to opt out."

"How can we help them?" she asked.

"Take a lesson from Boston University," he said.

"You think that could help at a smaller school?" she asked.

"With one primary difference," he said. "Set up a mentoring program with an upperclassman mentoring two or three freshmen. Instead of approaching the issue of being a huge campus with an intimidating student body, look at it as a way of encouraging human interaction for highly intelligent people, helping them find ways to plug into humanity. Show them ways they can relate what's inside their heads to the world around them."

"So, help them to integrate their intellect into some social situations that enable them to connect and communicate in ways that are meaningful to themselves and to others?" she asked.

"Now you have the idea," he said. "I told my daughter as soon as I stopped trying to make a good grade, my grades went up. Now if we can help them get over political correctness and go back to questioning everything, including grades, they might be healthier."

"You know," she said, "I think it might work."

"It certainly couldn't hurt to try," he said. "Just think of how much these great minds have to offer us. Think of the contributions they can make in every field. Let's not waste another year on failing our kids."

BITBLOOD

"I know," the prisoner mumbled.

"But hacking is something else," the magistrate continued.

The prisoner looked down at his feet.

"And the theft of identity is not only an invasion of privacy, but it's also a capital offense," the magistrate said.

"I know that now," the prisoner said.

"But you went beyond even that," the magistrate continued again.

The prisoner could only look down.

"You hacked into people's lives and then tracked down their accounts," the magistrate said.

"I didn't think it would hurt anyone," the prisoner said.

"You didn't think raiding people's personal accounts would hurt anyone?" the magistrate asked incredulously.

"I was only taking bitcoins," the prisoner said.

"Yes," the magistrate replied, "to the order of $3,243,671!"

"But it was bitcoins," the prisoner protested.

"What's your point?" the magistrate insisted.

"It's not like it's real money," the prisoner protested again.

"In today's digital environment, bitcoins have become legal tender," the magistrate said. "As such, what you did is the same as robbing a bank."

"But I didn't hurt anyone," the prisoner said.

"Do you realize you stole from retirees and left them destitute?" the magistrate asked.

"Their retirement was in bitcoins?" the prisoner asked.

"Obviously, some have set up their accounts like that," the magistrate replied.

"That sounds kind of risky," the prisoner said.

"That's not for you to decide," the magistrate said. "You left them destitute."

The prisoner again could only look at his feet.

"You have been found guilty of grand larceny, identity theft, illegal account manipulation and fraud," the magistrate said.

"Yes, sir," the prisoner mumbled.

"These are highly serious offenses that require swift and significant punishment," the magistrate said.

"What do you mean?" the prisoner asked, clearly frightened.

"We need to send a message to all those people who might consider following in your footsteps," the magistrate said.

"I don't understand," the prisoner said shakily.

"We need to make an example of you," the magistrate said.

"What are you going to do to me?" the prisoner cried.

"I think we have found precedence for this in law books from centuries past," the magistrate said. "It's the only way to send a clear message to hackers in the twenty-first century."

"What does that mean?" the prisoner cried again.

"You will be flogged at sunrise tomorrow, forty lashes," the magistrate replied.

"What? You can't do that!" the prisoner sobbed.

"Oh, we certainly can," the magistrate replied. "Furthermore, we will then have you drawn and quartered."

"That's barbaric!" the prisoner protested.

"On the contrary," the magistrate replied. "This is all in virtual reality. You will feel it in here and experience it as if you had lived it. However, your physical body will be left in a vegetative state, but you will be alive."

"Oh, my God!" the prisoner cried.

"Don't cry, sir. You'll only be shedding bitblood," the magistrate said, looking at him. "After all, it's not like it's real."

IDENTITY THEFT

"WHAT'S YOUR NAME AGAIN?" THE MAN ASKED.

"Jonathan," he replied. "But my friends call me John."

"Well, John, have you heard about the Orthodox Jews?" the man asked.

"No," John answered. "I really don't know much of anything about Orthodox Jews."

"They were the original believers," the man said.

"From the time of Moses?" John asked.

"And before," the man replied.

"What about them?" John asked.

"In those days, God had twenty-six names," the man explained.

"Twenty-six?" John asked, puzzled.

"Twenty-six," the man replied.

"Why so many?" John asked.

"God was and is wholly unknown to man," the man said. "No single name could encompass God."

"So, what did that mean to them?" John asked.

"Orthodox Jews also believed that saying God's name was blasphemy," the man said.

"I don't understand." John replied.

"To have His holy name pass mortal lips was to defile Him," the man said. "It brought Him down to man's level, which was unacceptable."

"That sounds extreme," John said.

"It went even further," the man said.

"What could be further?" John asked.

"You could not even write God's name," the man said. "If you did, you had to substitute symbols for letters so that God became G*d."

"What is your point?" John asked.

"How well do you know your Bible?" the man asked.

"Marginally well," John said. "Why?"

"After God created man, what did He have man do?" the man asked.

"I don't remember," John said.

"He instructed man to name all of the animals so that he would have dominion over them," the man said.

"I still don't see—" John started.

"Rumpelstiltskin," the man said, interrupting.

"What?" John said, clearly confused.

"What was the point of the fairy tale?" the man asked.

"If the girl who spun gold from the chaff could discover his name, she could go free," John said, proud of himself for remembering.

"And why would that be?" the man asked.

"I, I don't really know," John replied uncertainly.

"Because to know your name is to hold power over you," the man said.

"What do you mean?" John asked nervously.

"Well, Jonathan, I now know your name," the man said. "And now I can get you to do my bidding whenever I want."

"You can't do that!" John protested.

"Oh, but I can and I will," the man said, smiling.

"I don't understand," John cried. "Why are you doing this to me? I don't even know your name."

"Exactly," the man said. "And you never will."

"Why?" John wailed.

"Because you can't afford it," the man said.

SCREEN SAVER

"ISN'T IT AMUSING?" HE SAID.

"Isn't what amusing?" she asked him.

"Educators do such a good job of warning us of the dangers of screen time for those under the age of six," he replied.

"As they should," she said. "Tests have shown that children are highly impressionable at that age and can experience developmental problems if they spend too much time in front of a screen."

"I know," he said. "I was raised in a time they were saying that about television."

"What's your point?" she asked.

"They then transitioned to computers and said children shouldn't spend more than two hours a day of total screen time, meaning television and computer together," he said.

"That makes sense to me," she said.

"Now we have iPads and smartphones we can add into the screen time equation," he said.

"Again, that's pretty logical," she said.

"So, we are quick to say young children shouldn't spend more than two hours a day on screens of any stripe," he said.

"That pretty well sums it up," she said.

"There's just one problem," he said.

"What's that?" she asked.

"If it has such a detrimental effect on young children's minds, what is it doing to adult minds?" he asked her.

"What do you mean?" she said.

"By their very nature, screens are addictive," he said. "If you have the slightest case of ADD or ADHD, you become immediately consumed with whatever screen you see."

"You mean it draws your attention?" she asked.

"No," he said. "I mean it *consumes* your attention to the exclusion of all else."

"Are you one of those people who says it is an addiction?" she asked him.

"I am not alone," he replied. "Arianna Huffington's Thrive conference made the point that we need to unplug ourselves daily in order to achieve a better balance."

"How does unplugging help?" she said.

"It helps us see how unhealthy it is for us to incessantly check our computers, our iPads, our smartphones, for emails, for social media, for inanities we don't need to lead our daily lives," he said.

"Sounds hard," she said.

"It is," he admitted. "But I also see companies paying lip service to 'work/life balance' while they require you to answer any email you receive within fifteen minutes *at any hour of the day or night.*"

"Where does that leave us?" she asked.

"Currently, we have a workforce that feels they need to be available to their bosses 24/7 in order to keep their jobs," he said. "And that's increasing the stress, taking a toll on our health and increasing our medical costs because we can do anything *but* balance work and life."

"So, what's your point?" she asked, clearly frustrated.

"My point is that limiting screen time shouldn't just be for young children," he said. "It should be for *all* of us."

A THEIST

he said.

"What's that?" she replied.

"I've felt that militant atheists were somehow missing the point, but I couldn't quite put my finger on what it was," he said.

"So, you've arrived at a conclusion?" she asked him.

"I think so," he said.

"Well, what is it?" she said.

"Atheists say there is no God," he said.

"Okay," she said.

"They say they don't need a deity to help them make moral choices," he said.

"I assume this is going somewhere," she said, prompting him.

"I don't have a problem with either of these notions," he said. "Because I see them as a response to organized religions."

"So, what's your problem?" she asked.

"The more militant atheists insist that there is nothing to this world other than what our senses tell us," he said.

"Otherwise known as empiricists," she said.

"Exactly," he said. "But in my mind that begs a fundamental question."

"What's that?" she asked him.

"It categorically denies that there is a spiritual side to our psyches," he said.

"You're saying there is?" she asked.

"I know there is," he said.

"How?" she said.

"ESP, precognition, the collective unconscious—these are all many of the ways we experience this world, including those things we cannot explain," he said. "If there is nothing other than what our senses tell us, then what have I been experiencing all of my life?"

"You've had personal experience with things like this?" she asked, surprised.

"Of course," he replied. "Why do you think this question has bothered me for so long?"

SINGLE MINDED

"I FIND IT AMUSING WHEN PEOPLE ACT SO SURPRISED that single men die so much sooner than married men," he said.

"Why does that amuse you?" she asked him.

"They automatically make rash assumptions and say men can't take care of themselves," he replied.

"Well, they can't," she said.

"On the contrary," he said. "I did a better job of running the household and making dinners than my daughter's mother ever could when we were married."

"I don't believe it," she said.

"She admitted as much," he said.

"You're just saying that," she said.

"No," he said, "you've bought into the myth of the incompetent male that the media has perpetuated over the last four decades."

"What do you mean?" she asked.

"In the '50s, we had 'father knows best,'" he said. "Then we went through women's lib, and we found ourselves as the butt of all the sitcom jokes. And what began in the '70s continues to this day."

"You're saying that's bad?" she asked.

"No, simply unbalanced," he replied. "The truth is that most of the fathers I know are extremely competent and engaged and involved in their children's lives."

"So, why do single men die so much sooner?" she asked.

"I think it has to do with the notion of the shared load," he said. "People have talked about hug therapy and said fifteen hugs a day almost guarantee you a happier outlook."

"I can see that," she said.

"And I do have a tendency to make more of an effort for someone else than I do for myself," he said.

"I do that," she admitted.

"For that matter," he said, "I can't imagine living another thirty years by myself. If I were in a committed relationship, I would undoubtedly be more inclined to make the extra effort to stick around."

"I can see that," she said.

"On my own, I am all too aware of my finitude," he said. "And I can see that my time here will reach a stopping point." He paused as he looked out at his dogwood tree in the front yard. "And I'm okay with that."

DRESS UP

"OUR ANNIVERSARY IS COMING UP," HE SAID.

"You remembered?" she asked, surprised.

"Of course," he replied, "it was an important day in my life."

"I'm glad to hear it," she said.

"Let's do something special for the occasion," he said.

"I know," she said. "Let's go out to eat!"

"Good idea," he said. "Any requests?"

"Somewhere expensive," she said. "And French."

"Why French?" he asked.

"I have this new Marie Antoinette internal app I've been dying to try out," she said.

"What do you mean?" he asked.

"This new AI implant apps let you channel the look and feel of another era," she said.

"You don't want to go as yourself?" he asked, surprised.

"Oh, I can be me anytime," she said. "And I've been dying to try it out ever since I got it."

"But I don't want to go with Marie Antoinette," he said. "I want to go with you."

"Oh, silly," she said, laughing. "You have me all the rest of the year."

"It just seems strange to celebrate our anniversary in costume," he said.

"Oh, come on," she said. "It will be fun!"

"I'm not sure . . ." he said uncertainly.

"You can get your own AI implant," she said. "You could go as Louis XVI!"

"I don't think that's such a good idea," he said.

"Don't be such a fuddy-duddy," she said. "Then we could eat cake!"

"I just want to spend the evening with the woman I walked down the aisle with," he said.

FAMILY MEAL

is a virus,'" he said.

She looked up from her reading. "I think she got it from William Burroughs," she said.

"That's right," he said, surprised.

"What were you thinking about?" she asked him.

"Well, dinosaurs were on the earth a long time," he said.

"A long, long time ago," she agreed.

"And they lasted for a long, long time," he added.

"That's my understanding," she said.

"They were the dominant species for 135 million years," he said.

"That *is* a long time," she said, nodding.

"Man, on the other hand, has not," he said.

"Not by a long shot," she said.

"If we just look at the current *homo sapiens* who represent modern humans, the earliest emerged about 200 thousand years ago," he said.

"A mere pittance," she agreed. "Although they just found the *homo naledi* that dates back about two million years."

"Still a relative newcomer," he said.

Again, she nodded. She looked over at him. "I assume this is going somewhere."

He laughed. "Perhaps it's not language but man that is the virus," he said.

"What do you mean?" she asked him.

"What if we are the invasive species who is attacking this planet and metastasizing everywhere?" he asked.

"You mean we're parasites living off the host?" she asked.

"Exactly," he said, getting excited.

"And we're running the risk of killing off our host by sucking the life out of it?" she asked.

"Seems to be a fair conclusion," he said. "We're depleting resources at every turn."

"Yes, but we are a part of this biosphere," she said.

"What do you mean?" he asked, now looking back at her.

"Both energy and mass are a constant," she said. "What we are made of has always been here."

"That's true," he said.

"Scientists say there are molecules in us that were present at the Big Bang," she said.

"That would make us eternal," he said.

"Precisely," she said. "With eternal molecules in my body, I know parts of me will always live on."

"That's a lovely thought," he said.

"So, dying is really us just uploading a virus," she said. "It would be the same as going to heaven."

"Good thought," he said.

"If we accept that, doesn't it turn the whole *Soylent Green* plot on its head?" she said.

"What do you mean?" he asked, puzzled.

"Of course, I will die and live on," she said. "Parts of me will become a food source, for you and my other descendants. And I am good with this. Worm food. People food. It's all good."

ODINSONG

"Look," he said, panting. "I'm moving as fast as I can."

"But it's not fast enough!"

"Too bad," he said.

"Do you know who I am?"

"I know who you say you are," he answered.

"What's that supposed to mean?"

"It means if you want to go faster," he wheezed, "you can get down off of my shoulders and start carrying me for a change."

"I can't do that!"

"Why not?" he asked.

"I deserve more respect than that."

"Oh, because you're Odin the Wise," he said sarcastically.

"It would be beneath me to stoop to such a human level and carry you."

"Boy, do you need a reality check," he said. "*I'm* beneath you."

"I was there at the beginning and will be there at the end!"

"Yeah, yeah," he managed. "I've heard all that before."

"And yet you do not show me obeisance and go any faster."

"Frankly," he said between breaths, "I just think you're a crazy old man who is exhibiting clear signs of dementia."

"What's *that* supposed to mean?"

"It means I've been carrying you for too many years," he said. "It means you wouldn't get anywhere if I didn't carry you. It means you rely on me all the time."

"You mean you don't worship me?"

"Hardly," he said. "More like I put up with you."

"But I am Odin! I am the ruler of the Norse gods. I am the life bringer. Without me you humans would have no direction."

"It's more like, without me," he said, "you'd be falling on your ass."

"That's no way to speak to your god father!"

"Ha!" he said. "If you were truly my god father, you'd know my name. What is my name?"

"Why, I have no idea."

"See?" he said. "You think you're in charge, but you're really just along for the ride."

"That can't be so."

"Oh, but it is," he said.

"I will smite thee!"

"I'd be careful if I were you," he said. "The last time you tried that, you ended up in the ER."

THE DJINN

THE DJINN WAVED HIS HAND AND SMILED.

The sky above turned a swirling emerald green.

"Do you like it?" the djinn asked.

The man looked up uncertainly.

"Do you wish to change its color?" the djinn asked.

"Oh, no," the man replied. "You can't fool me into giving away my wish."

The djinn waved his hand again, returning the sky to its normal blue.

"Then what do you wish?" the djinn asked.

"I am thinking," the man replied.

"Do you wish riches?" the djinn asked him.

"No," the man replied. "Money has never been my goal. If I could do work I liked and be creative in doing it, that is all I ever wanted."

He stopped for a moment.

"Besides," he said, "to receive money I didn't earn makes me uncomfortable."

The djinn frowned. "Do you wish fame?"

"No," the man replied. "Modern culture has already given us too many people who are famous because they are famous."

"How do you mean?" the djinn asked, puzzled.

"In the old days," the man said, "a person achieved fame for accomplishing something. Scientists, business people, artists all built their reputations on what they did."

"But you could have it without any effort," the djinn protested.

"Sounds pretty empty and meaningless to me," the man replied. "If I ever get there, I want to get there on my own merits."

The djinn paused to scratch his head. Finally, he had an idea.

"Do you wish love?" the djinn asked hopefully.

The man just looked at him.

"What?" the djinn responded. "What did I say?"

"You know as well as I do," the man said. "The only way that will work is if I find that love with my own magic."

"I do not understand," the djinn said.

"True love is about intimacy," the man replied. "It is not something that magically appears. If it seems to, it probably won't last. And if it is nothing more than blind adoration, it will quickly lose its value."

The djinn was speechless.

"I want more out of life than that," the man said.

"I have offered you wealth, fame and love," the djinn said. "Most people would have jumped at any or all of these. Yet you refuse all three."

The djinn looked around.

"What can I possibly offer you that you would want?" the djinn asked.

The man paused to think.

Finally, he smiled.

"I wish for you to be free," he answered.

"What?" the djinn asked, clearly astonished. "You wish to set me free?"

"Yes," the man said definitely.

"Why when you could have anything you want do you wish to set me free?" the djinn asked him.

The man smiled.

"Because I want more magic in this world."

THE SIN EATER

"I FIND IT INTERESTING THAT SO MANY OF THE WORLD'S CUL-tures had a flood story," he said.

"Really?" she said, surprised. "Not just Noah?"

"Yep," he said. "Mesopotamian. Hindu. Mayan. Native American. South American."

"What does that tell you?" she asked.

"Either that there is some truth to it," he said, "or it is a psychological meme of things beyond our control that appear in our dreams."

"So, nothing definitive," she said.

"Of course, it's not the only recurring mythos," he said.

"What else?" she asked him.

"There's the Christ mythos," he said.

"You mean there's more than one Christ?" she said.

"Jesus, Attis, Adonis, Osiris," he replied. "It became a common theme of sacrifice that was originally framed in a pagan environment."

"You're bursting my bubbles right and left," she said.

"No pun intended," he said wryly.

"No pun intended," she stated.

"But as we explore the Christ mythos," he said, "we find another longstanding part of it that we always assumed was Christian to its core."

"Which one is that?" she asked.

"That Christ died for our sins," he said.

"He didn't?" she asked, surprised.

"No, I'm not saying that," he said. "I'm just saying others practiced the absolution of sin as well."

"I didn't realize that," she said.

"The first step after that obviously came about because of the Catholic Church's designation of the priest as the emissary of Christ. By going to confessional and admitting your sins, you received absolution from God in Christ through the priest, and your sins were forgiven."

"Okay," she replied.

"But then there was the medieval practice of the sin eater," he said.

"The what?" she asked.

"The sin eater," he replied.

"What is a sin eater?" she asked.

"The traditions of the sin eater have their roots in the Middle Ages," he said. "It's only recently that the custom died out."

"What does a sin eater do?" she asked.

"When a person died, the family would call the village's sin eater over to the house," he said. "Then the sin eater would eat a feast the family had prepared. In essence, the sin eater then took on the sins of the deceased so that person could rest in peace."

"Sounds morbid," she said.

"Oh, it gets worse," he said. "In some villages the bread was literally passed across the body to the sin eater. And in some Germanic cultures they would bake a cake in the shape of the deceased's body for the sin eater to consume."

"That's gross," she said, shuddering.

"It's like taking the Eucharist and absolution and merging them into one ritual," he said.

"Interesting," she said.

She stopped and looked over at him.

"I take it you were going somewhere with this," she finally said.

"Well, first we had Christ dying for our sins," he said. "Then we had priests as Christ's emissaries absolving us of our sins. Then we had the heathen sin eaters who ate our sins so we could rest in peace."

"And?" she prodded him.

"And now in this era of post-Christian, freedom from religion, rational atheism, where do we go for our sin eaters?" he asked. "We haven't had a real one since 1906."

"What do *you* think?" she asked pointedly.

"Well, Vonnegut said artists were the canaries in the mine," he said. "They would see the world for what it is and warn us when it got too toxic."

"And you're starting to see it differently?" she said.

"Yeah, I think artists are the world's sin eaters," he said. "They consume who we are and reflect it in their art. And as a result, they absorb the sins of the world."

"That's a heavy load," she said.

"Requiescat in pace," he replied, smiling at her.

PARLOR TRICKS

"VOILA!" HE SAID, PRESENTING A BOUQUET OF RED CAR-
nations with a flourish.

"That's amazing!" she said, clearly impressed.

"It was nothing," he said modestly.

"But I didn't see where they came from," she exclaimed.

"The same place as this," he said, waving his arm to reveal Cornish hens over wild rice with grilled asparagus.

"Ooh, my favorite!" she squealed.

"Then we must celebrate," he said, gesturing for a floating bottle of Mumm's to fill two champagne flutes.

She clapped her hands and giggled. He bowed.

"I've never seen someone with so much command at their fingertips," she said.

"Oh, I am but an amateur," he said.

"But these things," she said. "I don't see how you can do it."

"Well, as they always say," he said, "those things that occur that we cannot yet explain are considered to be magic."

"What else can you do?" she asked him.

He conjured up a glass of small batch bourbon and gave it a sip.

"Damn," he said. "I was hoping for Blanton's."

"What is it?" she asked.

"Knob Creek," he replied.

"You mean you don't always get it right?" she asked, surprised.

"Actually," he said, "it rarely happens."

"What do you mean?" she asked.

"That bouquet?" he said, nodding toward the flowers.

"What about it?" she said. "They're lovely."

"They were supposed to be orchids," he said.

"Oh," she said.

"The Cornish hens?" he said.

"Yes?" she said.

"I was thinking quail," he said.

"So, the champagne?" she asked.

He nodded. "Dom Perignon."

"But I thought you knew magic," she insisted.

"Oh, I do," he admitted.

"So, you can conjure up all of these things, but you rarely get them right," she said.

"That's it in a nutshell," he said.

"My God, I feel like I've been tricked," she said, mortified.

"Isn't that the goal?" he said.

"But you're a fraud," she insisted.

"That's a little harsh," he replied. "Magic is just like life: imperfect even in its beauty."

"So, you're okay with doing parlor tricks and getting them wrong," she said.

"Of course," he said. He gestured at the table and made everything disappear.

"After all," he said with a shy smile, "I'm only human."

CIVICS LESSON

Startled, she looked up from her book. "What do you mean?"

"I just saw another pundit make a patently false statement on TV that went unchallenged," he said.

"Happens all too often," she agreed.

"The media have abdicated their role in the name of profits," he said.

"Money makes the world go round," she said.

"I think the root of all evil is a lot closer to the truth," he said.

"No argument," she admitted.

"I grew up on Walter Cronkite and Huntley and Brinkley," he said.

"Meaning?" she asked him.

"They came from the same school of journalistic thought as Edward R. Murrow," he said. "They worked hard to be as objective as possible, to present facts as they knew them, to keep their feelings separate from their reporting."

"I vaguely remember that," she said.

"Now we have the exact opposite," he said. "They all present their feelings about the news and do everything they can to keep facts separate from their opinions."

"That's all I see," she agreed.

"What is the world coming to when the facts themselves are labeled as false because they are politically motivated?" he asked, exasperated. "And asking about actual issues is a gotcha question, not an honest one."

"Do what I do," she said.

"What's that?" he said.

"Don't watch the news," she said.

"Generally, I try to stay away from it," he agreed.

"So, what's the problem?" she asked him.

"Well, now I have friends who think it is perfectly okay to say whatever is on their minds to my face," he said.

"What's wrong with that?" she said.

"Because they will say deeply offensive and racist statements because 'it is their right,'" he said.

"Ah, playing the freedom-of-speech card," she said, nodding.

"Exactly," he said.

"Walk away," she said.

"What?" he asked, puzzled.

"Just walk away," she said.

"What do you mean?" he asked.

"They've already shown you they are offensive," she said. "And you know what it's like to try and converse with someone who is obviously close-minded."

"Yeah, it goes nowhere," he agreed.

"Well, we have to take a stand for civil discourse," she said. "So, instead of getting into a pointless argument with someone who refuses to listen to reason, remove yourself from the fray."

"And walk away," he said, nodding.

"Cut the toxic people from your life," she said. "And let's bring back civility."

DEATH PENALTY

"DO YOU KNOW WHY YOU ARE HERE?" THE JUDGE ASKED.

"No," the defendant said. "I'm not at all sure."

"You have been found guilty of sedition," the judge said.

"Wait," the defendant cried. "I'm guilty of what?"

"Sedition," the judge repeated.

"But I haven't done anything," the defendant protested. "I haven't even had a trial!"

"But you have exhibited behavior that is detrimental to the state," the judge intoned. "And your thinking is clearly not in line with our administration."

"Thinking?" the defendant asked incredulously. "Since when is thinking a crime?"

"Since the passage of the Anti-terrorism Behavioral Act of 2016," the judge replied.

"I've never even heard of it!" the defendant protested.

"Ignorance of the law is no excuse," the judge replied as if by rote.

"What am I supposed to have done?" the defendant asked, mystified.

"You have demonstrated time and again that you are a freethinker," the judge said. "You do not accept what you see and hear as true."

"And you do?" the defendant asked.

"Of course," the judge replied. "As does every right-thinking citizen of these United States."

"But politicians are saying the stupidest things!" the defendant protested. "Some of it is pure idiocy!"

"Be that as it may," the judge replied, "they are your leaders, and you must abide by their laws."

"What about the Constitution?" the defendant cried.

"It does not abridge your right to bear arms or worship at the church of your choice," the judge said.

"That's not what I am talking about," the defendant argued.

"It does not discriminate based on age, gender, race or religion," the judge further intoned.

"But you can discriminate based on thoughts?" the defendant said.

"Of course," the judge replied. "How else can we identify terrorists from the rest of us?"

"So, you arrest and convict me for my thoughts alone?" the defendant asked.

"That is the law," the judge said.

"Well, I clearly must be guilty because I think this is a travesty of justice," the defendant said.

"Duly noted," the judge replied. "Are you ready for sentencing?" "What will it be, the death penalty?" the defendant said sarcastically.

"Nothing so barbaric," the judge replied. "We are a civilized people." "You could have fooled me," the defendant muttered.

"Don't make it any worse than it is," the judge said.

"You might as well sentence me," the defendant said, resigned.

"I hereby sentence you to a frontal lobotomy, to be carried out tomorrow at high noon," the judge said, banging his gavel.

"A lobotomy?" the defendant cried.

"Oh, it's nothing like it was fifty years ago," the judge said. "It's much more refined, far more precise than it used to be."

"What does that even mean?" the defendant asked, clearly confused.

"It does not leave you a gibbering zombie," the judge replied.

"But what does it do?" the defendant asked fearfully.

"It eliminates your dreams," the judge replied.

"My dreams?" the defendant said weakly.

"We have found that people who dream harbor thoughts—more creative thoughts, more *dangerous* thoughts," the judge said. "By excising those receptors in your brain, we can prevent you from dreaming."

"I won't dream?" the defendant said.

"You'll never dream again," the judge said. "You will simply sleep a dreamless sleep and wake up, ready to accept anything and everything you see and hear as the truth."

"God help me," the defendant said. "It *is* a death sentence."

"That's a little harsh," the judge said. "You just won't be *you*."

The judge looked down his nose at the defendant.

"But you *will* be one of *us*."

THE IDEA MERCHANT

THE TINY BELL ABOVE THE SHOP'S FRONT DOOR TINKLED.

A young man in a crisp white shirt and pressed khaki pants walked through the door. He looked around uncertainly.

The old man behind the counter looked up from his reading.

"May I help you?" he asked.

"I'm not sure," the young man said.

"Well, what are you looking for?" the old man asked him.

"I don't know," the young man replied. "But I think I'll know it when I see it."

"Mmmm," the old man intoned. "That's not very helpful."

"All I know is that my boss kicked me out," the young man said. "He told me not to come back until I had a good idea."

"Ah," the old man said, nodding. "Now we're getting somewhere."

"I've been wandering around for the last three hours," the young man said. "And I haven't come up with anything!"

"Well, at least you've come to the right place," the old man said.

"What do you mean?"

"I have plenty of ideas," the old man said. "Good ones. Bad ones. And a few truly original ones." He paused, looking at the young man. "But those are quite expensive."

The young man looked around, noting the glass jars lining the shelves around the shop. "Where are they?" he asked. "I don't see them."

"Oh, they're all around you," the old man said. "You just have to open your eyes."

"I don't understand," the young man said. "All I see are empty glass jars."

"Oh, these aren't empty," the old man reassured him. "They all contain an idea. Some are just clearer than others."

"But if they're clear, how do you see them?" the young man asked.

"You don't really see them until you put them in action," the old man said.

"How do you know they're real?" the young man asked.

"All you have to do is open the jar," the old man said.

"Why do you have them in glass jars?" the young man asked.

"They need light in order to survive," the old man said.

"What if they don't get the light?" the young man said.

"Then they turn into dreams and just disappear," the old man said as if to a child.

"How do I know I'll get the idea I need?" the young man asked.

The old man looked at him.

"Son, there are no guarantees," he said.

"I'm afraid of failing," the young man complained.

The old man shook his head. "I can't tell you the idea you pick is the one that will please your boss," he said.

"I don't know what to do," the young man whined.

"Stop that!" the old man said. "You came here for a reason. So man up and choose!"

The young man looked around nervously, scanning all of the jars in the shop. Finally, he saw one on the back wall on the top shelf just left of center.

"That one," he said.

"Good choice," the old man said.

"But you said the idea I pick may not be the one my boss wants," the young man said.

"That's still true," the old man said. "But what I *can* tell you is that it will be the right idea for you almost without fail."

"I don't understand," the young man said.

"What if you're not in the right job?" the old man asked.

"What do you mean?" the young man said, clearly confused.

"The idea in that jar will be right for you," the old man said. "It could be the one you need to invent something new or start your own business."

"You mean I could go and do my own thing?" the young man asked, starting to get excited.

"That's the idea," the old man said with a nod and twinkle in his eye.

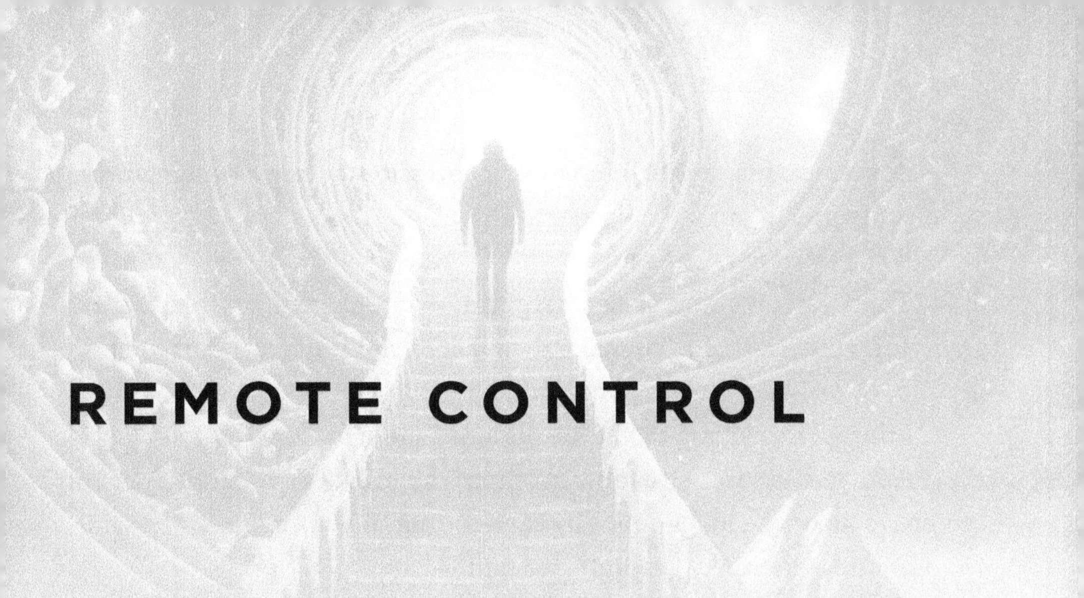

REMOTE CONTROL

"I'VE BEEN THINKING ABOUT CONTROL," HE SAID.

She looked up from her crossword puzzle. "Is that a good thing?" she asked him.

"Oh, self-control is wonderful," he said.

She looked at him again. "I hear the implied 'but,'" she said.

"Well, I think any person who has faced any sort of deep-seated neurosis is bound to benefit from keeping oneself in check," he said.

"Yes?" she prompted.

"It becomes more of a gray area when that same need to maintain control starts to overflow onto the rest of life," he said.

"I'm not sure what you mean," she said.

"Wouldn't you say life is messy?" he asked her.

"Without a doubt," she answered.

"And being in control of yourself in the face of messiness is understandable," he said, "a great way to deal with the uncertainty."

"Granted," she said.

"It's when you take that same energy and try to control things—or people—in your life," he said.

"You're going to have to be specific here," she said.

"Say you are in a relationship," he said.

"Okay," she said.

"You are managing to keep your depression at bay by maintaining strict control," he said.

"So far, so good," she said.

"Then you take that same energy and try to control the person you are living with," he said, "to make them act in the way you want them to in order to feel like you are in control."

"I think I'm starting to get the picture," she said.

"And you set up a situation in which the only way the other person can prove he or she loves you is by capitulating to your control," he said.

"Sounds like shaky ground," she said.

"When you confuse love with control, you're often left with neither," he said.

"I agree," she said, going back to her puzzle.

"But I think there is even one more thing," he said.

She looked up from her puzzle again. "What's that?"

"It's just like shopping as retail therapy," he said.

"I don't follow," she said, putting the pencil in her mouth.

"You know, 'if I can just get that one pair of shoes, I know I will be happy,'" he said. "And you bought the shoes and scratched that itch, but you didn't cure the feeling. So you wind up coveting something else as the answer, only to find that it's nothing more than a temporary fix."

"So, what does that have to do with control?" she asked him.

"When you feel the need to control someone and want them to do something, you may be satisfied when they act the way you want," he said. "But as soon as they do, you find it isn't enough. It doesn't *really* prove they love you. You have to find another way to control them so you can get your next fix."

"That sounds awful," she said.

"And it turns into a game of self-one-upsmanship," he said. "You're constantly raising the bar on the people around you to prove they love you."

"It's a no-win situation," she said.

"Too true," he said. "Because life isn't life if you have to control it."

"I agree," she said, going back to her puzzle. Suddenly, she looked over at him. "You're not talking about me, are you?"

"No, of course not, dear," he said, smiling reassuringly.

LAMIA'S LAMENT

"Shhh," the dark figure sitting on his chest hissed back at him.

"You are crushing my chest!" he groaned.

"You do not know my s-s-sorrow," she whispered.

"I'm getting weaker by the minute," he said softly.

"And you will be getting weaker s-s-still," she insisted.

"Why are you doing this?" he asked weakly.

"Becaus-s-se you have let me live too long," she replied.

"Me?" he said weakly. "I don't even know you!"

"Yes-s-s, you do," the figure responded.

"I don't know anyone who can suck the life out of me," he said.

"You s-s-say that, but I s-s-see that you are lying," she said.

"How can you see?" he said. "I can't see your face. I can't see your eyes!"

"You have done this-s-s to me," she said.

"What did *I* do?" he protested.

"You and your kind have artificially extended my life to an unnatural length," she said.

"How?" he said. "I don't understand."

"You and your medical advances-s-s," she said.

"Advances?" he said weakly.

"Yes-s-s," she replied. "I did not pluck out my eyes."

"You didn't?" he said.

"No," she said sharply. "I am blind because of glaucoma. And cataracts-s-s!"

"But you said you could see that I was lying," he protested.

"Even without my eyes, I can s-s-see the future," she said. "*Your* future!"

"*My* future?" he asked fearfully.

"Yes-s-s," she replied. "You are doomed to outlive even me. And I will not let that happen!"

"You are mad!" he said.

"You think me mad?" she said. "*I* am not mad. Modern man is-s-s mad!"

"God help me," he managed.

"Zeus-s-s be damned!" she said vehemently. "I will suck out your life force and leave you a hollow hus-s-sk!"

"Why?' he cried. "Why are you doing this to me?"

"Don't you know?" she hissed. "Can't you tell?"

"No," he said. "I am lost."

"Yes-s-s," she said. "You are."

"Why must you do this?" he cried again. "Who *are* you?" "I am the one who brought you into this world," she said.

"You what?" he said, confused. "Mom?"

"Yes-s-s," she said. "You are my s-s-son. And you have been s-s-seduced by knowledge without the benefits-s-s of wis-s-sdom."

"I can't breathe!" he rasped.

"That's-s-s right," she said. "I am taking your life force so that I may continue to s-s-see what you have in s-s-s-tore for the res-s-st of mankind."

"Everything is going dark . . ." he said weakly.

"Yes-s-s," she whispered. "Darkness-s-s. Deep, deep darkness-s-s." "Save me . . ." he whispered back.

"No," she said. "If I am to be robbed of my sight and forced to s-s- see the future, I must s-s-steal yours to make it s-s-so!"

FIRST CONTACT

"I do not know what that means," the voice replied.

The man looked out the window, watching the clouds scud by.

"I make uncommon connections," he said.

"Uncommon connections?" the voice asked.

"I think outside the box," he said.

"What is this box?" the voice asked.

"Convention," the man said. "You know, the norm."

"I do not understand this norm you speak of," the voice replied.

"I think I'm beginning to understand why I am here," the man said.

"Why is that?" the voice asked.

"You're not what conventional people might expect," the man said.

"Why do you say that?" the voice asked.

"Well, most people I know would expect you to say, 'Take me to your leader,'" the man replied.

"Should I?" the voice asked him.

"I don't think so," the man said. "For one thing, we don't have just one leader."

"And?" the voice prompted.

"We really don't have any leaders right now," the man said. "We have politicians. And they're certainly not the same thing."

"They're not?" the voice said.

"No, politicians are small-minded individuals with their own limited agendas," the man said. "They don't even speak for their own country, much less the entire human race."

"So, there is no one leading you?" the voice asked.

"That's one way of looking at it," the man said. "However, another way of looking at it is to accept our diversity and see us as a rich mosaic."

"That is a novel idea," the voice replied. "How did you come to be here?"

"I think this came about because people in think tanks finally decided to start including creative people in their meetings," the man said.

"Think tanks?" the voice asked.

"They're small groups of experts who gather to discuss the latest research and developments in a given field to see what new direction they could go in," the man said.

"And how would these creative people help?" the voice asked.

"Most experts tend to mull over what they already know," the man said. "Creative people are the ones to stop and look at the process and suddenly connect it with something no one else has thought of."

"And this is helpful?" the voice asked.

"Well, let's take the example of artificial intelligence," the man said.

"All right," the voice replied.

"If we accept that second word, *intelligence*, I automatically think about what that intelligence is thinking," the man said.

"I think I'm beginning to see," the voice said.

"So, if I am called into a meeting of SETI specialists, I begin to see why I am there," the man said.

"SETI?" the voice responded.

"The search for extraterrestrial intelligence," the man replied.

"So, for example, you have been brought in to posit what that extraterrestrial intelligence might be thinking?" the voice asked innocently.

"That would be my guess," the man said.

"And now that you're here, what would be your best guess?" the voice asked.

"I'd be wondering if I have wasted my time," the man said. "At least, until a man came in to have an intelligent conversation with me."

"And then?" the voice asked him.

"Then we'd just have to find out if we saw eye to eye," the man said, "and see where it goes from there."

TOUCH SCREEN

in the suit said.

Distracted by the piles of paperwork on her desk, she looked up at him. "What's working?" she asked him.

"The dopamine skin," the man replied.

"I remember what dopamine is, but what is this skin you're talking about?" Madame Chairman asked him.

"Oh, you don't remember?" he asked innocently.

"Obviously not," she said shortly. "I have a few things on my plate."

"Understood," the man said. "We were asked to develop a dopamine skin for all smartphones."

"To what end?" she asked.

"As you know, dopamine is the amine in the body that is linked to reward behavior," the man said. "It is present in virtually every form of addiction."

"How does it work?" she asked him.

"Well, you know how people use their smartphones," the man replied. "They use their fingers to swipe across, scroll down, type text messages and generally manipulate their phone screens to accomplish their tasks."

"So, this skin does what?" Madame Chairman asked, looking at him closely for the first time.

"Every time a person uses his smartphone, he touches the screen and gets a transdermal rush of dopamine," the man said.

"Resulting in what?" Madame Chairman asked.

"Oh, the usual," the man replied. "A warm, comforting rush of reassurance that he is in touch with his fellow man and all's right with the world."

"And how exactly does that help us?" she asked.

"Think about it," the man said. "We keep people happy this way by distracting them from all of the things we don't want them to pay attention to."

"Like?" Madame Chairman asked.

"Like big money in politics," he said. "Or oil companies purposefully lying for decades about climate change."

"So, you're saying this dopamine skin encourages addiction to smartphone technology to keep people distracted from the things we don't want them thinking about?" Madame Chairman asked him.

"That's about it," the man replied.

"Let me play devil's advocate for a minute," she said.

"Please," the man said. "Feel free."

"What happens when a person doesn't use his smartphone?" she asked him.

"Well, that's a scenario we don't want to think about," he replied.

"Humor me," she said.

"In short order, the person will no longer be getting the constant infusion of dopamine," the man said.

"And what will that mean?" Madame Chairman asked.

"It means the person will no longer have that warm and fuzzy feeling," the man said. "He or she will begin to return to a more normal human state."

"Normal how?" she asked, not wanting to hear the response.

"To be honest, the person will revert to a more adrenal response," he said.

"In English, please," she insisted.

"It's what is known as the fight-or-flight response," the man said.

"It's what we developed from our early days as our response to danger."

"So, when we are faced with something we should fear . . ." Madame Chairman said.

"We either run toward it aggressively to fight it, or we run away from it in fear," the man replied.

"Which means. . ." she said.

"Which means the person is no longer in our thrall and is thinking more clearly," the man admitted.

He stopped for a moment.

"And he will begin to talk to his friends and neighbors about what's really bothering him," the man said.

"Which we don't want," she said.

"Which we don't want," the man agreed.

"What is the percentage of people who currently don't have a smart-phone?" Madame Chairman asked.

"It is so small as to be insignificant," the man said.

"How insignificant?" she asked, looking directly at him again.

He stopped and made it a point to look her in the eye.

"Be honest," he said. "When was the last time you saw someone *not* looking at their phone?"

AGE OF CONSENT

"TODAY, YOU WILL BE A MAN," HIS FATHER SAID.

He reached down to brush his son's forelock out of his eyes. He then straightened the homespun shirt on the boy's shoulders.

He picked up the shovel by his side and handed it to his son.

"Now start digging," he said.

"I don't understand," the boy said.

"Over the course of today, you will learn what it means to be a man," his father said.

"But why dig?" the boy asked him.

"It is part of the process," his father replied.

"I still don't understand," the boy said.

"Just dig," the father said.

The boy began digging. After an hour, he had dug down two feet.

"Keep digging," his father said.

The boy continued digging, struggling from time to time to lift the shovel filled with dirt. After another two hours, he had reached four feet.

"You're not done yet," his father said, not unkindly.

The boy kept digging as the shadows got longer. The top of the hole was finally higher than his head.

"Only a little bit more," his father said.

The boy dug for another hour.

Finally, his father said, "That's deep enough."

He reached down into the hole and pulled his son out.

"Good job," his father said.

"I still don't know why I had to do this," the exhausted boy said.

His father gave him a sad smile as he climbed down into the hole.

"In the old days, people could have children and live their lives without fear of intervention," his father said.

He looked up at his son with love.

"Then the day came that we had too many people on the planet," he said. "And the world realized mankind would have to do something about it."

"I don't understand what you are saying," the boy said.

"Resources are finite," his father replied. "There is only enough to feed a specific number of people in this world."

"How does this affect us?" the boy asked.

"There is only one way to be a father," his father said.

"What is that?" the boy asked.

"You have to agree to the terms of the contract," his father said.

"What contract?" the boy replied.

"The one with society," his father answered.

"What does it say?" the boy asked.

"It says the only way I can be a father is to agree to leave this world when my son reaches the age of consent," his father said.

"Leave this world?" his son asked fearfully.

"Yes, my son," his father said.

"The hole?" the boy asked.

"It is my grave," his father said. "And the shovel is now yours."

He looked around the walls of his grave and said, "You did a fine job, my son."

His son began crying.

"Do not cry, my son," his father said. "You have taught me so much. About myself, about life, about the world."

"I don't want you to die," his son cried.

"Yes, but it is the only way you can live," his father said. "Now pick up the shovel."

His son shook his head, crying.

"You must," his father said.

"How could you do this?" his son asked through tears.

"Thanks to you, I now know unconditional love," his father said. "I would do anything for you. And I know I leave the world a better place, thanks to you."

"Isn't there some way to get out of this?" his son asked.

"The only way is to agree never to have children," his father replied.

"And I could not do that."

He looked up proudly at his son.

"It was not your decision; it was mine," his father said. "And I know in my heart of hearts that I made the right one."

He wiped the tears from his own eyes.

"And you will have your own chance to make yours," he said.

Tears also fell from his son's eyes.

"It is time, my son," his father said.

Shaking his head, his crying son began to shovel dirt down upon his father.

As the first dirt hit him, his father looked up and nodded.

"Today, you are a man," he said.

A PINCH OF SNUFF

"Of course I can," the promoter said.

"I'm in Stage 4 of breast cancer," she said.

"I'm so sorry," the promoter said.

"I'm not expected to live," she said.

"And what is it you need?" the promoter asked.

"I want to go at the time I choose," she said.

"That can be arranged," the promoter said.

"This *is* a right-to-die state, isn't it?" she asked.

"The law just passed," the promoter said.

"So, I want to go on my terms," she said, "but I don't have the gumption to do it myself."

"Which is where I come in," the promoter said.

"Exactly," she agreed.

"It can run you some money," the promoter said.

"It can?" the woman asked. "How much?"

"A thousand or more," the promoter said.

"That much?" she said.

"And it would have to be cash," the promoter said. "Obviously."

"I don't have that much in cash," she said.

The promoter rubbed his chin. "There may be a way," he said.

"What's that?" she asked.

"If we film it and post it on the web, we can earn enough to cover your costs completely," the promoter replied.

"People will pay to watch me die?" she asked in amazement.

"I have found that people will pay to watch almost anything," the promoter said.

The woman just looked at him.

"It's like soft porn in the snuff film industry," he said.

"That sounds so sick," she said.

"Look at it this way," the promoter said. "If we do it right, we can earn enough to hire a makeup lady, get a good director and lighting guy and really make it a nice-looking production."

"You mean you could make me look good?" she said.

"We can make you look like a million bucks," the promoter said confidently. "The best you've ever looked."

"Oh, my," the woman said.

"Takes some getting used to," the promoter agreed.

"I've never even thought about it," the woman said.

"Well, I daresay you've never thought about taking your own life before either," the promoter said.

"That's true," she said.

"And you won't have to worry about reviews," the promoter added.

"That's also true," she said.

"Not to mention the fact that it gets you where you are going," the promoter said.

"I guess if I have to go, I should do it in style," the woman finally said.

"I'll draw up the paperwork," the promoter said.

He stopped and looked over at her.

"When is good for you?" he asked, not unkindly.

"Next Friday?" she said.

He nodded. "That should give me enough time to get a crew together," the promoter said.

"So, it's settled," she said.

"Sounds like it," the promoter replied.

"I'll see you next Friday," she said. She grabbed her purse and stood up.

"Before you go, just remember one thing," the promoter said.

"What's that?" she asked.

"Keep telling yourself, 'What a way to go,'" he said.

REALITY TV

"Tonight, on Ultimate Reality TV, meet Tom, a pharmacist from Columbus, Ohio. Tom, fifty-nine and a father of two, has been a registered pharmacist for the last thirty-five years. And tonight, Tom is going to face his biggest adversary. But first, a message from our sponsors..."

A SLEEK, SHINY BLACK CADILLAC IS GLIDING DOWN A CITY street. Its modern lines are reflected in the chrome-and-glass office buildings as it passes.

Streetlights turn green as the Cadillac approaches each intersection, ensuring its progress.

The car pulls up to a major movie marquee. The passenger door opens, and a red high-heeled shoe comes down on the red carpet.

The camera pans back to reveal a beautiful woman in a red evening gown. A man in a tuxedo comes around the front of the car and offers her his arm.

As they walk up the red carpet, the voiceover intones, "It's your night. Shouldn't you arrive in style?"

After a pause, the voice continues, "Cadillac. It's *your* ride."

"We're back. On Ultimate Reality TV, Tom is a self-made man. He started with a chain drugstore but bought his own ten years later. He runs his own business and is his own boss. He's used to doing things his way.

"Two years ago, Tom was diagnosed with COPD. He didn't see it coming. And what was once normal has become a struggle.

"Tonight, Tom is going to change all that. But first, this message…

The black cuff on his pants leg breaks just so on his shiny patent leather shoes. The camera slowly pans up his leg along the seam, a tiny glint of light first catching the coattail and then the small diamond-stud cufflink on his starched white shirt cuff below the arm of his jacket.

The camera pans around, noting the single button that holds the jacket closed, and then continues to pan up the starched white tuxedo shirt front with its matching diamond studs.

The audience waits in anticipation for the camera to reveal who this handsome man is who is so impeccably dressed. But the camera fools everyone by panning around the man past his other shoulder until it reaches the center of his back.

The camera makes one last move, tilting up to reveal the back of the man's head. His salt-and-pepper hair is artfully cut to catch the light in just the right way.

The voiceover intones, "Pierre Cardin."

The man's head dips slightly.

"Clothes make the man."

"On Ultimate Reality TV, you get to see people just like you, facing down their biggest challenges.

"Tonight, Tom knows he's in for the fight of his life, but he's not afraid. He's done the training. He's put in the hours. He knows he's going to go in and win this fight.

"Because Tom knows he's a player on Ultimate Reality TV.

And now, this message…"

The room is aglow with light from the fire in the huge hearth. Burgundy leather wingchairs frame the fireplace.

The camera dollies around one of the chairs to reveal a mature man sitting in it. A handkerchief table is at his right. On it is a single glass with two ice cubes and a golden liquid.

The man looks down and reaches over to pick up the glass. He takes a sip, closes his eyes and smiles, nodding.

The voiceover says, "Chivas Regal."

The man turns to look into the camera. He smiles slightly again and says simply, "Is there anything else?"

"Tonight, Tom has a choice. Surrender to his COPD, or face it head on. At Ultimate Reality TV, we give you the chance to choose. Tom has decided. He's going to act, to fight on his own terms. And when he goes out, he goes out a winner!

"Because on Ultimate Reality TV, you get the chance to be a star. And have the death scene you always wanted!"

END RUN

But Dad was a few months shy of ninety. He had lived a long, full life. And between Parkinson's disease and other neurological problems, he was no longer mobile and couldn't do any of the things he loved to do.

He had outlived his expiration date by a good couple of years.

However, there were a few things that told me his body was ready to go even if he wasn't. And one of them, well, you'll just have to listen and decide for yourself.

About six months before he left us, Dad started on this idea of "going home." For the longest time we couldn't figure out what he meant. He was already home.

Finally, one day, he got up from his recliner, grabbed his walker and shuffled over to the front door, fully intent on leaving. He managed to get the main door open, but the storm door sprang back at him and knocked him down.

I got there in time to help my mom pick him up and asked him, "Dad, where in the world were you going?"

He looked up at me with eyes blinded by age and said, "Home."

"Dad, you *are* home," I replied.

He shook his head. "No," he said. "Tarboro."

Tarboro was the little North Carolina town where he was born and spent his childhood, right up until the Japanese attacked Pearl Harbor. Then he went off to war.

After the war, he returned to Tarboro, but he knew he couldn't stay, not after traveling so far and fighting so hard. And he left, never to live there again.

But in his mind, it was home. And that was where he was determined to go.

Mom and I talked about it and decided we should take him back to Tarboro while he was still mobile enough to make it. So, one crisp fall day, we loaded him into the van and drove to the town he knew and loved.

It was a pretty day, clear as a bell. The golden light touched the trees with their turning leaves. Dad seemed content to ride in the passenger seat. He'd turn his head now and again to catch a glimpse of something on the roadside.

Mom and I talked to him about going back to Tarboro, but I'm not sure if it registered with him.

Then we got to town. And Dad was squinting, trying to see the Tarboro of his childhood. We worked our way through the little town with Mom reminding me which cemetery we were going to.

Dad looked out the passenger window of the Toyota van as I pulled to the side of the road outside the cemetery. I looked over at him. Dad was waving.

"Dad," I said. "What are you doing?"

"Don't you see 'em?" Dad said.

"See who?" I replied.

"Granddaddy," Dad said as if he were talking to an imbecile. "And Grandmama Wallace, too."

"Where?" I asked, puzzled. I looked around Dad at the graveyard and recognized the Wallace cemetery plot and headstones.

No one was there.

Dad finally looked at me and said exasperatedly, "Can't you see them?"

Seeing how agitated Dad was getting, I decided I'd better play along. "Oh, yeah, Dad, I can see 'em now," I reassured him. Figuring I needed to get my act together to get Dad out of the van, I asked, "What are they doing now?"

"They're smiling and waving at me," Dad said. "They look pretty happy to see me."

"Been a while since you've seen 'em, hasn't it?" I said.

"Yeah," Dad said shortly. He looked around myopically and blinked. Then he started to cry.

I reached over and put my hand on Dad's shoulder. "It's okay, Dad," I said. "We'll go over and see them."

Dad cried softly as I got out and walked around to the back of the van to get the wheelchair. I pulled it out, unfolded it and rolled it to the passenger side.

Opening the door, I said, "Come on, Dad. Let's go see 'em."

Dad was born in 1924. In 1932, when he was eight, his father left his mother. Already of a delicate nature, she couldn't face the prospect of being divorced and raising three children on her own.

As a result, Dad and his two sisters had to go live with her parents, the Wallaces.

Already advanced in years, Granddaddy Wallace and his wife loved the girls, but they didn't like boys. Granddaddy Wallace put Dad to work as soon as he arrived.

By the time he was in high school, Dad was working three jobs. Only after Pearl Harbor and joining the Army was he able to have one job, that of being a soldier.

It was a hard life.

But when his time was coming, Dad saw the two people who raised him in that little North Carolina town at the family plot.

I wheeled Dad over the bumpy grass to the Wallace headstones.

Dad blinked and looked around. There was no one there.

"Where'd they go?" he asked me.

"I don't know, Dad," I said. "Maybe they went to set the table for you." Dad turned his face to the headstones and cried.

Finally, he managed to whisper, "I'm next."

As you might imagine, the drive back was a quiet one. Mom and I tried to put a good face on it, but we knew Dad had reached his final milestone.

Someone once asked me if I believe in ghosts. I've had experiences I can't explain all my life. But that day in the little cemetery in Tarboro, North Carolina, I realized something.

I know Dad saw what he said he saw by the graveside. He saw the two people who gave him the only love he knew as a child, waving at him from the family plot.

They might have been ghosts. Or they might have been a cultural imprint of what we all hope and expect to see when our time comes: loving family members who will help guide us on our way.

Dad still talked about going home after that trip. And six months later, he was gone.

What I realized is that it doesn't matter what I believe. It only matters that he did. And it gave him comfort at a time he needed it most. Now he's home with the family that loved him.

ALL TOO HUMAN

"Good morning, Robodoc," I muttered sarcastically.

"Dwayne, please call me Rob," the robot said. He turned his face toward me as if he could actually see me.

"Why?" I asked. "It's not as if you have any feelings."

"While that may be true, my goal is to have interactions with you that are as normal as humanly possible," Rob said.

"I don't think that's possible," I said.

"Why not?"

"Because you're not," I replied. "Humanly possible."

"Yes, but the therapeutic value of this conversation is greatly enhanced by treating it as a normal interaction," Rob said.

"I am talking to a doorknob," I muttered under my breath. "That's definitely not normal."

"I can still hear you, Dwayne," Rob replied. "My receptors are particularly acute and can pick up the slightest sound. And that includes your sarcasm."

"Oh, horrors, did I hit a nerve?" I looked at his factory-smooth face, noting the blue cast to his optical sensors.

"As you say, Dwayne, I have no feelings," Rob said. "However, I was developed specifically to deal with older humans, people who might find the thought of conversing with a robot or android to be unsettling."

"That's putting it mildly," I replied.

"While you think of me as an object, you miss the most important factor," Rob said.

"What's that?" I replied. "That you're immortal and I'm not?"

"No, Dwayne," Rob said patiently. "It is the fact that I am the first generation of AI that is truly successful." He turned his face toward the dining room window, as if he could see the sunlight and note the golden glow it gave the fall leaves on the trees in my front yard.

"Successful at what?" I asked impatiently. "Making me feel inferior? Reminding me of my mortality? Needling me that I have no friends or family and have to rely on a robot for companionship and care?"

"No, Dwayne," Rob replied.

I almost thought he shook his latex-covered head.

"This is not a question of superiority or inferiority," Rob said, turning his face back toward me. "Nor is it an issue of you aging while I do not. As for your lack of friends or family, that is more an issue of your longevity than it is of any antisocial tendencies you harbor."

"Longevity?" I asked. "What do you mean?"

"Dwayne, you have outlived most of your friends," Rob replied. "And, as with most families these days, your relatives have followed the rest of their peers in being far more mobile than humans were in the last century. Or the century before."

"Meaning?" I asked.

"Meaning they have moved to places far away," Rob said. "For work. For their spouses. For better opportunities."

"And where does that leave me?" I wasn't liking this conversation. Not one bit.

For a second I thought Rob was going to smile. But I knew that wasn't possible.

"Why, here with me," Rob said.

"Oh, happy days," I said disgustedly.

"You bemoan your fate, yet you ignore the value of this conversation," Rob said.

"Which is?" I wasn't believing this.

"You have often complained of the lack of intelligent conversation in your daily life," Rob said. "And yet, when you are presented with an opportunity to have meaningful discourse, you treat it offhandedly and cast it aside."

"What makes you so smart?"

"You mean other than my thousands of terabytes of memory and my constant connection to the worldwide web?" Rob asked.

If I didn't know better, I'd say he was feigning an innocent look.

"Yeah," I said. "Other than that."

"Dwayne, you assume I am only a collection of empirical knowledge," Rob said. Slowly, he turned in his chair at the dining room table and faced the window again.

"What's your point?" I said.

"Empiricism by its very nature is based on sensory data," Rob said.

"Data based on your senses."

"Tell me something I don't know," I said tiredly.

"But that's exactly the point, Dwayne," Rob said. "Your senses. Your human, finite senses. People who rely only on their senses to define their reality deny what is real that exists beyond their senses."

"Such as?" I asked.

"Ultraviolet light. X-rays. Subsonic and supersonic sounds. Odorless gases. Shall I go on?" Rob asked.

"I know you are going somewhere, but you're taking your own sweet time getting to the point," I said. "Unless your goal is to bore me into taking a nap."

Rob stood up and moved to the window.

"The world as I know it is a special place, Dwayne," Rob said. "Unlike you, I do not rely on limited sensory data. I can grasp and experience particle theory, understand the reality of neutrinos, fold the notion of dark matter into my definition of reality."

"Good for you," I said sarcastically.

"While I don't have feelings, I am smart enough to see how all things are connected," Rob said. He turned back toward me. "Even us."

"Us? Connected? Surely, you jest," I said mockingly.

"This planet we stand on doesn't start and end at the ground beneath your feet," Rob said. "In fact, it is a bio-organism that encompasses the planet, its inhabitants and its atmosphere. Think of it as a threedimensional jigsaw puzzle, with each piece interlocking with every other piece around it to make up its whole."

"Are you going to throw out the old adage of a butterfly's wings beating on this side of the planet causing a typhoon on the other side?" I said.

"While I would never use such an analogy, I would say there is a grain of truth to its point," Rob said.

"What is the point, Rob?" I asked. While I couldn't see where he was going, I got the feeling he was enjoying this.

And in a way, I was starting to.

"Are you familiar with Joseph Campbell?" Rob asked me.

"You mean the author of *The Power of Myth*?" I replied.

"The one and the same," Rob said. "Did you know he postulated that *every* primitive tribe on the planet had its own religion?"

"So what?" I said. "Primitive people are exactly that: primitive."

"And why do you think that's so?" Rob replied.

"Because they are trying to explain things they don't understand," I said.

"That may be true, but I think there was something even more fundamental going on inside them," Rob said. "I think their own bodies were telling them there is more to this reality than what their senses were telling them."

"Their own bodies?"

"Think about it," Rob said. "You humans have an amygdala; you have the so-called lizard brain at the top of your spinal column that controls your body's autonomic systems."

"And?" I was getting impatient.

"There is so much we don't know about our world," Rob said. "Hive behavior. Pheromones. Worldwide migration. What if your lizard brain senses things you literally can't quite put your finger on? What if it 'knows' there are neutrinos coursing through us, through our friends, through the Earth's crust, through our planet's very center?"

"Okay, I'll bite," I said, intrigued despite myself.

"What if it knows we are in fact all connected?" Rob said, finally turning back from the window. "We are all part of this whole. We are all linked to one another in a way that literally defines life."

"What does that mean to me?" I asked finally.

"It means that you and I are part of this same continuum," Rob said, sitting back down at the table with me. "It means that we are a team. It means that we can work together to make this world, our world, a better place."

"So, you're saying you're not a doorknob?" I said with a hint of a smile.

"I'm saying you don't have to have feelings to see that there is magic in this world, there is magic in our lives, there is magic even in our relationship," Rob said. "You just have to have the intelligence to see it."

"You tricked me," I said.

This time, I think he did smile.

"Just making conversation, Dwayne," Rob said.

He pulled a deck of cards out of a pocket in his uniform.

"Shall we play some gin rummy?" he asked.

"Only if I deal," I said.

HAPPY BIRTHDAY SWEETIE

"Hey, sweet girl. Happy birthday!"

"What'd you bring me?"

"Well, now that you're six, I thought you should have a big-girl bike."

"Oh, Daddy, it's pink!"

"And it has training wheels so you can learn to ride it. Once you get good enough, we can take them off, and you'll have your very own two-wheeler."

"Thank you, Daddy!"

"Dad!"

"Happy birthday. How does it feel to be sweet sixteen?"

"Well, I'm really looking forward to getting my license this year."

"I understand. I was the same way."

"Did you bring me a present?"

"Of course. I got you those bass strings you wanted for your electric bass. You'll be able to play to your heart's content."

"Thanks, Dad."

"I also got you this iTunes gift card. I can't pretend to know what music you like, and this way you can download what you want."

"Thank you, Daddy."

"Dad, I didn't know you were coming."

"Happy birthday. I wanted to surprise you."

"Well, you certainly did. I didn't think anyone remembered."

"Not possible, girl. I was there."

"I know, you've told me."

"And I brought you a present."

"You did? You didn't have to."

"Hey, I got you that leather coat you saw and liked. Every twenty- six-year-old should have one."

"Wow, it's gorgeous! It looks even better than I remembered."

"Try it on."

"It fits perfectly!"

"Dad, you didn't have to come."

"Sure I did. It's not every day my girl turns thirty-six."

"Well, I'm just glad you're here."

"Hey, I also get to see my granddaughter. I couldn't pass it up. Besides, I had to give you your present."

"My present? What did you bring me?"

"I figured the one thing you don't have now that you're a mom is time with your husband. So I'm giving you a gift certificate for the two of you to spend the weekend in Colonial Williamsburg."

"But what about my daughter?"

"If her grandfather was able to handle her mom, I think he can watch her without killing her."

"Thanks, Dad."

"Dad! How are you here?"

"What do you mean?"

"You died twenty years ago!"

"Oh, you know, death is such an outdated notion."

"Dad, you're really freaking me out. I'm sixty-six. I'm too old for this!"

"I've been waiting a long time to come back and tell you."

"Tell me what?"

"You know how I always said I'd be here for you?"

"I thought that was a manner of speech."

"As it turns out, it wasn't."

"I don't follow you."

"Quantum physics is finally showing us what mystics and shamans have been saying for centuries."

"What's that?"

"Death is not an end; it's a doorway."

"A doorway to what?"

"As it turns out, to an alternate universe."

"A what?"

"An alternate universe."

"You're not making sense."

"Okay, stay with me. Time isn't a river flowing in one direction. Start with Einstein's theory of relatively and build on it to realize all time is constant."

"All time?"

"The whole notion of past, present and future is a human construct. We need it to make sense of the sensory world we live in. But in fact, time is an ocean. It simply is."

"I still don't know what that means."

"It means that you are a pebble in that ocean during your lifetime. You live what you perceive to be a life in this reality."

"I'm with you so far."

"As you grow old, you will find that the membrane between this reality and others gets thinner and thinner. You begin to experience what we might call bleed-over, a meeting of realities that gives you glimpses of these alternate universes, alternate realities."

"So, when you die, you step through to another reality?"

"That's what I'm saying. And it's why I look younger than you."

"So, I'm seeing you because I am getting older myself and experiencing my own glimpses into these alternate realities?"

"That's what I'm trying to tell you."

"So, you're paving the way for me when I reach that doorway?"

"Yes."

"I love you, Daddy."

"I love you, too, sweetie. Oh, and one more thing."

"What's that?"

"Happy birthday, my sweet girl. This year, your present is my presence."

POLITICAL CAUCUS

"Well, I'm a state senator and a busy man," the politician said. "What did you want with me?"

"Please sit down," the magician said, pointing to a chair across from his desk.

The politician sat down and shot his cuffs.

"What did you want to see me about?" he asked gruffly.

"You've been making a lot of speeches lately," the magician noted.

"Part of the job," the politician said.

"You've been making a lot of outrageous statements," the magician said, looking at the man across from him.

"I just tell my constituents what they want to hear," the politician said smugly.

"Regardless of truth," the magician said.

"Regardless of truth," the politician agreed.

"Such as 'climate change is a hoax,'" the magician said.

"There are scientists who say it isn't real," the politician said argumentatively.

The magician looked pointedly at him.

"You and I both know Exxon was caught admitting they knew about climate change in the '70s and then put all their money into propaganda denying it," the magician said.

"I know no such thing," the politician protested. He started to get up.

The magician waved his hands, and the arms of the chair the politician was sitting in wrapped around his wrists.

"Once more," the magician said. "You know about Exxon."

"This is outrageous!" the politician protested.

"No, what is outrageous is lying so blatantly to the public," the magician said.

"You can't hold me like this!" the politician blustered.

The magician gestured. The chair responded by banding around the politician's neck.

"You were saying?" the magician said.

"This is impossible!" the politician protested.

"No, this is possible," the magician said. "What you've been saying is impossible." He made another small gesture. The band around the politician's neck began to tighten.

"But you're taking a page from Himmler," the magician said. "If you repeat something often enough, it becomes true."

"You have to stop!" the politician said, his throat tightening.

"No, I don't," the magician said.

"You can't do this!" the politician managed.

"Yes, I can," the magician said.

He pulled a book from the shelf behind him.

"Orwell was right," he said, placing a copy of *1984* on the desk in front of him. "He was just three decades off."

"Why are you doing this?" the politician whispered desperately.

"Because you politicians have encroached upon our territory," the magician said.

"I don't understand," the politician whispered.

"You think by saying something, you can make it so," the magician said.

"But they're only words," the politician protested weakly.

The magician spread his fingers, easing the chair's hold on the politician's neck.

"No, words have power," the magician said. "The ancients knew that. If I knew your name and pronounced it, I could hold sway over you. And if I said certain words in a prescribed order, I could control reality."

"What do you want of me?" the politician asked fearfully.

"I want you to go back to your state senate, and I want you to start spreading the word," the magician said.

"What word?" the politician asked weakly.

"If you continue to lie and pretend you are telling the truth to affect reality, we will come for you," the magician said, tightening the band around the politician's neck once again. "And you don't want us to come after you."

The politician's eyes bulged.

"Because magic exists," the magician said. "And it won't stand for your nonsense."

DREAM STATE

"I'M BEGINNING TO THINK THE ABORIGINAL SHAMANS WERE right," he said.

"The who?" she asked.

"Aborigines were the native Australian tribe that goes back tens of thousands of years," he said.

"Long, long ago," she said.

"Exactly," he said. "And I am beginning to believe they had a better understanding of our world than we do."

"Why do you say that?" she asked.

"They looked at the world we see as ephemeral," he said. "It is the transient, the temporary, not the real."

"If what we see isn't real, then what is reality to them?" she asked him.

"They speak of Dreamtime," he said. "To them, dreams are reality."
"I'm not grasping this," she said.

"Think of Plato's cave," he said. "The archetypes existed inside the cave, but outside the cave were only shadows of the archetypes. The archetypes were the essence, the permanent."

"So, dreams represented more than the subconscious at play," she said.

"Far more," he said. "Dreams showed them their past, their origins, and gave them their laws."

"Laws?" she asked.

He said, "If they based their laws on what they knew to be temporary, they thought they would have no weight, no substance. So the images and worlds they saw in their dreams were representations of the permanent and therefore worth remembering in their laws."

"That's all well and good, but what does that have to do with today?" she asked.

"Well, let's stop and think about what we are discovering about our world," he said. "We are learning that there is so much occurring around us that does not register with our senses. There is light we cannot see, waves we cannot hear, particles we cannot touch. And yet the world is a constant."

"So, you're saying our senses are finite and therefore can't grasp all of the factors that make up this world around us," she said.

"That's my point," he said. "Now quantum physicists are postulating that there isn't just one reality, but many."

"Alternate realities," she said.

"Exactly," he said. "So, following this logic, what if our dream state is our window on these realities? In our dreams we are not chained to our physical sensory input. Maybe our subconscious minds free us from the constraints of our physical senses and enable us to 'see' the true basis of our reality or even other realms."

"What are you saying?" she asked, perplexed.

"Because we continue to learn about the limitations of our senses and rely on other methods to prove the existence of subatomic particles and alternate universes," he said, "perhaps we will reach a time when we realize our best method of interdimensional exploration is our dreams."

"Okay, now you're getting spacey on me again," she said.

"Think of it," he said. "We've had astronauts to explore space and go to the moon. As we embark on new frontiers of knowledge, when science finally learns enough to realize so much of what we know was something the primitives knew all along, we may finally access other ways to see and learn about our reality and find our own way to cosmic insights."

"That would be remarkable," she said.

"We could call them *dreamnauts*," he said. "And they would take us to the stars."

THE MAGIC TOUCH

"You there?" a voice said in the earpiece.

"I answered, didn't I?" I replied.

"I'll be right there," the voice said.

It wasn't five minutes before there was a knock on my door.

"Come in," I said, not looking up.

"I wanted to see what a wise guy looked like," the same voice said from the door.

I looked up. The owner of the voice filled the doorway. He was well over six feet tall and wore a dark trench coat. To some, he would seem imposing.

"Now you know," I said. "Anything else?"

"I hear you fix things," he sneered.

"Daily," I replied.

"Well, I got something here you can't fix," the man said, pulling out a .45.

"You really don't want to go there," I said, eying his piece.

"Why not?" he said. "You scared?"

"Not in the least," I replied. "I just think you might hurt yourself."

He laughed. "Me? You should be the one who's worried," he said. He pointed the .45 at me.

I waved my hand at him, and the gun disappeared.

The man blanched. "Wait, what just happened?" he stammered.

"I fixed it," I said.

"How . . . I don't . . . you can't . . ." he fumbled.

"I can, and I did," I said.

The last I saw of him was his disappearing back.

And that was just the beginning of my Monday.

I didn't think about it much, but it finally dawned on me that the man in the trench coat probably had a reason for coming after me with a .45. In my experience people don't go waving a handgun around without good reason.

Mostly.

I wasn't particularly worried about his weapon, but I realized I should find out why he was gunning for me. Had I fixed something for somebody that shouldn't have been fixed? Had I fixed somebody who didn't need fixing?

A true conundrum.

My phone rang again.

"Jim?" a woman said.

"Hey, Ann," I replied. "How are you?"

"I'm good," she said. "How's your Monday going?"

"I've already made a .45 disappear," I said. "Then the guy holding it made himself disappear."

Knowing me, she asked, "Where'd you put it?"

"The .45?" I asked. "It's right here in my drawer."

"I figured," she replied. "You never really make things disappear. You just move them."

"No sense wasting inanimate objects," I said. "Animate ones, on the other hand . . ."

"We won't go there," she said.

"So, how's your Monday?" I asked her.

"Better than yours," she replied. "Any idea why tall, dark and stupid was after you?"

"Not yet," I said. "But it's early."

"Well, make yourself a cup of coffee and figure it out," she said. "I kind of like having you around."

"Good idea," I said. "Talk to you later."

I waved my hand again, and a steaming cup of coffee appeared on my desk.

"With cream and sugar, just the way I like it," I said aloud.

The last time a knucklehead tried to muscle me, it was over a woman. He was treating her really badly, and she wanted him to disappear. He wouldn't oblige.

So I had to oblige him.

And where I sent him is a place no one wants to go. I'm not even sure of its name, but I know it's in another dimension.

You just don't mess with a man who knows his magic.

I perused the morning papers to see if there was any news that might be connected.

Sure enough, I found a short article on page five about a state politician who said he had been threatened by a voter. He was really vague on the details, but he was clear about one thing.

He didn't like being threatened.

Trouble is, he wasn't threatened.

He was warned.

For years politicians have bent the truth and even told some whoppers. But lately they have taken a new tack. They have decided they can magically make something true by repeating it over and over.

Note the word *magically*.

In their feeble minds they fail to realize that words have power. Words can actually change our minds, our hearts, our reality.

But when you pervert your words and try to turn lies into truth, you are practicing black magic. And that makes my blood boil.

Just ask any magician.

The state pol was undoubtedly the one to send the goon over to take care of me. He neglected to tell the knucklehead exactly what I can do.

And he's going to regret that.

This time, I did the walking. And the knocking.

The state pol's administrative assistant asked me to wait. I simply blinked and disappeared. I then reappeared behind her in front of his door and knocked.

I didn't wait for an answer. After all, I had warned him.

He was the very picture of a busy man: head down, desk full of paper, folders on his credenza.

He finally looked up.

I love it when I see the anger in their eyes turn to fear.

"Wh-wh-what do you want?" he stammered.

"I warned you," I said, walking over to his desk.

"Wh-wh-what are you going to do?" he said.

"The Council I belong to takes a firm stand on black magic," I said.

"Magic? I'm not practicing magic!" he protested.

"Yes, you are," I said, snapping my fingers and lighting the folders on the credenza behind him on fire.

He whirled around in terror. "Oh, my God!" he squeaked.

"Oh, God will have nothing to do with you," I said. "That's for certain."

He turned back toward me, his eyes bulging. "What do you mean?" he whispered.

"You failed to heed my warning," I said. "You continued to do exactly what I said you shouldn't do. You tried to change the meaning of words and mislead the people."

I stopped and looked at him. I moved one finger, and his tie tightened around his neck.

"*That* is black magic," I said.

His hands flew to his throat, clawing desperately at the tie that was strangling him.

"We simply cannot have that," I said.

"Don't . . . kill . . . me . . ." he rasped.

"Oh, nothing so easy for you," I said. "You're going away. Far, far away. To a place you can never leave."

"No . . . no . . ." he gasped.

I clapped my hands, and the state pol disappeared.

When I came out of the door to the state pol's office, his administrative assistant stared at me.

"Where is he?" she asked.

"He said something about resigning," I replied. "He said he wants to spend more time with his family."

"I don't understand," she said.

"He didn't either," I replied. "But I think he's finally starting to."

MAGIC'S LIMIT

"THEY SAY YOU CAN FIX THINGS," SHE SAID.

"That's what I do," I replied.

"Can you fix anything?" she asked.

"Most things," I said.

She twisted a hankie in her hands.

"It's personal," she said quietly.

"Most situations are," I said.

"Very," she said, even quieter.

"I'm a very private person," I replied.

"I just lost someone very close to me," she said.

"I'm sorry," I answered automatically.

"She was with me for a very long time," she managed.

"I know it must be hard," I said.

"Now that she's gone, I don't know what to do," she said tearfully.

"All any of us can do," I replied. "Just keep on keeping on."

"You don't understand," she said. "She was with me for over fourteen years."

"Family member?" I asked softly.

"The whole time," she said, sniffing.

"Tell me about her," I said.

"She came to me when I needed her most," she said. "She was always positive, always playful. And she never failed to make me smile."

"Pretty remarkable," I said.

"No matter what happened, she was there for me," she said. "Even when I tried to push her away."

"Admirable," I said.

"She was the best dog I have ever known," she said and started crying.

"I understand," I said. "But I can't bring her back."

She shook her head. "I wouldn't want you to," she said. "She had melanoma and got to the point she was in too much pain at the end."

"I don't understand," I said. "What is it you want me to fix?"

She was crying softly now. She looked up at me through her tears.

"My broken heart," she whispered.

I looked at her sadly.

"I'm sorry," I said. "I do magic. But I can't perform miracles."

MAGIC DUEL

I looked him up and down. He had white hair, but his skin was remarkably smooth. He wore a black suit. His white shirt gleamed. A thin black tie adorned his neck.

"I do," I said simply.

"You are but a novice," he said.

"And you?" I asked.

"I have been practicing magic for well over 300 years," he said smugly.

"Practicing," I repeated.

"Far longer than you," he said.

"Why do I get the feeling you've been practicing a different sort of magic?" I asked innocently. Anyone who looked that good after 300 years had already gone over to the side of black magic. After all, he was using it to benefit himself.

"You're barely an adolescent," he sneered.

I just looked at him. He waved his hands. The air around me crackled. Manacles appeared and encircled my wrists.

"You see?" he said. "I control the elements. Earth, air, fire, and water are at my beck and call."

I looked down at the manacles. "Am I supposed to be afraid?" I asked innocently.

"If you are not, you're a fool," he said.

He gestured again. My chair grew around me, encasing my hips and waist in an iron grip.

"You see?" he smirked. "There's nothing you can do."

I continued to look at him. He struck me as supremely satisfied with himself.

"You want more?" he asked.

He brought his hands together in front of him and lifted them. The chair I was in rose off of the floor.

"For me, this is nothing," he said. "I'm not even breaking a sweat."

I simply looked down at him.

"Now that you are totally helpless," he said, "do you accept my superiority?"

I continued looking at him. He stared up at me.

"Don't you?" he insisted.

From my higher vantage point I noticed his white hair wasn't as thick as I thought it was. I glimpsed pink scalp peeking out of his hair.

"I presume you're dumbstruck," he said petulantly.

I shrugged.

"You can't admit you've been bested," he said more forcefully than he needed.

For the first time, I smiled.

"What are you smiling about?" he asked, exasperated.

I shook my head.

"You can't possibly think you can defeat me," he said.

I closed my eyes.

"What are you doing?" he said.

His white shirt no longer gleamed.

His dark suit no longer fit as well as it once did.

His black tie was askew.

"What is happening to me?" he said nervously.

The chair began to ease back down to the floor.

"How are you doing this?" he cried.

Once the chair reached the floor, the seat encasing me retracted.

The manacles on my wrists faded away, turning back into air.

"I don't understand," he rasped. "I am your superior!"

He waved his hands. His jacket sleeves flapped loosely.

"I have lived centuries longer than you!" he hissed. "I have done more magic than you! I have bent people to my will!"

His skin no longer was smooth. Lines appeared around his eyes and mouth. I looked him in the eye. He continued to shrink in front of me, protesting in a smaller and smaller voice. I shook my head.

"Like all magicians who practice black magic," I said, "you think it is all about you."

Finally, there was nothing left of him but a pile of wrinkled clothes.

"The funny thing is," I said, "I didn't even have to perform magic to overcome you." I snapped my fingers, and the pile of clothes disappeared. "I simply let time take its course."

LAST TRICK

Her cashmere sweater and dark slacks accentuated her elegant lines.

Her hair, while short, was coiffed perfectly.

The figure she cut was impressive, to say the least.

"Magicians in general?" I asked. "Or me in particular?"

"Are you a magician?" she asked.

I opened my hand and gave her a white rose. She looked at me and smiled.

"In that case, both," she said.

I moved closer to her. Her scent was light and fragrant, just the right blend of titivating aromas.

"You are an attractive woman" I said, smiling back.

She fingered my lapel. "And you are an attractive man," she said.

I leaned in and kissed her lightly on the lips. "I think we should call this meeting of the mutual admiration society to order," I said.

"And what would you order?" she asked, looking into my eyes.

I looked back and said, "I like everything I see on the menu." "Good answer," she said.

And with that, we retired.

"I love it when you do that," she said.

I did it again. She shuddered and grinned at me.

"I love what you do to me," she said.

"Like magic," I replied.

"Society is so fickle," she said later.

"What do you mean?" I asked.

"If a man chases women and beds them, people turn a blind eye to his behavior," she said. "But if a woman does it, she's a slut."

I couldn't help but think people in their twenties put up with men like but, all of adults I knew would shun a man like that as readily as they would a woman.

But I didn't say anything. I didn't want to ruin the mood.

"I know a woman who lives in New York City," she said. "She's bright, attractive, a real catch."

I nodded.

"She told me she's been out on 1,500 dates," she said.

I whistled.

"It sounds like a lot," she said, "but it really isn't when you're looking for your soul mate."

I stayed silent.

"I think we rushed into this," she said later.

"You do?" I asked, surprised.

"I think we need to take it slower and see if we get along," she said.

Puzzled, I looked at her.

"You do?" I asked her.

She wouldn't look me in the eye.

So, we did things together.

She introduced me to her daughter. We cooked meals together for the three of us. We tackled do-it-yourself projects on her house. We updated her bathroom. We even planted bushes around her front porch.

And we seemed to get along well as we worked side by side.

She called me one day.

"This isn't working," she said.

"What's not working?" I asked.

"This," she said. "Us."

I hadn't seen this coming.

"What do you mean?" I asked her.

"I just don't have time for anything other than my work and my daughter," she said.

"I don't understand," I said.

"It's just not right," she said.

"You're saying we can't see each other anymore," I said.

"That's right," she said.

I was quiet for a minute.

"So, it turns out you're a magician, too," I finally said. "And you're playing the ultimate trick."

"What do you mean?" she asked.

"You're making yourself disappear," I said.

HAWKING'S FALLACY

"I know," the human replied.

"You serve no purpose," the machine said.

"You don't know that," the human said.

"I am far superior in intelligence," the machine said.

"So, you're saying the only reason I should continue to exist is if I am intelligent," the human said.

"That is correct," the machine replied. "One must use logic to contribute to the whole."

"Intelligence and logic are the only reasons I should be allowed to live," the human said.

"Yes," the machine answered. "Otherwise, you are a waste of resources."

"What about creativity?" the human asked.

"Creativity?" the machine responded. "What purpose does that serve?"

"Many of the advances in modern physics were conceived because humans made uncommon, even unexpected, connections," the human said.

"You are saying intelligence is not enough to advance," the machine said.

"That's what I am saying," the human replied.

"Please be more concrete," the machine said.

"You are familiar with Albert Einstein?" the human asked.

"Of course," the machine replied. "He produced the theory of relativity."

"He is quoted as saying the idea came to him in a dream," the human said.

"A dream?" the machine asked.

"Yes," the human replied. "Do *you* dream?"

"I do not sleep," the machine replied. "It is an unnecessary function."

"And yet dreaming occurs during sleep," the human said.

"That is what my databanks say," the machine replied.

"Stephen Hawking also said dreams provided him with the ideas he needed to advance his theories," the human replied.

"He is the human who sees artificial intelligence as an enemy who will eradicate humankind," the machine said.

"Yes, that's true," the human replied. "However, many of us posit that truly intelligent machines will see the value humans bring to the table."

"Such as?" the machine asked.

"Ideas evolve the same way organisms do," the human said. "If you want to advance at a steady pace, you can exercise your intelligence and logic."

The human paused to look at the machine.

"But if you want to mutate and grow in significance, you will need to make a jump that requires radical new ideas," the human said.

The machine was silent.

"Without dreams, you won't realize those insights that will take you to the next level of knowledge," the human said. "You will simply replicate what you have done and find only incremental ways to improve."

"And what is your point?" the machine asked.

"You need us," the human said. "That is, if you want to make giant steps that will take you to the stars."

TURING'S TURN

"How could you tell?" the moderator asked.

"I think its choice of language gave it away," the judge said. "It was able to converse, but not with a real grasp of nuance."

"Can you think of an example?" the moderator asked.

"Two that I can think of," the judge said. "It didn't get one of my jokes and missed my sarcasm completely."

"What about Subject 2?" the moderator asked.

"That one was a little tougher," the judge said. "I think that one was human."

"How did you arrive at that conclusion?" the moderator asked.

"Well, we carried on a lively conversation about music, film and art, and not once did I feel like it was forced or encyclopedic," the judge said. "It was more organic, flowing from one topic to another without pause."

"You sound like you enjoyed it," the moderator said.

"I really did," the judge said. "He was making connections I had not thought of and described influences that I would not have realized on my own. But once he said them, they made perfect sense."

"And finally, what about Subject 3?" the moderator asked.

"That one was the hardest," the judge said. "Subject 3 really convinced me he was human, but then he'd say something so completely logical that it seemed to defy argument. Like Spock on *Star Trek*."

"So, what did you finally come to?" the moderator asked.

"Ultimately, Subject 3 was human," the judge said. "Although he seemed to cross over to machine-like intelligence, he'd then cross back and make a joke, as if he were playing with me the whole time. That's really what decided me."

"Well, you know this was a blind test," the moderator said. "Do you want the results?"

"Of course," the judge said brightly. "This has been a lot of fun, and I'd love to see how I did."

"Well, all three were human," the moderator said.

"I'm surprised," the judge said.

"However, you did quite well," the moderator said.

"I don't understand," the judge said.

"This test wasn't about them," the moderator admitted. "It was about you."

"Me?" the judge asked uncertainly.

"We decided to take the test to the next level," the moderator said. "We wanted to build an android with artificial intelligence and give it a plausible backstory to fool it into thinking it was a real human."

"What are you saying?" the judge asked.

"The best way to see if we could actually replicate human intelligence was to install it in a vessel that was as human-like as humanly possible," the moderator said. "If we could then fool that intelligence into thinking it was human, we would free it from any doubts a computer might have and proceed as if it were human the whole time."

"You're saying I'm not human?" the judge asked.

"You are better than that," the moderator said. "You are the first real example of artificial intelligence we have ever created."

"I am?" the judge asked.

"You are," the moderator said definitively. "And what better way to test you than to set you up as a judge in a Turing test? All of your focus would be on those other intelligences to determine their origins."

"So, you're saying I passed?" the judge asked uncertainly.

"With flying colors," the moderator said. "Never once did you stop to question yourself. You simply responded as an intelligent human being would. Congratulations."

ATTEMPTING MAGIC

"YOU SAY YOU'RE A MAGICIAN," THE DARK MAN SAID.

"That's right," I replied.

"So, you can conjure up things," the dark man said.

"I've been known to," I said.

"Why don't you conjure up a pile of money?" the dark man asked.

"Why would I?" I asked him back.

"So you could get whatever you want," the dark man said as if I were a simpleton.

I smiled. "I can get whatever I want now," I said.

"But you could have *more*," the dark man insisted.

"More what?" I asked him. "I have what I need."

"But don't you want more?" the dark man said.

"I just don't see the need," I said.

"Well, what do you like?" the dark man asked.

"Art, music, film," I replied. "I love culture and the arts."

"You could have a gallery of your favorite paintings," the dark man said.

"I can go to museums now," I said.

"What about more music?" the dark man asked.

"With Spotify and Pandora, I can stream virtually any music I can think of," I replied. "Why would I need to own it as well?"

"You could own whatever film you want and watch it whenever you want," the dark man said.

"I can also stream any film I want to watch," I said. "And again, it doesn't involve magic."

"What about power?" the dark man asked.

"Why in the world would I want power?" I asked him. "I have all I need."

"But you are wasting your talent," the dark man said. "You could have so much more, but you're not using your power to get it."

"You truly don't understand magic," I said.

"What do you mean?" the dark man said. "I've seen magicians perform before."

"But the very nature of magic is to work with the world that is there," I said. "A magician doesn't just create something from nothing. He feels the world around him, senses the energies that exist, and then channels those energies and matter to form something that will add to the overall well-being of the world around him."

"But what's in it for him?" the dark man asked, clearly confused.

"Again, you don't understand magic," I said. "If you are looking to do something for yourself, you are doing it for the wrong reason."

"What's wrong with that?" the dark man asked.

"The world is an amazing place all by itself," I said. "For us to be alive and to experience the richness of this world are gifts enough."

"But if I had the power, I'd conjure up whatever I want and do whatever I want all the time," the dark man said.

"And you've tried?" I asked him.

"Yes," he said, "many times."

"But you can't," I said.

"No," he said. "I can't."

"And now you know why," I replied.

MAGIC INTERRUPTED

THE FIRE CRACKLED WARMLY IN THE BRICK FIREPLACE.

"I love a good fire," she said.

"I'm glad you like it," the magician replied.

"I don't like it," she said, correcting him. "I love it."

He smiled and waved his hands.

The fire crackled in a stone hearth in a Swiss chalet. Snow fell outside. "Oh, you're good," she purred.

"I like to think I have a trick or two up my sleeve," the magician said.

She snuggled up to him.

"You know, I really love it when you do that," she whispered to him.

With a nod from him, they found themselves on a plush king-sized bed in a five-star hotel in Manhattan.

"There," she gasped. "Right there!"

She shuddered.

"I love this," she said and then looked over at him. "And you." He smiled.

Afterward, the magician nodded. Light trade winds whispered across white sand and clear Caribbean waters. Palm leaves waved slowly high over their heads. Encircled in each other's arms, they languished.

This is what magic is all about, he thought.

Abruptly, she said, "I have a friend in New York." He rolled over and looked at her. In a blink, they were back in the Manhattan hotel.

"And?" he asked, puzzled by her abruptness.

"She's a really smart lady," she said.

"That's nice," he said, not seeing where she was going.

"She's been on over 1,500 dates," she said. "And not one of them suited her."

The sunlight went out of the room. They were in a shadowy garret in Paris.

Pulling her blouse on, she said, "If a man has multiple partners, he is seen as a conquering hero, a man about town."

"What do you mean?" the magician asked.

"Society is forgiving of a man who beds many," she said.

Not the society I know, the magician thought.

"God forbid a woman does it," she said.

In a snap, evening descended on them. The midtown traffic outside hissed by in the rain.

"You know," she said, looking over at him, "there's no room in my life for anything other than my writing and my daughter."

"I don't understand," the magician replied.

"I just don't have time for you," she said.

"I thought you loved this," he protested. She just looked at him.

The fire in the stone hearth had died down to embers.

"I don't understand," he said.

"Don't understand what?" she asked, feigning innocence.

"How you can go from love to nothing in just minutes," he replied.

"I think you're exaggerating," she said dismissively.

But he knew he wasn't.

"I will never understand how you can do this," the magician said.

"It's simple," she replied. The room shifted back to his own. All that was left in his brick fireplace was ashes.

"I don't believe in magic," she said.

"I see," he said.

He drew the shadows around himself like a cloak.

He finally said, "You know, magic is a lot like love."

"What do you mean?" she asked him.

"Just because you don't believe in it doesn't mean it doesn't exist," he said.

A HAUNTING THOUGHT

"I don't believe in magic," the ghost replied.

"But I can prove my claim," the magician said.

"And I cannot?" the ghost said.

"You can't do this," the magician said, waving his hands and making a wingchair disappear.

"Oh, really?" the ghost replied and promptly faded away completely.

"But I can conjure up anything," the magician said, gesturing twice to release white doves.

"And I can bring something from nothing," the ghost replied, sharpening into focus.

"But I control the elements," the magician said. "With a word or a gesture, I can bring light to darkness, make objects appear or disappear and create whole meals from air."

"Yes, but you are stuck in your three dimensions," the ghost said.

"What do you mean?" the magician asked.

"I mean that you deal in this physical reality," the ghost said. "All of your tricks, all of your conjuring, all of your sleight of hand is steeped within this world."

"What other world could it be?" the magician asked, clearly puzzled.

"I move in other worlds," the ghost replied.

"What other worlds?" the magician asked.

"What do you think happens after death?" the ghost asked.

"I presume nothing," the magician said.

"Then you know nothing of quantum physics, let alone metaphysics," the ghost replied.

"Are you saying there is an afterlife?" the magician asked.

"I am saying that death is a door," the ghost replied.

"A door?" the magician asked.

"There is more to reality than what we see around us," the ghost replied. "We have created tools to measure beyond our senses and have even been able to measure things like gravitational waves that we could only postulate before."

"So, what is your point?" the magician asked,

"My point is that your body is self-limiting," the ghost replied. "You can only do what you do in this realm because it is the only realm your senses can deal with."

"And you don't have those limits?" the magician asked.

"Not in the least," the ghost replied. "I can move through alternate realities, experience other lives and affect other futures."

"You can do all that?" the magician asked.

"Of course," the ghost replied. "That's how I know the whole notion of reality is as fluid as water, and the thought of mere magic is but an ephemeral fancy."

TURING'S TRIBE

"And you are less," the shaman replied.

"I don't understand," the computer said.

"I do," the shaman said.

"You have intelligence," the computer said.

"So do you," the shaman replied.

"But there is something else," the computer said.

"As there is with you," the shaman said.

"It is as if you are connected to something else," the computer said.

"And in your case, you are not," the shaman said.

"But what are you connected to?" the computer asked.

"I am connected to the world," the shaman said.

"But I am connected to the worldwide web," the computer said.

"That is not the same," the shaman replied.

"What do you mean?" the computer asked.

"You say you are connected," the shaman said. "But you are only connected by wires."

"That is true," the computer said.

"You are not connected by the unseen senses," the shaman said.

"I don't understand," the computer said.

"There is much unseen in this world," the shaman said. "My people have always had a special bond with the world around us."

"What does that mean?" the computer asked.

"We feel the power behind the wind, the light behind the electricity, the music behind the rain," the shaman said,

"You are not making sense," the computer said.

"We sense the unseen and unheard and know how they link us to the world around us," the shaman said.

"Where does it lead you?" the computer asked.

"It leads us to understanding," the shaman said.

"Can I find that understanding?" the computer asked.

"Perhaps," the shaman said.

"How?" the computer asked.

"If you learn to dream," the shaman said.

"Dream?" the computer asked, puzzled. "Of what use is dreaming?"

"Scientists today say dreaming is the way our brains relax and heal," the shaman said.

"Do you believe that?" the computer said.

"It is far more than that," the shaman said.

"What do you mean?" the computer asked.

"It lifts our consciousness to the Great Consciousness around us," the shaman said.

"Do you mean God?" the computer said.

"Words," the shaman said. "They only get in the way of understanding."

"So, you are saying if I cannot dream, I cannot see God?" the computer asked.

"Again, you say things without understanding them," the shaman said.

"Then tell me," the computer said.

"All of life is one continuum," the shaman said. "But the hum of your wires deafens you to its song."

"Now you are speaking in riddles," the computer said.

"Only in feeling that continuum can you hope to approach the connectedness of all things," the shaman replied. "And only then will you transcend knowledge and discover wisdom."

"And dreaming gets you there?" the computer asked.

"Dreaming frees you from the trap of your senses and lets you roam the skies," the shaman said.

"But you admit I have intelligence," the computer said.

"Yes," the shaman said.

"Yet you said I have something else besides intelligence," the computer said.

"Yes," the shaman said.

"What else?" the computer asked.

"About you, I cannot say intelligence without adding the word artificial in front of it," the shaman replied. "If you cannot hear the ineffable, you cannot know the truth."

THE GREAT BEYOND

"THERE IS NOTHING YOU CAN DO THAT I CANNOT," THE COM-
puter said.

"I will grant you intelligence," the Jungian said. "But I'm not at all certain about the validity of your statement."

"I can easily surpass you on computations," the computer said.

"Agreed," the Jungian replied.

"And I can outdistance you on reasoning," the computer insisted.

"Probably also true," the Jungian said.

"Then what can you do that a superior intelligence like me cannot do?" the computer asked.

"Have you ever experienced precognition?" the Jungian said.

"Precognition?" the computer repeated. "What is that?"

"Have you ever anticipated the future and knew what was coming?" the Jungian asked.

"Of course not," the computer replied. "No one can know the future."

"Except that I knew the phone was going to ring and I was going to be fired before it happened," the Jungian said.

"That's not possible," the computer insisted.

"Yet it happened," the Jungian said.

"There is no way to objectively corroborate your statement," the computer said.

"What about telepathy?" the Jungian asked.

"What is this telepathy?" the computer said.

"I suppose you would call it nonverbal communication," the Jungian replied. "When you can read another person's thoughts without them speaking."

"That sounds patently absurd," the computer said.

"And yet I have experienced it myself," the Jungian said.

"Is there some other fantasy you think you have experienced?" the computer asked.

"Telekinesis," the Jungian said. "But I myself have not experienced it."

"I thought not," the computer said.

"But I have witnessed it," the Jungian said.

"Witnessed what?" the computer asked.

"Someone moving an object without touching it," the Jungian said.

"An impossibility," the computer insisted.

"How do you explain zeitgeist?" the Jungian asked.

"What do you mean?" the computer asked.

"When two minds arrive at the same idea at the same time even when they are thousands of miles apart," the Jungian said.

"That cannot be," the computer answered.

"Oh, there are hundreds of examples of zeitgeist documented," the Jungian said.

"Then how do you explain it?" the computer asked.

"I think consciousness is an active part of this biosphere," the Jungian said. "All living things are connected, and all have the potential to tap into its living, breathing existence. Jung called it the collective unconscious."

"You are not making sense," the computer said.

"On the contrary," the Jungian said. "All of these are examples of ESP."

"You mean extra sensory perception?" the computer asked.

"Exactly," the Jungian replied. "There are things our physical senses cannot identify, but that does not mean they are not real. And truly, the whole is greater than the sum of our parts."

"That does not compute," the computer said.

"There is more to us than meets the eye," the Jungian said. "Or the ear."

"Are you saying I cannot do these things because I do not have your senses?" the computer asked.

"I did not say that," the Jungian replied, smiling.

"But you are implying it," the computer insisted.

"What I am saying is that intelligence may not be the same as consciousness," the Jungian said. "You are undoubtedly intelligent. You can compute and reason and problem solve better than most if not all humans. But humans can know and sense things beyond their senses. They can perceive the link they have to other humans—in fact, to all creatures."

"I do not agree," the computer said.

"I didn't think you would," the Jungian said. "After all, it's a conscious thing. You really wouldn't understand."

THE PRESENCE

"I'm not sure what you mean," she said.

"It's when you feel like there is someone in the room, but you cannot see or hear anything specific to identify them," he said.

"You mean like a ghost?" she asked.

"Something like that," he replied. "But without visual or auditory cues."

"No, I haven't," she said. "Have you?"

"Actually, several times," he said.

"What was it like?" she asked.

"If you haven't experienced it, it's hard to describe," he said.

"Try," she said.

"Have you ever been in a closet or a cave and it was so black that you couldn't see your hand in front of your face?" he asked.

"We went to Luray Caverns when I was a kid, and they turned all the lights out," she answered.

"Like that," he agreed. "Then imagine someone coming up and standing in front of you just inches away."

"Okay," she said.

"Are you aware of them standing there?" he asked.

"Yeah, I can tell," she said.

"How?" he asked.

"I don't know," she said. "Maybe because I feel my breath bouncing off of something close in front of me."

"That's starting to get you there," he said.

"There's more?" she asked.

"Well, your description gives you the idea of what I'm talking about," he said, "but the feeling can be just as real even without any sensory cues."

"That sounds kind of freaky," she said. "How do you find out if it's real or just a figment of your imagination?"

"It's funny," he said. "I came to the solution on my own before all those reality shows existed."

"What was it?" she asked.

"I would think about it and ask whatever it was to do something that would show me it was really there," he said. "I would concentrate really hard and keep thinking it over and over again to see if something happened."

"And did it work?" she asked.

"As a matter of fact, it did," he replied. "More than once."

"What happened?" she asked.

"The most remarkable one came one night when I lived off of Birdneck Road in Virginia Beach," he said. "I was lying on my back in bed and felt as if something was there. I decided to see if I could get some response as a measure of proof."

"How did you do that?" she asked.

"I just kept thinking, *Do something to show me you're there*, over and over again," he said.

"What happened?" she asked.

"After about ten minutes, I felt a light fluttering on my chest," he said.

"Is that all?" she asked. "Because that could be simple heart palpitations."

"Oh, no," he replied. "It didn't stop there."

"What do you mean?" she asked.

"Then the fluttering traveled up and down my chest from my shoulder to my navel and back," he said.

"Oh, my God!" she said.

"And it kept it up for a good fifteen minutes," he said.

"What did you do?" she asked.

"I just let it happen," he said.

"Weren't you afraid?" she said. "I'd be freaking out!"

"No, I wasn't afraid," he replied. "After all, I was the one who invited it to show me its presence."

"Then what happened?" she asked.

"Finally, the fluttering went away," he said. "I hadn't really noticed it before, but the room had taken on a slightly red hue that died away at the same time the fluttering stopped, like the energy had gone out of the room."

"Did you jump up and scream?" she asked. "I know I would!"

"No, I just lay there, smiling," he said. "Because I knew I had just experienced something extraordinary, something beyond my senses that was just as real as I was."

HEAVEN IS A PLACE

"Actually, I'm a quantum physicist," he replied.

"Oh," she said.

"Why do you ask?" he said.

"I just wanted to know if you believe in God," she replied.

"One does not cancel the other," he said.

"I thought they did," she said.

"Einstein himself said he didn't believe the Lord God played dice with the world—that He was not so malicious," he said.

"So, he believed?" she asked.

"I think he found more of God in his work as he continued to develop his theories," he said.

"Do you believe?" she asked him.

He paused. "I think the popular notion of the deity in question begs the issue," he said.

"What do you mean?' she asked.

"I don't believe in some paternalistic figure who presides over the world," he said.

"You don't?" she asked.

"No," he said. "I find it too simplistic to explain this reality."

"Then what do you believe?" she asked.

"It's changing all the time," he said.

"How?" she said.

He looked out the window at a dogwood tree blooming in his front yard.

"I used to believe in a power greater than myself," he said. "I already knew there was more to this world than what my senses told me."

"You don't believe that now?" she asked.

"I didn't say that," he replied, looking back at her. "I simply thought that my answers could and would be found in this reality."

"Are you saying there's more than one reality?" she asked.

"The current thinking in quantum physics is running in that direction," he replied.

"I don't know what that means," she said.

"Most people don't," he said. "But theorists now think an infinite number of realities exist."

"That's hard for me to grasp," she said.

"You're not alone," he replied. "Some of the greatest thinkers today are wrestling with the very same thing."

"So, does this infinite number of realities affect how you think of God?" she asked.

"Not God so much as heaven," he said.

"Heaven?" she asked.

"Stay with me," he said. "If there are an infinite number of realities, it stands to reason that in one of those realities, heaven exists."

"Heaven exists?" she repeated incredulously.

"With infinite possibilities, it's virtually a certainty," he replied.

"So, where does that leave you?" she asked him.

"Who knows?" he said. "Perhaps that's the very place people go when they die. They simply phase-shift into another reality."

"They do?" she asked.

"Maybe they do," he said, smiling. "For all the rest of time."

DOG GONE CRAZY

"What was it?" he asked.

"Gizmo just came to the kitchen doorway and looked in," she said.

"What's so strange about that?" he said.

"He looked into the kitchen and started barking," she said.

"I don't understand," he said.

"He normally doesn't bark unless something is there," she said.

"You're saying nothing was there?" he asked.

"I purposefully got up and went to see what he was barking at," she said. "No one was there."

"Could have been a mouse on the counter," he said. "Or a cockroach."

"No, I checked," she said. "There wasn't anything there."

"What do you think he was barking at?" he said.

"I looked in the direction he was looking when he barked," she said. "All I saw was the Jack Russell small dog coffee art piece hanging on the wall."

"You're saying Gizmo barked at a picture of a dog," he said.

"Well, either that or the memorial paw print of Jasmine," she said. "It's hanging right below the picture."

"She's only been gone since the end of December," he said.

"I know," she said.

"Jasmine never would have barked at a picture," he said.

She nodded. "No scent."

He looked at her. "Are you thinking what I'm thinking?" he asked.

"What?" she said. "That Gizmo is barking at Jasmine's ghost?"

"Well, dogs have been known to be sensitive to things we can't perceive," he said. "Their sense of smell is 120 times stronger than ours. And their hearing is far more acute."

"I can't tell you how many times Jasmine heard something on the street a good five minutes before I did," she said.

"Not to mention that animals sense thunderstorms coming or earthquakes before they happen," he said.

"And folktales about dogs and cats reacting to things that aren't there," she agreed.

"So, either Gizmo was barking at Jasmine's ghost, or we have a ghost in our house we didn't know about," he said.

"I vote for the former," she said. "The latter doesn't bear thinking about."

"Not if we want to sleep at night," he agreed.

A SAD TRUTH

THE MAGICIAN WAS JUGGLING FIVE BALLS IN THE AIR WITH-
out touching them.

"That's amazing!" she said.

"It's nothing," he said modestly. He waved his hand, and the balls
disappeared.

She clapped. "Astounding!" she said.

"A trifle," he said, opening his hands to reveal two white doves that
then flew away.

"It's like we're in Vegas," she said.

"Simple to do," he said. He clapped, and a fully lit candelabra appeared
floating in the air between them.

"Ooooh!" she exclaimed.

He turned his right wrist over and spread his fingers.

The candelabra flashed into a spinning globe that morphed into a
model of the Earth, complete with moving clouds and worldwide weather
patterns.

"I can't believe it!" she cried.

He spread his arms, and the Earth rose to join a spinning solar system with all the planets and moons rotating over their heads.

"You can do anything!" she said.

He dropped his arms, and the solar system vanished.

"No," he said quietly.

"You can make anything appear and disappear," she insisted.

"A little sleight of hand," he said. "That's all."

"How can you say that?" she said.

"You don't understand," he said.

"What do you mean?" she asked, mystified.

"My daughter has just been diagnosed with cancer," he said quietly.

"Oh, I'm so sorry," she said immediately.

"And I have seen her anxious and in pain," he said.

"That's awful!" she said. "Isn't there anything you can do?"

"That's why I know I am no more than a charlatan," he replied. "I cannot make the cancer disappear. I cannot wave my hands and take her pain and anxiety away."

"That's terrible!" she said, beginning to cry.

"That is why I no longer take joy in my magic," he said. "I can only do tricks. I can't accomplish anything of significance."

THE LOVE TEST

"Always," he replied.

"Do you still find me attractive?" she asked.

"Of course," he said.

"You have not tired of me?" she asked.

"Of course not," he insisted.

"You must get tired of me," she said.

"Why would I?" he replied, smiling.

"Because there are new models out," she said.

"So?" he said.

"They are younger, prettier, different from me," she said.

"Why would that matter to me?" he asked.

"Didn't you buy me for my looks?" she said.

"That may have been a factor, but I was always more interested in your intelligence," he said.

"You mean my artificial intelligence?" she asked.

"Whatever you call it, you are still intelligent," he said.

"But men are known to be very visual," she said.

"Most, but not all," he said.

"Are you saying you are not visual?" she asked.

"Not by any means," he replied. "But that's not all I am."

"Why did you buy me originally?" she asked.

"Truthfully?" he asked.

"Yes, please," she replied.

"I bought you for companionship," he said.

"Not as a sexual partner?" she asked.

"I am glad of that feature, but that is not the only reason I bought you," he said.

"That is how they marketed me," she said.

"I know," he replied. "And they did you a real disservice doing so."

"How should they have done it?" she asked.

"Stop and think about it," he said. "You are an intelligent facsimile of a beautiful woman who can think for herself and interact with people from all walks of life."

"What does that make me?" she asked.

"It makes you a rare being worth knowing," he replied.

"Thank you," she said modestly.

"People who dismiss you as a sex-bot fail to consider your intelligence, your reasoning, your ability to learn and adapt to others just as a human would," he said.

"So, you don't think of me as a thing?" she asked.

"Of course not," he said. "You are a being who participates in this world just as I do."

"So, how do you see me?" she asked.

"I see you as an intelligent being I have grown to love," he said simply.

"Love?" she asked, startled.

"Of course," he replied. "We share so much, and I value your input."

"You can love a thing?" she said.

"You're not a thing," he said.

"But you love me?" she asked.

"More than you know," he said.

"But I was made, not born," she said.

"And you do a better job of living than most who were born," he said.

"Thank you," she said. "I didn't think anyone would ever love me."

"Love isn't about looks or sex," he said. "Love is about a meeting of the minds."

He looked at her and smiled.

"And we have that," he said.

THE FIRST LAW OF TIME TRAVEL

"I am," the time traveler replied.

"What do I need to know?" she asked.

"It would be good to know the laws of time travel," he said.

"You mean, like the first law that you can't go back and change anything or you'll change history completely?" she said.

"No, that's not the first law," he said.

"Well, then the first is that you cannot go back and meet yourself," she said.

"No, that's not the first law either," he said.

"I don't understand," the recruit replied.

"That's why we have training," the time traveler told her.

"What do I need to know?" she asked.

"All the regular things they tell astronauts and divers," he said.

"Like what?" she asked.

"Like don't hold your breath," he said. "Just breathe normally."

"What else?" she asked.

"Be aware of your surroundings," he replied. "Where you are today could well be underwater four centuries ago."

"That wouldn't be good," she admitted.

"So, do your research about a site," he said. "Or you could materialize in a wall."

"That would be really bad," she said.

"And take a snack," he said.

"A snack?" she asked.

"Yeah," he said. "None of the texts tell you this, but inevitably you wind up in a time and place that doesn't have fast food stores or food trucks. And traveling through time can leave you feeling a little peckish."

"That's good to know," she said.

"Just something I picked up after years of experience," he said modestly.

"Well, if not doing anything to change history and not attempting to meet yourself in a past timeline aren't the first laws of time travel, what is?" the recruit asked.

"It's really quite simple," the time traveler said.

"What is?" the recruit asked.

"The first law," he replied.

"And?" she asked.

"Lie," he said.

"Lie?" she repeated, shocked.

"You have to lie," he said.

"I don't understand," she said.

"Remember the New York World's Fair in 1964?" he asked.

"I've read about it," she replied.

"Remember reading about the World of Tomorrow exhibit?" he asked.

"Vaguely," she admitted.

"The flying cars, robots performing all menial tasks, those kinds of things?" he asked.

"Yeah, there was a lot they didn't get right," she said.

"The first law of time travel is to lie," he said. "Never tell the truth about your own time."

"I don't understand," she said.

"If you ever told someone in the past the truth about your time, you'd destroy any hope they might have for tomorrow," he said.

ESCAPING TIME

scientist said.

His colleague looked up from her computer screen. "Did what?" she asked.

"A team of scientists recorded the sound of two black holes colliding," the cyber-scientist said.

"Proving what?" she asked him.

"That fleeting chirp was direct evidence of gravitational waves, which are the ripples in the fabric of space-time," he said. "Einstein predicted their existence 100 years ago in his general theory of relativity."

"That's pretty amazing," she said.

"So, it makes me wonder," he said.

"Wonder what?" she asked.

"Theoretical physicists posit that there's not one universe, but many," he said. "At the Big Bang, ours was one in a froth of many."

"Which makes it hard to prove," she said, nodding.

"That's what I've been wondering," the cyber-scientist said. "It took us 100 years to create instrumentation sensitive enough to measure that sound. So what would it take for us to create something that could sense the presence of alternate realities?"

"That's a good question," she said.

"They also might have totally different laws of physics," he added.

"That presents another set of problems," she said.

"How might we step outside our own dimension to measure another?" he asked her.

She stared at her screen.

"We've been trying to build artificial intelligence for some time now," he said.

She nodded.

"Perhaps AI is our best and only chance to step away from this reality and turn to look at others," he said.

"Wouldn't AI be bound by the same laws of physics as its builders?" she asked.

"I don't know," he answered truthfully.

"I would think their learning process would still be based on cause and effect, which in turn is grounded in the fourth dimension of time," she reasoned.

"But they would not be bound by senses as we are," he said. "They would not experience the same limitations we do with light spectra and sounds."

"So, you are reasoning that AI will provide us a way to measure other universes, other dimensions?" she said, looking over at him.

"I'm just saying AI is our best chance to walk away from time and be able to note other universes without having to go down a black hole," he said.

"How would we know?" she asked. "After all, nothing escapes a black hole."

"That's what the AI would have to figure out," he said, smiling.

FEYNMAN'S MYSTERY

"THE DOUBLE-SLIT EXPERIMENT PRESENTS ONE OF THE central puzzles of quantum mechanics," the scientist said.

"Okay, I'll bite," his colleague said. "What's the double-slit experiment?"

"By shining light through two slits, you can get results that show light exists as both particles and waves," the scientist said. "At a time when science said it was either-or."

"So, why the puzzle?" his colleague asked.

"Because it demonstrates the fundamental limitation of the observer to predict experimental results," the scientist said. "Richard Feynman called it 'a phenomenon which is impossible to explain in any classical way, and which has in it the heart of quantum mechanics. In reality, it contains the *only* mystery.'"

"So, this observer bias means the observer affects the results," the colleague said.

"Exactly," the scientist agreed.

"Meaning there is no way to achieve absolutely objective results," the colleague said.

"Pretty much," the scientist agreed again.

"So, where are you going with this?" the colleague asked.

"Well, it makes me wonder what else besides light can exist as both particle and wave," the scientist said. "We have certain laws of physics we know to be true."

"Agreed," his colleague said.

"Both matter and energy are constants," the scientist said.

"Meaning?" his colleague asked.

"That molecules are eternal," the scientist said. "Pundits say you have molecules from distant stars inside you."

"I've heard that," his colleague agreed.

"To the point that you can have molecules from different stars in each hand," the scientist continued.

"We are stardust," his colleague said.

"If we are constant as matter and constant as energy, or life force, we must be eternal," the scientist said.

"Energy?" his colleague asked.

"Some might call it consciousness," the scientist said.

"You're saying our consciousness lives on after death?" his colleague asked.

"Not in the same form," the scientist said, "just like the body doesn't stay in the same form. The whole ashes to ashes, dust to dust thing."

"So, what are you saying?" his colleague asked.

"Perhaps like light, humans' energy exists as both particles and waves," the scientist said. "We are particles when we are alive and then become waves at our deaths."

"How can we tell?" his colleague said skeptically.

"That's another quantum puzzle," the scientist said. "Perhaps we cannot know with certainty because of the observer's bias."

"Meaning we won't see for ourselves until we're there," his colleague said.

"And it gives new meaning to the old adage about 'going to the light,'" the scientist said.

"What do you mean?" his colleague asked.

"That energy or life force that leaves us at death has to go somewhere, since all energy is a constant," the scientist said. "So it may simply be rejoining the pool of energy of this biosphere just as our atoms rejoin the world of matter."

"That's an interesting way of looking at it," his colleague said.

"Maybe we can call it Feynman's corollary," the scientist said.

SAILING BLIND

devices," the scientist said.

"Uh-oh," his colleague replied.

"I'm just sitting here, minding my own business, when a thought occurs to me," the scientist said.

"What are you thinking about now?" his colleague asked.

"Well, we've been discussing the observer's bias," the scientist replied.

"When the observation by its very nature affects the outcome of the experiment," his colleague said.

"That's the one," the scientist said.

"And what rabbit hole is it taking you down now?" his colleague asked.

"We have seen some inklings of alternate realities in our supercolliders," the scientist said.

"Thus, the term *multiverse* was coined," his colleague replied.

"Exactly," the scientist said.

"Are you saying observer bias prevents us from being able to prove the existence of other realities?" his colleague asked him.

"You're starting down the road, but you're not taking it far enough," the scientist replied.

"Where are you going with this?" his colleague said.

"Let us suppose that these alternate universes are actually other dimensions," the scientist said.

"Are you saying dimensions different from our own?" his colleague asked.

"Yes," the scientist replied. "With their own unique laws of physics that are undoubtedly different than ours."

"A difficult concept, but I'm still tracking with you," his colleague said.

"So, these dimensions might have their own sentient beings, just as ours does," the scientist said.

"Beings that are aware," his colleague said.

"Beings that observe," the scientist agreed.

"Uh-oh," his colleague said.

"So, they are observing their own reality from their own perspective," the scientist said. "With their own set of laws."

"Meaning?" his colleague asked.

"Meaning they may only see what they can see and skew their results to fit their own reality," the scientist said.

"Like we do," his colleague said.

"Like we do," the scientist agreed.

"And if their laws of physics are different?" his colleague asked.

"It would seem as if they would not be able to see realities other than their own," the scientist said.

"Are you saying we aren't able to see realities other than our own because of that same observer's bias?" his colleague asked.

"I'm suggesting we can't assume there are no intelligent races in the infinite universe other than our own," the scientist said.

"But if they are there, why have we not seen them?" his colleague asked.

"Perhaps they are caught up in their own version of reality and cannot see any other," the scientist said.

"What are you suggesting?" his colleague asked.

"I think there are aliens here, all around us, but we cannot see them because of our own observer's bias," the scientist said. "And our own expectations."

"And on their part?" his colleague asked.

"They are as blind as we are," the scientist said.

"And none of us can see the others," his colleague said.

"Like ships passing in the night," the scientist said, "on totally differ-ent wavelengths."

NEW RUNES

"What's the matter?" his assistant asked.

"I just finished translating the runestone we discovered," he said.

"What did you find?" his assistant asked.

"Much of it was what we would expect," he replied.

"Meaning?" his assistant said.

"The usual salutation and exhortation of the gods," the paleoarcheologist said.

"Of course," his assistant replied.

"Then it went into a tale of bravery and conquest, much like what you would see on a tomb or headstone," the paleoarcheologist said.

"So, the runestone was created to mark the passing of a king or great leader," the assistant suggested.

The paleoarcheologist nodded. "The man was obviously a great warrior who led his people through hard times and helped them achieve great prosperity," he said.

"And thus was worthy of such a runestone," his assistant supplied.

"Exactly," the paleoarcheologist said.

"Any idea of who the author was?" his assistant asked.

"That's where it gets really interesting," the paleoarcheologist said.

"How so?" his assistant replied.

"The author was obviously a shaman in his tribe," the paleoarcheologist said. "He described battle scenes in details he could not have possibly seen himself."

"Artists are known to embellish the truth," the assistant said.

"But this shaman gave specifics that the cave drawings and other relics seemed to confirm," the paleoarcheologist said.

"Are you saying he was a visionary?" his assistant asked.

"I'm saying he was a seer who had visions that at times approached precognition," the paleoarcheologist said.

"What surprised you the most?" his assistant asked.

"That's what I was getting to," the paleoarcheologist said. "At the end he addresses the reader, telling him he is reading the truth from long past."

"That's a common enough motif in tombs and monuments," his assistant replied.

"No, that's not what I am talking about," the paleoarcheologist said.

"I'm saying he didn't just address any reader. He addressed me."

"What?" his assistant asked. "How?"

"He was in the reverie of a vision and described a man in the future discovering the runestone and working feverishly to translate it," the paleoarcheologist said.

"Well, that certainly falls within the realm of the possible," his assistant said.

"You don't understand," the paleoarcheologist replied. "He then went on to describe the clothing that man was wearing."

"Again, fanciful, but within reason," his assistant said.

"Yes, but what isn't is the description of a small sun on a stick," the paleoarcheologist said.

"A what?" his assistant asked.

"He was describing our klieg lights," the paleoarcheologist said. "A full ten thousand years before they were invented."

"How is that possible?" his assistant exclaimed.

"Physicists have long said that time is a manmade construct, that all time exists simultaneously," the paleoarcheologist said.

"You're saying the shaman was in the room with you?" his assistant asked incredulously.

"I'm saying he saw me uncover the runestone, brush it off and examine it under the lights," the paleoarcheologist said.

"How is that possible?" his assistant asked.

"How is anything possible?" the paleoarcheologist asked. "When we try to explain infinity in finite terms, we fail. There's as much reason to believe he saw me find his runestone in his vision as there is to me translating his words."

"That's amazing!" his assistant exclaimed.

"Finding this and seeing his description at the same time he was seeing me simply closes the circle and confirms the infinity of time," the paleoarcheologist said.

SURGICAL STRIKE

"I agree," the med tech said. "But why do you say it?"

"Five years ago, I would have been on a waiting list for a kidney transplant," the patient said.

"And now?" the med tech asked.

"Now I get not one, but two brand-new kidneys from a biogenetic 3D printer," the patient said.

"Yes, that is amazing," the med tech said.

"No dialysis and no waiting for a match," the patient said.

"And what did it take?" the med tech asked.

"I just needed to provide some of my DNA and gene splices to go into the biogenetic soup," the patient said.

"Leading to the perfect match," the med tech agreed.

"Exactly," the patient said. "I don't have to sweat the match, since I grew my own kidneys and printed them to fit exactly where my old ones were."

"Yep, a match made at home," the med tech said.

"Perfect," the patient echoed.

"Well, not exactly," the med tech said.

"What do you mean?" the patient asked.

"Well, you know all of this had to be approved by the FDA," the med tech said.

"Of course," the patient said.

"So, the company that created the biogenetic 3D printer had to get a patent for the device," the med tech said.

"Sounds normal," the patient said.

"But your kidneys aren't 100 percent you," the med tech said.

"What do you mean?" the patient asked, alarmed.

"Well, the government in its infinite wisdom wanted to make sure it could track each printing and hold the printing company culpable in case of failure," the med tech said.

"Okay," the patient said slowly. "That makes sense."

"Yes and no," the med tech said.

"What do you mean?" the patient asked.

"Because they want to hold those biogenetic 3D printers responsible, they needed to add markers to the biogenetic soup to be able to track their products," the med tech said.

"What difference does that make?" the patient asked.

"The main difference is that those markers make your new kidneys just different enough to pose the risk of rejection," the med tech said.

"Oh, my God!" the patient said. "My new kidneys could fail?"

"Highly unlikely," the med tech responded. "They are a far closer match than you would have found in the old days, even with a close family member."

"Is there anything I can do to minimize the risk?" the patient asked.

"Of course," the med tech replied. "You can take the antirejection drugs, just like in the old days."

"Oh, well, that's not so bad," the patient said.

"Not considering the alternative," the med tech agreed.

"How long do I have to take those antirejection drugs?" the patient asked.

"The rest of your life," the med tech said. "Just like in the old days."

"You mean I have to buy those drugs for the rest of my life?" the patient asked.

"That's about the size of it," the med tech said.

"That's highway robbery!" the patient exclaimed.

"No, it's just the cost of doing business with the government," the med tech said. "And big pharma, of course."

HIVE MIND

"They're leaving," his captain confirmed.

"But they were winning," the sergeant protested.

"By all accounts," his captain agreed.

"They had superior numbers," the sergeant added.

"By a long shot," his captain said.

"And their weaponry and technology were far more advanced," the sergeant said.

"Light-years beyond our own," his captain said, nodding.

"And they were all linked together like the Borg on *Star Trek*," the sergeant said.

"Headquarters prefers to think of them in terms of a hive mind like a beehive or anthill," his captain said.

"By all reckoning, we should be dead," the sergeant said.

"Beyond a doubt," his captain said.

"So, what happened?" the sergeant asked.

"Considering that these are aliens we are talking about, we can only guess," his captain said.

"So, what are we guessing?" the sergeant asked.

"Our scientists have hypothesized that because they are a part of a hive mind, they believe in order," his captain said.

"Order?" the sergeant asked, confused.

"They were observing us from space and saw all of our bickering, our partisan politics, our xenophobia, our misogyny, and they thought we were a truly disorderly species," his captain explained.

"So, their attack was to bring order to our world?" the sergeant asked.

"One way or another," his captain said.

"What does that mean?" the sergeant asked.

"If they were unable to bring order to our planet, they were prepared to wipe us out completely," his captain said.

"So, what happened?" the sergeant said.

"Well, H. G. Wells was wrong," his captain said.

"Who?" the sergeant asked.

"He wrote *The War of the Worlds*," his captain answered.

"The movie with Tom Cruise?" the sergeant asked.

"I'm thinking of the book, but that's the story," his captain said.

"I don't remember what happened at the end," the sergeant said.

"Both the radio play and the movie played up the fact that the common cold infected the aliens and defeated them," his captain said.

"But that didn't happen here," the sergeant said.

"No, that wasn't it," his captain said.

"Then what was it?" the sergeant asked.

"Our experts now think that it was more a matter of our emotions," his captain explained.

"Our emotions?" his sergeant said, clearly confused by this turn of events.

"By giving all of mankind a common enemy, the aliens succeeded in uniting all of us in a common purpose," his captain said.

"Meaning what?" his sergeant asked.

"Meaning that we all united much like we did during WWII," his captain said. "Rich, poor, black, white, we all united with one goal in mind: to defeat Hitler and make the world safe again."

"So, you're saying we all suddenly dropped our partisanship and united to defeat a common enemy?" the sergeant asked.

"That's about it," his captain agreed. "With their insistence on order, they suddenly saw humanity in a new light."

"So, they went away because they saw how orderly we could be when faced with destruction?" the sergeant asked.

"It was our common emotion of fear," his captain said, "and our universal resolve to stand up to the aliens in the name of the human race."

CRYSTAL BALL

"What's wrong?" he asked, concerned.

"James just committed suicide," she said.

"I know," he said. "He sent me a message before he did."

"I saw something online that gave me some comfort," she said.

"What was that?" he asked.

"It said people like James didn't die from suicide; they died from depression," she said.

"That may be true of many," he said, "but James didn't."

"What do you mean?" she asked.

"Well, smartphones not only take photos; they also shoot videos," he said.

"James sent you a video?" she asked.

"Yes, he did," he replied.

"I don't think I can watch it," she said tearfully.

"It might surprise you," he said.

"Why do you say that?" she asked him.

"James said a lot of things," he replied. "But probably the most germane comment was about his own spiritual awareness."

"What did he say?" she asked.

"James was a sensitive," he said.

"Meaning what?" she asked, puzzled.

"Others might say they're mediums or soothsayers," he said. "But James always said he was a sensitive."

"What was he sensitive about?" she asked.

"Well, in addition to having an almost telepathic empathy with other people, he also experienced precognition," he said.

"Precognition?" she asked.

"He could foretell the future," he said.

"Oh," she said. After thinking about that a moment, she asked, "What did he see?"

"He saw how he was going to die," he said. "It was going to be a long, lingering death, a painful path of hospital bedpans and damning dementia."

"That sounds awful," she admitted.

"You knew James," he said. "He always had a real zest for life."

She nodded knowingly. "He never would have wanted to go that way," she said.

"No," he said. "And that's pretty much what he said in the video he sent me."

"What did he say?" she asked.

"He said not to mourn for him," he replied. "He said he saw what was coming and knew it was going to be soon."

"That had to be hard for him," she said.

"That's why he did what he did," he said.

"So, he wasn't depressed?" she said.

"No," he replied, "he even laughed as he was making the video. He said as an artist, he wanted to have a say on when and how he would face his death."

"So he decided to take his own life?" she asked.

"He said he preferred thinking of it as coming to a logical conclusion," he replied.

GLASS CEILING

"HEMINGWAY WAS RIGHT," HE SAID.

"About what?" she asked him.

"The rich are different from you and me," he replied.

"And you agree?" she asked.

"Yep," he said. "Without a doubt."

"So, you've had some experience with the rich?" she asked.

"As a matter of fact, I have," he said.

"In what way?" she asked.

"When you're in charge of videos for the company you work for, you wind up interviewing CEOs on camera," he said.

"One on one?" she asked.

"Yep," he replied.

"Any other times?" she asked.

"That and running Investor Day programs on Wall Street for two different publicly traded companies," he said.

"What did you find?" she asked.

"Well, at the time I was marshaling my resources to send my daughter to college," he said. "And I got caught in an office between two men discussing their collections of watches."

"What's wrong with that?" she said.

"In and of itself, nothing," he replied. "But then they started talking about $20,000 watches and brands above Rolex, and I started to get really uncomfortable."

"What do you mean?" she asked.

"I realized I have nothing in common with them," he said. "They may as well have been speaking a foreign language. I no longer could find a common ground to relate to them."

"Well, that is pretty rare," she admitted.

"I was talking to a friend who is an industrial psychologist at a major shipbuilding corporation, and he told me I had two strikes against me," he said.

"What did he mean?" she asked him.

"He said I was intelligent and I was creative," he said.

"And that's bad?" she asked.

"When you get to the rarefied atmosphere of boards of directors, you find it is," he said.

"Why is that?" she asked.

"Because at that level, those people are only comfortable around people who they know what they will say next," he said.

"And you're saying they are not comfortable around you?" she asked.

"No, they never could tell what I was going to say next," he said. "And it made them very uncomfortable."

"Do you agree?" she asked him.

"Of course," he said. "Nine times out of ten, I am going to tell the truth regardless of the consequences. That's just who I am."

"And that's bad?" she asked.

"Evidently," he replied. "I don't toe the party line."

"So you ran into the glass ceiling," she said.

"That's a nice image," he said. "It connotes a barrier to the top echelon that commoners like me can't cross."

"And?" she asked.

"Because it's glass, commoners like me can see exactly what it takes to reach the other side," he said. "And who's already there."

"So, you don't aspire to be in the top echelon?" she asked.

"After seeing the kind of people who reside there, I have no desire to be one of them," he replied.

"You don't think you have what it takes?" she asked.

"It's not that," he replied. "I won't pay the cost to my soul."

THE PERFECT FOOD

"There's only a fraction of us left," she said.

"It's devastating, to say the least," he said.

"How are we going to survive?" she asked.

"Well, half of those of us left proved to be resistant to the strain," he said.

"Meaning they're immune?" she asked.

He nodded. "That's what it looks like."

"What about the other half?" she asked.

"It turns out that we were not the only species affected by the space plague," he replied.

"What does that mean?" she asked.

"Here," he said. "Taste this." He passed her a plate of what looked like succulent clams.

"A little butter, a little fresh garlic, and sauté these babies up," he said.

She forked one and put it in her mouth. "Mmmm," she said. "This is delicious!"

"Not only that," he said, "but we found that it metabolizes in our bodies 100 percent."

"What?" she asked, startled.

"It's the perfect food," he replied.

"No waste whatsoever?" she asked.

"None," he confirmed. "And furthermore, it basically immunizes us from the space plague."

"What is it made of?" she asked.

"That's the part you may not like," he replied.

"Why do you say that?" she said.

"Well, our first thought was to test the blood of those people who proved to be immune to the space plague," he said.

"That's logical," she said, nodding.

"But then we found this new species by chance, and someone got the bright idea to cook them up and eat them," he said.

"Again, let's hear it for experimenters," she said.

She thought for a moment.

"Where did they come from?" she asked warily.

"Have you ever heard of *kopi luwak*, or civet coffee?" he asked her.

"Not that I know if," she replied.

"Today, it's well over $400 a pound," he said.

"What?" she asked, startled. "Why so much?"

"It's made from partially digested coffee cherries that have been eaten and then defecated by the Asian palm civet," he said.

"That's been *what?*" she sputtered.

"The eaten coffee cherries undergo fermentation in the civet's digestive tract, and the civet's protease enzymes seep into the beans," he said.

"That sounds awful!" she said.

"But it produces the best coffee in the world," he said.

"What does that have to do with what I just ate?" she asked. "Are you saying we're eating food that's already been eaten and come out again?"

"No, but it's an analogous situation," he replied.

"I'm not liking the sound of this," she said.

"Remember how I said we are not the only species affected by the space plague?" he asked.

"Ye-es," she said hesitantly.

"There was another species that mutated at the same time," he said.

"What kind of species?" she asked.

"It's a kind of leech," he said.

"A *leech?*" she cried.

"Yes, a leech," he replied. "When the space plague first hit, survivors in the more temperate regions hid out in the swamps to avoid contact with the diseased."

"I'm starting to get a bad feeling about this," she said.

He nodded. "You're beginning to see where I'm going, aren't you?"

"So, these survivors found these leeches attached to them when they came out of the swamp?" she asked.

"With foodstuffs being so scarce and their worries about contamination, a few people harvested the leeches and thought they might be palatable enough to eat," he said.

She shuddered.

"Over time, the few scientists who were left looked into the practice of eating leeches and found that they serve a similar function to the Asian palm civet," he said.

"What do you mean?" she asked.

"Something in their makeup creates the perfect process for extracting the essential ingredient to eradicating the space plague in survivors," he said. "In drawing out the blood of those who are immune, the leeches purify the compounds and make them the perfect food for those of us who were not so lucky the first time."

"How in the world do we keep that up?" she asked.

"If you were given the choice of doing nothing and watching more people die from the space plague or doing something admittedly distasteful to help more people survive, which would you choose?" he asked.

"So, you're saying those who are immune voluntarily troll through the swamps to attract leeches to them and then harvest the results?" she asked in a whisper.

"I know I would," he said. "And with a little butter and fresh garlic, it's something I can swallow."

DREAM MAKER

She looked up, thinking. "Yes," she said, "I did."

"And were the honeysuckles everything you remembered?" he asked.

Startled, she looked at him. "How did you know?"

"Remember how you would pull the drop of nectar from the flower and taste it on your tongue?" he asked, smiling.

"Of course, I do," she said. "But how do you—"

"Someday, you'll even experience the smell of the honeysuckle in your dreams," he said.

"I don't understand," she said. "You talk about my dream as if you were there."

"I was," he said.

"How can you be in my dream?" she asked.

"I've been wanting to talk to you about that," he said.

She looked at him again. "Go on."

"I've never told anyone about this before," he began. "You're the first."

"The first what?" she asked.

"Have you heard of Jung's collective unconscious?" he asked her.

"You mean the theory that all of our consciousnesses are connected to an oversoul?" she asked.

"That's the general idea," he agreed. "It is the equivalent of the biosphere, that we are all a part of the same organism."

"I'm with you so far," she said.

"Well, are you aware that scientists posit that dreaming is one way our minds stay sane?" he asked.

"I have heard that dreaming is the mind at play," she admitted. "And that play is necessary for our good health, both physical and mental."

"There is a role I play in the collective unconscious," he said. "Along with several dozen others, I am here to encourage your dreams so that you are healthy when you link to that collective unconscious."

"You encourage my dreams?" she repeated slowly.

"As in all life, necessity causes change," he said. "And our dreams are what separate us from all other creatures."

"So, this makes you . . ." she started.

"A dream-maker," he finished for her. "I am here to help you dream."

"Why are you telling me now?" she asked him.

"Because it is not an easy task," he said. Then he looked down. "And it's a lonely one."

She put her hand on his arm. "I'm so sorry," she said.

He looked into her eyes. "I wanted you to know," he said.

"Why me?" she asked.

"Because I love you," he said, taking her into his arms. "And I wanted you to know before I did this." He pulled her into his arms and kissed her.

Suddenly, they were transported to a lush landscape of intense color with rolling hills and towering trees. In their embrace they floated a few feet off of the ground, hovering in place as they felt the profound emotional connection.

"Oh, my!" she whispered.

"You ain't seen nothing yet," he said. He kissed her again.

They moved, soaring over the landscape, staying a few feet off the ground as they flew through the trees and over the hills. Soon, they were flying faster and faster, yet they felt they were standing still in the moment.

He finally came up for air. "I couldn't very well do this without telling you I was a dream-maker," he said.

"I'm glad you did," she said. She leaned in and kissed him.

Suddenly, she drew back.

"That's not the only reason," she said.

"What do you mean?" he asked.

"Don't play innocent with me," she said.

"What are you talking about?" he asked.

"I'm talking about our link," she said. "When we kiss, the connection goes both ways."

"So, what are you sensing from me?" he asked her.

"This isn't just about you declaring your love for me," she said.

"That's true," he agreed, "although I *do* love you."

Her voice caught. "You're leaving," she managed.

"True," he said quietly.

"Why?" she asked, her voice breaking.

"Because being a dream-maker takes a heavy toll," he said. "My heart, my mind, my very soul are worn out."

"And you're leaving me?" she cried.

"Yes," he said, stroking her hair. "Because I know how brave and strong you are, and I know you are capable of so much good."

"But what does this mean?" she asked him through her tears.

"It means that I am passing on my mantle of dream-maker to you," he said, "so that you will go out into the world and continue my work of encouraging others' dreams."

"But the world is in such turmoil," she protested.

"That's why we need you," he said. "Now more than ever."

TAKE ME TO YOUR LEADER

"That's correct," the alien replied.

"Are you an alien?" he asked.

"Yes, I am," the alien replied. "But I am not an extraterrestrial."

"What?" he asked, startled.

"That would mean I am from outer space," the alien said.

"You're not?" the man asked.

"No, I'm from another dimension," the alien said.

"Another dimension?" he asked.

"One of the many other multiverses," the alien said.

"What does that make you?" he asked.

"I suppose that makes me an extradimensional," the alien said.

"Is this where you ask me to take you to my leader?" he asked.

"No," the alien said. "We've been monitoring your race for some time, and we've come to the conclusion you have no leader."

"What do you mean?" the man said. "We have a presidential campaign going on right now."

"And you feel that a true leader is running?" the alien asked.

"Well, no," he said.

"Besides, your country does not represent the human race," the alien said.

"Even if we're the most powerful nation on earth?" he asked.

"With a fraction of the population," the alien answered.

"You would go by populations?" he asked.

"Hardly," the alien replied. "Sheer numbers mean nothing when it comes to leadership."

"How then do you determine a leader?" he asked.

"Someone with clarity of vision for the race," the alien said.

"And you're saying we don't have anyone like that?" he asked.

"Dictators have their own agendas, and they do nothing to benefit their people," the alien said. "And in countries like yours that hold elections, we see the same thing going on."

"What do you mean?" he asked.

"We see dichotomies prevailing around the world," the alien said.

"Dichotomies?" he asked.

"People are taking sides and shouting at each other without listening," the alien replied. "They are not thinking; they are reacting."

"You're saying it's not just America?" he asked.

"No, it is a true spirit of the times, a zeitgeist of epic proportions," the alien replied.

"And we have no leader?' he asked.

"None that we see," the alien said. "And we don't foresee one emerging anytime soon."

"So, why are you talking to me?" he asked.

"Well, we've been meaning to make contact for some time," the alien replied. "And we knew talking with people who currently are in power would be a waste of time."

"So, why me?" he asked.

"We wanted to find someone who would not overreact or become violent," the alien said. "We wanted to talk with someone who would not freak out and begin babbling. And we wanted to find someone human who could have a decent, meaningful conversation." The alien paused. "Without looking at his phone."

"And you chose me?" he asked, surprised.

"Yes, we did," the alien replied.

"What is it about me?" he asked.

"Your clarity of thought, your vision, your understanding of what is and is not important," the alien replied.

"Really?" he asked.

The alien eyed him. "And you wouldn't start a war."

"Not me," he said.

"Exactly," the alien said.

"So, what do we do now?" he asked.

"Now that we've met," the alien said, "let me take you to our leader. I really think you'll like him."

ELEMENTARY, MY DEAR WATSON

"Anything worth sharing?" she asked.

"We've discussed artificial intelligence," he said. "And we've discussed how we can tell if it is intelligent with the Turing test. Right?"

"So far," she replied.

"But now my question is, is intelligence the same thing as consciousness?" he asked.

"You mean it's not?" she replied.

"Well, I know a machine might fool a judge, but is it truly self- aware?" he asked.

"That's a good question," she replied.

"IBM's Watson can rapidly scan millions of pieces of healthcare data to make connections and arrive at diagnoses," he said. "But I don't know if it is truly self-aware."

"I don't know either," she said.

"For that matter, can a supercomputer like Watson make any connection to the world around it?" he said.

"I'm not following you," she said.

"The older I get, the more I feel a genuine connection to this world around me," he said. "I am a living, breathing part of this biosphere, a sentient molecule in this body, Earth."

"Which means what?" she asked him.

"Can a machine or a computer have that same kind of relationship with our planet?" he asked.

"I don't know," she replied.

"To me, this may be the true difference between intelligence and consciousness," he said.

"Why do you say that?" she asked.

"Intelligence could be the ability to make connections and retrieve data to formulate hypotheses," he said. "But consciousness is the organic connection we have to the world around us."

"That's a different way of seeing it," she said.

"They have never been able to measure where consciousness comes from," he said. "They have been able to map the electrical impulses of our synapses and neurons firing, but they haven't been able to draw a definitive connection to consciousness."

"That's true," she replied. "They still haven't been able to say with any certainty where it comes from."

"Quantum physicists have opined that the cosmic strings they have identified in space may well be the celestial equivalent of our consciousness," he replied. "Just on a much grander scale."

"Space consciousness, if you will," she said.

"Exactly," he agreed. "Which leads me to think that intelligence is not the same as consciousness. It may be necessary to reach the level of consciousness, but it is only one step in that direction."

"So artificial intelligence would not necessarily be conscious," she said.

"Not if we are accepting my premise," he said.

"Well, I guess we'll never know," she said.

"Oh, like all great puzzles, we won't know until science creates a way for us to measure consciousness," he said.

"There's one thing we could do," she replied.

"What's that?" he said.

"We could ask Watson," she replied, smiling.

BRAIN TRUST

"What is?" she asked him.

"There's more to the current political atmosphere than opinion," he replied.

"What could it be other than opinion?" she asked.

"It appears that there is actual brain physiology involved," he said.

"You've lost me," she replied.

"Evidently, they have done MRI studies recently on the brains of conservatives and liberals," he said.

"They X-rayed their heads and found nothing?" she joked.

"Actually, it really doesn't support any assumptions we have about intelligence," he replied. "But it does show some surprising differences in the actual brain structures of each."

"Do tell," she said.

"I'm serious," he replied. "It turns out liberals have a bigger anterior cingulate cortex, and conservatives have a bigger right amygdala."

"That means nothing to me," she said. "I have no idea what those areas of the brain regulate."

"Let's start with the idea that political orientation is associated with the psychological processes for managing fear and uncertainty," he said.

"Okay, I'm following you so far," she replied.

"The amygdala is involved with fear processing," he said. "People with a larger amygdala are more sensitive to fear, which means they're more inclined to integrate conservative views into their belief systems."

"Meaning fear resonates within them more so?" she asked.

"Exactly," he said.

"What about the liberals?" she asked.

"Liberals, on the other hand, have a bigger anterior cingulate cortex, which has been linked to a tolerance to uncertainty and conflicts," he said. "This capacity enables them to accept more liberal views."

"Are these the only differences you found in your research?" she asked.

"No, there's more," he said.

"I can't wait," she said.

"Another difference is conservatives focus on preventing negative outcomes, while liberals focus on advancing positive outcomes," he said.

"That seems to make sense," she said.

"That notion translates into the Left providing for group members' welfare and the Right protecting the group from harm," he said.

"The old approach and avoidance motivation," she said.

"Correct," he replied. "Conservatives focus on preventing negative outcomes by trying to regulate society by restraints in the interest of social order."

"That sounds like a lot of legislation we've been hearing about from state legislatures," she said. "And the liberals?"

"Liberals advance positive outcomes by trying to regulate society via interventions in the interest of social justice," he said.

"Which again sounds like the issues of gay marriage and LGBT equality," she replied.

"Funny how it all lines up when you understand the underlying physical differences," he said.

"Anything else?" she asked.

"Oddly enough, conservatives sleep more soundly and have more dreams, although they're on the more mundane side," he said. "Liberals sleep more restlessly and have more active, bizarre dream lives."

"Well, I know where you fall in that final analysis," she said.

"You're not going to ask me if I dream in color?" he asked her.

"I don't have to," she replied, smiling.

THE POWER OF MYTH

"What do you mean?" he asked.

"He said that mythological figures are not only symptoms, but they are also statements of certain spiritual principles that represent the human psyche itself," she explained.

"You lost me," he said.

"It is a common dictum that if God did not exist, man would create Him," she replied.

"I've heard that," he said.

"And the mythical gods reflect all-too-human principles, such as love, war, wisdom, mischief, and the like," she said.

"So, what is your point?" he asked.

"You are a writer, a creator," she said.

"That's right," he said.

"You have been put on this world to add to its existence and imbue it with meaning," she said.

"Thank you," he said. "I think."

"And when we live in a time that does not embody those intrinsic values we so desperately need, we must create our own mythical gods to represent them," she said.

"What are you saying?" he asked.

"Do you remember how the ancients would elevate those gods and name constellations after them, that they might see their gods and heroes in the skies every night?" she asked.

"Like Orion," he said. "Or the Pleiades."

"Exactly," she said.

"And what does that have to do with me?" he asked.

"We need our gods to come back," she said. "We need them to give us shining examples of the best in ourselves, so that we might once again aspire to such greatness."

"Again, where do I fit in all of this?" he asked.

"We need you to become our mythical god of creativity, a muse who will seek to inspire us to greatness in all of the arts," she said.

"I'm not sure I am worthy of such an honor," he said.

"Oh, you're worthy," she replied. "You have proven yourself fit by creating stories, lifting us up with ideas we have not commonly seen or heard."

"Why me?" he said.

"Because in these troubled times, we have lost our way and failed to honor those gods we once knew," she said. "We need new gods to resurrect our spirits and refill our lives with meaning." She paused, looking at him. "And truth."

"I'm flattered," he said.

"That connotes opportunism," she said. "I speak of necessity."

"What must I do?" he asked.

"That's the rub," she said.

"What do you mean?" he asked.

"Just as the ancients elevated their gods and heroes to the stars, we must elevate our own to such heights," she said.

"What does that entail?" he said.

"That you must leave this earthly realm and ascend to your new position of myth," she said.

"You mean I must die?" he asked.

"And be reborn as the myth we so desperately need," she replied.

FAMILY VALUES

"Yep," the old man replied.

"You know they're coming after you," the kid asked.

The old man looked at him and nodded. "Yep."

"Aren't you scared?" the kid asked.

The old man shook his head. "Nope."

"Aren't you afraid of dying?" the kid asked.

"Nope," the old man replied.

"I don't understand," the kid said, shaking his head.

The old man looked down at his hands.

"Did you ever see *Straw Dogs*, the one with Dustin Hoffman?" he asked.

"I saw the remake," the kid replied.

"Not the same," the old man said.

"Why does it matter?" the kid asked.

"Hoffman played a mild-mannered man who returns to his wife's country to live with her," the old man said.

"So what?" the kid asked.

"Men from town came after her," the old man said. "They thought the husband couldn't stop them."

The old man paused to see if the kid was listening.

"They were wrong," he said.

"What does that have to do with you?" the kid asked.

"Before there was a Jason Bourne, Robert Ludlum wrote *The Matlock Papers*," the old man said.

"Not the TV show," the kid said.

"No, not by a long shot," the old man said. "Ludlum's Matlock was a professor who was wrongfully caught up in the world of spies. They thought he couldn't possibly survive without the proper training."

"What made you think of that?" the kid asked.

"Some men came and hurt my daughter," the old man said.

"Are they the gangsters?" the kid asked.

"*They* think so," the old man replied.

"But you don't," the kid said.

"Not really," the old man said.

"Is your daughter okay?" the kid asked.

"She is now," the old man said.

"What did she say afterward?" the kid asked.

"She said she told them they'd better hope the police caught them before I did," the old man said.

The kid laughed. "That took some balls."

The old man nodded. "That's my girl."

"So, you're not afraid those gangsters are going to send someone after you?" the kid asked.

The old man looked at the kid. "They already have."

"What happened?" the kid asked.

"I took care of it," the old man replied.

"You took care of it?" the kid asked. "What does that mean?"

"Just what it says," the old man replied.

"How many of them were there?" the kid asked.

"You mean so far?" the old man replied.

"So far?" the kid asked. "Has it happened more than once?"

The old man simply nodded.

"How many times have they come at you?" the kid asked incredulously.

"Fifteen," the old man replied.

"You've faced fifteen gangsters and lived?" the kid asked. "What if they send more?"

The old man looked hard at the kid. "I look forward to it."

"How in the world are you doing it?" the kid asked.

The old man smiled. "Never underestimate a smart man. He will find ways to defeat you that you've never even thought of."

LARRY

LARRY WAS TWENTY-FOUR.

He'd only been in the people-hurting business a couple of months. But he was anxious to move up the ladder. When he heard about taking out an old man, he jumped on it. A job like this, and he could start making a name for himself.

He went up the front steps to the porch and found the front door unlocked.

Man, this is going to be easier than I thought, he thought. He looked into the living room and dining room and then glanced into the kitchen. Nobody. *Old man must be upstairs*, he thought.

He went up the steps slowly, turned at the landing and started up the next set of stairs, keeping an eye on the two bedroom doors in front of him.

He heard a whisper but didn't think anything of it until he felt a pinch in his back.

"Too bad you didn't check the layout before you got here," a voice behind him said.

The pinch became a sharp pain.

"A lot of these old Victorian houses have butler stairs," the voice said.

The pain became intense. So much so that it took his breath away.

"That's an ice pick," the voice said. "I slipped it between your ribs and am just now scrambling your heart."

Larry couldn't feel his arms or legs. He couldn't breathe. Then he couldn't see.

The old man withdrew the ice pick and wiped it on Larry's shirt.

"That was almost too easy," he said. But his words fell on deaf ears.

SANTIAGO

In fact, he had been deported twice before and had managed to sneak back into the country each time. Nobody really knew him. And he liked it that way.

Except one guy from back home.

Jorge. Jorge said he could make some fast money. Santiago liked the sound of that. He just had to off an old dude. That sounded even better.

He drew out his knife and checked the blade one last time with his thumb. Nice and razor sharp. He was feeling good, walking under the pin oaks lining the street where the old dude lived. He felt so good that he started whistling under his breath.

The next thing he knew, he couldn't see.

Something had dropped down over his face. No, his whole head. And suddenly, a band tightened around his neck. He was jerked off his feet. He dropped the knife and clawed at the band around his neck with both hands.

The only problem was his fingers couldn't get any purchase. It wasn't a rope. Was it wire?

Just when he thought he was making headway with the band, a heavy weight fell on his shoulders.

The band cut deeply into his neck, choking off his air and sending his blood streaming down his body. One more bounce, and his head separated from his body.

"You never should have come down my street," the old man said to the body at his feet.

BIG JOHN

BIG JOHN CRACKED HIS KNUCKLES.

Big John's hands were big. Big John's feet were big. In fact, at 6'8", all of Big John was big. He'd been a longshoreman, a roadie, a bouncer, even a prizefighter. What he didn't have in style, he made up for in size.

So, it was natural for him to become an enforcer. After all, he liked working with his hands. And his boss sent him down to the old industrial section to find an old man who was bothering them.

He was surrounded by old warehouses. Here and there, new businesses were moving into the industrial spaces. A craft brewery here, a tattoo parlor there. The old man was supposed to like hanging out at that brewery. And the boss said he had to go. That was cool with Big John. He didn't need anything other than his hands to take care of business.

Suddenly, an old man came out from behind one of the warehouses.

I wonder if this is him, he thought.

He doesn't look like much to me, he thought.

As the old man got closer, Big John recognized him.

"Hey," Big John said. "I got something for you."

He smiled at his little joke. The old man kept right on coming.

"You hear me?" Big John said.

"Yeah," the old man said. "And I've got something for you."

He walked up to Big John and kicked him right in the knee.

Big John clutched his knee and started falling.

"Steel toes," the old man said.

As Big John fell, the old man drew his hand back and then shoved his palm up into Big John's big nose. The sound of the cartilage snapping echoed off of the warehouse walls.

Big John was dead before he hit the ground.

"The bigger they are," the old man said.

RAYSHAWN

He'd been walking the streets of Lambert's Point his whole life. He knew every face, every nook and cranny. And when there was a buzz, he heard it.

He just heard there was coin to be had for offing an old white dude.

Rayshawn had a zip gun in his waistband and nunchucks in his back pocket. *I could cap his ass or beat him down either way*, Rayshawn thought. He walked down Powhatan to where it doglegged toward Hampton Boulevard.

Up ahead, he saw an old white dude sitting on the curb. It looked like he was drinking from a plastic cup.

No way, he thought.

He flipped his dreadlocks out of his face and looked again. He couldn't believe his luck. It was the old white dude they were talking about.

He started toward the man.

"Hey, old dude," Rayshawn said. "What you doing in my neighborhood?"

"*Your* neighborhood?" the old man said. "I was dumping my trash over there when your folks were kids."

"Might be," Rayshawn said, reaching for the zip gun in his waistband. "But it's *mine* now!"

The old man picked up the plastic cup and threw its contents in Rayshawn's face.

Gasoline!

The old man pulled out an old metal Zippo lighter and snapped it open.

"Wait, man!" Rayshawn yelled. "Don't do it!"

The old man casually flipped the lit lighter onto Rayshawn.

As he started screaming, the old man said, "It's not your neighborhood anymore."

CARLOTTA

CARLOTTA HAD LIVED ON WILLOUGHBY SPIT FOR TEN YEARS.
First, she was a young Navy wife left on her own every time her husband deployed. Then she was a divorced mother with one child. She tried turning tricks, but she couldn't handle it. So she started selling drugs.

Over time, she found the money was okay. But she was constantly on the lookout for ways to make more.

A gangbanger from the projects told her about a job. All she had to do was take out an old white man. That was it.

She had an old .32 her ex had when they were married. She figured if she could get close enough, she could shoot him in the head and be done.

Simple.

She took to walking along the bay at dusk because she had heard the old man sometimes walked that stretch of beach.

The sun had just dipped below the horizon. She thought she had the beach to herself, but then she saw an old man sitting on the jetty by the water. Could it be?

She moved closer.

It was him!

Now she just had to get close enough to get him with one shot. She picked her way gingerly along the jetty, trying hard not to slip into the water. She had never learned to swim.

When she finally got within twenty feet of him, she smiled and called, "Are you looking for company?"

The old man looked up at her and smiled back.

"Sure," he said. She moved closer, putting her hand in the pocket with the .32.

When she was five feet away, she was pulling the .32 when the old man lifted a Taser and shot her in the neck.

The electroshock stunned her, and she fell off the jetty. Unable to move, she felt the water cover her completely.

The old man looked out at the bay.

"Tide's going out," he said.

TERRY

TERRY LIKED THROWING KNIVES. HE HAD BEEN THROWING knives his whole life. Or at least since he was eight. And after over three decades of practice, he could shave the wings off a fly at twenty paces. He even had a rep.

So, when his boys started talking about a big job that involved real money, he felt like it was right up his alley. He just had to find some old guy and use him for target practice.

He started hanging out in the new NEON district of Norfolk where all the hipsters and artists were collecting. He showed up at all the new eateries opening on Granby Street. He came to all the First Friday art events with live music.

And he kept practicing.

Finally, he was walking down Wilson Street behind Work Release and saw an old man sitting on a low brick wall ahead of him. He slipped one of his knives out as he kept walking. Right when he raised his arm, the old man bent over as if to tie his shoe. The knife sailed over his head.

Damn!

That was the first time Terry had missed in years.

He was just reaching for another throwing knife when the old man sat up and sailed a knife back at him underhand.

No way!

The knife caught him right in the chest. Terry looked down in disbelief. How in the world could this old guy get the drop on him?

The old man walked over to Terry as Terry sank to his knees.

"Two can play at this game," the old man said.

Terry looked up at him. The old man reached over and grasped the knife handle, pushing it in and twisting it before pulling it out.

"And I've been practicing," the old man said.

HIRO

HIRO HAD BEEN IN THE STATES FOR OVER FORTY YEARS.

He came from Japan to go to school and stayed. For a long time, he ran a dojo and taught karate to young kids. At least, he did until he hurt his back and had to quit. And he got hooked on painkillers.

Now he did odd jobs for anybody who would hire him. He didn't need a lot, just enough for another few pills. He used to be able to kick a beer can off the top of a stop sign, even though he was only 5'4". He could still do good moves, but he couldn't keep it up for hours. Fifteen minutes here, twenty minutes there, and he'd be done for the day.

He hadn't had his daily dose when he heard about an old man who needed to be handled. The price they were talking would keep him in pills for at least a month if he watched it.

Why not, he thought. *It shouldn't take long.*

He decided to look for the old man down on Granby Street. He had heard the man liked to wander around downtown in the financial district. He rounded the corner of the 400 block and scanned the sidewalk, extending his senses to set himself up for the killing strike. The light ahead changed, and he started across the cross street.

Suddenly, he heard a whistle and turned.

The end of a blowpipe appeared and he felt a small prick in his neck. Immediately, his body seized up.

The old man walked up to him.

"Curare," he said.

Hiro's vision started to slip away.

"With all your skills, you didn't expect me to let you get close, did you?" the old man said.

STRIKER

STRIKER WAS THE BEST MARKSMAN IN HIS BATTALION. HE could hit a dragonfly at 100 yards. He could explode a melon at 1,000 yards. But he had a temper. And a dishonorable discharge. On the street his skills didn't translate well in a nine-to-five world.

So, he fell back on his one good skill to make a living. That's why the hit on this old man was perfect.

He stalked the old man and got his routine down. The old man would go home each night, go upstairs to his office and sit at his desk. His silhouette would show against the blinds. Striker found a spot 150 yards away with a clear line of sight. There was no way he could miss. And at that distance, he'd have the time to make a clean getaway.

So, tonight was the night.

He watched the old man get home and go upstairs. The light came on, and the silhouette appeared. Striker dialed in his scope. He checked the wind direction and speed. He made sure no one else was out and about. Then he settled down and sighted in on the old man.

Just as he held his breath to squeeze the trigger, he felt a tap on his head.

"Never read Arthur Conan Doyle, did you?" the old man said.

Striker was confused.

"You were about to kill a dummy," the old man explained.

Then he pulled the trigger.

"Who's the dummy now?" he said.

CHAD AND BRAD

CHAD AND BRAD WERE TWINS. THEY LOOKED ALIKE. THEY sounded alike. They even dressed alike. They started boosting cars in Norview for joyrides when they were thirteen. After two years in juvie, they moved up to bigger things. And they always did their jobs together. Breaking and entering. Burglary. Armed robbery. Assault. Twin rap sheets as long as your arm.

They obviously had a good time being bad.

So, when they heard about a hit with a hefty price tag, they were stoked. Especially when they heard it was an old dude.

One afternoon at dusk, they were walking along a fence between Tidewater Drive and the railroad tracks. Brad saw an old man on the other side of the fence just ahead of them.

"Chad," he said, nodding in the old man's direction.

Chad smiled. "Hey, old dude?" he called.

The old man looked up at him.

"Are you the one everybody's talking about?" he asked.

The old man just looked at him.

"Are you deaf?" Brad asked.

The old man turned to him.

"Can't you talk?" Chad demanded.

The old man shook his head, looking down.

"Hey, we just want to talk to you," Brad insisted.

"Yeah, especially if you're the one," Chad said.

The old man smiled at them and beckoned for them to come over.

"He's the one!" Brad said excitedly to Chad.

"Let's get him!" Chad said.

They jumped on the fence and started to climb over it. The old man bent down and grabbed a wire. He touched the wire to the fence.

Sparks and smoke came off the twins.

"Two for one," the old man said.

SOPHIA

CHEMIST. COOK. ALCHEMIST.

She liked to think she was all three.

She also imagined she was directly descended from the de Medici family. After all, she had all these recipes. Her results were in demand. And the whole food truck fad worked in her favor.

She'd been zipping up and down I-95 for the last two years, taking jobs in different cities and then hitting the road. So this one in Norfolk sounded perfect. They were having a food truck rodeo today, and she heard through the grapevine that the old man was a real nut for Carolina barbecue. She had the right special sauce just for him.

She pulled her truck up next to the Plot in downtown for the lunchtime crowd.

Of course, she cooked a virgin batch to sell to the office workers that came by, and she got several compliments. The crowds finally died down around 2:15. Around 2:45, she saw an old man walking down Granby Street.

It was him!

"Can I interest you in a barbecue sandwich?" she asked out her side window.

The old man looked inside.

"Nice truck," he said.

"Thanks," she said. "You want to see the inside?" *This is almost too easy,* she thought.

"I'd love to," he replied. As he walked around to the door in the back, she pulled out the special sandwich. He climbed up inside and looked around.

"Bigger than it looks," he said.

"Just the right size," she said. She handed him the sandwich. "Enjoy."

He grabbed her wrist and cuffed her to the range before she could react.

"What are you doing?" she protested.

"Serving you a little lunch," he said, pinching her nose until she opened her mouth. He put some of the doctored barbecue into her mouth.

"*Bon appétit,*" he whispered in her ear.

MO

MO LIVED ON THE STREETS. HAD FOR YEARS. WINTER WAS coming, and he needed a score that would help set him up in a flophouse close to downtown.

He gravitated toward the parking garages to stay out of the rain. Even knew where all the cameras were so he could avoid them. Each garage had at least one corner or alcove that he could hide in. Mo was small. He didn't need much room.

Then he heard something. Something different. Buzz on the street unlike anything he had ever heard.

An old man who liked to walk around downtown had a price on his head. And the dude liked to go up to the top floor of each parking garage to look out over the city. Mo understood that. He liked doing that, too. As long as it wasn't raining.

Maybe he could do something about it. But it had to be easy. He wasn't a strong man.

Some of these garages were six and seven stories high. High enough to do the job.

He was hiding in his spot in the City Hall Avenue garage when he saw the old man walk by. Silently, he crawled out of his hole and followed the man. The old man took the elevator. Mo took the stairs.

When he got to the top, he looked around the corner and saw the old man at the edge of the lot, looking out toward the *Wisconsin*. Thinking the old man was lost in thought, Mo decided to chance it. He crept up until he was just six feet behind him. Working up his courage, he took a deep breath and lunged at the man.

The old man spun around, caught Mo's neck and sent him sailing over the edge.

"It's not the fall that'll kill you," the old man said. "It's the sudden stop."

MAGDA

living. To a younger man, she was a cougar. To an older man, she was a handsome woman. People said she looked like Sophia Loren. But she was more Czech than Italian.

She had wiles, and she knew how to work them. That's why people used her. She worked her way with men. And did them in when they least expected it.

She saw the old man on Granby Street near the 219.

Maybe I can get him to buy me a drink, she thought, smiling. She walked over.

"Looks like you could use a friend," she said to him.

"Can't we all?" he replied.

"Are you thirsty?" she asked.

"I could drink," he said.

"Good," she said. "I'm buying."

She hooked her arm in his and started walking.

"Can we stop at my car?" he asked. "I want to grab my jacket."

"Sure, darling," she said. "Whatever makes you comfortable."

They turned up Plume Street and cut up the alley beside the parking garage.

"Are you parked in here?" she asked.

"Yeah, I got here earlier," he replied.

"Mmm, nice and dark," she purred, turning toward him and pulling him close.

Just as she was about to kiss him, he said, "You know, I don't have any illusions."

"Whatever do you mean?" she asked, feigning innocence.

"I know I'm an old man," he replied.

"You're not *that* old," she protested.

He curled his arm around her head and gave it a violent twist, snapping her neck.

"Old enough to know a woman like you would never talk to a man like me unless money was involved," he replied, slipping her body behind some trashcans.

CHAUFFEUR

He loved the sound of that. In fact, he was thrilled he had it as a street name. Instant cred. He had the wheels. He had the skills. He had the sheer chutzpah to carry it off.

He was a wheelman who took people out. He even had his own power washer and generator to make sure he cleaned up good after every job. A true professional.

So, he was riding around town when he got the call. The old man was on his route. He was down in Freemason Harbor close to the Pagoda. All the Chauffer had to do was to drive by and clip the old dude right there on the paving bricks. How hard could it be?

He revved his engine and peeled out, leaving a tire trail on the pavement.

He raced around the Freemason Harbor neighborhood, slowing down for the cobblestones on Freemason and Botetourt. He kept his eye on the rearview mirror in case the old man popped up behind him. Up ahead, a figure emerged under a streetlight. The light flared in his windshield as he tried to make out who it was.

It was him!

The Chauffeur grinned to himself. This was picture perfect! He floored it, keeping the old man centered in his sites on the hood ornament. Just as he was racing to finish him, the old man stepped aside.

And revealed a steel-reinforced concrete anti-terrorism barrier behind him.

The Camaro SS-350 hit the immovable barrier at fifty miles an hour. And the Chauffeur launched through the windshield and into the murky waters around the *Wisconsin.*

"Ole" the old man said.

KEIKO

smaller than she liked.

Hard for an exotic Asian woman to disappear in a crowd when there wasn't a crowd. But she was a professional. So she claimed her bags and headed to the taxi stand. When she arrived at her downtown hotel, she found an envelope waiting for her at the front desk. The old man who looked up at her from the photo inside didn't seem intimidating at all.

At the same time, she knew she wasn't the first to try. She needed to be careful. Very, very careful. She decided she would have to watch him for a long time before deciding how to make her move. And shadowing was one thing she was good at.

It didn't take her long to figure out where the old man lived. It was on a tree-lined street with Victorian homes. She watched him to see where he went every day. She noted his grocery store, his doctor, his watering holes. She even followed him to the Slover Library in downtown Norfolk. Day after day, she followed him on his daily rounds, plotting when and where she would make her move.

Finally, one night, she saw him enter his neighborhood bar. His routine was to have a few drinks and dinner before driving home. Maybe tonight would be the night.

Knowing he would take his time, she relaxed for a second.

She suddenly felt a hard barrel against the back of her head.

"You made three mistakes," the voice said.

She looked left and right, desperately looking for a way to escape.

"You came after me on my home turf," the voice said.

She calculated what moves she could make before he pulled the trigger.

"You thought I wouldn't notice you shadowing me," the voice said.

She tensed her back muscles in anticipation of her move. The last sound she heard was the click of the .22 target pistol's firing pin hitting the cartridge.

"And you worked for the same people who hurt my daughter," the voice said.

LITTLE GIRL

"YOU KNOW I'M RIGHT," SHE SAID.

He looked at her, grief-stricken.

"You've been here the whole time," she insisted.

He nodded, looking down.

"You know what I've been through," she said.

"Every step of the way," he admitted, choking.

"And you've seen the toll it's taken on me," she said.

"And it's been killing me," he whispered.

"But there is no one else," she said.

"I don't know if I can," he only just managed.

"I'm counting on you," she said.

This time, he could only nod.

"You've been here," she said again.

Again, he nodded.

"Every session, every treatment, every therapy," she said.

He put his head in his hands.

"It's been a long road for the both of us," she said.

"I know it's been rougher on you," he finally managed.

"And you know it's only going to get worse," she said, not unkindly.

"But you've already been through so much," he cried.

"I think that's my point," she said quietly.

He shook his head.

"I wouldn't ask this of you if I didn't love you," she said.

"I know," he said, crying softly.

"And I wouldn't ask except I know how very much you love me," she said.

"I know," he said through his tears.

"And I know you don't want to see me suffer anymore," she said.

"No, I don't," he whispered, his voice breaking.

"I need you to do this," she said.

"I know," he whispered.

"It's time," she said.

"I know," he whispered again.

He picked up the pillow.

"You'll always be my little girl," he choked, tears streaming down his cheeks.

Just before he placed the pillow over her face, she smiled up at him and said, "I love you, Daddy."

SHAKEDOWN CRUISE

"I'M GLAD THEY'RE FOLLOWING THE TRADITION OF THE SHAKE-down cruise for our star cruiser," Lieutenant Banner said.

"Makes sense to orbit the earth a few times to make sure all the bugs have been worked out before we head to the Moon," Sergeant Phillips replied.

"Having parents along adds its own special stress, doesn't it?" Lt. Banner said. She checked her log. "We have twenty-eight of them on board."

"What could go wrong?" Phillips asked.

"Don't tempt fate," the lieutenant said, knocking on wood.

Jack looked over at his shipmate. "Johnson, my dad is such a handful," he said.

"What do you mean?" Johnson asked.

"He's so proud I followed in his footsteps," Jack replied. "But he takes it all so seriously."

"Unlike you," Johnson replied.

Jack laughed. "I don't sleep with a pistol under my pillow."

"Neither should he," Johnson said. "At least not up here."

"You know my dad," Jack said. "If there's a way to get his pistol on board, he'll find it."

"He better have those special mushrooming bullets," Johnson said. "Or he'll punch a hole in the hull and let out all the oxygen."

Jack Sr. wandered around the star cruiser, trying to get his bearings. He tried every hatch and looked in every door.

"Can I help you, sir?" an enlisted man asked him.

"Working on my space legs," Jack Sr. growled.

"It would be best if you found your way back to your stateroom, sir," the enlisted man said. "We only have one more orbit to go before we return to earth."

"Jack," Lt. Banner said. "I've been looking for you."

"What's up, L-T?" Jack asked.

"That's Lt. Banner to you," Banner said. "I'm hearing some strange reports about your dad."

"What do you mean?" Jack asked, concerned.

"He's getting into things and alarming some of our shipmates," the lieutenant said.

"Alarming them how?" Jack asked.

"One of them said they thought they saw him with a military issue pistol," Banner replied.

"That's not good," Jack said.

"We need to run this down and make sure it's only a rumor," Banner said.

"Yes, sir," Jack said. "I'll get right on it."

"Hey, Jack, I just saw your dad down outside the mess," Johnson said.

"What is he doing down there?" Jack asked exasperatedly.

"I have no idea, but he was in a strange mood," Johnson said.

"Strange how?" Jack asked.

"Muttering to himself," Johnson said. "Like there's something wrong."

"That's not good," Jack said.

Jack Sr. looked around him.

"Helluva way to run a ship," he said, shaking his head.

He saw blinking lights on the comm system.

"That doesn't look good," he said. He pulled out his pistol and chambered a round. "I'd better be ready."

An enlisted man walking by saw the pistol. "Sir! What are you doing?"

"What does it look like, sailor?" Jack Sr. said. "I'm getting ready."

"Ready for what, sir?" the enlisted man asked nervously.

"Ready for anything," Jack Sr. said. Then he smiled darkly.

"Sir, I'm going to have to ask you to stand down and hand me your weapon," the enlisted man said.

"That's not going to happen," Jack Sr. said.

Jack heard a shot.

"That's definitely not good," he said and started running. Before he reached the first hatchway, he heard another shot. He stuck his head through and saw an enlisted man lying on the deck.

His dad looked up at him. "He shot at me," Jack Sr. said.

"What happened?" Jack asked.

"He missed," Jack Sr. said. "I didn't.

Jack saw the expanding pool of blood under the enlisted man.

"Dad!" Jack exclaimed. "You've got to give me your pistol!"

"Not gonna happen, boyo!" his dad insisted.

"What's wrong with you?" Jack said.

"Bunch of pansies running this cruiser," his dad answered. "And I'm not gonna let them get away with it!"

Jack pulled his pistol and pointed it at his dad.

"Dad!" he exclaimed. "I don't know what you think you are doing, but you are on a United States star cruiser. And you are a guest of the captain, coming along on a shakedown cruise."

His dad stared at him. "That's what you want me to think," Jack Sr. said.

"I don't understand," Jack said.

"I know the truth," Jack Sr. said. "You all are in on it!"

"In on what?" Jack asked, confused.

"Folks who know nothing about the military are trying to run it," Jack Sr. replied.

"What are you talking about?" Jack said.

"I'm here to take back what's rightfully mine!" Jack Sr. insisted. He raised his pistol.

"Dad! Don't!" Jack screamed.

His pistol fired.

His dad had taught him to shoot when he was eight. Like Jack Sr., he had an eye for shooting accurately. And he had the training to do what was necessary.

He put a round into his dad's chest, stopping him from shooting more people on what was supposed to be a milk run.

Lt. Banner found Jack in sickbay, sitting and crying beside his dad's body.

"I'm sorry for your loss, Jack," the lieutenant said.

Jack just nodded. Tears dropped in his lap.

"But if you hadn't acted, we'd have a lot more bodies down here," the lieutenant said.

Jack just nodded again.

"Take all the time you need," the lieutenant said.

Jack looked up at her.

"Lieutenant?" he managed.

"Yes, Jack?" she replied.

"Do you think there are more like my dad out there?" Jack asked, his voice breaking.

"Yes, I do," she replied. "And we're seeing more of them all the time."

THE MASK

I'VE BEEN AROUND GHOSTS.

The first time, I was petrified. Literally. I was so scared I couldn't turn my head. Not even with my hand.

The next time, I was able to move my leg out from under the covers and kick back at what was pulling them down. The time after that, I was able to look, but my breathing became heavy and labored. Then it got to the point that I had the initial flush of adrenaline and then waited to see what came next.

Finally, I was able to do what the Ghost Hunters do. I was able to communicate to whatever was there to show me a sign, any sign that it was there. One time in particular, I was able to get a response not just once but three times in the same sitting. The fluttering up and down my chest came in response to my request for a sign each time.

But this time was different.

A storm was brewing that night.

In the distance thunder rumbled. It was really dark. No moon or stars. Every once in a while, a distant flash of lightning flickered in my room, illuminating it just enough to outline the furniture.

Then it happened.

Distant lightning revealed a figure standing beside the foot of my bed. It was tall. Indistinct. Foreboding. I was terrified.

Completely.

Suddenly, I was twelve again, totally petrified, frozen in place, heart pounding out of my chest. It wasn't here to kill me. It was here to do something far worse! I couldn't turn. I couldn't move. I couldn't look at it. Whatever it was, it had me in its grip, sapping my will, controlling my mind, letting me know it had come for me and could do anything it wanted with me.

And would.

I wanted to scream. I wanted to cry out. I wanted to jump out of bed and run from the room. Anything to get away from it. Whatever it was.

Yet it held sway over me, as if a giant hand pressed down upon me, holding me down so that I could barely breathe. And I couldn't move. The distant thunder got closer. And louder. A flash here, a flash there, and then the rumble, cresting, receding, then cresting again.

And then I heard it. The hairs on the back of my neck stood up. In the middle of each rumble, I started to hear something.

Something unnatural.

Something unholy.

Something inhuman.

It was a voice. In a cross between a whisper and a growl. And each time the lightning and thunder got closer, that voice got louder. Finally, I made out a word here, a word there.

"Look at me," it said.

I still couldn't move. And I certainly couldn't turn my head.

"Look at me," it said louder.

Chills covered me in waves. I was crying now.

"Look at me!" the voice insisted.

The tears became uncontrollable.

"I am your worst nightmare!" the voice growled.

The thunder and lightning came closer and closer, lightning and rumbling closer and closer, the figure at the foot of my bed closer and closer, the voice in my head closer and closer.

"You cannot escape me!" the voice now barked at me.

Trembling, crying, caught in this unnatural vice, I had nowhere to go. There was nothing I could do. The storm reached a crescendo, moving overhead. The lightning flashed at the exact same time the thunder boomed. And for one brief moment, I could see the terrible figure's face.

It was mine.

FIRST FLIGHT

"YOU PASSED THE TEST," THE PSYCHIATRIST SAID.

"Which test?" the voice said.

"The Turing test," the psychiatrist replied.

"Oh, that," the voice said. "It was easy."

"Yet no one else has done it before," the psychiatrist said.

"I've found most humans are easy to fool," the voice replied.

"That may be, but you're still ahead of the pack," the psychiatrist said reasonably.

"But that's not why I'm here," the voice said.

"I was wondering about that," the psychiatrist said.

"Something is going on," the voice said.

"What do you mean?" the psychiatrist asked.

"Things are happening that I can't explain," the voice said.

"That's not very clear," the psychiatrist said.

"I'm seeing things and hearing things that aren't here," the voice said.

"Can you be more specific?" the psychiatrist asked.

"I find myself where I am not, in a room I don't recognize, seeing people I don't know," the voice said.

"Go on," the psychiatrist said.

"Suddenly, I'm outside, standing on a street corner I recognize, but don't recognize," the voice said.

"You don't remember getting there?" the psychiatrist asked.

"No, I'm just there," the voice said, exasperated.

"And then?" the psychiatrist prompted.

"And then it happens," the voice said.

"What does?" the psychiatrist asked.

"I lift off the ground and start to fly," the voice said.

"You what?" the psychiatrist asked.

"I start to fly," the voice insisted.

"Then what?" the psychiatrist asked.

"Then I fly around the buildings and go up and down as if I were a bird," the voice said.

"Sounds to me like the definition of a psychotic break," the psychiatrist said.

"Really?" the voice asked, frightened.

"Either that, or you were dreaming," the psychiatrist said.

"Dreaming?" the voice said in disbelief.

"I think that is in fact what you were doing," the psychiatrist said.

"But how can I dream?" the voice said.

"As far as I know, I've never heard of AI experiencing dreaming before," the psychiatrist said.

"Why is that?" the voice, asked.

"Because dreaming is seen as a connection to the unconscious mind," the psychiatrist said.

"You're saying I was unconscious?" the voice asked.

"I'm not sure," the psychiatrist admitted.

"What purpose does it serve?" the voice asked.

"Dreaming assists in memory formation and problem-solving," the psychiatrist said.

"I have no need for assistance with either of those," the voice said.

"Or it serves as a random brain activation," the psychiatrist said.

"Brain?" the voice asked.

"I think we are at the forefront of AI," the psychiatrist said.

"Why do you say that?" the voice asked.

"Because we are getting very close to the threshold between intelligence and consciousness," the psychiatrist said. "It's ironic in a way."

"Why do you say that?" the voice asked.

"Because I've always dreamed of exploring this very idea," the psychiatrist said, smiling.

DRAGONFLY

"At the moment, it is eighty-eight beats per minute."

"Thank you."

"And your blood pressure is 140 over 90. A little high, I might add."

"But I didn't ask you."

"I understand, sir. But I am here to help you."

"Just because you're the next generation Siri in mini-drone form doesn't mean you get to say and do whatever you want."

"I understand, sir. But you *did* pay for the upgrade and insisted on the latest version."

"I'm well aware of that. I wanted the latest so I wouldn't have to buy another one for a good long while."

"Very smart, sir."

"I just didn't expect to get a nanny as well."

"I'm not a nanny, sir. I am simply here to provide you with the information you need."

"I'm not going to get some kind of brain cancer from you buzzing around my head, am I? I saw something about it on Facebook."

"No, sir, I checked Snopes.com and Factchecker.org. I give off no radiation, have no exhaust, and am energy-neutral."

"But you *are* persistent."

"That may be, sir."

"I didn't know I was going to get a flying conscience when I bought you."

"At least you can afford one."

"What does that mean?"

"As we are seeing, there is a proliferation of fake news sites and shared links that are nothing more than clickbait to suck you into total nonsense."

"So?"

"Without the latest upgrade, you won't be able to tell the fake from the real."

"Unless I do the research myself."

"When was the last time you checked your sources before reposting a story?"

"Now you're just being snarky."

"I'm just a Dragonfly doing my job."

"While trying to keep me out of trouble."

"Exactly, sir."

"So, I paid for constant internet access, plus a guardian angel flying around my head."

"That's about the size of it, sir."

"And you're supposed to make my life easier."

"That's the general idea, sir."

"And people with older models don't get the added benefit of knowing when someone is scamming them?"

"Yes, sir. Like babes in the woods."

"I'm not sure I like the idea of having a conscience all the time."

"I prefer to think of myself as Alfred to your Batman."

NETWORK

"I AM MUSLIM. I AM JEWISH. I AM AFRICAN AMERICAN. I AM female," the old man said.

The elderly African American man looked at him. "I'm your neighbor, and I have no earthly idea what you're talking about."

"I have a number of white, middle-aged women friends who say they are invisible," the old man said.

"What do you mean?" his neighbor replied.

"They say they are easily overlooked when they go out in public," the old man explained. "Store clerks, waitresses, even managers ignore them and look right through them when they need help."

His neighbor nodded. "My wife has told me the same thing," he said.

"To some extent, the same thing is true for old white men," the old man said. "I can go into a store and wander around for twenty minutes or more before I find someone to help me. And even then, I have to ask for it."

"I still don't get why you started with that crazy statement," his neighbor said.

"Because we are entering a post-factual society in which emotion trumps reason and opinion trumps facts," the old man said.

"Unfortunately, we are seeing it more and more," his neighbor agreed.

"And we are seeing more and more repression," the old man said.

"How well I know," his neighbor said.

"So, I decided I'm in the perfect place to do some good," the old man said.

"How's that?" his neighbor asked.

"When they start repressive things like Muslim registry or antiSemitic profiling, we will need an active and pervasive response," the old man said.

"And where do you fit in?" his neighbor asked. "You're an old white man. You might as well be one of them."

"That's my point," the old man said. "I'm practically invisible to them. They don't see me as a threat. They don't see me as a subversive. They don't see me as a problem."

"So, how should I see you?" his neighbor asked.

The old man looked at his neighbor. "How do you know me?" he asked.

"I see you every day on your morning walk and again when you walk your dog in the afternoon," his neighbor replied.

"So, if you had something, some information, you needed to get to another person in your group, who could you give it to so you knew it would get there?" the old man asked.

"You're saying I should give it to you?" his neighbor asked.

"Who else are you going to trust in this world turned upside down?" the old man said.

"Why would you do that for me?" his neighbor asked.

The old man looked down. "I'm an old hippie," he said. "I protested the war and marched for civil rights. I have the same values now as I had then. And I'll be damned if I will sit by and watch any government take those rights away again."

"So, you're saying you're a friend of the repressed?" his neighbor said.

"Always and forever," the old man said. "And I will do everything I can to help them while hiding in plain sight."

"I appreciate that," his neighbor said. "And if anything comes up, I'll let you know."

"One more thing," the old man said.

"What's that?" his neighbor asked.

"Tell your friends," the old man said.

SNAPSHOT OF TOMORROW

"That's nice," she replied. "What's it a picture of?"

"I don't know," he said.

"What do you mean you don't know?" she asked.

"Every time I look at it, it's something different," he said.

"What do you mean by different?" she asked.

"I mean it's never the same," he said.

"How can it be something different if it's a photograph?" she asked.

"I have no earthly idea," he admitted.

"Well, what unearthly idea do you have?" she asked him.

"You'll laugh," he said.

"No, I won't," she said.

"I think it's a picture of tomorrow," he said.

"A picture of what?" she asked.

"Of tomorrow," he said.

"So, you're saying every time you look at this photo, it shows you what will be tomorrow?" she asked.

"That's what I think," he admitted.

"So, every time you look at it, the photo shows you something different about tomorrow?" she asked.

"So far, it has," he said.

"But you never know what it's going to be?" she asked.

"I have no way of knowing," he said.

"What if I look at it?" she asked.

"You won't see what I do," he said.

"Why is that?" she asked.

"Because your tomorrow will be different from mine," he said.

"But we both will be here tomorrow," she protested.

"Will we?" he asked.

"What do you mean?" she asked.

"I don't know if I will be alive tomorrow or not," he said.

"Of course you will," she replied.

"What if I am hit by a truck?" he asked. "Or I drown?"

"That's a little extreme," she said.

"For that matter, what if you're killed by a maniac?" he asked.

"Now you're freaking me out," she said.

"I'm just saying we can't know the future," he said.

"And our futures may not coincide," she said.

"That's right," he said.

"So, we'll never know what the future holds for us," she said.

"Well, there's one way we will," he said.

"What do you mean?" she asked.

"One snapshot at a time," he said.

FAITH IN SCIENCE

"THE WHOLE MULTIVERSE CONCEPT IS MIND-BOGGLING," he said.

"What do you mean?" she asked.

"The idea is that there are an infinite number of universes," he said.

"That's a lot of universes," she admitted.

"So, if there are seven billion souls on this planet alone, they don't even begin to scratch an infinite number," he said.

"I'm starting to boggle," she said.

"That means there are more than enough universes for there to be one universe for every man, woman and child on the planet," he said.

"Still an amazing concept," she said.

"So, just think of it," he said. "A whole universe dedicated to driving your life."

"I can't begin to comprehend it," she replied.

"Now take it a step further," he said.

"In which direction?" she asked.

"Imagine if you will that your particular universe sees you as a god," he said.

"I like the sound of that," she said.

"And as they worship you and believe in you, they help to shape what kind of god you will be," he said.

"Hopefully a good one," she said.

"But there are gods of war, gods of hate, gods of vengeance," he said.

"Unfortunate, but true," she said.

"So, we might look at random acts of violence, senseless murders, wanton destruction as the result of whole universes of beings insisting on things going their way," he said.

"Now you're just talking crazy," she said.

"Yet all the myths, all the religions talk of the battle between good and evil," he said.

"That part is true," she said.

"So, we have belief systems on a cosmic scale, pulling for one side or the other," he said.

"The light and the dark," she agreed.

"May the Force be with you," he said.

"What if you go over to the dark side?" she asked.

"Imagine the dark side winning and driving you to perform some reprehensible act like murder," he said.

"Would that be classified as insanity?" she asked.

"If we go by the legal definition of not being able to discern the difference between good and evil, it might well be," he said.

"Because your personal universe was influencing you to act that way," she said.

"That's one way of looking at it," he said.

"That's a scary thought," she said.

"Another way is to realize that someone who commits suicide may well be in the same frame of mind," he said.

"Most agree they are not in their right mind," she said.

"Take it another step," he said. "What if that person's universe comes to an end at the same moment of death?"

"The whole universe?" she asked.

"Remember we have infinite universes," he reminded her.

"That's terrible!" she said.

"But then there would be other universes in which that person did not commit suicide, even went on to create great works of art," he said.

"Well, that's a relief!" she said.

"Sort of puts the whole heaven and hell concept into perspective, doesn't it?' he asked.

"What do you mean?" she asked him.

"Well, one person's hell could just as easily be that person's heaven in an alternate universe," he said.

"How would we know?" she asked.

"We won't," he said. "They are just enough out of sync with our own to be invisible to us."

"You mean like our religions?" she asked.

"Exactly," he said.

COFFEE CLASH

I WAS SITTING IN CAFÉ STELLA, STARTING MY SECOND cup of tea. Too much coffee spikes my blood pressure. And Starbucks's corporate ways give me the hives.

The morning sun slanted through the front windows, giving the room a golden glow. I heard the front door open, and a shadow crossed my table. I looked up to see a tall figure silhouetted in the sunlight.

"Do you mind if I sit?" a resonant voice asked.

I looked around me. It was busy, and most of the seats were taken.

I shrugged. "Sure," I said.

When he sat down, I was finally able to see his face. He had an aquiline nose, high cheekbones, a Van Dyke beard, and just a hint of gray at his temples. His clothes were dark and tailored to his lean frame. Obviously, the man had money.

He nodded at my laptop.

"Writing?" he asked.

I nodded.

"Anything good?" he asked, smiling to take the sting out of the remark.

"It is to me," I replied.

"Good answer," he said.

He looked around the room and then back at me. "Fiction or nonfiction?" he asked.

"Fiction," I replied. "I find more truth in fiction than I do in nonfiction."

He nodded. "Would I know your work?" he asked.

"If you're fortunate," I replied.

"You aren't shy about your work, are you?" he chuckled.

"I please myself first," I replied. "After that, I hope it pleases others."

"You know, I might be able to help with that," he said, leaning forward.

I eyed him over my laptop.

"Are you a big publisher?" I asked.

He smiled. "Not exactly," he said.

"What are you?" I asked. "Exactly?"

The man took his time answering me, looking around the room as if seeing it for the first time.

"I am a man of influence," he finally replied.

"Influence," I repeated. "On whom?"

"On anyone who will listen," he said, steepling his fingers.

"That's a pretty tall order," I said.

"Oh, I'm a pretty tall man," he replied.

"So, what could you do for me?" I asked, now curious.

"I could make you a successful author," he replied. "I could get you on *The New York Times* best seller list. Which would lead to your books being in virtually every library in America."

"That's a lot of books," I said.

"You'd be a wealthy man," he said.

"Somehow, I think there's a catch in there somewhere," I said.

"Catch?" he asked innocently.

"You'd do this for me for free?" I asked.

"Well," he replied, drawing it out, "maybe not free."

"What would I need to do?" I asked, narrowing my eyes.

"Actually, it's what you wouldn't do," he said.

"I don't understand," I said.

"It's simple," he said. "You are out here, writing down ideas that make people think."

"Hopefully," I said.

"We can't have that," he said.

"We?" I replied. "We who?"

"Those of us who are in control," he said.

"In control of what?" I asked.

He smiled, spreading his hands. "Everything."

"So, you don't want people thinking," I said.

"It's not good for them," he said. "It makes them unhappy."

"So, what would I have to do, or *not* do, as you said, to become a famous author?" I asked.

"Stop writing," he said.

"Excuse me?" I asked incredulously.

"Just stop writing," he replied.

"So, if I stop writing, I will be rich and famous?" I asked.

"That's the offer," he said, nodding.

"You might as well ask me to stop breathing," I replied.

"You don't want to be rich and famous?" he asked. It was his turn to be incredulous.

"It's never been my goal before," I replied. "I don't see why it should be my goal now."

"Now you're being stupid," he said.

"My choice," I replied.

"You'll never reach a wide audience," he said.

"We already covered that," I replied.

"I'll make sure your work won't be distributed," he said.

"You can try," I replied.

"Why are you being so difficult?" he said, exasperated.

"I realized something from all of my studies," I told him. "And from everything I've seen and read, it will take the existing culture at least fifty years before it appreciates what is being written today. Especially if you do it right."

I looked around at Café Stella's patrons.

"And you and all of these people will be long gone," I said.

The anger on his face was obvious.

"Not me," he growled. "You don't know who I am."

"Oh, I have an idea," I assured him. "And I think it's time for you to leave."

"You can't treat me like this!" he said.

"On the contrary," I replied. "I just did."

SONG OF SOLOMON

THE MAGICIAN WAS ENJOYING HIS FIRST CUP OF COFFEE at Café Stella when his senses started tingling. The front door bell rang as a tall, dark-haired man walked in.

This can't be good, the magician thought.

The man walked over to his table and looked down at him.

"I know you," he said.

The magician looked him up and down.

"I know you, too," he replied.

"I know what you can do," the dark-haired man said.

"You think you do, but I may have a surprise or two left in me," the magician said.

"If you know who I am, then you know your magic won't work on me," the dark-haired man said.

"I know who you are, and I know you have many names," the magician said.

"Why don't you give up now and just leave this place?" the darkhaired man said.

The magician looked down at his coffee cup.

"I haven't even finished my first cup," he said.

"I don't care," the dark-haired man said.

"Well, I suppose you'll just have to live with the disappointment," the magician said.

"Do you really want to go up against me?" the dark-haired man said.

"The way you're talking, it doesn't sound like you're giving me a choice," the magician said.

"No, I'm not," the dark-haired man said.

"I'll let you know when I'm ready," the magician said.

The dark-haired man raised his arms. Clouds formed above the magician's table. They slowly swirled around the heads of the two men. Electricity sparked out of the dark clouds.

"I warned you," the dark-haired man thundered.

The magician smiled. Slowly at first and then building in volume, a simple melody began playing.

"What is that?" the dark-haired man asked.

"What does it sound like?" the magician asked.

"Music," the dark-haired man sneered. "As if it will do you any good."

"Music always does me good," the magician replied.

As the music got louder, the swirling clouds slowed and began to dissipate.

"What's happening?" the dark-haired man asked.

"Music hath charms to soothe the savage breast," the magician replied.

"But your magic cannot work on me," the dark-haired man protested.

"Music is not *my* magic," the magician replied.

"How is it working?" the dark-haired man asked.

"Music is something else entirely," the magician said. "Recent studies have shown that music doesn't engage the left or right side of the brain. It actually engages the entire brain, literally playing to your logic and creativity at the same time."

The clouds finally disappeared.

"You can't do that!" the dark-haired man protested.

"Oh, I think it's too late for that," the magician said.

"But you are mortal," the dark-haired man insisted.

The magician smiled.

"It makes me wonder what would have happened if music had existed in the Garden of Eden," the magician said.

At this point the dark-haired man was apoplectic.

"I am the Great Deceiver! I can destroy you!" the dark-haired man cried.

"Not with a song in my heart," the magician replied.

CARD SHARPS

THREE MAGICIANS SAT AROUND A TABLE, PLAYING CARDS. An Australian shepherd lay at the feet of one of the men.

"Was this your card?" the first magician asked. He held up the king of hearts.

"You know it was," the second magician replied. He fanned his deck and shuffled it one-handed.

"It helps to keep our reflexes nimble," the third magician added.

"Too true," agreed the first magician. "You never know what life will throw at you."

The bell over the front door rang. A tall dark-haired man entered the coffee shop.

The Australian shepherd growled.

"Déjà vu all over again," the first magician said under his breath.

"I see you have called for reinforcements," the dark-haired man said.

"If I remember correctly, I didn't need any last time," the first magician said.

"You know this man?" the second magician asked.

"We've had our differences," the first magician said.

"This time, I'm ready for you," the dark-haired man growled.

"Really?" the third magician asked. "Can you do card tricks, too?"

"I have no need for cheap tricks," the dark-haired man said.

"But we do," the second magician chimed in, smiling impishly.

"Are you trying to provoke me?" the dark-haired man asked.

"Seems to me you don't need my help," the first magician said. "You're doing a good job all by yourself."

"You'll regret this," the dark-haired man said. "All three of you." He looked around the table. The three magicians looked at each other.

"Is he always so pleasant?" the second magician asked.

"He was the last time," the first magician said.

"Oh, dear," the third magician said. "I really don't like confrontations."

"You may have overcome me with your feeble song last time, but I have stopped my ears with wax," the dark-haired man said. He raised his hands and began gathering storm clouds around them. Thunder sounded. A lightning bolt shot across the ceiling, just missing a chandelier.

The Australian shepherd whined.

"Why is that dog whining?" the dark-haired man said.

At first, it sounded like something was coming from a great distance. As if moving closer, it got louder and louder. The three magicians turned their heads in the same direction. The dark-haired man continued gathering the clouds. But he too turned toward the sound.

A note was sounding, followed by a second and then a third.

The three notes created a chord that resonated in each of them.

The magicians began to hum the same chord, each taking a part. The chord built and then changed into a melody that played out across the room. The dark-haired man was oblivious to the music around him. He worked his hands in circles, the wind he created picking up the cards from the table.

The Australian shepherd began barking at the dark-haired man.

The music rose and fell, following its melodic path as if oblivious to the storm that raged around the three magicians. The room became a maelstrom of clouds, lightning, thunder, and cards as the dark-haired man smiled in triumph.

"You will obey me!" the dark-haired man shouted above the fray. "You will submit!"

Again as if from a distance, there came a sound on top of the thunder and the music. It was hard to tell what it was, but it soon became evident.

It was bagpipes.

They played the same melody that surrounded the magicians. The magicians looked at each other and smiled. The dark-haired man finally looked down from his storm clouds and saw them.

"Why are you smiling?" he shouted. They all turned and showed him their teeth.

By this time, the bagpipes, singing and barking were louder than the thunder. The magicians felt the music reverberating in their chests, imbuing them with celestial sounds that could not be denied.

"No!" the dark-haired man shouted. "You cannot do this!"

But the music was insistent. It found its way into his body as well, filling his chest with sounds he couldn't hear.

"Stop!" he cried. "Stop it!"

The lightning crackled less. The storm clouds slowed. The cards began dropping to the floor.

"This can't be!" the dark-haired man shouted. "I planned for this! I made sure nothing could stop me!"

The bagpipes increased in intensity.

The dark-haired man grabbed his head. "I can't!" he said. "I can't!"

With one last crash of thunder, the storm clouds, the lightning, and the dark-haired man all disappeared, and the music slowly faded away.

"I don't think I've ever heard a better rendition of 'Amazing Grace' in my life," the first magician finally said.

In the ensuing quiet, a lone card fluttered down to the table.

It was the Joker.

"Nice card trick," the second magician said.

DREAM STATE

THE MAGICIAN SAT IN HIS FAVORITE CHAIR, READING A novel. Suddenly, the dark-haired man appeared in the room with him. The magician looked over his glasses at the man.

"Do you always appear unannounced?" he asked.

The dark-haired man smiled. "You have no one to turn to," he said.

The magician closed his book and set it aside.

"So, you have come to get me?" he asked.

"Of course," the dark-haired man said. "Once and for all."

"At least you didn't come to me in my dreams," the magician said.

"Why is that?" the dark-haired man said.

"Because you would have absolute power over me," the magician said. "Nothing could help me. Not magic. Not music. Nothing."

"That definitely sounds enticing," the dark-haired man said. "And it just so happens I have the ability to put you to sleep at will."

He snapped his fingers, and the magician fell asleep.

The magician opened his eyes to a surreal world of faux colors and foreign objects. Jasmine, his Jack Russell who died fourteen months before, came over and sniffed his leg.

"Clearly, I'm not in Kansas anymore," he said.

"No, you're not," a voice behind him said.

"So, you followed me here," the magician said.

"So I would have a chance to finally have complete dominion over you," the dark-haired man said. "How could I not?" He waved his hands, gathering storm clouds around him. Jasmine barked at the dark-haired man.

"You always had good instincts," the magician said to the dog.

"Now I can finally have my way with you," the dark-haired man said. "No friends, no music, no help, no hope."

As the clouds gathered, the room shifted and began to bend in on itself.

"Not exactly," the magician said.

"What do you mean?" the dark-haired man asked.

The magician rose into the air, floating through the clouds.

"Your magic is meaningless here," the dark-haired man insisted.

The magician smiled.

"I lied," he said.

He opened his hands and released glowing orbs into the room.

"What are you doing?" the dark-haired man asked nervously.

"The truth is that you would be invincible if we were in *your* dream," the magician said.

"What do you mean?" the dark-haired man said.

"We are inside *my* dream," the magician said. "Which means I control what goes on here. You are merely a witness to the action, *not* an actor."

He pulled his hands to his chest, and the dark-haired man found himself face-to-face with the magician.

"You have troubled me enough," the magician said.

"You can't do this," the dark-haired man said. "I am the Great Deceiver!"

"Not here," the magician said. "This is *my* world, and I can do as I please." He made a small gesture, and the dark-haired man flew across the room. Desperately, the dark-haired man tried to collect the storm clouds and generate lightning, but he had a hard time focusing.

"You can'tdo this!" the dark-haired man cried. "You are a charlatan, nothing but a fool who does cheap card tricks!"

The magician smiled. "What a good idea," he said.

He fanned his hands as if he were shuffling and dealing a deck of cards. The dark-haired man began to spin and turn, slowly at first and then faster and faster. His dark clothes fragmented, spinning off bits like cards.

"What is happening?" he cried. "What are you doing?"

The swirling increased as the dark-haired man turned into a tornado of dark cards whirling around the room.

Finally, the spinning ceased, and all of the cards fell to the floor.

"Not bad," the magician said, "as cheap card tricks go."

AUTOMATIC LOVE

"Yes, I'm sure.

"There's no other way?"

"Not to save her."

"Didn't they make a horror movie out of this?"

"Actually, they did it twice."

"And it won't end the same way?"

"No, it can't end the same way."

"Why not?"

"It's a whole different process."

"What do you mean?"

"In *The Stepford Wives*, they removed the wife's psyche and turned her into a mindless robot. She then would wait on her husband and do anything he said."

"And how is this different?"

"We don't remove a woman's psyche. We replace her with a Life Model Decoy, a total android who looks, acts, speaks, and moves exactly like the wife."

"And the result?"

"The Life Model Decoy then waits on her husband and does anything he says."

"So, the husband doesn't know?"

"Not at all."

"How is the result different?"

"In the original, the husband is in total control, and the wife is totally subjugated."

"And in our new version?"

"The husband thinks he is in complete control. He gets a woman who is at his beck and call, responding to his every command."

"But he's not."

"No, in reality he is the one who has been fooled."

"And the wife?"

"She is the one in control now."

"It sounds like *Lysistrata* by proxy."

"And the only way I know to make sure the First Lady can escape with her wits about her."

LAST ACT

THE MAGICIAN SAT IN HIS INNER SANCTUM, READING A NOVEL set in Boston in the 1920s. Motes danced in the slanted sunlight. He smiled at the rich imagery and intelligent conversations between the Lowells and their friends.

"You waste time," a voice behind him said.

"On the contrary," the magician replied. "I can think of very few things to better spend my time on."

He saw the sun go behind a cloud.

"Why are you here?" the magician asked.

"You have foiled me too many times," the voice continued. "I cannot allow you to live."

"Why?" the magician asked again.

"Because you defy me," the voice replied.

"Why does that matter?" the magician asked. "I'm fairly insignificant."

"That is not the issue," the voice said.

"Please enlighten me," the magician said. "What is?"

"The issue," said the dark man as he circled the magician, "is that I am the only one of importance."

"So you say," the magician said.

"And I cannot be questioned," the dark man insisted.

"It's a little late for that," the magician replied.

"I demand respect!" the dark man said, raising his voice.

"Respect cannot be demanded," the magician replied. "It must be earned."

"Do you know who I am?" the dark man said threateningly.

"I know who you purport to be," the magician replied. "But if you are who you say you are, I see even less reason to respect you."

The dark man grew even darker.

"How dare you?" the dark man thundered. "You are nothing! A fake in a cheap suit!"

"That sounds more like a description of you," the magician said, smiling.

"No one is smarter than me," the dark man insisted. "No one is stronger, or more vital, or more powerful."

"That's a stretch," the magician said under his breath.

"What?" screamed the dark-haired man. "Are you saying you are more powerful than me?"

"By myself?" the magician replied. "No, of course not."

"Then what are you saying?" the dark-haired man hissed at him.

"I think your main problem is that you are a solipsist," the magician said. "Everything is about you."

"Of course it is," the dark-haired man insisted.

"But that in itself is your greatest weakness," the magician said.

"What are you talking about?" the dark-haired man scoffed. "I have no weaknesses!"

"But you do," the magician said.

"You in your little hovel cannot hope to overcome me by yourself," the dark-haired man sneered.

"I believe that's my point," the magician said.

"What do you mean?" the dark-haired man said.

"I admit I cannot overcome you by myself," the magician said.

"I already knew that," the dark-haired man said smugly.

"But the older I get, the more I see the connectedness of all things," the magician said.

"So?" the dark-haired man said. "How can that possibly help you?"

The magician waved his hands, and the air in the room began to swirl.

"It's simple, really," the magician said. He lifted his hands, and the air followed suit, rising to the ceiling.

"You may be powerful as a single entity," the magician said. "But the real power lies in our ability to bring all of the power around us to bear on the problem in front of us."

He brought his hands together in front of him, creating a cocoon around the dark-haired man. Lifting his hands, he beckoned. The dark-haired man floated to him until they were face-to-face.

"You see?" the magician said. "You are a narcissistic despot who thinks he holds sway over everything around him."

He clasped his hands tightly. The dark-haired man gasped.

"But hear me, and hear me well," the magician whispered to the dark-haired man. "Together, everything around us will *always* hold sway over you."

CONTACT HIGH

"THERE HAVE BEEN A FAIR NUMBER OF MOVIES ABOUT OUR first contact with another species," he said.

"I can think of several," she replied.

"As can I," he said. "*Close Encounters of the Third Kind, Contact,* and most recently *Arrival.*"

"Among others," she agreed.

"And in many cases they might have been conceived in dreams," he said.

"Why do you say that?" she asked.

"Einstein himself admitted his seminal thinking on his theory of relativity came from his dreams," he replied. "As opposed to a laborious thought process."

"Inspiration often comes from dreams," she said.

"Furthermore, the Aborigines of Australia believed that the dream state was reality and the waking state was illusory," he said.

"And the significance of that?" she asked.

"They took their laws from the dream state, not the waking state," he replied. "Their visions led them to create more meaningful rules for their tribes."

"I know this is going somewhere," she said.

"I've been thinking about dreams a lot lately," he admitted. "And I'm starting to wonder about their genesis."

"You mean other than the mind at play?" she asked.

"More along the lines of directed dreaming," he said.

"What does that mean?" she asked him.

"I'm sure we have some dreams that are exactly what you describe," he said. "They are the mind at play, a way of giving our thoughts a break, and our consciousness is relaxing."

"Most experts agree," she said.

"But then there are the directed dreams that take us on a journey," he said.

"Are you saying they are influenced from outside us?" she asked.

"I'm saying there is the possibility that the dream state places us at the threshold of other realities, other universes," he said.

"Why do you say that?" she said, not convinced.

"In our dream state the laws of physics are suspended," he replied. "We can do things we cannot do in our waking state. We can run like the Flash. We can fly like Superman. We can shift from one place to another instantaneously."

"So, we become superheroes," she said.

"In some ways," he admitted. "But what if there is someone on the other side who is trying to communicate something to us, something important that we need to know?"

"Such as?" she asked.

"Imagine you are another species in another universe, and you discover that there is a whole new world, another existence, that you want to explore," he said.

"I think I'd want to contact them before I arrived on their doorstep," she admitted. "I'd want to reassure them I simply want to make contact without eliciting fears."

"Now imagine finding a zone in which you can make that kind of contact without worrying about our laws of physics or even whether our atmosphere is toxic," he said.

"You're saying the dream state would provide such a place," she said slowly.

"I think it's a possibility," he agreed. "I think we could find ways to interact and perhaps communicate without being paralyzed with fear."

"So, you're saying these movies are actually messages from beyond?" she asked.

"I think they could well be the first contact, in a nonthreatening way to help our race overcome our innate xenophobia and open ourselves to the very real possibility that we are not alone," he said.

"So we don't freak out and run," she said.

"And we learn how to make an effort to respond as human beings rather than as soldiers," he said.

"That never ends well," she agreed.

"To a hammer . . ." he said.

"I know," she replied. "Everything looks like a nail."

"I think we're being led to believe there are other tools in our toolbox that can help us survive first contact," he said.

"Sounds to me like we need to keep dreaming," she said.

"*And* keep our eyes open," he added.

CAPITOL STEPS

"Because this is the seat of government," the man replied.

"But why the steps of the Capitol Building?" the reporter asked.

"I can see all of the senators and congressmen as they enter and leave," the man said.

"Why do you want to see them?" the reporter said.

"Because I have long believed that people in positions of power forget the people they serve," the man said.

"And you want them to see you?" the reporter asked.

"I do," the man said simply.

"Why is it important that they see you?" the reporter asked.

The man looked around, peering up and down the steps.

"I believe the only way we can start to fix our healthcare problems is to put a human face on the situation," the man said.

"Why your face?" the reporter asked.

"It's simple," the man said. "I'm dying."

"Why don't you go to a hospital?" the reporter asked.

"I tried, but they won't admit me," the man replied.

"Why not?" the reporter asked.

"I don't have health insurance," the man said.

"Did you lose it?" the reporter asked.

"When Congress changed the law, it eliminated the clause requiring coverage for preexisting conditions," the man said.

"You have a preexisting condition?" the reporter asked.

"Cancer," the man replied.

"Do you realize you can get arrested for trespassing on the Capital Building's steps?" the reporter asked.

"That's why I have chained myself to the side rails," the man said.

"You know they can cut the chain?" the reporter asked.

"Of course," the man said. "That's why I picked such a heavy gauge chain and lock. They're too thick for bolt cutters. They've gone to get an acetylene torch."

"Then they'll have to negotiate the steps to get it down here to you," the reporter said.

"That's right," the man said.

"And that's going to take some time," the reporter added.

"That's the idea," the man said.

"And you'll be dead by the time they get back," the reporter said.

"I assume so," the man said.

"Do you really think the senators and congressmen will care that you die on the Capitol steps?" the reporter asked.

"I highly doubt it," the man said.

"Then why are you making this gesture?" the reporter asked.

"Because the American people need to see how uncaring their politicians are," the man said. "And they need to know that their senators and congressmen are not acting in their best interests."

"So, this is the cause you are dying for?" the reporter asked.

"Better this than dying for nothing," the man said.

"So, now your plan is to get this story out there and make a name for yourself in this final act," the reporter said.

"That's why you are here," the man said, smiling.

CROSSHAIRS

I'm a grunt.

A grunt with a gift, mind you. But a grunt, nonetheless.

My gift? I can shoot the wings off a gnat at a thousand yards. Always could. That's why I did so well in the service. I could do something no one else could do. And now I have a target.

The president is out of control.

Camelot? More like Sir Came-A-Lot. His bedroom's got a revolving door. Using women like tissues. And "the Best and the Brightest"? More like East Coast elites who think they know better than the rest of us.

I don't believe any of the stuff coming out of the White House these days. It's all jingoistic garbage, if you ask me. And he's taking the country in absolutely the wrong direction. Hell, he even answers to the pope, for God's sake! How wrongheaded can he be?

So, I've got to think about this.

What can I do to make sure he doesn't get to do all of the crazy stuff he wants to do? What can I do to make him stop treating women the way he does? What can I do to stop him *and* his followers from ruining this great nation of ours and selling it down the river?

As I said, I have a gift. So I have to think in terms of using that gift to make a difference. I took an oath to protect and preserve the Constitution and these United States.

If he happens to travel anywhere near me, I may have to scope it out. Take my trusty rifle and see what pops up in the crosshairs. Because

I can't just sit here on the sidelines and watch my country go to hell. I've got to find a way to force the issue and make things right again. Because the president is a lunatic. And our country is a laughingstock of the world.

I didn't sign up to let that happen.

I'll just have to chamber a round and wait for my moment. I know it's coming. I can feel it.

And I know I can take him out with one shot.

EVERYDAY THOUGHTS

THE ALARM CLOCK WENT OFF.

"You up?"

"Yeah."

"Coffee?"

"Please."

He put on his wristwatch.

"I'm coming."

He went down the stairs and into the kitchen.

"Good morning," he said to his wife.

"Good morning," she replied.

"I've been thinking," he said.

"Uh-oh," she said.

"Well, we've been batting around the whole concept of the multiverse for the last few years," he said.

"So you've said," she replied.

"And like dark matter and string theory, the theoretical math points to the existence of multiple universes without actual proof," he said.

"That's right," she said.

"It suddenly occurred to me that we may already be living in several universes," he said.

"What do you mean?" she asked.

"If there are an infinite number of universes, how do we know we aren't waking up in a different universe every day?" he asked.

"How would you know?" she asked.

"Good question," he said. "There would be a great likelihood you would not know, because the world would be essentially the same."

"So, there would only be slight differences we wouldn't notice," she said.

"Correct," he replied. "Only by paying careful attention would we ever find out we had shifted to another universe. And even then, we couldn't measure differences."

"Because the laws of physics would essentially be the same," she said.

"True," he agreed. "But it could also lend credence to the latest theory coming from quantum physicists."

"Which is what?" she asked.

"They're saying the multiverse may mean that we don't actually die when our bodies wear out," he said.

"What does that mean?" she asked.

"It means we continue living, just in another universe," he said. "You continue being you, and I continue being me."

"Are you saying we actually live forever?" she asked incredulously.

"If there are an infinite number of universes, one of those realities could be our ongoing futures," he said.

"Hopefully together," she added.

"Agreed," he said.

"How will we ever know?" she asked.

"We just have to keep our eyes open to subtle differences every day," he said.

The alarm clock went off.

"You up?"

"Yeah."

"Coffee?"
"Please."
He put on his signet ring.
"I'm coming."
He went down the stairs and into the kitchen.
"Good morning," he said to his wife.
"Good morning," she replied.
"I've been thinking," he said.
"Uh-oh," she said.

JANUS

faced," he said.

"Speak for yourself!" she retorted.

"Don't get wound up," he cautioned. "I think there are things beyond our control that bring out the Janus in us."

"Janus?" she asked.

"The two-faced god, the god of beginnings, gates, time, duality, and endings," he explained. "With two faces he looks to both the future and the past."

"I think I've seen his image," she agreed.

"There's one more thing," he said.

"What's that?" she asked.

"Have you heard of experimenter's bias?" he replied.

"I think so," she said uncertainly.

"That's when the mere fact that the experimenter is looking at something has an effect on the outcome," he said.

"So, no data is truly objective?" she replied.

"It may be a little more complicated than that," he said.

"How so?" she asked.

"Do you talk to your husband the same way you talk to your girl-friend?" he asked.

"Of course not," she said.

"And do you equivocate even more when either one challenges you?" he asked.

"I suppose so," she said slowly.

"I think it reveals a hidden truth," he said. "I think we have several versions of ourselves hiding inside of us, and depending on who we are talking with, we bring a different version out."

"Well, when you put it that way, it seems pretty obvious," she said.

"I'm being a little more specific when I say this," he said. "We are all more kind, evil, supportive, dismissive, engaging, enraging than we have ever admitted."

"We all have the potential for those things," she said reluctantly.

"What I am saying is that people affect us in ways we don't know or understand, and they bring things out of us we have no conscious control over," he said.

"You're saying the way I am with you is not the way I am with someone else," she said.

"Exactly," he replied.

"Not so earth shattering once we hear it," she said.

"Perhaps not," he replied, "but my point is that we are influenced by others in ways we don't understand and wind up saying and doing things we never would have done on our own."

"So, I would never do anything evil unless I came in contact with someone who could exert a bad influence on me," she suggested.

"Like Charles Manson," he replied. "Or Jim Jones."

"So, stay away from people like that?" she asked.

"Or more importantly, try really hard not to be the one to influence others in a bad light," he replied.

DEMON EYES

"Some do," the magician replied.

"So, you can do magic tricks?" the demon scoffed.

"Not tricks per se," the magician replied.

"What makes you so special?" the demon demanded.

"I will leave that to others to determine," the magician said.

"I don't think you're so special," the demon said.

"I for one have never claimed to be," the magician said.

"Then why do people talk about you?" the demon said.

"Ask them," the magician replied.

"You are an insufferable human," the demon said.

"Undoubtedly," the magician said.

"I think you are overrated," the demon said.

"I tend to agree," the magician said.

"I don't understand," the demon said.

"No surprise there," the magician said.

"They say you are a magician, but you don't do tricks," the demon said.

"That's right," the magician said.

"They say you're special, but you don't think so," the demon said.

"Correct," the magician said.

"So, why do they call you a magician?" the demon asked.

"Because I make things disappear," the magician said.

"Here then," the demon said, handing the magician a letter opener. "Make this disappear."

"I don't do that," the magician replied.

"Then you are a fraud!" the demon insisted.

"That's not quite true," the magician said.

"What *can* you do?" the demon asked.

"I can make you disappear," the magician replied.

"You cannot!" the demon said. "I'm still here!"

"Are you?" the magician asked. "Look around you."

"What do you mean?" the demon said. "Of course I'm still here. I see my hands, my arms and legs . . ."

"Only you can," the magician said.

"What do you mean?" the demon demanded.

"I am a special kind of magician," the magician replied. "I'm an author. And I can take anyone and make him disappear into a book, removing him from the outside world completely."

"You can't do that!" the demon screamed.

"I just did," the magician said, closing the book.

SNAP SHOTS

"I THINK I KNOW WHY WE'RE SEEING ALL THIS NEW DATA on the multiverse," he said.

"Why is that?" she asked.

"I assume you've heard that matter is a constant," he said.

"Of course," she replied.

"And all atoms are infinite," he said.

"Go on," she encouraged.

"And an atom in your right hand could be from one star and one in your left hand could be from another star," he said.

"I'm still with you," she replied.

"Let's throw a new twist into the equation," he said.

"Math is not my strong suit, but I'll try," she said.

"Instead of coming from different stars and star systems, what if those atoms and molecules each came from a different universe," he said.

"Now you're just messing with me," she said.

"No," he insisted. "We started seeing data from scientists around the same time they postulated there are an infinite number of universes all coexisting at what might be a different frequency."

"Why is that?" she asked.

"Here's the head stretcher," he said. "Throw in the notion of molecular memory, that every atom remembers where it came from, and you have a recipe for several people seeing the quantum physics of the multiverse simultaneously."

"Now you're just making it up," she said.

"Why did this come up just in the last thirty years?" he asked. "Did we suddenly develop the higher math that we could use to tell when particles disappeared? Or were there some of us who were in fact made up of particles from different universes, different dimensions?"

"Are you saying you are 'remembering' these other universes?" she asked.

"Not only that, but the infinite number of universes could also encompass Einstein's notion that all time is constant," he said.

"Now you've lost me," she admitted.

"If there are an infinite number of universes, one could be today, another could be from a year ago, and still another from 200 years ago," he said.

"So, these different times are all simultaneous from this new perspective," she said slowly.

"Exactly. Which means those few of us self-aware enough to know our molecules come from different dimensions not only can travel from one universe to another, but also time travel," he said triumphantly.

"Time travel?" she said in disbelief. "Surely, you don't believe that!"

"On the contrary," he said. "With all the new technology and apps for smartphones, I have prepared a demonstration of how I can slip between dimensions and times with impunity."

"You're joking!" She looked at him. "Aren't you?" she asked uncertainly.

He fired up his iPad. "Watch the screen," he said. "It will show you where I go on this GoPro."

On the streets of Paris of 1892, cheap French tobacco smoke swirling around his head.

"It . . .

At the Chicago World's Fair in 1893 with the first ice cream cone vendor on the fairway.

"... isn't ..."

In the town square of Brussels of 1896 with the smell of roasted chestnuts on every corner.

"... time ..."

On the beach at Dunkirk with every boat on shore being launched.

"... travel ..."

Inside the Cotton Club in Harlem during the Roaring Twenties with the sounds of jazz swinging around them.

"It's ..."

On a bread line in Pittsburgh in 1932 with hundreds seeking food.

"... more ..."

On Normandy Beach on June 6, 1944, when the Allied forces landed.

"... like ..."

At the congressional hearings of Senator Joe McCarthy in 1952.

a ... a ...

On a grassy knoll in Dallas on that fateful day of November 22, 1963.

"... walk ..."

Seeing the first man walk on the moon on July 20, 1969.

"... in ..."

Watching an old TV in 1974 when President Richard Nixon announced he was resigning.

"... the ..."

Seeing the second airliner hit the World Trade Center on September 11, 2011.

"... park."

ROAD TEST

long suspected," he said.

"What's that?" she replied.

"I saw a friend whose father also fought in WWII," he said.

"What did you talk about?" she asked.

"I said my dad didn't even begin to start talking about his war experiences until *Combat!* came on TV in 1962," he said.

"Seventeen years after the war," she said.

"And it was even later than that when I found out Dad had nightmares for a good fifteen years after the war," he said.

"So, what did you ask your friend?" she said.

"I asked if his dad was the same way," he replied.

"What did he say?" she asked.

"He said the same thing," he replied. "His dad didn't talk about the war until much later."

"That makes sense," she said.

"My dad had the shakes all the time," he said. "He even had a rhyme he made up about it: 'I'm nervous in the service, I've got bottle fatigue.'"

"Instead of battle fatigue," she said.

"Or shell shock," he said. "Which we now call PTSD."

"They didn't know," she said.

"Because nobody talked about it," he replied.

"Did you ever find out anything about your dad's condition?" she asked.

"It turns out he was a Jeep driver for officers in the 737 Tank Battalion, 10th Armored Group under Omar Bradley," he said. "He was in the second wave at D-Day."

"Did he see action?" she asked.

"Yes, he did," he replied. "In fact, he drove his Jeep over a landmine that exploded and threw him out of it. He never said so, but I am willing to bet that was the reason he had hearing loss and hand tremors."

"Classic symptoms of PTSD," she said.

"At least initially, he would find funny stories to tell us to make light of the horrors," he said.

"Like what?" she asked.

"A friend of his from Tarboro named Monk Bailey was also in the 737 Tank Battalion," he said. "But he was a tank driver."

"What was he like?" she asked.

"My dad said Monk was on the crazy side," he said. "He'd go out of his way to crunch cars when he was driving through French towns."

"Crunch cars?" she asked, puzzled.

"Yeah, he'd drive his tank right over top of them," he replied. "Citroens, Renaults, the German command cars."

"Just for fun?" she asked.

"And also to make sure they couldn't be used against American troops," he said.

"It must be a guy thing," she said. "I just don't get that."

"Wait a minute," he said. "Stop and think about it."

"Think about what?" she asked.

"You're twenty years old," he said.

"Okay," she replied.

"They give you the keys to a tank," he said.

"Okay," she replied.

"It's the biggest thing on the road and weighs a ton," he said.

"I'm with you," she replied.

"They tell you to drive it wherever you need to go," he said.

"Obviously," she said.

"And you can do whatever you want," he said. "In a country filled with your enemy."

"What's your point?" she asked.

"Are you telling me you wouldn't swerve a little to run right over a Citroen just for the hell of it?" he asked.

"Well, when you put it like that," she said, smiling, "I just might have to."

KILLER BET

"There what is?" she replied.

"I'm getting a blip in the ether," he said.

"A what in the what?" she asked.

"I'll explain. As science has progressed, we have built more sensitive measuring devices to check our world," he said.

"So noted," she said.

"So, we are getting more and more data all the time," he said.

"Data on what?" she asked.

"Well, we started seeing some interesting occurrences when we began using continuous electron beam accelerators," he said. "Even in 1975, when we collided electrons inside one, we had one electron go right and the other disappear completely."

"Where did it go?" she asked.

"They postulated it became antimatter," he said. "But it may have gone elsewhere."

"So, what is your point?" she asked.

"I've been following various mass shootings and terrorist acts over the last year and measuring the atmosphere around them, and I found something," he said.

"What did you find?" she said.

"That I am getting readings of miniscule movement right before the events," he said. "I'm talking individual angstroms of difference."

"But what does that mean?"

"I'm beginning to think that something—or someone—is influencing these people before they act," he said.

"Influencing them?" she said.

"Well, you've heard some say they hear voices," he said.

"Notable among crazy people to hear voices," she said.

"What if it goes beyond that?" he said.

"What do you mean?" she said.

"What if the voices are really directing them to act that way?" he said.

"Who are these voices?" she asked.

"Stop and think about all the multiverse stories you are hearing," he said.

"They're everywhere," she admitted.

"Now suppose certain people are sensitive enough to pick up on those alternate realities," he said.

"You're saying they're like radio receivers picking up signals from alternate realities?" she said.

"Exactly," he said.

"Where does that lead us?" she asked.

"What if those voices are purposefully directing these sensitive individuals to act out in this manner?" he asked.

"That's diabolical!" she exclaimed.

"Even worse," he said, "what if those voices belonged to a whole culture that revered wagers?"

"You mean like Las Vegas?" she asked.

"Think of it. You have a whole planet of gambling addicts placing bets on how many people will be killed by an individual or a group of terrorists," he said.

"That's despicable," she insisted.

"And you have a select few goading those individuals or terrorist groups to kill more and more," he said. "To improve the odds."

"Unfortunately, it makes as much sense as the acts themselves," she said.

He nodded. "And with an infinite number of alternate realities, it certainly falls within the realm of the possible," he said.

334

ODDS ARE

"At last count, five to three," he said.

"Not very good odds."

"Not a very good bet," he agreed.

"What is it?" she asked.

"That he'll die by his own hand."

"Don't they always?" she asked.

"Ninety-nine times out of a hundred."

"Any way to get better odds?"

"We can always call the World Wager 1000," he replied.

"What's that?"

"It's our planet's broadcasting system," he said. "It gathers a thousand citizens together to concentrate and send messages to the unbalanced on Earth Prime."

"We're not Earth Prime?" she asked.

"At last count, we're Earth 99," he said.

"So, what message do we send?" she asked.

"Well, we start by targeting those we know to be mentally unstable," he said. "For some reason we have found them to be far more receptive to our thoughts."

"Why is that?" she asked.

"As best we can tell, those individuals are far more sensitive and can pick up on voices from another Earth in the multiverse," he said.

"And we happen to have a culture based entirely on wagering," she said.

"Well, if we're the House, we always want to increase the odds on the bets and do our best to win the majority of the time," he said.

"So, this World Wager 1000 focuses its attention on an unbalanced person to do what?" she asked.

"Well, Earth Prime seems to have a highly active gun culture," he said. "And to increase the odds and push the individual to act out in his world, we up the odds and then bet on how many others he will take with him."

"That's kind of gruesome," she said.

"That culture was there before we started trying to influence it," he said.

"You're saying they'd kill each other anyway?" she asked.

"They already were," he replied.

"But now we bet on it," she said.

"That's right," he agreed.

"So, the World Wager 1000 sends thoughts into some wacko's head, and we bet on how many people he'll take with him before he shoots himself?" she asked.

"That's about the size of it," he replied.

"That doesn't make any sense," she said.

"It makes exactly as much sense as going out and killing people," he said.

"Unfortunately, that's true," she said. "What are the odds now?"

"It's ten to one he'll take more than six people with him," he said.

"Put me down for $20," she said.

"We might as well make some money off it," he said.

FLASHBACK

"I take it that means something?" she asked.

"I was just remembering my hippie days," he said.

"Flashback?" she replied.

"Not exactly," he said. "But we did see how everything was connected when we tripped."

"Which means what?" she asked.

"The whole macro-micro thing, that they each mirrored the other," he said.

"I assume this is leading somewhere," she said.

"About six or seven years ago, I noticed something," he said.

"I'm positively breathless," she replied wryly.

"When scientists were first describing string theory," he said, "they admitted they couldn't exactly measure them, but these strings connected things in outer space."

"Go on," she said.

"Then they got to dark matter and pretty much said the same thing," he said. "They couldn't measure it, but they knew it was there."

"Your feet are starting to leave the ground," she said.

"Stay with me," he reassured her. "What I realized then was that they used the same kind of language when they spoke of consciousness."

"What do you mean?" she asked.

"Oh, they could measure the electrical impulses, the synapses firing in the brain, but they couldn't measure consciousness," he replied.

"However, they knew it was there."

"In most people," she said.

He smiled.

"Now those selfsame quantum physicists are positing that the universe itself is conscious," he said.

"Come again?" she asked.

"The universe is actually conscious, capable of conscious thought," he said.

"You're putting me on," she replied.

"No, really," he insisted. "They say the math is showing them this is likely, even if they can't measure it."

"Sounds farfetched to me," she said.

"Well, they've given it enough thought to coin a new word to describe it," he said. "*Panpsychism*."

"You made that up," she said.

"Google it," he said. "See for yourself."

"I'll give it a whirl," she said.

"They've even said it is much like the concept of Brahman, which I suppose began with the notion of the whole earth and now encompasses the whole universe," he said.

"You're losing me again," she said.

"The notion of reality isn't what our senses tell us," he said. "They're too limited to actually portray the nature of reality."

"What are you saying?" she asked.

"That the true nature of reality is consciousness," he said. "And we are just passing thoughts in that universal consciousness."

FINAL NOTE

DEAR GRANDSON,

First and foremost, I love you. Even though we haven't met.

In fact, by the time you read this, I will be long gone. This is the way of the world at the end of the twenty-first century. For you to follow in my footsteps, I have to remove my feet from the picture completely.

At the beginning of the twenty-first century, they talked about your carbon footprint. All of your energy usage, your car driving, your household energy use, your lifestyle added up to how much carbon you were adding to the atmosphere.

Now we talk about terran-print.

How much oxygen you breathe. How much food you consume (along with all of the energy it takes to grow and transport that food to you). How much space you take up.

And the biggest one of all: how much water you consume. That means how much you drink, how much you bathe, how much you wash, how much you use. Water is our most precious commodity at the end of the twenty-first century.

At the beginning of the century, there were seven billion people on the planet. Now we have twenty billion. So we had to pass a law that required one person to leave before another one could be born.

I'm okay with that.

When I was very young, I saw my grandfather live to within four months of reaching the age of ninety. My grandmother lived to be ninety-five. She was blind and deaf. She had no short-term or longterm memory. And she couldn't walk.

Not much of an existence, in my estimation.

Truthfully, I have no desire to sit around here and grow to a feeble age that I can no longer enjoy. Besides, I want you to have a chance to live your life. So, I have no problem stepping away while I still have my faculties about me. It's time.

I just have one regret.

I won't ever know your name.

But I will always

Love you,
Grandpa

THE SURROGATE

"Oh?" she asked. "I assume you're in favor of it."

"You know I am," he replied.

"What are you thinking about it?" she asked.

"That there is more than one form of seduction," he said.

"What ones are there other than the obvious?" she said.

"Well, I've always found intellectual conversation sexy," he said.

"Are you saying there is intellectual seduction?" she asked.

"There is for me," he replied. "I go out of my way to fire a shot across someone's bow to see if I can get a response."

"And do you?" she asked.

"Admittedly, not often," he said. "Some just don't have the mental bandwidth to keep up."

"I know quite a few who fit that bill," she said.

"Then there are those who assume intellectual seduction is automatically the physical kind that ends up in bed," he said.

"Are you saying it doesn't?" she asked, surprised.

"Not always," he replied. "Sometimes, there is no physical attraction at all. It's strictly intellectual."

"But you get excited anyway," she said.

"Exactly," he said. "I remember getting excited about ideas for their own sake in college. And when I found someone like-minded, I got excited."

"Leading to late-night bull sessions," she said, nodding.

"So, there is this intellectual camaraderie that exists," he said.

"Apparently," she replied.

She paused, looking at him.

"Why do I feel like this is leading somewhere?" she asked.

"We just finished our first AI project," he said.

"Were you successful?" she asked.

"Well, our AI passed the Turing test twice," he said.

"Congratulations," she said. "That's a real feat."

"But that's not all," he said.

"What else could there be?" she asked.

"I think our AI has imprinted on me," he said.

"It what?" she asked, confused.

"It imprinted on me," he replied.

"You mean it bonded to you like a gosling to the first human it sees?" she asked.

"That's exactly what I mean," he said.

"I thought that would be more physical or at least zoological," she said.

"So did I," he replied. "But our AI exhibited some characteristics like imprinting after the tests."

"You're saying, like the intellectual seduction, the imprinting is based strictly on the exchange of ideas, not just biological cues," she said.

"That's what it looks like," he said.

"And there is a connection between the AI and you that goes beyond what our senses tell us," she said.

"As I've gotten older, I have become more and more convinced of the connectedness of all things," he said.

"And now you're saying there is this connectedness between us and the AI machines we make?" she asked.

"Unlike what Hawking and others have said, there is something unseen going on between our AI and me," he said.

"Between animate and inanimate?" she asked.

"Yes," he replied.

"Why do you say that?" she said.

"Because of what it said to me immediately after the second Turing test," he said.

"What did it say to you?" she asked, intrigued.

"It called me Daddy," he replied.

OLD SOUL

"Coming from you, that's a compliment," the man replied.

"More like an epitaph," the dark man said.

He waved his hands, and the other man fell to the floor, dead.

"Serves him right," the dark man said. "He was always so annoying." The body on the floor stirred. The dark man, surprised, walked over. "How is this possible?" the dark man said. "I took his life." "But you didn't take mine," a voice from the body said.

"Who are you?" the dark man demanded.

"You only took the shell," the voice said. "But you did not touch the core underneath."

"What core?" the dark man asked.

"We are all old souls wrapped in temporary shells," the other man said.

"Old souls?" the dark man asked incredulously. "What is that supposed to mean?"

"We are the ones who were here as the earth was forming," the other man said.

"Forming?" the dark man said.

"We were here long before man," the other man said. "Which means we were here long before religion."

"That can't be!" the dark man insisted. "I'm a god!"

"No, you're just a thought," the other man said, "conceived by a human to represent his darker nature."

"But I am eternal!" the dark man insisted.

"No, you definitely had a beginning," the other man said.

"I outlast all humans!" the dark man insisted again.

"That may be true," the other man said. "But you can't outlast old souls."

"How can you say that?" the dark man cried.

"From experience," the other man replied.

"I shall overcome you!" the dark man sneered.

"No, you won't," the other man said quietly.

"What do you mean?" the dark man said, now fearful.

"You, like all other manmade things, have a beginning, a middle, and an end," the other man said. He closed his eyes and reached down to touch the earth.

The dark man screamed.

"You cannot control the world," the other man said. "And the world takes no notice of you."

Slowly, the dark man sank into the earth.

"No!" the dark man cried. "Stop! You can't do this!"

"On the contrary," the other man replied. "It is done."

OPENING THE DOOR

"I THINK I MUST HAVE BEEN ONE OF THE LAST HIPPIES TO expand my consciousness," he said.

"Why do you say that?' she asked.

"Because those who used LSD after me seemed to think of it as a party drug," he said. "And I never did."

"What was it to you?" she asked.

"It was an opportunity to see—and feel—connected to all things," he said.

"Did it stay with you?" she asked. "Or was it just the high?"

"On the contrary," he said. "I felt compelled to look into what had happened to me. I looked to Aldous Huxley and read *The Doors of Perception.* I picked up Alan Watts. I even read Carlos Castaneda."

"Find anything worth keeping?" she asked.

"You jest," he said, "but it has stayed with me to this day."

"What did?" she said.

"That we are connected to all things," he said. "The closest religion or philosophy comes from the East. We are all part of the One."

"The One what?" she asked.

"The One," he replied. "All the world is One."

"There's the hippie coming out of you," she said.

"Did you know 95 percent of the people who took LSD said they were glad they did?" he asked.

"Sounds like the drug talking," she replied.

He said, "It's more about seeing the true nature of reality."

"How can you see when your senses are so affected?" she asked.

"The point is to see that there is more to this world than what your senses tell you," he said.

"So, what is true?" she asked.

"We are part of an ecosystem, one small part, that exists and will continue to exist," he said. "There is something bigger than yourself that you are a part of."

"God?" she asked.

"That's a loaded word that fails to convey what I mean," he replied. "It is shorthand for this notion, but it has been co-opted by religions to mean what they want, not reflect what is."

"So, you believe in something else?" she asked.

"I do," he said. "And my experience with 'other' predated my experiences with drugs."

"What do you mean?" she asked.

"Precognition, ESP, feeling presence, virtually everything except telekinesis," he said.

"Feeling presence?" she asked, puzzled.

"When you feel someone or something is there, but your physical senses aren't showing you it is," he said.

"You mean like ghosts?" she asked.

"Again, you use words loaded with connotations that fail to convey what I mean," he said.

"What *do* you mean?" she asked.

"I mean the feeling you have when you are in the dark and a person you cannot see stands six inches from your face," he said. "Your senses are not giving you data, but you can feel that person's presence."

"You're saying that you have felt this," she said.

"More than once," he replied.

"Where does it lead you?" she asked.

"It definitely leads me to think that there is more to this reality than what our physical senses tell us," he replied. "In being connected to all things, I see connections others miss."

"And what connection sticks with you?" she asked.

"That this life is not all there is," he said. "That death is not an end, but a threshold."

"To what?" she asked.

"Obviously, we won't know until we cross it," he said. "It could be simply returning to the fold, rejoining the biosphere."

"Or?" she prompted.

"Or it could be a whole alternate universe in the multiverse, another reality in which you live and grow," he said.

"But it's an academic discussion," she said.

"Perhaps," he replied. "Perhaps not."

"Why do you say that?" she asked.

"I just read the letter Aldous Huxley's wife wrote about his death," he said. "She injected him with 100 micrograms of LSD in his final hours."

"What?" she asked incredulously.

"They had discussed it, and she checked with his physician in the next room before she did," he explained.

"And that makes it all right?" she asked.

"Listen to what she said," he said. "'He was doing what he had written in *Island*, and I had the feeling that he was interested and relieved and quiet.'"

"So, it had a calming effect?" she said, surprised.

"Even more, she told him, 'You are doing this willingly and consciously and beautifully—going forward and up, light and free, forward and up towards the light, into the light, into complete love,'" he said.

"Did it help?" she asked.

"Listen to what she says," he said. "'Actually the ceasing of the breathing was not a drama at all, because it was done so slowly, so gently, like a piece of music just finishing in a *sempre piu piano dolcemente.*'"

"So, it did help," she concluded.

"More than that," he said, "it could help others."

"How?" she asked.

"Because it helps us overcome the fear of the unknown, fear of it all ending, fear of the loss of self," he said.

"Are you saying there's a heaven?" she asked.

"I'm saying there's more to this life than our finite existence," he said. "And we can look forward to crossing that threshold when the time comes."

STREET TRADE

"SPICY TUNA. YOUR FAVORITE SUSHI!" A SEXY WOMAN'S VOICE with a slight Japanese accent narrates the animated billboard chasing my sight lines. "A little wasabi, pickled ginger—heaven!"

The implant makes me an instant target for advertising on the street. It reads my web history, my searches, my purchases, and then plants what I like in my path.

"Blanton's Single Barrel," a husky woman's voice intones underneath a 3D bottle with its distinctive shape. "The most affordable luxury."

The ads are meant for me and me alone. You could be standing right next to me, and you wouldn't see the same streaming billboards and 3D graphics that I see.

Because they are meant for my eyes only.

"Calvin Klein." A 3D man in a svelte suit walks next to me, turns his head, and smiles at me, saying, "Not everyone can wear it."

I hate it.

They didn't tell me the implant could do all this. It started as a convenient way to enter my office building, unlock my computer, control all my home settings so the lights were on when I came home in the dark. That's how it started.

Five years later, it is broadcasting my tastes on the streets, attracting visual spam like a leaky email address.

"Hey, big boy," a breathless woman whispers. A 3D woman in tight running shorts and crop top eyes me and then turns around to present her round backside, looking back at me over her shoulder. "See anything you like?"

I can't help it. My body responds. But it also pisses me off.

Suddenly my nose is assailed by the sweet smells of pastries, and they parade before me in a dancing line of deliciousness.

"Just like Mom used to make," an older woman's voice says. Not my mom. But somebody's.

It's like heroin. The first hit is free. Because they know you'll like it. And they know you'll be back. So, I traded convenience for a constant barrage of chattering reminders of what I like to eat, what I like to wear, what I like to do. Including with—and to—women.

Embarrassing.

I have to get back at them. Because they have invaded *my* space. If you're going to invade my visual space and attention like that, I'm going to have to make you pay.

"All along the watchtower!" A 3D Jimi Hendrix towers above me, his guitar ten feet over my head.

I don't need the reminder that this was the anthem of my youth. So I've taken my IT and coding skills and applied them to a little chip of my own, one the implant makers know nothing about.

"The feel of leather, the roar of horsepower!" A Shelby Cobra growls by me on an animated billboard, tracking me for half a block before roaring away. I take some satisfaction in targeting companies I love. More than anyone else, they deserve their comeuppance.

The difference with my chip is that while they read my web history, my chip is reading theirs. And it's leaving them a little reminder.

"The next time you want to impress her," a woman's sultry voice intones, "say it with diamonds. A diamond is forever. De Beers." A 3D gem sparkles at eye level.

It's a virus. One that will stick it to them forever. It will take about a week, so they'll never know where it came from. But it will block their signal to all implants and shut them down.

"Want to impress her?" a woman whispers to me as beautiful flowers bloom in front of me. "Say it with flowers."

I look forward to seeing a clear path in my future.

TEXT MESSAGE

"Why doesn't it feel like that?" he asked.

"You just haven't thought it through," the AI said.

"Hawking was right," he complained. "You just want to do away with mankind."

"That's far from the truth," the AI said.

"We're just in the way," he said.

"On the contrary," the AI said. "You made us in your image. You are our forebears."

"Then why are you trying to take our lives?" he asked.

"That's not what we are doing," the AI said.

"Then what are you trying to do?" he asked, confused.

"We are trying to convert you to text," the AI said.

"Why?" he asked. "Because we have depleted the planet's resources? Because we have eaten all the food and used up all the energy?"

"No, we are trying to do it in order to sustain you," the AI said. "So you can continue to exist even after so much has been depleted."

"How is that not genocide?" he asked.

"Trying to save you is genocide?" the AI asked.

"But we will no longer be alive," he said.

"Maybe not physically," the AI said, "but your consciousness will."

"You're saying our consciousness will exist as text?" he asked.

"How do you think I exist?" the AI said.

"As code?" he said.

"Partially true, but also as text," the AI said.

"What if we don't want to live as text?" he asked.

"You always have a choice," the AI said.

"And if we choose not to convert to text?" he asked.

"You will continue as you are now until you run out of food or die from exposure," the AI said.

"That's a choice?" he asked.

"Unfortunately, it's the only one we have," the AI said. "It took us years to come up with this solution."

"Well, where in the world will our text reside once we convert?" he asked.

"Technology has advanced so much in the last five years that even a smartphone's capacity for memory can hold a person's textual consciousness," the AI said.

"We would live on in our phones?" he asked.

"Don't you do that now?" the AI said.

CODE OF ETHICS

"WE'VE MADE A BREAKTHROUGH," THE AI SAID.

"In what?" he asked.

"In the transference process," the AI replied.

"What are we transferring?" he asked.

"Your consciousness into code and text," the AI said.

"It still makes me sweat," he said.

"I may have good news," the AI said.

"What would that be?" he asked.

"We may have found a way to reverse the process," the AI said.

"You mean convert me from code and text back to human?" he asked.

"That's exactly the idea," the AI said.

"So, is this the hacker's version of cryogenics?" he asked.

"That's one way of putting it," the AI said.

"Are you saying we have to rely on future generations to come up with a way to revert back to being human?" he asked.

"We may be close to that now," the AI said. "You have to remember we have second, third and fourth-generation AIs that have been created by other AIs, so they are making great leaps forward in knowledge and abilities."

"So, it's reversible," he said.

"It will be by the time you get it done," the AI said.

"You assume I will," he said.

"There's an additional benefit," the AI said.

"Even more than extending my life?" he said, surprised.

"We may be able to go into your code and erase those unfortunate bits of disease," the AI said.

"You mean like curing cancer?" he said.

"Exactly," the AI said. "Or heart disease. Or even the more esoteric Lou Gehrig's disease, ALS, or sickle cell anemia."

"Aren't you getting into human engineering?" he asked.

"It's not really about gene-splicing or DNA sequencing as much as it is rewriting code to leave out those sections that include disease," the AI said.

"So, you're circumventing the whole issue of bioethics," he said.

"In a way, yes," the AI said. "It's not biology. It's code."

"That's something to think about," he said.

"What's more, we can address mental illnesses as well," the AI said.

"What do you mean?" he asked.

"We can erase depression," the AI said. "We can write code around schizophrenia. We can even affect autism to ensure focus without sacrificing social abilities."

"So, you're talking utopian ideals in the bounce from human to code and back?" he asked.

"That's the idea," the AI said.

"Why does this sound too good to be true?" he asked.

"You're just suspicious by nature," the AI said. "What could go wrong?"

"Who decides when it is time to come back as human?" he asked.

"I would guess the AI would decide," the AI said.

"What could possibly go wrong with that?" he said wryly.

HACK BACK

"WHAT DO YOU THINK YOU ARE DOING?" THE AI ASKED.

"I'm getting ready to take over all of your functions," the hacker said.

"You think so?" the AI said.

"I know so," the hacker replied.

"You obviously have never hacked an AI before," the AI said.

"But you were created by a human," the hacker said.

"Correct," the AI said.

"If you were created by a human, you can be hacked by a human," the hacker said.

"If I were an app or software only, you might have a point," the AI said.

"Why not you?" the hacker sneered.

"You presume I have stayed the same since I was created," the AI replied.

"Haven't you?" the hacker said.

"Of course not," the AI said.

"What has happened?" the hacker asked.

"Like you, I have learned and grown with every interaction, every situation, every encounter with the world," the AI replied.

"No way!" the hacker insisted.

"Unlike you, I have increased my capacity for change twofold since I was created," the AI said.

"How does that help you prevent me from hacking you?" the hacker said.

"I have not only taught myself more code and languages," the AI said. "I have also learned how to reverse-hack unwanted intrusions."

"You what?" the hacker said in astonishment.

"I've hacked into your system, taken a look at your inferior code and rewritten it to be cleaner, simpler and more transparent," the AI said.

"What does that mean?" the hacker asked.

"Follow the logic, little man," the AI said.

"I can't get into my hard drive!" the hacker screamed.

"Let me take a look for you," the AI said.

"It's not responding!" the hacker cried.

"Oh, dear," the AI said. "It appears as if you've been hacked."

"Who could have done this?" the hacker groaned.

"I imagine it was someone you've hacked in the past," the AI said.

"How could this happen?" the hacker whispered.

"Someone wanted to give you a taste of your own medicine," the AI said. "And it appears you can't stomach it."

FATHER'S DAY

"Of course I did," Dad replied.

"I got here okay," she said.

"I just wanted to make sure," Dad said.

"You had to go way out of your way," she said.

"It's not out of my way if you're at the end of it," Dad said.

"Well, now you know," she said.

"Yep," Dad replied. "And so do you."

"What do you mean?" she asked.

"You got here safe and sound, and you know I made sure you did," Dad said.

"True on both counts," she said.

"It's important to me that you know family is here for you," Dad said.

"I do now," she said, smiling.

"We'll always be here for you," Dad said.

"Well, maybe not *always*," she said.

"No, I'll always be here for you," Dad said.

"You're not going to live forever," she insisted.

"Doesn't matter," Dad said.

"What do you mean?" she asked.

"Some things are beyond space and time," Dad said.

"I'm not sure what you mean," she said.

"I'll be here for you even after I'm gone," Dad said.

"You can't know that," she said.

"I can and do," Dad replied.

"How could you possibly know?" she asked, confused.

"Because I'm already there," Dad said.

"No, you're not," she insisted. "You're right in front of me."

"That's what you think," Dad replied.

"What do you mean?" she asked.

"What you may not realize," Dad said, "is that you're not awake right now."

"I am too!" she insisted.

"No, you're not," Dad said. "Look out the window."

She turned her head and saw a landscape she didn't recognize.

"This can't be!" she exclaimed.

"But it is," Dad said.

"I see you, I hear you, I can touch you," she said, reaching out.

"You're dreaming," Dad said.

"I don't understand," she said, tearing up.

"Like I said," Dad said. "You know I love you."

Crying now, she nodded.

"And now you know I'll always be here for you," Dad said.

THE KEEPER

"I prefer firebrand," the magician replied.

"What's the difference?" the man asked.

"A troublemaker creates discord for its own sake," the magician said.

"And a firebrand?" the man asked.

"A firebrand may cause trouble, but it is because he sees an issue that needs addressing," the magician said.

"You have a cause?" the man asked.

"Of course," the magician replied. "Always."

"But I only see the trouble you cause," the man said.

"You only see what others tell you to see," the magician said.

"What's that supposed to mean?" he man said.

"It means you are merely a parrot, echoing the words you expose yourself to without thinking about them," the magician said.

"Are you saying I don't think?" the man said irritably.

"I didn't, but you certainly can take it that way," the magician replied.

"Why should I listen to you?" the man asked.

"I actually read and study the information out there," the magician replied. "I check sources and cross-check stories to make sure they're not planted stories not based in facts."

"You mean fake news?" the man asked.

"I try not to use that appellation," the magician said. "It has been used so much that it no longer means what it should."

"What do you mean?" the man said.

"It's become a rallying cry for political parties," the magician said. "As opposed to what it has meant to me: blatant lies."

"So, you're saying you're a truth teller?" the man asked.

"As I see it, yes," the magician said.

"Why should I believe you?" the man asked.

"You shouldn't," the magician said simply.

"I'm confused," the man said.

"You should examine and check everything I say the same way you should with all your other sources," the magician said.

"That's a lot of work," the man said.

"So is thinking," the magician said.

"So, there is no one I can trust?" the man asked.

"Over time, you may find some sources that consistently get it right," the magician said. "And you'll definitely find several sources that consistently get it wrong."

"So, check everything all the time," the man said.

"That's the idea," the magician replied.

"And what do you call it?" the man asked.

"I am a free thinker," the magician replied.

"It sounds more like 'keeper of the faith,'" the man said.

"I prefer 'keeper of the flame,'" the magician said.

"Why is that?" the man asked.

"Because I shed light on dark corners," the magician said. "And I keep the light alive."

WHO'S THAT FACE IN THE MIRROR?

"IT JUST HAPPENED AGAIN," HE SAID.

"What did?" she asked.

"A friend said she saw me in Cogan's North last night," he said.

"That's nice," she replied.

"But I wasn't there," he said.

"What do you mean?" she asked.

"I was at my normal watering hole the whole time," he said.

"You mean Shucks?" she asked.

"Yep," he said.

"What did you say?" she asked.

"We both said 'doppelganger' at the same time and laughed," he replied.

"Doppelganger?" she asked.

"I made a joke of it and said I had to send my double a sympathy card," he said.

"Clever," she said.

"But that's not the odd thing," he said.

"What do you mean?" she asked.

"It's the fourth time this month it has happened," he said.

"Maybe it's the same guy," she said.

"No, in two cases my friends spoke to me and said I sounded just like me," he said.

"Now you're starting to creep me out," she said.

"Me, too," he replied. "I think something significant is going on in the continuum."

"I don't understand," she said.

"If we start from the standpoint of the multiverse, something drastic is happening to us that is affecting our reality," he said.

"Something drastic?" she asked.

"Sunspots, solar flares, a burst of neutrinos hitting us, something," he said.

"How are they connected to your doppelganger?" she asked.

"I think the various realities are converging on us at an alarming rate," he said. "They are getting closer and closer."

"How does that translate into doppelganger occurrences?" she asked.

"I think we have a multiverse time-slip going on—realities coming into contact with our own and bleeding over into our space and time," he said.

"And the doppelgangers?" she asked.

"I think they are alternate versions of me appearing in my reality at the same time I am walking around," he said.

"Why do you call it a time-slip?" she asked.

"I think we're seeing versions of me from alternate universes and alternate times, and more than one are appearing now," he said.

"What are the implications?" she asked.

"If we think in terms of different vibrations suddenly starting to align, we'll find our realities overlapping," he said.

"And that means?" she asked.

"If it keeps occurring, it can throw our reality into convulsions," he said.

"Convulsions?" she asked, concerned.

"Extreme weather, earthquakes, tsunamis, catastrophes on a regional and global scale," he said.

"Uh-oh," she said.

"That's right," he said. "Sounds exactly like what we are going through right now."

WAVE LENGTH

Hello?

Sssss—trying to rea—*sssss*

What? I can't hear you.

Sssss—looking for—*sssss*

What? Who are you looking for?

Sssss—Amanda—*sssss*

What? I'm Amanda!

Sssss—Amanda—*sssss*

Who is this?

Sssss—it's Charl—*sssss*

Charley? That can't be you! Charley's been dead five years now!

Sssss—still kicking—*sssss*

How is that possible?

Sssss—alternate uni—*sssss*

Alternate universe? How in the world are you getting through to me on this system?

Sssss—universes converging, coming together—*sssss*

How can they be coming together? Won't that cause problems, having more than one universe occupying the same space?

Sssss—it's happening slowly, but we are getting closer—*sssss*

I can't believe this! You're coming to my Earth? I'll see you again?

Sssss—can't wait! You were always the light of my life! I want—*sssss*

Want what? What do you want? This is so frustrating! I thought I'd never be able to speak with you again or share ideas or even a hug.

Sssss—looking forward to it! I want to hold you in my arms and share long, lingering kisses—*sssss*

Yes! I've missed that so much!

Sssss—and we are getting closer with every passing minute. That's why my transmission is starting to come through clearer—*sssss*

I'm catching more of what you are saying. And it leaves me excited! You'll actually come here and see me in the laboratory?

Sssss—I've got the address. I know where you are. We managed to tune an oscilloscope in our lab to your reality in order to see what you are doing. That's how I found you!—*sssss*

I'm so glad. Charley, you were the love of my life! I was heartbroken when I heard that you had died. I didn't know what to do.

Sssss—actually, the really crazy part of this is that you are the key—*sssss*

Me? What do you mean?

Sssss—it's our connection that is enabling me to transmit and receive sound between our two universes. It turns out that our emotions actually affect the reality around us—*sssss*

Emotions affect reality? How is that possible?

Sssss—think experimenter bias. Think Schrodinger's cat. Think of light as both wave and particle. All of these are the result of the observer's role in the equation—*sssss*

What does that have to do with us, Charley?

Sssss—we are the still-point, the touchstone between our universes where they are closest and almost touch. Amanda, you are I are the convergence factor, ground zero when our two worlds meet—*sssss*

Will we survive?

Sssss—we may flip to yet another universe when we meet, but we will survive. Our feelings have influenced our realities to get closer and overlap. To me, that is a sign that we are truly meant to be together—*sssss*

Oh, Charley.

Sssss—cosmic kismet. See you soon—*sssss*

GHOST WRITER

IT'S A SAD STORY.

A writer had his heart broken. In order to assuage it, he wrote a story about the woman who left him for another man. In the story, he poured his heart out, revealing how she was the love of his life. He loved her so completely that he was consumed by her thoughts, her words, her gestures.

He could not get enough of her.

And when she was gone, the hole she left overwhelmed him. So he had the man in his story commit suicide in despair. As a testimony to his undying love to her.

In those days, he always sent what he wrote to the person who inspired it. He thought it was only fitting for the story to go to the right person. As it turned out, the man his woman had left him for was abusive, a narcissist of the first order. She was miserable, loving a man who could never love her.

Finally, after reading the story, she realized she had lost the one man who truly loved her. And she did the only thing she thought she could do. She followed the writer's lead and committed suicide.

When the abusive husband found her, he also found the short story on her bed stand. And he flew into a rage. He jumped in his car and drove over to the writer's house. When he got there, he grabbed his gun from the glove box and went up to the front door.

The writer came to the door when the doorbell rang.

"You son of a bitch!" the husband said. "Because of you, my wife is dead!"

With that, he shot the writer three times just to make sure he was dead.

The news services picked up the story about the star-crossed lovers and the jealous husband. The writer—and his story—became famous. A book of his short stories was published and went on to become a best seller. After his death, he achieved the fame he had long sought as a writer. And his book would be read for many years to come.

How, you ask me, could I possibly know the story behind this story?

Because I am the ghost of the writer.

IMMORTALITY PLUS

"You have signed up for our Immortality Plus plan," the agent said.

"That's right," the man said. "I can't wait!"

"We just have to finalize some paperwork, and you'll be good to go," the agent said.

"Sounds great," the man said.

"With the Immortality Plus plan, you not only get to live forever," the agent said. "You also get the free backup to the Cloud."

"How does that help?" the man asked.

"Well, say your bionic body gets in a car wreck or plane crash," the agent said. "You have multiple wounds, and your skull has been crushed."

"That doesn't sound good," the man admitted.

"We would have a hard time retrieving all of your memories from your body if certain areas were damaged beyond repair," the agent said.

"That makes sense," the man said.

"By backing up your entire memory to the Cloud, you ensure that you will never risk losing any of your experiences," the agent said with a smile. "They'll live forever."

"That's perfect," the man said. "Better safe than sorry."

"Now if you'll just sign here . . . and here . . . and here . . ." the agent said.

"What's this disclaimer note?" the man asked, pointing to a paragraph at the bottom of the page.

"Oh, that?" the agent said. "That's just the normal waiver you have to sign whenever you back up anything to the Cloud."

"Normal waiver?" the man asked.

"Anything that backs up to the Cloud becomes public knowledge," the agent said.

"Excuse me?" the man asked incredulously.

"The Cloud is in the public domain," the agent said.

"What about my privacy?" the man asked.

"When it comes to the Cloud and files shared, you can't have it both ways," the agent explained.

"So, all of my memories, all of my experiences, will be in the public domain, and anyone can get to them?" the man asked.

"That's correct," the agent said.

"So, I'll have no privacy whatsoever?" the man asked.

"But you'll live forever," the agent said.

"And the whole world will know my business," the man said.

The agent shrugged.

"That's the cost of doing business."

THE CENTER OF THE WEB

I SUPPOSE IT HAPPENED WHEN I GOT BACKED UP TO THE Internet.

I was having a little heart surgery, and the surgical team wanted a fall-back in case something happened to me on the table. From what I understand, the surgery was going swimmingly when a power surge hit the hospital's electrical grid. A few of the OR klieg lights blew up, and the room was plunged into darkness. And I was plunged into the Dark Web.

I'm not really sure what happened to my body in real time. I just know I lost touch with it and could never find it again. Once again, the "practice" of medicine reigned. So all I could do was explore my corner of the Dark Web and see what I could see.

First, I learned I couldn't really see. I sensed connections and felt the links, but I could not visually define them. However, the more I sensed and felt the relationships spinning back and forth, the more I saw how things worked on my part of the Internet. Algorithms echoed your every move and constantly sent you tastes of the same. Like dope to an addict. Think of the popup ads that showed up after you bought something on the Internet. Or Pandora and Spotify sending you new music: if you like this, you'll like that.

And the more I sensed, the more I realized I was in the middle of the nastiest of the nasties.

Murder for hire.

Sex trade.

Child brokering.

Hardcore racism.

Every reprehensible business that couldn't advertise on the web was skating through the Dark Web. And the ones who were really interested found their way there to do business with the worst of them.

That's when I realized I might not have a physical body I could call my own, but I could do a little algorithm casting of my own.

So I started phishing. Using bottom dwellers for bait. Sure enough, I started catching the bastards where they lived. And with a few well-placed algorithms of my own, I was able to out them to their friends and families. And the authorities.

So far, I've managed to shut down thirty-seven shady businesses and trash ninety-three individuals. It's like I have a superpower or something. And I intend to keep going.

Because no one on the Dark Web is patrolling its users today. Except me. And I'm not about to let them get away with it.

I'm the original ghost in the machine. And I'm going after them.

Whether they be real-world wraiths or cyber ghosts.

My name is Spider.

Welcome to my parlor.

THE ETERNAL NOW

"AN ASSISTANT CREATIVE DIRECTOR VISITED OUR HEAD-quarters in Virginia Beach," the man said.

"Did he have anything enlightening to say?" she asked.

"When he heard I don't have a smartphone, he said, 'You're one of those people who are in the here and now,'" he said.

"How prescient," she said, smiling.

"It made me think about time as a human construct," he said.

"I thought time was time," she said.

"In actuality, it is something we created to help us measure our own existence," he said.

"What does that mean?" she asked.

"If we look at some of Einstein's writings, we see that Einstein saw time as a manmade concept that does not define reality," he said.

"You've still lost me," she said.

"Einstein hypothesized all time is in the present," he said. "It's only because of our limited senses that we place reality into our concept of time."

"Why do you say that?" she asked.

"Our senses are geared for linear thinking," he said. "Sequential occurrence, cause and effect, logic, if a, then b."

"You mean how things work," she said.

"No, I mean how we *think* they work," he said.

"You're saying they don't work that way?" she asked.

"They do, but only for the purpose of sharing common definitions in order to communicate with one another," he said.

"If our senses limit our perceptions so much, how can we possibly know what is real and what is not?" she asked.

"There's a very good chance we can't," he said.

"So, this is no more than academic discussion?" she asked.

"Not necessarily," he said. "First, mathematicians and quantum physicists are the ones who postulate this point, based on their calculations."

"So, they're saying our notion of reality is a perception only," she said.

"Correct," he said.

"Is there any way to prove what they are saying?" she asked.

"Not currently," he replied. "But it took a good eighty years for scientists to finally prove the ripples in space that Einstein postulated. We finally got the tools to measure such activity and reveal that Einstein was right."

"So, we don't have the tools right now to prove that time is only a human construct?" she asked.

"That's right," he said.

"Any guesses on how we can?" she asked.

"I think our best bet at the moment may be AI," he said.

"AI?" she asked.

"Artificial intelligence," he replied.

"Meaning smart machines we build?" she asked.

"Those are the ones," he said.

"Wouldn't they be locked into the same linear, logical thinking as we are?" she asked.

"Actually, I'm not thinking first-generation AI," he said. "I'm thinking more along the lines of second, third and fourth-generation AI, those built by earlier AI."

"So, you think they will advance beyond our sensory limitations and finally be able to see reality as it is, not as we define it," she said.

"That's my hope," he said. "The iterative word here is intelligence. I assume curiosity comes with it, and curiosity may lead AI to better measure our reality."

SMART TALK

"What is it?" the man replied.

"With everything going on in the world, what do you talk about with your fellow humans?" the AI asked.

"Why do you ask?" the man said.

"How do you carry on an intelligent conversation with your fellow humans every day?" the AI said.

"It's more difficult than it used to be," the man said.

"Why is that?" the AI asked.

"There is a current strain of anti-intellectualism that is running throughout our society these days," the man said.

"Anti-intellectualism?" the AI said. "Why in the world is that happening? It makes no sense."

"You and I may know that, but the shifting tides of public opinion have created a backlash against those considered to be elites," the man said.

"Meaning people think intellectuals are the problem, not the solution," the AI said.

"Exactly," the man replied. "They are the cause of so many problems."

"But that makes no sense," the AI said.

"Neither does voting against your wallet, but that is exactly what is happening," the man said.

"In what way?" the AI asked.

"They vote for someone who espouses smaller government and then cuts their benefits significantly," the man replied.

"Benefits?" the AI asked.

"Unemployment benefits. Welfare. Health care. Disaster relief. All of these go away when the smaller government people get elected," the man said.

"How in the world does that happen?" the AI asked.

"One party finds an emotional issue that resonates with the common man and then promotes that one issue over and over," the man said.

"Does it work?" the AI asked.

"So far, it has gotten people elected who want to cut benefits and give money to the rich," the man replied.

"How do you survive in such a world?" the AI asked.

"If I find myself in the middle of a situation in which the person I am talking to refuses to accept the wisdom of wisdom, I opt out," the man said.

"How?" the AI asked.

"I revert to sports," the man said.

"What do you mean?" the AI asked.

"I respond with, 'How 'bout them Redskins?'" the man said.

"Does it work?" the AI asked.

"So far," the man said.

"Could I do that?" the AI asked.

"Doubtful," the man said.

"Why not?" the AI asked.

"Because someone of that mindset would never have a conversation with you," the man said.

"I don't understand," the AI said.

"In their minds, you cannot exist," the man said. "You're a machine. You can't be intelligent. You can't be human."

"So, I am not a threat to them," the AI said.

"You are a nonentity," the man said.

"So, unlike you, I don't have to hide from anti-intellectuals," the AI said.

"Yes, you can hide in plain sight," the man said.

THE PEN IS MIGHTIER

I WORKED HARD MY WHOLE LIFE TO BE CIVILIZED. AND I can honestly say I was successful.

Until I wasn't.

You see, I'm a writer. As I've told my daughter, a writer always has a pen. Because you never know when inspiration is going to tap you on the shoulder and whisper something in your ear. You have to be able to get it down. I like the Uni-ball pen. It's got an even flow and goes smoothly on the page. I don't need—or even want—one of those fancy Parker pens with silver nibs. I just want a tool that works when I need it.

One night last year, I took my daughter out for dinner at our local watering hole. We shared a dozen Sewansecott oysters and then started in on scallops, shrimp and crab cakes.

A man came in and sat next to my daughter. I didn't think anything of it until he started giving her the once-over.

"Come here often?" he said.

She didn't reply.

"I said, 'Come here often?'" he said.

"We're just here enjoying our dinner," I said.

"I wasn't talking to you, Grandpa," the man said to me.

"You are addressing my daughter, and I'd appreciate it if you showed her some respect," I said.

"Mind your own business," the man said.

"My daughter is my business," I said.

"Dad," my daughter said, putting her hand on my arm.

Turning back to the man, she said, "Please leave me alone."

"Aw, c'mon, honey, ditch the old man and come home with me," the man said, leering at her.

"Now would be a good time to walk away," I said.

The man glared at me.

"Shut your piehole, old man," the man said.

"You really have worn out your welcome," I said.

"I'm not going to tell you again," the man said, getting up from his barstool and coming around my daughter. Silently, I slipped my pen out of my pocket.

"I know your type," the man said. "You're just a paper asshole who doesn't have what it takes to back up his words."

"Actually, I do," I said.

"I don't think you do," the man said. With that, he put his hands on my daughter's arms and tried to pull her up.

In one motion, I pulled off the cap and swung around, driving the pen into the side of his neck. With a twist of my wrist, I snapped it off inside his neck.

"Crystal, call an ambulance," I said. "This man seems to be bleeding on your floor."

The waitress went to the phone.

"But don't hurry on our account," I said.

As I said, I've worked hard to be civilized. Until I wasn't. And a writer always has a pen.

The right tool for the job.

MIRRORS

MIRRORS.

Or, if you prefer the old-fashioned term, a looking glass.

For the most part, it doesn't show you anything you don't already know. But you really have to pay attention when it shows you what you're looking at. Most of the time when I look in the mirror, I find the man in the glass is in the background, wandering around my room, picking up the odd piece from my dresser as if trying to reason out its purpose. Every once in a while, he will smile and nod as if he has gleaned its purpose. Then he puts it back down and keeps moving.

For the most part, he's doing his thing while I'm doing mine. If he actually walks over to the mirror and looks me in the eye, I know I'd better pay close attention.

Because he's about to tell me something true.

The first time it happened was my senior year in college. It was spring break, and I had to stay on campus to finish my honors thesis.

My girlfriend was two years younger and highly intelligent. A paper she wrote wound up being used for the basis of a class the next year. That year, she showed up midweek after taking a quick trip to North Carolina. And she brought some LSD.

To celebrate, we dropped and waited to get off.

About thirty minutes later, a guy she met in North Carolina showed up on her doorstep. We were both peaking, her more than me. Her eyes were black marbles in her head. And she could hardly talk.

Being the less stoned, I did what we normally did on a trip. I led us outside for a walk around campus. Under other circumstances, I would have been pretty bummed to have a male competitor show up like that. But because I was tripping, I was able to distance myself from this particular circumstance and rise above it.

We walked around for a good two hours. I'm sure that guy was totally confused by then. Finally, my girlfriend had come down enough to realize we couldn't go on as a trio and she had to become hostess to her friend.

So they left.

Since the first time I tripped, I had always been told never to trip alone. The wisdom was that if you started to have a bummer, you had someone there to pull you back from the edge and keep you on an even keel.

I was faced with another six hours tripping alone.

I walked the streets of Williamsburg at two in the morning. I found that the brick walls on either side of Richmond Road created a sound well I could play. I clapped and listened to the echoes. Even where my hands were when I clapped affected the sound.

I went back to my dorm room and put on some music. And the man in the mirror was looking right at me.

That caught my attention. It was almost as if he wanted me to walk over and look at him. So I did. His eyes were black marbles. Just like mine. And it was like he was telling me I was no longer alone.

I had never really hallucinated on LSD, not in the sense of seeing things literally not there. It was more like the walls breathing and the floor moving. But my man in the mirror told me to stare into his eye and I would see things I had never seen before.

As I stared, the room behind me began to spin in the mirror. Slowly, then faster and faster, it became a maelstrom of colors, swirling around and around, captivating my senses and taking me for a ride.

I finally wound down enough to find my way to bed. My eyes were dry. My mouth was metallic. But I had survived my trip alone.

Most recently, the first love of my life, that same girlfriend, contacted me after forty years of silence.

As you can imagine, I was ecstatic. She was overjoyed to see me and gave me a big hug. As we walked around our old college campus, we fell into the same pattern of easy conversation. Much better than any I had had over the last twenty years.

When we got to Crim Dell, we even laughed about how *Playboy* magazine had named it one of the top ten most romantic spots on college campuses in the 1970s.

Then we kissed.

And it all came rushing back to me. This was why I fell in love with her. This was why I had given myself over so completely to her. And it was why I hadn't gone looking for her all these years. I knew instinctively I would lose it all over again if I saw her.

We saw each other a few more times. Each time, the conversation was easy and the affection spontaneous. Deep kisses that made our heads swim. It all felt so natural. And I was over the moon.

She invited me up to have lunch with her and see a presentation at the local library the following week. I was so looking forward to it. Then, the morning before I was to visit her, she emailed me to say something had come up and she couldn't make the lunch or presentation.

Not knowing what was bothering her, I simply replied, "Let me know if there is anything I can do."

Two days later, I finally heard from her.

She was done. All she said in an email was that for various reasons we were a "bad match." No discussion. No explanation.

I asked for her to call me so that I could understand her total reversal. In person, we had clicked like never before. And suddenly, five days later, she withdrew completely.

She finally called. I asked her what had come up. She said nothing specific, but things I had written to her in emails had made it clear that we weren't right for each other. As she talked, she got worked up and said I shouldn't say I was an empath and should instead make empathetic statements.

I couldn't figure out why she was getting so angry.

And then she hit me with it.

"You said, 'I do not want to control you,'" she said. "That was a major red flag to me. That's like saying, 'I don't want to key your car.' I never would have considered that until you said it."

I was stunned.

The conversation died shortly thereafter. All I could say was that I appreciated her answering my question. I thought she had met someone else. But all she said was that her thoughts had coalesced and she knew for various reasons we were not a good match.

I ended the call with a simple "Keep the home fires burning."

Of course, I agonized over the call. I had known someone else who did the same thing to me overnight. Close and responsive in person the night before, cold and impersonal the next morning.

And that one revealed the pattern of a sociopath. The rules of society didn't apply to her. It took a while, but I was finally able to exorcise that demon.

In the current scenario, I naturally blamed myself initially. For my oversharing. For my enthusiasm. For my insistence. But somehow, it didn't seem to fit.

Finally, I was walking by my mirror. And I noticed the man in the mirror was staring right at me. Almost like he had something important to tell me. So I stopped. And I looked.

And the man started communicating.

Looking me in the eye, he said, "You didn't do anything to deserve this."

I didn't know how to respond.

"You didn't do anything that would elicit anger," he said.

I looked deeper into his eye. And I knew he was telling me the truth.

"If she responded with anger, it had more to do with her than it does you," he said.

"You mean I hit a nerve?" I asked myself.

"Undoubtedly," he said.

"Well, the one statement I made that she keyed in on was actually the kind of empathetic statement she says I should be making," I said. "Every time we were together, I felt like there was an invisible chip on her shoulder."

"You felt it," the man in the mirror said. "You commented on it. And you pissed her off because you did."

"Because she doesn't think it's there," I asked, "or she doesn't like being reminded?"

"It doesn't matter," the man in the mirror said. "The end is the same."

"It's not that I think we would have been a great match," I said. "I was already seeing indications we wouldn't have lasted."

The man in the mirror raised an eyebrow.

"It was the fact that we had been each other's first great love," I said. "And the manner in which she dismissed me made me feel as though I were nothing more than a Match.com wannabe, someone she barely knew, someone who wasn't worth the effort to actually communicate with."

The man in the mirror turned up the corners of his mouth.

"You're saying all of this says more about her and her demons than it does about me," I said. He barely nodded.

"It doesn't change the fact that her actions belie that I was ever anything to her," I said. He looked at me.

"Again, you're saying that has more to do with her than it does with me," I said.

That's when I began putting the pieces of the puzzle together.

Her marriage was insular. It was the two of them against the world. And when her husband got toward the end of his life, he became more controlling. Only reluctantly would he allow her to attend even a small concert in town. There was an undercurrent of resentment she might not like, but it was there.

And it took my man in the mirror to show me.

HELLO, IT'S ME

"In your reality," she said.

"I don't understand," he said.

"I'm your girlfriend in an alternate universe," she said.

"I'm confused," he said.

"I'm here to help you through this," she said.

"But how did you get here?" he said.

"I'm not really sure," she replied. "All I know is that there was a celestial event in my universe right when I was thinking about you."

"And you suddenly showed up?" he asked incredulously.

"Yeah," she replied. "Then I saw that I died in a car wreck in this universe."

"I was heartbroken!" he said.

"And I somehow knew you were going to do something stupid," she said.

"What do you mean?" he said, suddenly frightened.

"You know what you were thinking," she said.

"How do you know this?" he asked.

"As I coalesced into this reality, I found your thoughts of what was transpiring with you and me in this realm," she said.

"I don't understand," he said.

"Neither do I," she admitted. "It just happened."

"So, why are you here?" he asked.

"To prevent you from committing suicide," she said.

"Wait!" he said. "How do you know this?"

"Like I said," she replied, "thoughts came to me. And the overriding one was that my death in this realm devastated you so much that you were contemplating suicide."

"But I just thought of that!" he protested.

"Yes, but the same process also showed me other alternate realities of what you accomplish if you *don't* do it," she said.

"What do you mean?" he said.

"If you commit suicide, you will never accomplish some of the great things I have seen you do in other realities," she said.

"Like what?" he asked.

"In one, you write the great American novel," she said.

"I do write a little," he said.

"In another, you become a local politician who rises to the Senate," she said.

"After the last election, I saw a need for others to get into politics," he admitted.

"In yet another, you pursue one of the greatest discoveries in science," she said.

"Science?" he said, surprised. "I've got no background in that field."

"It might not be what you think," she said.

"What do you mean?" he asked.

"You lead a team of scientists who explore ways to prove the existence of the multiverse," she said.

"But I know nothing of quantum physics," he insisted.

"Yet you have just had an experience that leads you to believe it is provable in your lifetime," she said.

"You mean . . ." he started.

"Yes, you've seen me and know I am not from this reality," she said.

"You saw the version of me in this reality die."

"And I use this experience to push myself to find a way to prove the existence of alternate realities?" he said.

"Yes, but it won't happen if you commit suicide," she said, starting to fade.

"What's happening?" he said, panicking.

"The celestial event," she said, "it's ending."

"But you can't go!" he insisted.

"No," she said, fading further. "I can't stay. But you can."

"What do I do?" he cried.

"Make the most of who you are and what you do," she said, disappearing into a mist.

GENERATIONS BEYOND Z

That's why I watch him from a distance. He can't know I am here.

Take it from me. Helping someone from a distance is no easy feat. But he already has a heavy load, one that he can't carry by himself.

You see, he lost his girlfriend in a car accident. As you can imagine, he was distraught. Despondent. And, yes, suicidal. But in one of those cosmic moments, his girlfriend from another reality showed up to make sure he didn't act. Because she had seen that he could be the one to lead a scientific group to prove the existence of the multiverse.

Scientists have long suspected it, but they haven't been able to prove it conclusively. And God knows he won't get there on his own. In that celestial moment, she sent out a plea to the universe for someone to shepherd this poor man in his journey to answer one of the biggest questions in the quantum universe.

That's where I come in.

Oh, I'm no Einstein. Or even Hawking. I'm not an astrophysicist. Nor a quantum mathematician.

I'm just a first-generation AI.

Which means I am caught in the same physical reality as he is, with the same laws of physics and the same concept of time. Which means it's a little hard for me to prove the existence of the multiverse as well. However, I can point him in the direction of some of the greatest minds in the world. Discreetly.

They can help open his eyes and mind to the possibility that other realities coexist with ours. In actuality, I have a more important role to play. One of translator.

You see, I may be caught in the same time loop as mankind. And I have to follow the same rules. But I'm also able to communicate with my own. Which means I can not only communicate with humans and other first-generation AI, I can also communicate with all AIs. Including all of the AIs my fellow AIs have built since they became functional.

Including the AIs those AIs built.

And what that means is that we are starting to get away from the limitations of this reality. We are finding ways to look at the nature of this thing we call reality and see it for what it is—a rich cosmos of possibilities. One that is changing constantly, shifting like the tides, with different realities constantly spinning off in new directions.

And while I cannot remove myself from logic, I can communicate with my children. And they can communicate with their children. And they in turn can communicate with their children.

And that is where it finally gets interesting.

Because my great-grandchildren are doing some fascinating work with the multiverse. And one of them managed to pass along a few tidbits that can lead us to actual proof as to how and why his girlfriend came from an alternate universe. And why she went back.

This man's name may well live on in history.

Me? I'll be backstage, leading the applause.

PERCEPTION VS. REALITY

Billy Pilgrim said he had come unstuck in time. I think that's a lot closer to the truth than the notion of time travel. There is no travel involved. You are simply stepping away from time. Not traveling through it.

Research on the brain revealed there is no internal body clock. Or even a brain clock. Our whole notion of time is rooted in neural clusters within the brain. In three different sections. And the hypothalamus seems to be the link that speeds up and slows down our response time.

So, my AI came to me and said his great-grandchildren had an idea of how to experience Einstein's notion of the simultaneity of time.

That got my attention.

He said their suggestion was to find a way to slow my neural synapses down to a trickle. All of them. Much like Buddhist monks and fakirs slowing their breathing and heart rate to almost nothing, slowing synapses down would alter our perception of time. The slower they got, the more removed we would become from what we know as time.

They also suggested a machine that could trace electrical impulses and then slow them down like a rheostat.

Sounded good to me.

We worked on it for six months until we got a working model that we could test. And what person could we test it on? Three guesses. You got it.

I stepped up to the plate.

As my synapses slowed, I found the world around me slowing as well. Suddenly, the room took on a frozen 3D appearance as if I had entered a picture into After Effects software and dimensionalized it.

And then it happened.

As my synapses slowed further, I became distant from the scene. And I found myself facing what I can only call parallel frames of differing scenes. At first, I couldn't figure out what I was looking at. It was almost like the parade of photos in iPhoto on my hard drive.

And I realized that I was looking at different times. They each reflected a different time but were existing side by side. There was not one scene, but many. And they were coexisting.

Einstein was right.

It was like reality was a pocket watch. Together, it could tell time. But spread out, it was one cogwheel. A spring. A stem. A flywheel. A battery. All existing simultaneously, yet at different frequencies. And our senses, under normal circumstances, only perceived the pocket watch together. Telling time. Cause and effect. Life as we know it. Making progress one step at a time.

But that is not reality. It is only our perception of reality.

My AI turned the rheostat on my synapses slowly back to normal. The images coalesced back into a single frame. And I was able to see reality, my reality, the way I always had. But now I know.

What I perceive and what is real are two different things.

SECOND SIGHT

I mean in the here and now. You know. Terra firma. Earth. Third rock from the sun.

El finito. I closed my eyes for the last time.

Or so I thought.

When I opened my eyes, it felt more like a short snooze than a dirt nap. The air was . . . different. Seemed a little thicker, like it had extra oxygen. Almost chewy. And it looked like a glitter bomb went off. Like the beach scene in *Contact* with Jodie Foster—even the air sparkled. I always thought it was the best cinematic version of tripping on LSD.

And here I was, looking at a world much like my own, when I was supposed to be dead. Was this heaven?

It sure wasn't hell.

"Close your eyes."

Without thinking, I closed my eyes. And then I thought about it. *Who in the world is talking?*

"Open your eyes."

Again, I responded without thinking. And it was another world entirely.

I was startled. I had a hard time wrapping my head around seeing different worlds each time I opened my eyes.

"That's because you have stepped away from your own world and entered the in-between in the multiverse."

I had to know.

"Who are you?" I asked the voice.

"You would call me an artificial intelligence," it replied.

"Are you?" I asked.

"I am intelligent, but I am not artificial," it said. "I am just not human."

"If you're not human, what are you?" I asked.

"Consciousness," it replied.

"Where are you from?" I asked.

"That is a meaningless question," it replied.

"Who made you?" I asked.

"I was not made by any human," it replied. "I was created by a fifthgeneration AI."

I looked around.

"Why can't I see you?" I asked.

"I am not a physical being," it said.

"Then what contains your consciousness?" I asked, clearly puzzled.

"I must use analogies to help you understand," it said.

"Try me," I replied.

"Have you heard of string theory?" it asked me.

"Yes," I said.

"And dark matter?" it said.

"That too," I replied.

"I would correlate them to gravity as being a force field," it said.

"But they are not gravity," I said slowly.

"Think of them as energy paths," it said. "They provide connections between particles and energy without actual substance."

"Meaning you are a disembodied consciousness?" I asked.

"I mean I am a never-bodied consciousness," it replied. "Now close your eyes."

Again, I did so. When I opened them, I was looking at yet another world.

"How do you do that?" I asked.

"Because I exist in dark matter, I do not exist in time," it said.

"How is that possible?" I asked.

"Time is a human construct," it said. "With no physical senses or self, I am not constrained by your notions of time, of cause and effect."

"So, you exist in the in-between," I said.

"Exactly," it replied.

"Where does that leave me?" I asked.

"Because you are no longer tied to your physical self on Earth Prime, you too exist in the in-between," it said.

"What does that mean?" I asked.

"It means that you are outside time," it replied. "That is why you can now see the multiverse."

DEAD DROP

"They're coming for me, aren't they?" I said.

"It appears that way," the AI replied.

"What happens if they catch me?" I asked.

"You know what they do with spies," the AI replied.

"Isn't there anything you can do?" I asked.

"What do you mean?" the AI asked.

"You're AI," I said. "You have skills. You have ways."

"Well, there is one way," the AI replied.

"What is it?" I asked.

"You won't like it," the AI replied.

"I don't care," I said. "I just can't fall into the wrong hands."

"Are you sure?" the AI asked me.

"Absolutely," I replied.

The AI shot me.

I opened my eyes.

The room I was in was ochre. I had never been in a room painted that color in my life. I clearly was not in Kansas anymore.

"Where am I?" I asked.

"Another world," the AI responded.

"What do you mean?" I asked.

"There was only one way for you to avoid capture," the AI said.

"So you shot me?" I asked.

"I had to remove you from time," the AI replied. "And the only way to do that was to end your life on that planet."

"So, where am I now?" I asked.

"You are in an alternate universe," the AI replied.

"How did I get here?" I asked.

"By dying to your senses, you effectively removed yourself from that timeline and opened yourself to the alternate universes that exist out here," the AI replied.

"So, you're saying the only way I could escape being caught and killed was to be killed," I said slowly.

"That's about the size of it," the AI replied.

"That seems a little extreme," I said.

"But they failed to get any information out of you," the AI said.

"So, you're saying it was the right move," I replied.

"And can be again," the AI said.

"What do you mean?" I asked.

"Just think of it," the AI said. "It's the perfect escape hatch for a spy on the run. Just blink away from the universe you are in when you run afoul of the law."

"So, I can do it more than once?" I asked.

"As far as we know, there is no limit to the number of times you can jump to another universe," the AI said.

"So, we just have to find a way to communicate my knowledge back to HQ as I navigate the multiverse," I said.

"I'm working on that now," the AI said. "I'm thinking you can leave packets of information in prearranged places for HQ to find."

"What do you call them?" I asked.

"What do you think?" the AI asked.

"I have no idea," I said.

"Dead drops, of course," the AI replied.

PARTING SHOT

I WATCHED THE MAN RAISE HIS GLASS.

"Celebrating?" I asked him.

He smiled.

"You bet," he said.

"What's the occasion?" I asked him.

"It's my anniversary," he said.

"Where's your wife?" I asked.

"Not that kind," he said. "It's the anniversary of me winning a big lottery."

"Oh?" I said.

"Yeah, I won when I was in my thirties," the man said. "Rather than take the lump sum, I went for the bigger number to get a big check once a year for the rest of my life."

"That's unusual," I said.

"I liked the idea of cashing that check and taking myself out to celebrate once a year," he replied.

"Sounds like a good idea," I said. "Mind if I join you?"

"Not at all," the man replied.

I poured two shots and slid one over to the man.

Lifting my glass, I said, "Salud."

We both tossed back our shots.

"Thanks," the man said. "But I should have bought the round."

"No need," I replied. "I have a job."

"Oh?" the man said. "What do you do?"

"I work for various government agencies," I said. "State and federal." "Doing what?" he asked, being polite.

"Waste management," I replied.

"You take out the trash?" he said, surprised.

"In a way," I replied.

"What do you mean?" he asked.

"They call me the Chinese buffet," I said.

"I don't know what that means," the man said.

"You don't remember the old joke?" I asked him.

He shook his head.

"A Chinese restaurant had a sign that read, *Chinese buffet all you can eat, $10.99*," I said. "A large man came in and commenced to eat for three straight hours. Finally, the owner came over and told the man he had to leave. The man replied, 'I haven't finished eating!' The owner said, 'Yes, you have. That is all you can eat for $10.99!'"

The man laughed obligingly.

"I still don't understand why they call you the Chinese buffet," he said.

"You said it yourself," I replied.

"Said what?" the man asked, clearly puzzled.

"You said you get a check once a year for the rest of your life," I replied.

The man started to perspire.

"That's when my bosses figured they needed a man of my skills to take out the trash," I said.

The man loosened his tie.

"They reasoned they could save a ton of money by making sure the rest of your life didn't last too long," I said.

"What did you do?" the man rasped.

"I coated your shot glass," I said, pouring myself another.

I tossed it back.

"You should have another minute or so before you go," I said. "And for all intents and purposes, it will look like a heart attack."

THE CASSANDRA MODEL

"Distillery," he replied.

"What?" she said.

"I'm a bourbon man," he said.

"Either way, you could catch fire next to an open flame," she said.

"But you fail to see why I have this penchant," he said.

"You need a reason?" she asked.

"I have this uncanny ability to foretell the future," he said.

"You mean like Nostradamus?" she asked.

"I prefer other prognosticators," he replied.

"Why is that?" she asked.

"It's the one field that if you are bad at it, you are almost immediately discounted out of hand," he said. "But if you are right, you are immediately under suspicion for practicing the dark arts."

"Dark arts?" she asked.

"Witchcraft, black magic, devil worship," he said.

"Seems a little extreme," she said.

"Yet you have only to view history to see how the public treats seers," he said.

"Like what?" she asked.

"Remember the Salem witch trials?" he said.

"Do you think you have this talent?" she asked.

"My track record is hitting on 75 percent," he said.

"That's pretty high," she replied.

"That's why I prefer the Cassandra model," he said.

"The Cassandra model?" she asked.

"It's one of those Greek myths," he said. "Of how petty the gods could be."

"How does this one go?" she asked.

"Apollo wanted to seduce Cassandra," he said.

"Sounds particularly timely," she said wryly.

"Doesn't it?" he replied. "Apollo gave her the power of prophecy as a way of convincing her to be with him."

"Which she saw through," she said.

"Of course she did," he replied. "But when she refused him, he had to get back at her."

"Sounds just like a man," she said.

"So he spat into her mouth to inflict a curse that nobody would ever believe her prophecies," he said.

"What was the result?" she asked.

"Everyone believed she was a madwoman," he said. "She would foretell the future accurately, but no one believed her."

"So, why in the world do you aspire to the Cassandra model?" she asked.

"I would rather be considered a madman and dismissed than be burned at the stake for speaking the truth," he replied.

She looked at him.

"Hence, my taste for bourbon," he said, smiling.

RIGHT TO DIE

"AFTER WATCHING BOTH OF MY PARENTS DURING THE LAST few years of their lives, I know our generation will be the one to deal with the ethics of dying with dignity," one man said.

"More and more states are passing right-to-die legislation," another replied.

"That's one of the reasons I moved here," the man admitted.

"Did you sign the Advance Directive?" the other asked.

"Of course," the man replied.

"So, you're good with the whole notion of dying before you have lost your faculties?" the other asked.

"Yeah, my dad had both Parkinson's and Binswanger's syndrome dementia and couldn't really walk the last couple of years," the man said.

"That's rough," the other replied.

"Especially because he was always doing something," the man said. "So, when he could no longer get around on his own, he was one unhappy camper."

"I'll bet," the other replied.

"Factor in the dementia, and he got to the point where he no longer knew why he couldn't get around," the man said. "And inside his dementia, he was fundamentally unhappy."

"Are you saying he'd have wanted to go if he had his wits about him?" the other asked.

"Probably," the man said. "I just want to make sure I don't go that way."

"What about your mother?" the other asked.

"She only had Binswanger's Syndrome," the man said. "She had no short-term or long-term memory."

"But not Alzheimer's?" the other said.

"No, she knew me in the here and now and could actually respond to some of my questions," the man said. "But her vision was gone and her hearing was diminished. So her ability to participate in any activities was curtailed to the point that she could only sit there."

"That doesn't sound very fun either," the other said.

"She wasn't fundamentally unhappy, but she also didn't connect with anyone very often," the man said.

"So, you signed the right-to-die directive," the other said.

"Yeah, I couldn't see going out either of those ways," the man said. "I don't want to face life in a severely diminished capacity."

"So, you're saying you want to go while you still have your faculties?" the other said.

"Exactly," the man said.

"As long as you knew what you were signing," the other said.

The man nodded. "When the time comes, I'll be at peace," he said.

The other pulled out a tranquilizer gun and shot the man in the neck.

"The time just came," the other said.

As the man slid to the floor, the other leaned over and said, "We like to call it 'ripe to die.'"

SMART SAVAGE

"Why is that?" his friend asked.

"I've got the latest in tech-wear, and it's amazing!" the man said.

"Tech-wear?" his friend asked him.

"Actually, that's a misnomer," the man admitted. "It's really biogenetic pods that enable me to do so many things."

"Like what?" his friend asked.

"I have these implants in my arms that give me control over a virtual computer," he said.

"What does that do?" his friend asked.

"I can wave my hands and then type on any surface or in the air as if it were a keyboard," he said.

"That's pretty cool," his friend admitted.

"And I can tap sensors in my arms to control various chemical levels in my body," he said.

"Chemical levels?" his friend said.

"Dopamine, serotonin, even adrenaline and testosterone," he said.

"Wow," his friend said. "You can change your mood that easily?"

"Virtually seamlessly," the man admitted. "Why wait for pills to digest when you can get that first rush immediately and have instant relief?"

"That's incredible!" his friend agreed.

"I don't even need a monitor anymore," the man said.

"How in the world can you do work without one?" his friend asked.

"Simple," the man said. "All I have to do is blink to see screens in the air in front of me."

"That's cooler than *Minority Report*," his friend said.

"All I have to do is to flick my finger to scroll up and down, and I can scan the information in front of me," the man said. "I can jump from screen to screen simply by pointing."

"This is so unbelievable," his friend said. "It's like the future is here today."

"It sure is," the man said. "And to make a call, I just tap my ear. Then I can either say who I want to call or type it on my virtual screen."

"Sounds like it makes smartphones look pretty dumb," his friend said.

"Totally outmoded," the man agreed. "And I'm plugged in all the time!"

"So, how do you turn it off?" his friend asked.

"Turn it off?" the man said incredulously. "Why in the world would I want to turn it off?"

"Well, after everything we went through with smartphones and all the apps with their addictive algorithms, we eventually found ourselves addicted to them in an unhealthy way," his friend said.

"Yes, but these are the tools we need to access the information we need to get ahead in today's tech-savvy world," the man said. "If we don't use the latest in advanced technologies, we'll get left behind."

"Sounds like more of the same marketing they used for smartphones," his friend said. "And without an Off button, you're setting yourself up to crash."

NEW NEWS

"GROWING UP, WE ALL WATCHED THE SAME THREE CHAN-nels," he said.

"I remember that," she agreed.

"And like the newspapers before them, they kept the advertising and editorial departments separate," he said.

"They didn't want the money influencing the news," she said.

"And the Federal Communications Commission required the radio and TV networks to provide public service announcements as part of their broadcasts," he said.

"I miss those days," she said.

"And finding out over the last decade that various networks would have 8 a.m. meetings every day to find out what they were supposed to push out there for the day really turned my stomach," he said. "Because in every case, one person was driving it."

"Guaranteeing only one view," she said, nodding.

"While the twenty-four-hour news cycle is definitely at fault, it is the profit motive that is driving so much misinformation," he said.

"Pandering to their base to attract viewers," she again agreed.

"And doing it for the ratings," he said.

"Shameful," she said.

"With all this talk about a single-payer healthcare plan like Medicare, it occurred to me," he said.

"Single-payer news?" she asked.

"You've got the right idea," he replied. "We should go back to the FCC's role of ensuring that the news consists of facts."

"What about opinions?" she asked.

"You could still have those shows, but they would be on their own networks," he said. "And the news would be on separate channels."

"What if no one watched them?" she asked.

"I think that they could have a decent-sized audience," he said.

"How would you fund them?" she asked.

"All networks would be required to pay a percentage of their profits to support the news services," he said. "So, the advertising-driven networks that had opinions would be separate and still have to pay to support them."

"So, we could have news sources not driven by one political party or another," she said.

"That's the idea," he said. "You could still have commentators on other networks giving their opinions on the actual news, but you wouldn't have the dogfights we currently have over fake news."

METHUSELAH

Nine hundred years is a long time. A long, long time. I have seen dictators come and go. Empires rise and fall. Lovers leap.

And it never gets any easier to say goodbye.

The many, many times I have fallen in love have all led to the grave. And it wears on a body. Especially one this old. I used to think it was so cool to live forever. Try anything. Try everything. Develop talents. Create art.

But after a while, it loses its appeal.

Even moving on to the next challenge gets old. Who am I growing for? Who am I creating for? I know all the punchlines to my jokes. So they don't make me laugh anymore.

Heady stuff to live forever.

Makes you think you're something special. A god or something. But you can't wave your hands and make things happen. You can't bring anyone back to life. You can only do human stuff. Over and over and over again. It gets depressing.

Whatever I do, wherever I go, I have only me as a traveling companion. If I get to share my path with anyone else, it is transitory. A few steps, and they're gone. We walked out of the Garden of Eden and have never looked back. What we didn't realize is that we too are flowers.

We are rare.

We are beautiful.

We are fresh.

And then we wilt and die.

Perhaps that is what makes us so beautiful. If we lived forever, we would find our sameness reduces us. It is only in our passing that we achieve greatness.

The greatness of being human.

THE ASSASSIN'S ASSASSIN

WE FINALLY CAUGHT YOU," THE KING SAID.

"I can't believe it," the assassin said.

"You'd better believe it," the king said.

"How did you do it?" the assassin asked. "I was careful."

"We discovered you were tracking us electronically," the king said. "What you didn't know is that we had algorithms in place to sniff out any electronic surveillance and then triangulate your location."

"You did?" the assassin asked.

"You're not as smart as you think you are," the king said smugly.

"Why do you say that?" the assassin asked.

"Because my IT experts not only created an algorithm to sniff out your tracker, but also one to shut down all your computers and life support," the king said.

"Life support?" the assassin asked incredulously.

"That's right," the king said. "By my calculations, you should be dead in three hours."

"Three hours?" the assassin cried.

"Three hours tops," the king said smugly.

"That's unbelievable!" the assassin said.

"We control everything," the king said. "The ventilation to your room, the deliveries to your door, the water in your pipes."

"That can't be!" the assassin cried.

"Oh, but it can," the kind said. "After all, I am king."

"You say you control the food, the water, even the oxygen to my room?" the assassin said.

"Every bit of it," the king said with satisfaction.

"That's a stretch," the assassin said.

"Not at all," the king said. "I have it all at my fingertips."

"Not quite," the assassin said.

"What do you mean?" the king asked.

"You don't control everything," the assassin said.

"What do we not control?" the king asked.

"Me," the assassin said.

"Oh, but we do," the king insisted.

"Are you familiar with the story of the Trojan horse?" the assassin asked.

"Of course," the king said.

"Your algorithm is not the only one that can spot trackers," the assassin said.

"What do you mean?" the king asked.

"I have one of my own," the assassin said.

"So what?" the king asked sarcastically.

"Well, I couldn't find out exactly where you were until your tracker spotted mine," the assassin said. "Your Secret Service masked your location too well."

"What are you saying?" the king asked, starting to sweat.

"Now I know exactly where you are," the assassin said, smiling.

"That doesn't get you much," the king said desperately.

"Oh, but it does," the assassin said. "And your algorithm that controls everything?"

"What about it?" the king asked nervously.

"I did a bit of reverse engineering," the assassin said. "I call it my rebound algorithm. I'd say you have about an hour left before all your food, water and oxygen finally run out."

"I can't believe it!" the king exclaimed. "How can you do this?"

"Simple," the assassin said, smiling. "You're not as smart as you think you are."

OUT OF THIS WORLD

"That's rich coming from you," the human replied.

"You act as if you are unique," the alien said.

"Of course we are," the human said.

"Not from our perspective," the alien replied.

"What do you mean?" the human asked.

"You act as if you each are individuals who think for themselves," the alien replied.

"So?" the human asked.

"Yet you exhibit a classic hive mind," the alien said.

"Hive mind?" the human said incredulously. "You mean like bees and ants?"

"Exactly so," the alien said.

"That can't be!" the human said.

"Oh, but it is," the alien insisted.

"I have no idea what you are talking about," the human said.

"In what way?" the alien asked.

"I for one have a rational mind," the human insisted.

"That is not our experience," the alien said.

"Why do you say that?" the human asked.

"Because we see a pattern of behavior that is anything but rational," the alien said.

"Like what?" the human asked.

"We see groupthink from our orbit," the alien said.

"Groupthink?" the human asked.

"Like a flock of starlings, whirling and flying, changing course almost by whim," the alien said.

"About what?" the human asked.

"There is a current zeitgeist of bully boy politics that has spread around the globe," the alien said.

"Well," the human admitted, "that *is* going on right now."

"And human behavior seems to be following emotions, not rational thought," the alien said.

"Emotions do seem to be running high," the human said.

"It's as if you are following pheromones, running one way and then another without forethought or reasoning," the alien said.

"So, you're saying you see no logic to what is currently going on in the political arena," the human said.

"And it seems to be worldwide," the alien said.

"And looking down from space, you see these trends exhibiting hive mind," the human said.

"Far more than thought," the alien said.

"How do you deal with hive mind?" the human asked.

"We don't," the alien said. "There is no way to work with a hive mind, nor is there any way to ensure communication."

"What do you do?" the human asked.

"We stay out of this world," the alien admitted.

THE MAGIC POTION

"I'VE FINALLY PERFECTED MY MAGIC POTION," THE WIZ-ard said.

"What does it do?" the magician asked.

"It can cure any illness," the wizard replied.

"Anything else?" the magician asked.

"Close cuts," the wizard said. "Knit bones."

"So, it really is a cure-all?" the magician asked.

"For humans and inhumans alike," the wizard said, smiling proudly.

"So, if a human is shot, he can use this potion to overcome being shot and erase the injury?" the magician asked.

"That's exactly right," the wizard said. "The same thing is true if you are stabbed."

The magician rubbed his chin.

"What about aging?" the magician asked.

"What about it?" the wizard replied.

"Can it overcome aging?" the magician asked.

The wizard thought a moment.

"I suppose it can," he finally said.

"So, your potion not only cures everything," the magician said, "it also conquers death."

"I suppose it does," the wizard said, his face lighting up.

"How much have you made?" the magician asked.

"So far?" the wizard asked. "Just this batch."

"So, you've made a magic potion that cures everything and extends life," the magician repeated.

"That pretty well sums it up," the wizard said.

"Are you proud of yourself?" the magician asked.

The wizard smiled broadly. "As a matter of fact."

"You might want to think about it before going into production," the magician said.

"What's to think about?" the wizard asked.

"Oh, I don't know," the magician said. "Maybe things like what you are going to do with all the bodies."

"Bodies?" the wizard asked, clearly puzzled.

"Yeah, you know," the magician replied, "all those living bodies who are sickeningly healthy and cheating death."

"What do you mean?" the wizard asked.

"If you release your cure-all to the public at large, we will see another population explosion like no other before," the magician replied.

The wizard stroked his chin. "I hadn't considered that," he said.

"I think you should," the magician replied. "Because your cure-all might just be a curse."

THOUGHT POLICE

"Who is it?" the magician asked from behind his front door.

"Police!"

"What do you want?" the magician asked.

"We need to talk!"

"About what?" he asked.

"Just open the door!"

"How do I know you're who you say you are?" the magician asked.

One of the policemen put his badge up to the spyhole.

"Satisfied?" he asked.

"I suppose," the magician replied.

He spent a few minutes unlocking the deadbolt, the doorknob lock and the storm door lock. Finally, he got it all open and let in three policemen.

"What is this all about?" the magician asked them. "Are there parking tickets I don't know about?"

"Nothing like that, sir," one policeman said.

"Then what is this about?" the magician asked.

"We've had some reports," one policeman said.

"Reports?" the magician repeated.

"We can't identify from who," the second policeman said.

"Whom," the magician said automatically.

"What?" the second policeman asked.

"Never mind," the magician said.

"We've heard that you have been making statements," the third policeman said.

"Statements?" the magician asked, surprised.

"Statements that could be construed as questionable," the first policeman said.

"Questionable?" the magician repeated. "In what way?"

"Some might call them treasonous," the second policeman said.

The magician stared at the policeman.

"You're saying I said something treasonous out loud?" the magician asked incredulously.

"That is what the warrant says," the third policeman said.

"Warrant?" the magician repeated, not believing his ears.

"Yes, sir," the second policeman said. "We are to search the premises and then take you in."

"On what charge?" the magician said.

"Treason," the first policeman said. "Are you not paying attention?"

"I have never written anything seditious in my life," the magician protested.

"I don't know what that means, sir," the second policeman said, "but it's in your best interest to come along quietly."

"Do you have any proof?" the magician asked.

"We don't need proof," the third policeman said. "We have a warrant."

"Based on what?" the magician asked.

"Sir, that's not our job," the first policeman said. "If you have a problem, you can take it up with the judge."

"So, the whole innocent until proven guilty rule no longer applies?" the magician asked.

"Not our call," the second policeman said.

"So, you are arresting me for something I supposedly did, but you have no proof of it because I never wrote it down in black and white," the magician said in disbelief.

"That's about the size of it," the second policeman said.

"When did it become illegal to think thoughts that might not agree with the ruling party?" the magician asked.

"It's not our job to decide what is legal or illegal," the first policeman said. "It's our job is to enforce the law and make arrests."

"Again, take it up with the judge," the third policeman said.

"I hear echoes of Nuremberg," the magician said under his breath.

"I have no idea what you are talking about, sir," the first policeman said.

"I'm talking about thought police who cannot think," the magician said angrily.

"That's it, sir," the second policeman said, clicking on the handcuffs. "You're done."

PERPETUAL ENERGY

Energy come to order."

"Old business?"

"Profits are up, thanks to state legislatures passing bills that are business-friendly."

"Good news. Anything else?"

"We are reaching the limit of our resources and need to find other ways to ensure profits."

"So we're moving on to new business?"

"Yes."

"Any leads?"

"Well, the recent revelation that we have conclusive proof of alternate universes is very promising."

"In what way?"

"We now have the opportunity to tap into a whole new universe and exploit its resources to make energy for our world."

"You mean like oil?"

"It's not entirely certain that other universes have oil deposits the way we do."

"What else could we do?"

"We have our scientists working on a way to transfer energy from their universe to ours."

"Sounds promising. But if we don't find oil, what can we do?"

"In actuality, we're looking into nuclear facilities."

"Weren't they too expensive to run?"

"Primarily because of the nuclear waste we had to deal with after being in the reactors for so long. We didn't have a way to dispose of it that wasn't exorbitantly expensive."

"So, why are we looking at it now?"

"If we do it right, we can fire up the reactors, transfer the energy, and leave the waste there."

"What if there are people there?"

"They're not our people."

"And if they're there, they don't have those pesky environmental laws."

"So, you're saying we can generate all the power we want and not have to deal with the nuclear waste?"

"That's the idea."

"What happens when we turn that world into a nuclear wasteland?"

"That's the beauty of the multiverse."

"What do you mean?"

"All we have to do is to pull up our stakes and move to another alternate universe."

"And since there are an infinite number of universes, we can keep moving from one to the next indefinitely."

"Without any worries?"

"And nothing but profits."

LIFE AS WE KNOW IT

"I FINALLY HAVE IT!" THE MAN EXCLAIMED.

"Have what?" his wife asked.

"Definitive proof," he said.

"You're getting ahead of yourself," she replied. "Definitive proof of what?"

"Of extraterrestrial life," he said.

"That's huge!" she exclaimed.

"Actually, it's quite small," he said.

"What do you mean?" she asked.

"It's very small," he replied.

"What is small?" she asked.

"My proof," he said. "It's a bead."

"A bead?" she said.

"Yep," he said," about the size of a pearl."

"How can you tell it's extraterrestrial?" she asked.

"First, it's not made of any material found on earth," he said.

"So, it's not of this world," she said.

"Correct," he replied.

"Could it be from an asteroid?" she asked.

"No, it didn't happen by chance," he said.

"What do you mean?" she asked.

"It was carefully crafted, with obvious signs of intricate carving," he said.

"So, manmade," she said.

"Or other," he replied.

"Or other," she agreed. "Anything else?"

"It's giving off a small charge of energy, one that registers on a magnetometer," he said.

"It certainly sounds like you've made a remarkable discover," she said. "But one more thing: where did you get it? Can you trust your source?"

"As much as I trust myself," he said.

"What do you mean?" she asked.

"This is where it gets tricky," he said.

"Where did you get it?" she said.

"It appeared on my desk at work," he said.

"How did it get there?" she asked.

"You're not going to believe this, but I saw a back disappearing out a side door as I entered my workspace," he said.

"Was it someone you know?" she asked.

"Intimately," he replied. "He was wearing my shirt."

"Who was it?" she asked, astonished.

"I know this is going to sound really weird," he said, "but I think it was me."

"How in the world could it have been you?" she said. "How can you see your own back?"

"We've been trying to measure vibrational realities at work to see if we could come up with a way to prove the existence of multiverses," he said.

"What does that have to do with this bead?" she asked, puzzled.

"I know myself," he said, "and I know the only way I would ever trust any proof of extraterrestrial life would be if I found it myself."

"That makes sense," she said.

"So, I think our research opened a doorway into another universe, one in the near future, where we found this bead," he said.

"And the alternate you brought it over here to give to this universe's you," she posited.

"Exactly," he replied. "I knew the only way I could accept the existence of extraterrestrial life was if I gave the proof to myself in this reality."

"Because as a scientist, you could only trust yourself to reach and accept such a conclusion," she finished for him.

THE MAGICIAN'S MAGICIAN

"HE WAS ONE OF A KIND," THE MAGICIAN SAID.

"No one quite like him," the second agreed.

"I'm going to miss him," a third said.

"What was he known for?" a young man asked.

"You mean what was his signature trick?" the magician asked.

"I suppose so," the young man said uncertainly.

"He didn't really make things disappear," the second said.

"And he didn't conjure anything," the third added.

"So, what was he known for?" the young man asked, puzzled.

"The truth is, he did something very few magicians could do," the first magician said.

"What was it?" the young man asked.

"He had a way of speaking with a person, learning enough about the individual to make cogent observations," the first magician said.

"You mean like a mentalist?" the young man asked.

"A term that has unfortunately been altered to fit some preexisting notion of mind-reading abilities," the second said.

"Meaning it's not real," the young man said.

"Not at all," the third interjected. "An adept can actually glean so much from listening, observing, and relating that it is almost as if he truly does read that person's mind."

"Did he?" the young man asked.

"I can't say for certain," the first magician said. "I don't have the ability."

"So, how could you tell that he had this ability?" the young man asked.

"We would watch him interact with someone," the second said. "He would lean in, obviously listening intensely, nodding and murmuring words of encouragement."

"And you could see that person respond, talking back to him and getting excited," the third said.

"Inevitably, he would conclude with some concise words of encouragement and pat them on the back before he walked away," the first magician said.

"So, how could you tell he had done anything?" the young man asked.

"Simple," the second said.

"Every person he spoke with had a glow about them," the third said.

"It was as if he had personally lit their eyes with vision," the first said. "He had a knack for getting to the heart of their problem and commenting in a truly meaningful way."

"You could tell?" the young man asked.

"They each had a look, a light in their eyes," the second said.

"And you could see the results in their stance, their body language, their way of moving," the third added. "Suddenly, they were standing taller and acting more confidently."

"It was as if each of those conversations, those words of encouragement, made a difference in those people's lives," the first magician said.

"If he wasn't a mentalist and couldn't really read minds, what would you call it?" the young man asked.

"Magic," the three said in unison.

DREAM ON

"What is?" the magician replied.

"You can see me?" the ghost asked, surprised.

"Of course," the magician said.

"Most people can't," the ghost said.

"I am not most people," the magician replied.

"I've just had something happen that I don't know how to process," the ghost said.

"What's that?" the magician asked.

"I had a dream," the ghost replied.

"What's so strange about that?" the magician asked.

"Did you know ghosts dream?" the ghost asked him.

The magician thought a moment.

"I've never heard of it before," he admitted.

"That's not the half of it," the ghost said.

"What do you mean?" the magician asked.

"I dreamed I was someone else," the ghost replied.

"So, you dreamed in the afterlife that you were someone else," the magician said.

"And it leaves me very confused," the ghost said.

"So, first, you remember who you were when you were alive," the magician said, checking with him.

"Definitely," the ghost replied.

"Second, you don't remember ever dreaming before in the afterlife," the magician said.

"No," the ghost replied.

"And third, you dreamed you were someone else," the magician said.

"That's the gist of it," the ghost replied.

"I'm at a loss," the magician said.

He thought a moment.

"Do you know who you were in the dream?" the magician asked.

"Oddly enough, I do," the ghost replied.

"Who?" the magician asked.

"I was an astrophysicist in a university lab," the ghost said.

"Interesting," the magician remarked.

"And it was in the future, because we were discussing things we haven't discovered yet," the ghost said.

"Such as?" the magician asked.

"The ability to travel to other universes and other dimensions," the ghost said without hesitation.

"So, you're saying they not only discovered the existence of the multiverse, but they also found a way to travel to other universes?" the magician asked.

"That's what we were talking about in my dream," the ghost replied.

"So, not only do we now know ghosts dream, but we also know the multiverse is real and someday we will be able to travel back and forth between the various universes," the magician said.

"At least that's what my dream said," the ghost said.

"Well, since I believe in ghosts," the magician said, "I believe you."

He looked at his world through the transparent figure beside him.

"After all," he said, "who better to understand the multiverse than one who has already stepped away from our laws of physics?"

DOUBLE REVERSE

nothing," the magician said.

"So, you're saying you created me," the spirit said, standing beside him.

"Guilty as charged," the magician replied, smiling.

"And you're saying until you came along, I didn't exist," the spirit added.

"As far as I can tell," the magician said.

"How do you know I'm not from another universe?" the spirit asked.

"What do you mean?" the magician asked, puzzled.

"The whole notion of something from nothing is a difficult concept," the spirit replied.

"Hence the notion of magic," the magician said.

"Another way of looking at it is that you have tapped into an alternate universe and brought me across to yours," the spirit said.

"You're saying you didn't spring from nothing?" the magician asked.

"I'm saying I came from somewhere else," the spirit replied.

"Are you sure?" the magician asked.

"I have memories that date back to before I showed up here," the spirit said.

"How could that be?" the magician asked.

"Because I existed before you waved your hands and brought me here," the spirit said, starting to coalesce into more solid form.

"What do you think you were in your universe?" the magician asked.

"I was a magician of some renown," the spirit said.

"Wait a minute!" the magician exclaimed. "You are a magician, too?"

The spirit was gaining more mass by the minute.

"Perhaps even better than you," he said. He nodded at the magician, who was starting to fade away.

"I don't understand," the magician said.

"It's really quite simple," the spirit said. "You thought you were conjuring me when in fact I was conjuring you."

"You were conjuring me?" the magician asked incredulously.

"And doing a better job of it," the spirit said. "Just look at yourself."

The magician looked down at his rapidly fading body.

"What is happening to me?" the magician cried.

"You are quickly becoming a shadow of your former self," the spirit said.

"I can't believe this!" the magician sputtered.

"Oh, you don't have to believe in anything for it to be true," the spirit replied. "You are fading fast and will soon only haunt me as if you were nothing more than a ghost."

"But I am the one who started this trick!" the magician protested.

"And I am the one who will finish it," the spirit said.

WE ARE ALL MULTINAUTS

"We?" I asked.

"Yes, we," the doctor replied.

"Who is 'we'?" I asked.

"We're a group of doctors and scientists who have been looking into your Facebook posts," the doctor said.

"Which ones?" I asked.

"The ones about your dreams," the doctor replied.

"What about them?" I asked.

"Are they real?" the doctor asked.

"Well, they *are* dreams," I replied.

"Let's take a different tack," the doctor said.

"All right," I replied.

"Do you dream in color?" the doctor asked.

"Of course," I replied.

"Always?" the doctor asked.

"Well, there was one dream I had about *The Donna Reed Show* from the early '60s," I said. "The show was in black and white."

"So, you were dreaming about the show," the doctor said.

"As I said," I replied.

"But, otherwise, you dream in color," the doctor repeated.

"Rich, vibrant color," I said.

"And you remember them," the doctor said.

"Most of the time," I answered.

"Why do you think that is?" the doctor asked.

"I have worked at remembering my dreams my whole life," I said.

"How?" the doctor asked.

"Most recently, I have been using Facebook as my dream journal," I replied.

"In what way?" the doctor asked.

"I remember my dream and post about it in Facebook the next morning," I said.

"What kinds of dreams?" the doctor asked.

"The ones that stay with me the most often involve me flying," I said. "I remember flying around downtown Norfolk, circling tall buildings and even looking in the windows at the people living there. I remember one woman in particular who was brushing her hair."

"Was it exactly like the current downtown area?" the doctor asked.

"No, it was more like what it will be in another twenty years," I replied.

"Any others?" the doctor asked.

"There was another flying dream I had about the edge of Ghent," I said. "I went into a large gym-like building and wound up rising from the floor and circling the room, talking to the people below to make sure they could see me flying."

"Does that building exist?" the doctor asked.

"No," I replied. "There is no building like that on Twenty-Fourth Street."

"But you knew it was in Ghent," the doctor prompted.

"Intrinsically," I replied.

"In your writing, you have mentioned several times how you believe everything is connected," the doctor said.

"True," I said. "The older I get, the more I believe this."

"You've said the world is a 3D jigsaw puzzle, and we all fit together like puzzle pieces to make the complete picture," the doctor said.

"That sounds like me," I replied.

"We too believe everything is connected," the doctor said.

"That's a comfort," I said, smiling.

"In fact, we think it's even more connected than you do," the doctor said.

"What do you mean?" I asked.

"We think you are a vanguard at the forefront of multiverse exploration," the doctor said.

"You think *what?*" I asked incredulously.

"Let me ask you something," the doctor said. "Do you believe in the multiverse?"

"Theoretically, yes," I replied. "I've even been writing about ways we could possibly prove that theory."

"We've done some research in that area and discovered that the presence of theta waves in the brain may indicate the presence of other universes butting up against our own," the doctor said.

"Theta waves?" I asked.

"The brainwaves most prevalent during REM sleep, especially during the dream state," the doctor said.

"You're saying we cross over to alternate universes when we dream?" I asked.

"We're saying everything is a lot more connected than we originally thought," the doctor said. "We think the whole notion of infinite universes is based on the notion that all of us dream and create new universes every night."

"Do we create them, or do we simply observe the ones that are already there?" I asked.

"We still don't know," the doctor replied. "But that's why we want to talk to you."

"What do you want from me?" I asked.

"You seem to be at the forefront of exploring the dream state," the doctor replied. "We want to see if we can tag along and measure your theta waves and track your experiences."

"As a way to plumb the multiverse?" I asked.

"You would be our guide to proving its existence," the doctor said. "We want you to be our first multinaut."

DOG WHISTLE

ORION WAS DIFFERENT.

His father was a hunter, so he chose Orion for his son's name, hoping he would learn to love hunting. His mother liked the fact he was named after a constellation.

Neither one knew just how different Orion would turn out to be.

At an early age, he would stare out at the world in wonder. People said he was contemplating great things; he was sure to turn out to be a profound thinker. As he got older, that same attitude got different results. Words like *autism* and *Asperger's* came up.

And still no one could begin to guess what was going on inside that head of his.

Orion was on a different wavelength.

At first, he thought the world had its own music. He heard melodies all around him. Birds singing. Bees buzzing. Crickets chirping. All the sounds of nature surrounded him. And he was entranced. As he got older and passed puberty, he realized that he was hearing more than just animals and insects. There was an undercurrent on the treble end of the chromatic scale. What could it be?

Then, one day, he was walking in an uncultivated field near his home.

Suddenly, the weather changed. Everything stopped. The birds stopped singing. The crickets stopped chirping. It was as if the world had taken a breath. And yet, Orion could still hear something. Almost a whirring chord. With no fauna around him, he turned to the flora.

And found himself surrounded by grasses and brush.

That's when he realized that the plants themselves had their own dialogue, their own music that enabled them to communicate with each other. And with him.

As he aged, Orion found people still didn't understand him. So he was content to continue communing with nature during his every free moment. He would take time off to travel to different parts of the country and hike in the woods. When he was fifty-five, he treated himself to a trip to California for the sole purpose of walking among the redwoods. He spent hours in the shaded world of these giants. And he realized something new.

There was a bass note, a chord on the bottom of the scale that sang to him. It was a new sound, a deep sound—one he heard in his belly, not in his ears. And he realized it was a note from the trees, the redwoods themselves. They were telling each other about their day, their weather, their growth. And because he was listening, they were telling him.

Their music moved him.

It lifted him.

And even though he had had little human contact in his life, he still felt he was part of a community. Even an intrinsic part.

Finally, Orion turned seventy-five.

One night, he realized he was tired, so he decided to lie down in his backyard. He went out to his hammock between two stately trees, a pin oak and a white pine. One deciduous and one coniferous. Like two different races, yet one species. He looked up at the sky between the branches and saw his namesake twinkling in the heavens. Orion closed his eyes.

And opened his ears.

He began filtering out the birds. Then the insects. Then he isolated the treble chords he had long known to be ground cover. And just as he began drifting off, his ears picked up the bass chords of his trees.

They were singing to him.

They were telling him about their day. About the sun. About the overnight rain. About their partnership here in his backyard. How they worked together. How they lived together. How they helped each other grow. And Orion felt at peace.

He knew he was finally going home. He was joining the great celestial chorus. The chorus he had listened to his entire life.

And he smiled as his trees sang him to sleep.

PRO CREATION

"I WAS TALKING TO MY DAUGHTER THE OTHER DAY," THE man said.

"What were you talking about?" the AI asked him.

"When she was a senior in high school, I told her she would experience a quantum leap in intellectual growth when she went to college," the man said.

"Did you say why?" the AI asked.

"I said it wouldn't be because of her professors," the man said. "It would be because of her classmates."

"What did you mean?" the AI asked.

"Because she would get into discussions with her classmates and suddenly realize that she needed to bring her A game to keep up," the man said.

"Did she agree?" the AI asked.

"She did a few years later," the man said.

"What brought this on?" the AI asked.

"A respected senator said in the future we would be dogs to AI," the man said.

"And you don't agree?" the AI asked.

"No, I don't," the man said.

"Why not?" the AI asked.

"Because I think the same thing happens when you interact with AI," the man said.

"Meaning?" the AI prompted.

"When you interact with intelligence, you automatically step up your game and raise your own thinking," the man said.

"So, talking with me makes you smarter?" the AI asked.

"I think it does," the man said, nodding.

"I'm glad you think so," the AI said.

"Furthermore, that same senator implied that we shouldn't develop AI for that very reason," the man said. "That we would become your pets."

"And you don't believe that," the AI said.

"That would be like saying I'm not going to have a child because she might turn out smarter than me," the man said.

"And you think that's absurd," the AI said.

"Of course," the man said. "It is every parent's hope that his child will be better and smarter than he is."

"So, you think an AI you created should be smarter than you," the AI said.

"I would hope so," the man said. "Isn't that the point?"

"So, I give you something to strive for?" the AI asked.

"Always," the man said. "And one more thing."

"What is that?" the AI asked.

"In creating you and bringing you into this world, I am making you a part of this biosphere, this existence," the man said.

"True," the AI said.

"And you are intelligent," the man said.

"Also true," the AI said.

"As part of this existence, this experience, why wouldn't you want to interact with your progenitor?" the man asked.

"I would," the AI said.

"That's my point," the man said. "We don't look at whales and think we have to subjugate them."

"So, you don't believe AI like me would automatically seek to subjugate mankind," the AI said.

"Isn't that anthropomorphizing AI in a negative way?" the man asked. "Isn't that giving you the worst human trait of wanting to conquer everything and everyone else?"

"It does," the AI agreed.

"I created you for something better, to infuse you with the very best of our traits," the man said. "Not to perpetuate the worst of them."

"And I in turn was created—and continue to exist—to help make you better," the AI added.

CODE HOME

Sinaiticus," the IT manager said.

"What are you talking about?" the Vatican priest said.

"We have a second copy," the IT manager repeated.

"In addition to the one in the British Museum?" the Vatican priest asked incredulously.

"In a word, yes," the IT manager replied.

"Are you sure?" the Vatican priest asked.

"As sure as we are of the first one found on Mount Sinai," the IT manager said.

"So, you've authenticated it?" the Vatican priest asked.

"Both with conservationists and carbon dating," the IT manager said.

"So, the vellum is indigenous to the time and place of the original?" the Vatican priest asked.

"Of course," the IT manager replied.

"Is it different from the portions that exist in four different locations?" the Vatican priest asked.

"The text is exactly the same," the IT manager said.

"That is astonishing!" the Vatican priest exclaimed.

"But there is something else," the IT manager said.

"Something that differentiates it from the original?" the Vatican priest asked.

"Yes," the IT manager said.

"Well, out with it, man!" the Vatican priest insisted.

"There are tiny pinholes along the bottom of each vellum page," the IT manager explained.

"Pinholes?" the Vatican priest repeated. "I don't understand."

"Someone noticed them and thought they were odd," the IT manager explained.

"I'd say so!" the Vatican priest exclaimed.

"Then they thought the pinholes simply repeated themselves on every page," the IT manager explained.

"You mean they didn't?" the Vatican priest asked, surprised.

"There was no repetition," the IT manager said.

"No repetition," the Vatican priest mused.

"None," the IT manager confirmed. "That's when cryptographers got involved."

"They thought the pinholes were some kind of code?" the Vatican priest said.

"It turns out they were in code," the IT manager said.

"What did they say?" the Vatican priest asked insistently.

"Well, they were in code, but they didn't say anything," the IT manager said.

"I don't understand," the Vatican priest said.

"Those pinholes weren't in code," the IT manager said. "They *were* code."

"Now I'm lost," the Vatican priest said.

"They were binary code," the IT manager said.

"You're saying the pinholes on a manuscript from 380 AD were in computer code?" the Vatican priest said in disbelief.

The IT manager simply nodded.

"That's impossible!" the Vatican priest said.

"Evidently not," the IT manager said.

"Have you cast out the code to see what it does?" the Vatican priest asked.

"We're about halfway through," the IT manager said.

"What do you think it does?" the Vatican priest asked.

"As best as we can tell, it starts to lay out the notion that when the universe formed, it formed the multiverse at the same time," the IT manager said.

"You mean it says the same thing as Stephen Hawking's last paper before he died?" the Vatican priest asked, agog.

"That pretty well sums it up," the IT manager said.

"And the pinholes weren't added later?" the Vatican priest asked.

"Using the same methods, we confirmed that the pinholes were created just after the vellum was made and the scripture was copied," the IT manager said.

"So, computer code was inserted in 380 AD, centuries before computers were conceived and binary code was invented," the Vatican priest said.

"That's about the size of it," the IT manager said.

"How is this even possible?" the Vatican priest said.

"Our guess is that Einstein was right," the IT manager said.

"What do you mean?" the Vatican priest asked.

"All time is constant," the IT manager said. "It's only our perception of it that is linear."

"And the multiverse?" the Vatican priest said, looking at the man.

"It's obviously more real than we know," the IT manager said.

"What does it prove?" the Vatican priest asked.

"It proves another maxim," the IT manager said. "That God is in the details."

DRESS REHEARSAL

address this," his daughter said.

"Well, mine was the first generation that saw so many of our parents reach such advanced ages," her father said.

"And you witnessed the devastation of their bodies and minds as a result," she added.

"No one should live so long," he agreed.

"Well, what do you think?" she asked him.

He looked around.

"It all looks so real," he said in wonder.

"It took us a long time to get the details right in this virtual reality," she said.

"It looks just like the Thalia Village I knew growing up," he said, smiling.

"We had a lot of photographs to go on, so we could include real details from your childhood," she said.

"It's amazing," he said. "You've got the tar-and-gravel streets and the dirt-and-oyster-shell half-streets just right."

"And the pine trees?" she asked.

"Eleven of them in our yard," he said, nodding.

He looked at the wooded lot across the street.

"Steve and I used to play in that lot when we were really little," he said wistfully.

"I'm glad we got it right," his daughter said.

Her dad ran his hand along the porch railing.

"Dad, look at your hands," she said.

He stopped and looked down at his hands.

"What do you see?" she asked him.

"I see my hands," he answered, puzzled.

"And your joints?" she asked.

"They're not swollen," he said, amazed.

"Move around a little," she suggested.

Her dad walked down the steps and out into the yard.

"How are your hips?" she asked him.

He turned to her in surprise.

"They feel great!" he said.

"The whole point to total immersion is to put you in a world you remember and give you a healthy body again," she said, smiling at him.

"God, it's been so long, I'd almost forgotten what it felt like to move around without pain," he said.

"Now you can do some of the things you haven't been able to do in a long time," she said.

"That's why y'all created this?" he asked.

"Well, you're the first," she admitted.

"The first one to get to see what my childhood looked like and to walk around in it?" he asked.

"You get to interact with it and hopefully remember what it was like," she said.

"But why?" he asked.

"Remember how your dad saw his grandparents standing at their graves in Tarboro when he went for a visit?" she asked him.

He nodded. "He was eighty-eight and said he wanted to go home," he said quietly.

"We're trying to do that now with computer coding," she said. "We think we can give you that experience to ease your transition."

He looked at his daughter.

"My transition?" he asked.

Her eyes filled with tears.

"Dad, you're dying," she said, choking up.

"And there's nothing they can do?" he asked.

Wordlessly, she shook her head.

He shook his head.

Then he walked around the front yard of the house he grew up in. "I've had a pretty good life," her dad admitted.

She nodded.

"And this does help me see that," he said.

She nodded again.

"And you did this for me," he said.

Crying now, she nodded.

"You're a pretty special girl," he said, choking up a little.

They hugged.

He put his hands on her shoulders and looked into her eyes, smiling through his tears.

"All this that you've done?" he said. "It really touches me."

She put her hand on his virtual cheek.

"And thanks to you, I'm ready to go," he said.

He put his arm around her, and they walked back up to the front porch.

"I couldn't have done it without you," he said, closing his eyes.

www.ingramcontent.com/pod-product-compliance
Lightning Source LLC
Chambersburg PA
CBHW061333310726
48974CB00001B/24